**MARVEL**

# WASTELANDERS: STAR-LORD

## SARAH CAWKWELL

ADAPTED FROM THE SCRIPTED PODCAST
BY BENJAMIN PERCY

ACONYTE

FOR MARVEL PUBLISHING

VP Production & Special Projects: Jeff Youngquist
Editor, Special Projects: Sarah Singer
Manager, Licensed Publishing: Jeremy West
VP, Licensed Publishing: Sven Larsen
SVP Print, Sales & Marketing: David Gabriel
Editor in Chief: C B Cebulski

FOR MARVEL DIGITAL MEDIA

Executive Producer: Dan Buckley
Executive Producer: Jill BC Du Boff
Executive Producer: Daniel Fink
Executive Producer: Ellie Pyle
Producer: Brad Barton
Producer: MR Daniel
Producer: Larissa Rosen

Special Thanks: Jenny Radelet Mast, Kimberly Senior,
Sarah Amos, Joe Quesada, Becca Seidel, and Stephen Wacker

© 2023 MARVEL

First published by Aconyte Books in 2023
ISBN 978 1 83908 227 6
Ebook ISBN 978 1 83908 228 3

Cover art by Steven McNiven

Distributed in North America by Simon & Schuster Inc, New York, USA
Printed in the United States of America
9 8 7 6 5 4 3 2 1

**ACONYTE BOOKS**

*An imprint of Asmodee Entertainment Ltd*

Mercury House, Shipstones Business Centre

North Gate, Nottingham NG7 7FN, UK

*aconytebooks.com // twitter.com/aconytebooks*

*For Josh, who believed in me.*

# PROLOGUE

Begin Recording...
Entry C1451Z2E
Location: *Outer spiral arm of the Milky Way, two light years off the perimeter of Alpha Centauri. An abandoned mining freighter owned by Stark Industries.*

Stark Industries mining freighter *Prosperity* drifted in space like a vast, battle-scored tombstone freed from its terrestrial bonds. The word "sleek" had never been less appropriate. It was a vessel built solely for durability and function. Tony Stark would have had little hand in its aesthetic as it lacked the bells and whistles (and what Quill called "fancy bits") that most of Stark's personal creations did. No, the *Prosperity* had once had purpose.

Now it drifted. Aimlessly. Directionless. Lifeless.

Well.

Lifeless, that is, unless you counted the hundred alien voices mingling with one another, shredding any silence and serenity that may have existed. The shrieking of the Brood – incensed by the trespassers and now slavering for the fresh, warm

7

bodies barricaded behind some mercifully sturdy doors – was a cacophony of horror. It invited visions of anguish, torment, and slow death, probably the sort where you begged them to stop eating you even as they chowed down.

The barrier standing between the Brood and their prey was one of the most important doors aboard the *Prosperity*. It was the access to the bridge. It was also, Quill reflected, all that was stopping him from becoming a Brood snack – a death he wouldn't choose for anybody.

Right now, he was pressed up against the door, although he couldn't have told you why that was. Perhaps it was born of a need to punish himself, to hear the bellowing from beyond and muse on the fact that perhaps what Rocket was saying was something he actually agreed with.

"We shouldn't have stopped," observed Rocket, the raccoon's tone dripping so heavily with sarcasm that you could easily have filled a bucket. "'*We haven't got time to stop, Quill. We've got a job to do, Quill.*' But did you listen? Hell, no. You *never* listen. You insisted we pay a visit to this… this… heap of tin. Now we're screwed." Rocket's anger was nothing new. Of late, Quill was fairly sure that his small friend was largely sustained by spite, rage, and bile.

Quill's need to placate and find the bright side of the situation overrode the need to admit he might have been wrong.

"We're not screwed, Rocket. Not as *such*…"

"I knew you were stupid, Quill, but I didn't think you were an *idiot*." Rocket pointed one clawed finger at the door. "In case you'd not noticed, there is a Brood swarm right outside that door! Their teeth are bigger than your fingers!"

Quill couldn't help it. He looked at his fingers.

He shuddered.

"Their exoskeletons are stronger than steel." Rocket was relentless.

Quill looked at the steel door.

He shuddered again.

Rocket gestured around expansively, taking in the abandoned bridge. Like the rest of the freighter, there was a thick layer of dust over everything, as though a volcanic event had occurred before finding something better to do. "We have *no* way out, Quill. No way out except maybe through the digestive tracts of the Brood. That, my friend, is the very definition of 'screwed.'"

Much as Quill hated admitting it, Rocket was right. But he still clung onto his misplaced sense of optimism.

"We couldn't just ignore an emergency beacon..." he began weakly and Rocket rode over him roughshod. The anger gave way to something worse. Mockery.

"'Whatever happened to the Guardians of the Galaxy?' he said." Rocket simpered in his best impression of Quill. Then he slapped his paw against the console. "'Let's go explore this abandoned ship that won't respond to our hails', he said!"

Rocket's tirade was interrupted by a keening wail from the other side of the bulkhead and a series of heavy *thuds* as the Brood battered at the barrier keeping them from their prey. There was a wet snarl and although it was unlikely, Quill swore he heard something out there licking its lips.

"If we die, my ghost is gonna haunt your ghost." Rocket moved away from the central console where he had been studying the primitive human technology. He prodded Quill's stomach, each word accompanied by a jab. "Because. This. Is. All. Your. Fault!"

"All right, all right!" Quill threw his hands up in exasperation. "Just… stop, OK? Let me think." He reached up and scratched at his bristled chin, casting his gaze around the gloomy bridge. The only illumination came from the light spheres they'd released, floating above their heads emitting a faint, greenish glow. They drifted lazily around the room and accented a metallic surface. Quill peered into gloom.

"OK, I got it. I got us into this mess. I am gonna get us out." He left his post at the entrance, ignoring the growing number of *thumps* shaking the door. He moved with as much alacrity as his body and the debris on the bridge would allow, hopping over a pile of disturbingly human bones to where he'd caught the glimpse of what he hoped was…

Yes!

He metaphorically punched the air, then *actually* punched the air. "Here!"

"Here what?" Despite his barely contained fury, Rocket followed Quill and stared at what he was indicating.

"This!" Quill pointed triumphantly at his quarry. "A robot of some kind."

The humanoid shape was crumpled in a heap on the floor of the bridge, sleek and more sophisticated than most of the other tech – if not the freighter itself. Synth-tech across the galaxy was extraordinary and many manufacturers had chosen to build in metallic elements to indicate that their creations were not, in fact, real.

Quill couldn't help but notice that the body had a definite set of feminine curves to it.

He was *great* at spotting those.

Focus, *Quill*.

"Let's see if we can get it up and running..." He was enthusiastic. This was a *great* plan!

Rocket rolled his eyes. "What's the point of..."

"Think about it, Rock! This could be some sort of battle bot, with lasers and hidden weapons! It could hold vital information on what's happened here. It probably knows more about the situation that's led to this point than we do. Just *look* at it. Please?"

Rocket opened his mouth to respond, but the hopelessness of Quill's tone stayed his biting retort. He glared upwards, throwing up his paws irritably. "Fine," he said, before shifting his attention to the automaton on the floor, crouching down and studying it more closely.

"Naw," he said. "This ain't no battle bot. Design's too synthetic. Probably an emissary of some sort. Maybe a translator droid." He studied it a little longer, then stood. "Probably motion activated. I got just the thing."

He punctuated the sentence with a swift kick to the bot's torso. Despite himself, Quill put out a hand.

"Hey, woah! Don't kick it, man! Look at it. I mean *her*. It's a *girl* bot. Don't kick..."

Rocket stared at him. Quill couldn't hold his gaze. He turned away to look at the bot, which suddenly emitted a burst of static and white noise. He was briefly put in mind of someone tuning an old radio, looking for a stable signal. Rocket smirked, folding his arms across his chest.

"See? There we go."

There was a sudden and violent burst of feedback and the bot's eyes flickered into life. They were a deep emerald hue, artificial of course, but projecting a curious sense of awareness. Quill waved a hand in front of them.

"Hello? Hello?" He turned to Rocket. "Do you think it can hear me?" He leaned in closer and just for good measure, and because there are certain conventions that cannot be denied in such circumstances, raised his voice. "Can you hear me?"

Nothing.

Quill drooped.

"I don't think…"

There was another burst of static, and another high-pitched whine, gradually ebbing to a barely audible hum from the bot's body.

Well, barely audible over the sound of hundreds of starving Brood.

"Rocket! Did you see that? Look! Her eyes! They're moving. She's awake. Good job, buddy! Good! Yes, yes! They flickered, did you see? I think her eyes flickered. Her eyes, Rocket! Did you see the eyes? Did you see them flicker?" His excitement was boyish and infectious but Rocket had long grown used to it.

"Yeah," he acknowledged sourly. "I saw them flicker."

The bot, which was laying on one side, shifted slightly and its arm dislodged a nearby bone. The bone skittered away across the metal floor of the bridge. Quill could barely contain the excitement he felt at this sudden development.

"It moved! Look! Its arm… *her* arm *moved*, Rocket!"

"Maybe. You could just be having a stroke, old man."

"Yeah, maybe, but no. No, I'm not. The arms are moving." He reached out and gripped Rocket's shoulder with one hand. "Look! She's gonna talk!"

The voice that came from the bot was rich and pleasant, modulated for composure and control. Anything else that might be gleaned at this stage was curtailed somewhat by the fact it presently had very little to say.

"Hell."

"Great," said Rocket. "At least it understands the situation."

"Hell. Hell. Hell."

Rocket snorted again. "I know *that* feeling, honey."

"Hell… o." There was a brief pause, another burst of static and then the voice spoke again, this time confidently. "Hello."

"Well, hi," said Quill, delighted by this development.

"I," said the robot, "am a Rigellian Recorder."

"Of *course* you are," said Quill, reaching an arm down. "Here. Let me help you up. Careful." He gallantly helped her stand. The automaton was reasonably sized, perhaps a little over five and a half feet in height and now that it stood, it was apparent that the builder had gone for a pleasing female aesthetic. Her metallic body was a perfect facsimile of a young human woman.

*Sometimes*, Quill thought, wistfully, *I worry I've been on my own with nothing but a ratty old doormat for company for too long.*

"Thank you," she said, displaying impeccable manners. "Thank… thank… thank you. I apologize. My vox unit is glitching."

"Ah, don't sweat it. Sometimes I feel glitchy myself when I wake up. One of the things that comes to you when you hit fifty…"

Rocket snorted. "Fifty. Of *course* you're fifty."

Quill waved a hand vaguely. "Fifty-ish."

"Oh, please," said Rocket. "Not *even*. Why do you live in constant denial of the fact that you're nothing more than a slowly rotting bag of human waste? Don't bother. I already know the answer."

Several thuds against the door suggested that if they didn't come up with a plan soon, then they'd all be reduced to quickly rotting bags of waste, human or otherwise.

"I'm an optimist, Rocket," said Quill.

"Where I come from, that's called 'delusional'. Now talk to the skinbot and figure out what happened." He shifted back to the central console and fixed Quill with a glare. "I'll try and get the mainframe back online."

Rocket busied himself with the console, using one of the many tools he carried with him to open the service compartment. He muttered and complained as he worked, commenting on the state of the system, the fact that they were just delaying their own deaths, and the futility of existence – all to the accompaniment of the howls and screams beyond.

There was an awkward silence as Quill found himself wondering how to open a dialogue with a synthetic. He scratched his beard and rubbed his nose. Then he scuffed his boots.

"So… hi."

*Great moves, Quill.* He tried again.

"Is everybody dead?" Not the *best* opening line, but at least it was to the point.

The recorder tipped her head to one side and studied him. "I am sorry," she said, sweetly. "I do not understand."

"Everybody. On the ship." Quill waved a hand. "We must've passed about fifty skeletons on the way here. Is everybody dead? The crew?"

"No, not everybody is dead," came the reply. There was an innocence there, a lack of guile that caught Quill by surprise. "You and your pet are alive."

Rocket's voice bellowed from the bowels of the console, filled with venom. "I am not his pet!" Even as he spoke, there was a fresh sound from outside the bridge: a heavy, resonant *DOOM* sound suggesting the urgency had grown, the Brood thrilled by the sound of Rocket's shouts. "I am his boss, thank you very much. If anything, he's my pet…"

*DOOM!*

*DOOM!*

The recorder nodded, turning away from Rocket to look back up at Quill. "You are correct: everyone *else* is dead."

*DOOM!*

"The Brood ate them."

Rocket sneered. "Well, I took at least five of them down in the hall before we got here," he said. "Few less mouths to feed…"

*DOOM!*

Quill's nerves were frayed to the point of snapping, and he held up his hands in a placatory gesture. "Keep it down, Rocket, you're getting them excited! Focus on getting this ship online. I don't know about you, but I do *not* want to be the prime rib special at today's Brood buffet."

Rocket resumed his task, muttering just loudly enough for Quill to hear him suggest that the Brood would skip his bloated torso and go straight for the meaty thighs. Then he tore off another panel and resumed cussing and swearing.

The recorder looked at Quill expectantly. He found another line of questioning. "So… um… how can you help us?"

"How can I help you?"

Quill was entirely unsure if her response was a question or an offer. Behind them, Rocket swore outrageously as two wires shorted close to his muzzle, burning a patch of fur clean off. Quill focused on the synth.

"I don't suppose you've got… I dunno. Missile launchers hidden in your hands? A master of kung fu perhaps?"

"No," came the reply he'd expected. "But I record."

"You record? What?"

"Everything. Audio, visual, heat and chemical signatures. Also, localized digital and radio transmissions. I am recording you right now."

That made him oddly uncomfortable, and Quill tried a different tactic.

"Why are you on this mining vessel?"

"It was bound for the third planet of this solar system."

Quill's brow furrowed. "But why were you…"

She interrupted him to continue her statement. "It is my understanding that Earth offers many wealthy possibilities for my research."

"Can you transmit? Are you transmitting anywhere right now? Could you maybe call in a rescue?"

"I have been aboard this vessel long enough that the Rigellians have listed me as lost. Therefore, they have cut off my communication relay."

"But… when… I'm sorry…" Quill was foundering now, confused by her words, puzzled as to why it… *she*… had been bound for Earth, frustrated that now was not the time to ask.

"Oh, for the love of… Quill! Stop with the dumb questions! Ask *smart* ones. Figure out what happened!"

"Rocket, please! I *am* asking what happened, but I'm doing it *my* way! You know. I like to… *massage* my way into conversations."

"Uh-huh, sure. Hey. You. Skinbot! What happ…"

"Commencing audio reference."

What then came from the recorder's mouth was nothing short of horrific. Sounds of chaos and panic, screaming and yelling. The impact of running feet and the louder impact of bodies hitting the floor. The horribly visceral and disturbingly wet sounds of bodies being torn apart. All the while, the rhythm of the Brood at the door kept up their ever-present counterpoint.

As the last sounds died away, Quill stared at her. "What… What was that terrible noise that just came out of your mouth?"

"You asked what happened," she said. "I played an audio segment from my archives."

"I don't want to hear that," said Quill, shaking his head vigorously. "*Nobody* wants to hear that!"

"Would you like to see the video of the merciless slaughter of the…"

"No!"

Rocket shook his head. Clearly even *he* had found the noise disturbing – not that he'd admit it. "What happened to this ship?"

The recorder turned to face Rocket. "The *Prosperity* was asteroid mining along the outskirts of Alpha Centauri."

"See, Quill? That's how you do it."

"They came for platinum, rhodium, gold, and silver. But one of the asteroids they mined turned out to be a Brood hive. Unfortunately, nobody realized this until after the hull was loaded."

"You know what I hate about the Brood?" Quill interjected. "Other than their unrelenting need to multiply and feast on anything they encounter, obviously."

"No," said the recorder. "I do not know what you hate about the Brood."

"They *look* disgusting," affirmed Quill. "Like what would happen if a wasp boned a cockroach. I *hate* bugs. D'you know, there was this one time I woke up and I swore there was a spider in my ear and…"

"OK, Quill," snapped Rocket. "So hey, skinbot. How long has this ship been adrift?"

"…I don't know how the spider got there…" Quill trailed off, his story thwarted. He waved a hand vaguely. "What he said."

"Thirty-two years," said the recorder sweetly. "Thirty-two years, twenty-six days, five hours, two minutes and forty-seven seconds."

There was a heavy pause and Quill shifted his gaze to his companion. "Nobody came to save the people here? Or to salvage the ship? In all that time?"

"A few salvagers have attempted to board the *Prosperity*," replied the recorder. "They were eaten."

"No," said Quill, firmly. "No. Earth would *never* let this happen."

"Are you implying that Earthlings are driven to do moral good at their own risk?"

"No. Yes. No. Look! What I'm getting at is that this ship… there's a *fortune* in minerals and precious metals in the hold. It's owned by *Stark Industries* for God's sake…" Rocket waved a hand dismissively and shrugged. "Must've decided to cut their losses. Too risky with the Brood on board. Who are still here, in case it's escaped your notice."

"No," said Quill, mostly to himself. "Tony Stark would never…"

"Tony Stark would never what?" The recorder's question was curious. An expression of discomfort and pain flickered across Quill's face as he replied.

"He would never leave his crew behind."

"Enough, Quill." Rocket's low voice held a private warning and Quill nodded, absently. Rocket directed his question back at the recorder. "So you've just been sitting around here all that time?"

"Sometimes I have been standing," she replied. "But yes, mostly I have been sitting. There was some lying on the floor, and…"

"For thirty years?" Quill was incredulous.

"For thirty-two years, twenty-six days, five hours, three minutes and fifty-one seconds."

Quill rubbed at his upper arm, more than a little worried by the situation. He was struggling to reconcile the concept of Stark abandoning his people with what he knew of the man. Fortunately, the recorder offered up a new distraction.

"If I may," she said, "what are your titles?"

"What are our what-nows?" He was pulled from his reverie by the question.

"How should I address you?"

"Oh. I'm Peter Quill, but…" He brightened.

Rocket groaned, looking up from his work. "Don't you *dare*. Don't!"

"You can call me… *Star-Lord*." Oh, man, it felt so *good* to say it. He said it with what he hoped was a brightness in his voice, a confidence remembered and re-applied with all the care and love of someone slapping a strip of duct tape over a broken window and hoping nobody would notice.

"Let me tell you something," said Rocket, his tone aggressive. "The only throne this lord sits on is the latrine. For a half hour after every meal."

"Star-Lord is my official title. It's true!"

"Does this mean you are nobility?" the recorder asked.

Quill beamed and tried to ignore the sound from outside that suggested some of the Brood had fallen to fighting among themselves.

"What it means is you are in *luck*. Because me and Rocket over there – we are the Guardians of the Galaxy!"

"Is this equal to being space police?"

"Not exact…"

"Space knights, then?"

"Nah, those guys *suck*. I guess you could call us… space cowboys. Or the Gangsters of Love. Heh."

The reference fell on deaf ears.

There was a clatter as Rocket dropped one of his tools to the ground. He picked up another. "You want the truth, lady? Here it is. I kick the mighty Star-Lord over there awake every morning. Then he whines and zombies his way through whatever work we gotta do… then we do it all over again. His hobbies include… eating, napping, playing *terrible* music. Not to mention his newest pastime of talking endlessly and pathetically about his long-gone glory days."

"That does not sound very impressive," said the recorder.

"And you know what?" Rocket was relentless in his attack and Quill knew that nothing would stop him. "You know why he *really* wanted to board this vessel? Because he figured he could salvage it for parts and then sell them…"

"Aw, c'mon, man." Quill was moved to interrupt, part

embarrassed, part annoyed – but Rocket was unstoppable.

"A long time ago, a long, *long* time ago, we were the Guardians of the Galaxy. But that, my friend, was before. This is *now*."

"What happened?"

All Quill could manage was a faint noise of discomfort. Rocket relented, shaking his head. "We don't talk about it. Now, we're just a couple of work-for-hire mercs. Smugglers, for the most part." He sighed, Quill felt a little over-theatrically. "Not exactly where I thought we were gonna end up, but there you go."

He turned back to his work and there was a loud hiss as the bridge doors ratcheted back a few centimeters. The commotion from the corridor, which had faded into muffled background, suddenly became loud and immediate. "Oh geez! Son of a flarkin'…"

"What did you do, Rocket?"

"I… must've hit the wrong button…"

"You've opened the *door*, man!"

"Only a little! Settle down. I got this!" He grabbed the ends of two sparking wires, twisting them back together. There was a pause of three heartbeats and the door slid shut. "See? I got this."

"They bent the door, Rocket," said Quill, unable to keep the faint hysteria from his voice. "They cracked the door!"

"Everything's under control."

"How much longer is this gonna take?"

"Let me see. How long to juice up a carbon-scored, rusted-out, iced-over ship that's been adrift for thirty…"

"Thirty-two years, twenty-six days…"

"For over thirty years? I'm sorry I can't do it in fifteen seconds, O great and mighty Star-Lord!"

The recorder shifted her position, clearly not detecting any hint of sarcasm, or perhaps simply ignorant of what sarcasm was. "I would like to hear the story of the great and mighty Star-Lord."

"No," said Rocket, bitterly. "You wouldn't."

"Hang on," said Quill. "Hang on…"

"Will you please tell me your story?"

"My story?"

"Oh, man," muttered Rocket. "This is gonna be *rich*."

"What part, sweetheart?" said Quill, adopting a casual stance and moving a few feet to show off a suddenly affected swagger. "What do you want to know?"

"Everything."

"Well, I don't really know where to start. There's so much to tell! All the romance, the intrigue… death-defying heroism. And dancing, of course, there's always the…"

"If I may," said the recorder, interrupting Quill mid-flow, "how about you begin with the story of how you came to save me… Star-Lord."

A slow grin spread over Quill's face.

"Oh, *yeah*," he replied.

"Oh, *no*," said Rocket.

Outside, the shrieking continued.

"You see," began Quill, "it's like this…"

# CHAPTER ONE
## OUT OF THE FRYING PAN

### THE INDETERMINABLE PAST
### (A FEW DAYS AGO)

Rocket had scored the job and Quill had not been in any position to turn down the lure of work. They were mercenaries, after all, and credits were running exceptionally low. So that was why they had found themselves aboard an unusual spaceship taking on a job that was absolutely unlike anything either of them could recall.

"What made it unusual?" The recorder broke into Quill's recollection, and he looked up, startled.

"For starters, we didn't know who our contact was and *that* was different. All we had were the rendezvous coordinates for the ship and I'll tell you what was different about that as well," he said. "*If* you let me carry on."

"Apologies. Please continue, Star-Lord."

"Sure. So. There's me and Rocket there, in the hangar of a

23

ship that looked like a haunted castle. You know what that is, honey?"

"Castle," she replied and thought for a moment. "Yes, I have enough references in my internal databanks to understand what you mean."

"It was like being in an episode of *Scooby-Doo*. A voice comes over an intercom, 'Peter Quill and Rocket Raccoon', it says. Female voice. Loud."

"Just Rocket, for your records, synthskin," Rocket growled.

Quill charged on, heedless of the underlying warning. The recorder paid close attention to the story and as he spoke there were faint sounds of whirring as she took everything down for posterity.

"Peter Quill and Rocket Raccoon!"

The voice reverberated through the hangar. The suddenness of it startled both Quill and Rocket into momentary silence, a state of affairs that never lasted long. Their surroundings were far from normal for a ship's hangar: there was a baroque feel to the décor and while perhaps it was less "haunted castle" and more "Halloween decoration", it was definitely unusual.

Quill had to assume that the thin, spindly things he occasionally spotted moving in the darkest corners were spiders. Imagining otherwise was the path to madness.

"Who's that?" Quill's voice was equally loud, but infinitely less imposing. "Sounds a bit like the Great and Powerful Oz to me..." His voice didn't reverberate anywhere near as impressively, but still echoed throughout the hangar. Rocket shifted uncomfortably.

"I don't like this, Quill," muttered Rocket. "When I don't

like things, I itch. I am real itchy right now, you know what I mean?" He shifted from paw to paw, clearly uncomfortable. As he spoke, a door opened with a soft swoosh in front of them, seamlessly retracting into the metal of the hull. Neither of them had noticed it until that moment.

"Rocket?"

"Yeah, Quill?"

"Do you think we're supposed to… y'know. Just walk on through? Into the glowy chamber beyond? Into the great unkn…"

"Proceed into the chamber." The female voice boomed around them as though responding directly to Quill's question.

He swallowed, nervously. "Guess that answers *that* question." He glanced at Rocket. "I suppose 'after you' isn't gonna cut it here?"

A brief tussle ensued as they jostled for the right to be the second person through the door. In the end, Quill took the lead and although he would never have admitted it, was grateful that Rocket remained close. They left the empty hangar space behind, passing into something very different. Within this part of the ship, someone had gone to great pains to build what Quill could only describe as a chapel. Not that it was particularly holy. There was a lot less iconography and considerably less musty smell of old parchment for starters. High, vaulted ceilings arched away above him and the sound of fluid bubbling in tanks loaned its own uniqueness to the environment.

Maybe less like a church, Quill thought as he studied his environs more carefully. More like a *museum*. He remembered a school trip to a museum when he'd been a kid. He recalled a faint sense of reverence around some of the exhibits. Mostly, there had been seeing what he and his friends could steal from the gift shop, but when their harassed teacher had finally corralled the class enough to pay attention, Quill had felt that sense of awe and wonder that came with seeing antiquities *in-situ*.

Those had been far less interesting exhibits than this, though. One of the tanks burbling away contained something that resembled a freakish cross between the head of the Hulk and an octopus. Another tank was filled with inky, black water, making it impossible to guess the actual depth – but if you looked closely enough, you could see the shine of a billion stars. An entire *galaxy*, contained within a glass case, floating within the dark liquid.

"Were you and Rocket there to make great discoveries? To find rare artifacts?" The recorder interrupted the flow of the story again, but Quill found it less jarring this time. A slow smile spread across his lips.

"Far be it from me to shatter your obviously accurate opinion of me as a hero, but no. Rocket and I were there to make a huge, stinking pile of cash. Discovering new adventures, ethics, and morality are all wonderful things, but they don't pay debts and they don't buy fuel or food. It's all about the credits. Sometimes, it's about the glory. But mostly, it's the credits."

Rocket nodded his agreement.

"Do you ever do anything that is not for credits? Say, for the greater good?"

Quill's eyes narrowed and he studied the recorder, attempting to determine if she was mocking him or not. Then he let out a hollow laugh. "Nah," he said. "The greater good can take care of itself. It's the money. That's all that matters nowadays."

"Was it not always that way?"

He didn't like the discomfort he felt at the recorder's question. Fortunately for him, any answer he might have made was put on hold as a new round of howling and thumping came from the Brood beyond the door. It reminded him starkly of their current situation. Quill and Rocket exchanged a look, the latter shaking his head and returning to the work on the console.

Quill pushed the sounds of the Brood out of his thoughts for now. They were trapped regardless so he may as well continue. "We were in this display room, or whatever it was," he said. "Rocket made a discovery."

"Hey, Quill, check these out!" Rocket had found a series of pedestals, each topped with a variety of items. Weapons, masks, jewelry – each was unique and fascinating. Quill tore himself away from the Hulk-topus to go see what Rocket had found.

A strange feeling passed over him and he swore *blind* that he heard distant, angelic music. The sound of harp strings sounded real, and he blinked.

"Do you hear that?"

"What? Use your *words*, Quill. Be more specific."

"The music…" His gaze shifted from pedestal to pedestal until it rested on a small harp. The strings, viewed from this distance, looked as though they might be spun of pure gold and they trembled slightly. "*That* music." He pointed.

"Don't hear nothing. You forget to take your pills again?"

"Ssh. It's… beautiful, Rocket. Can't you hear it? It's…" Quill took several steps forward, tipping his head to one side. He had the strangest urge: a desire to take up the instrument and to play it. He yearned to release the song locked within.

He reached out his hand.

"Stop!"

The voice filled the available space with absolute command and authority. The single word stayed Quill's hand and he froze in place. The music came to an abrupt halt, and he shook his head as though a spell had been broken.

"Do you have any idea what will happen if you play the Sacred Harp of Angels' End?"

"The sacred…? Harp of who's end?"

"Obviously not, Strange and Disembodied Voice," Rocket threw in.

The voice appeared not to be interested in his sarcasm and continued. "If you take this instrument up and play it, your body will be reduced to an empty shell as your soul becomes a song owned forever by the instrument in your hands."

"Really?" Quill asked.

There was a pause as though the Voice was confused that it was being questioned on this matter.

"Yes," it said, finally. "Really."

"Wow," said Quill, succinctly. "But you know what? Given some *other* options that have come my way in the past, that's not really a *terrible* way to spend an afterlife, is it? Can I choose my jam? The style of the song? Imagine being immortalized as Eighties hair metal…"

"Peter Quill. You are not here to touch the exhibits or to ask questions."

"All right," bawled Rocket. "Enough of this! Who *are* you?"

"I am," responded the voice, leaving what Quill felt was an unnecessarily dramatic pause, "the Collector."

"I know my interruptions are tiresome, Star-Lord," said the Recorder, sounding fascinated. "But what did this Collector look like? Did you ever see her? Or was she just a voice?"

"Oh, we saw her," said Quill. "She was… kind of… well, like a grape."

"I do not follow. Are you saying that the Collector was a sentient fruit?"

"No! More that… well, she was small and round. Purple. Like a mall-walking grandma in a tracksuit."

"Your descriptions are largely meaningless to me, Star-Lord, but they *do* remind me of songs."

"Well, isn't that handy, because I just so happen to write my own music."

"Badly. You write bad music, badly. Brood are still out there, Quill. You gonna get to the point?"

"Good point, Rocket. OK, well, yeah. The Collector…"

"I am the Collector."

Rocket blinked. "The Collector's a *chick*, now?"

"Time turns, Rocket Racoon."

"Just Rocket, thanks…"

"Time turns and power shifts. I *am* the Collector." The female figure who stepped out of seemingly nowhere to stand before them was somewhere between Rocket and Quill's height, wearing a long robe of a soft-looking fabric that draped artfully across her body. "If you care to look further, you will find that among my exhibits is the skeleton of he who was formerly known as the Collector." By her side was a small, canine creature wearing a collar of tiny bells that tinkled as it moved.

Rocket tipped his head to one side. "You're tinier and more purple than I was expecting."

She turned yellow eyes on him, the disdain palpable. "And you," she retorted, "have entirely more gray fur than I was expecting." Without the echoing theatrics, her voice was less impressive and yet she seemed to be bigger than her manifested self. Quill had the faintest hint that they were seeing what she wanted them to see, not what she actually was.

The dog barked incessantly, and she stooped to gather it up. "Oh, hush now, Mr Delicious. These are our guests. We should be kind to them. Unless they wrong us, of course. Then we'll make them suffer unimaginable pain. Isn't that right, Mr Delicious? Isn't that right?"

Mr Delicious *woofed* his agreement. At least, it seemed like agreement. The threat sat between them like an unexploded bomb until Rocket spoke.

"Let's talk about the job, lady. Implication was that it's a hush-hush transportation and delivery. What you got?"

"Straight to business. I *like* that in my employees. Very well, Mr Rocket. You see that display over there?"

They turned to where her finger indicated and, as one, they tipped their heads to the side to study it. Quill broke the silence first.

"A broken mirror?"

"Look more closely. This is an invaluable relic." She led them towards the pedestal and, as they approached, she nodded at Quill. "Pick it up."

"Me?" Her words about the harp were still at the front of his mind.

"Go on." His hand snaked out and she caught it. "Carefully."

Quill picked the mirror up, steeling his resolve. Nothing untoward happened and he let out a breath. He peered at the object. "It's not showing my reflection," he observed.

"Correct," said the Collector. "Keep looking."

"It's showing me…" He studied the image that he could make out and his heart leaped into his mouth. A planet. Blue and green, with a soft blue halo. He knew this world. He dreamed of it. "Earth?"

"Look closer."

"Closer?" As he stared at the rotating planet, it zoomed in, like he was watching a movie. "OK, not just Earth. That's America. *North* America, right?"

"Closer."

Another shift in the visual and Quill's eyebrows lifted into his receding hairline. "The plains region? South Dakota…"

"Closer."

"Look, lady, if he gets any closer, he's gonna have to start licking it."

"Hills," said Quill and his voice had a strange timbre to it. "The Black Hills. I went there once. When I was a kid. With my mom…"

"Closer, Peter Quill."

He shook his head. "There *is* no closer. There's nothing else to see. It shatters there."

"But what do you actually *see*? In that shattered moment? *Look.*"

He looked into the object again and the scene replayed

until something caught his eye. At first, it was just a flicker. A hint that solidified as though being brought into focus. Quill squinted like an old man to aid his vision. Much to his chagrin, it helped. "I can see *something*, hang on. It's a word. Mount... yep. Mountain. And there's something else, hold on... Moriah." He shook his head. "But then it fractures. It makes no sense. What *is* this thing?"

"What you're looking at isn't a mirror," the Collector said. "It's a map."

There was a sudden hum of sleeping systems coming online and a series of lights sparked to life across the central console. Rocket punched the air in self-congratulatory delight. "Yes! Now we're in *business*!" To punctuate his moment of success, the ship's computer voice came through loud and clear.

"Systems online."

"You did it?" Quill's story stalled and he turned to Rocket.

"You bet I did it."

"But Star-Lord. The mirror... the map. What did it look like?"

"What? Oh. It was small. About the size of my hand. It had this weird black frame. It was sorta spooky looking." Quill was distracted by the various chirps and whirrs coming from the console as Rocket worked. Not to mention the blood-curdling howling and slavering noises still coming from beyond the door.

"Almost there," said Rocket, urgently.

"Please, Star-Lord. What was it like? Please do not stop there. What was spooky about it?"

"Sure. The mirror part was, I guess, kind of coffin shaped.

Tall and rectangular. The frame itself was like a figure. A black, dead-eyed figure that looked as though it was holding the mirror within. Anyway, as soon as I saw it, I had a hunch as to what we were dealing with…"

"You did *not*." Despite working on the console, Rocket was clearly still listening for appropriate moments to interrupt.

"I did! I was just playing dumb, man. For *her* benefit."

"Well, it was a *very* convincing performance."

"What did the map lead to?" The recorder's focus was impressive, and she pulled the conversation back on track.

"An object of great cosmic power," said Quill and sounded a dramatic chord within the confines of his own imagination. "This thing called the Black Vortex."

"Hey!" Rocket dropped his omni-tool. "Hey, shut up! You're not supposed to tell anybody that, you idiot!"

"It's fine, Rocket."

The scratching and thudding at the door continued apace and the three of them stared at it for a moment.

The moment over, Rocket continued his tirade. "The Collector quite specifically said not to tell anybody. Now you've gone and told a living, flarkin' *archive*, no offense. Un-flarkin' believable, Quill."

"Will you show me this mirror?" The recorder continued her questioning.

"I mean, of course you can see it. But it's on the *Milano*, our ship. So, the first thing we've gotta do is figure out how to haul our asses from here to there."

There were a few more sounds from the console as Rocket narrowed in on how to operate everything on board the ship. His aptitude for technology was extraordinary and in all the years they'd been together, it never failed to impress Quill. Not that he said so. No point in inflating Rocket's ego any more than it already was.

"Two more minutes," said Rocket, gleefully. "Two more minutes and the Brood will be *toast*, baby."

"I did not realize that the human ass was detachable."

"I... wait, what?"

"You said you desire to return your ass to the *Milano*." The recorder's tone was serious.

"For real? Have you ever actually met anybody with a detachable ass?"

"Of course I have, Star-Lord."

That had not been the response he'd been anticipating and all he could manage in response was a weak little "oh."

"Please be patient with me, Star-Lord. I have over a million languages in my database, but English is one of the most challenging because it is so rarely literal. For example..."

"Enough," snapped Rocket. "Stop chatting up the skinbot. She's given us what we needed. Shut her down."

"Rocket!" Quill was mortified. "She's not like that mainframe you're gleefully ripping apart! She's practically a *person*."

"Quill. If she was just a square box with blinking lights and a keyboard, you'd not care. You're just distracted by the..." He waved a paw vaguely. "By the mask."

"Ignore him," said Quill to the recorder. "Rocket's useful, but he's heartless."

"He has no heart?"

"You can learn, right?"

"Yes, Star-Lord. That is my primary objective. To learn."

"Not just data, though. I mean, you can learn behavior."

"Yes. In order to better blend in and avoid causing offense, my programming allows me to observe and mimic societal codes. I do not actually experience what you would call 'emotion', but I comprehend its attendant behaviors."

Quill slapped his hand on his thigh. "I'd call that a big 'yes'. See, Rocket? She's more human than *you* are."

"As though being human is some great thing. No, Quill. That's not true. She cares what you think – which I don't, by the way – and *that's* the only reason you like her."

"Nobody likes Rocket," said Quill to the recorder. "Heck, I barely tolerate him and I'm his best friend."

Rocket made a noise between a snort and a laugh and then put his paws triumphantly onto the console. "I'm gonna try this now. And when it works, because it *will* work, you can thank me after. OK. Here goes. Wish me luck!"

"Sure, Rocket," said Quill in what he hoped was an encouraging tone. "Good luck, bro."

Rocket's claws clattered on the console, his dark eyes fixed firmly on what he was doing, and he pushed a slider upwards. The background whine went from low to high and then a steady *thrummmmm* filled the room. Lights flickered on, revealing the ship for the mess that it had become beneath the onslaught of the Brood. "Oh yeah," said Rocket. "Bow down before me, because I am a *god* among…"

"Raccoons?" the recorder interjected. The look Rocket shot her could have melted her circuits.

"No! I keep telling you all! I ain't a…"

There was a sudden change in the background sound, an audiological stutter and then the pause of a heartbeat. Rocket's look of triumph become one of panic. "Oh no."

"'Oh no' is never good," said Quill, abandoning his position by the recorder and moving to the console. "Why are you saying 'oh no', Rocket? What did you *do*?"

"I didn't…" There was a cessation of noise outside the door as the Brood simultaneously picked up on the same thing that everyone else did. The background noise ramped upwards to a pitch so high that it could possibly have attracted dogs from galaxies hitherto undiscovered. Rocket, who could pick up the ultra-high frequency of the sound, clamped his paws over his ears and said something in a language Quill did not know.

Then all the lights went out.

Even the dim glow of the emergency lighting had gone. They were enveloped in an all-consuming darkness of the kind that ate sound and vomited it back up as an ominous, silent threat: a certainty that any moment now, something would leap out and go "boo".

"Flark," came a voice in the darkness. There was a momentary pause and then first Rocket's and then Quill's portable lights flickered on, throwing them and the Rigellian Recorder into sharp relief. Rocket's paws flew across the console. "Flarking…"

"What happened?"

"I believe the whole system crashed," said the recorder, helpfully.

Rocket turned on her in a furious rage. "Flark you and flark this *flarking* ship, and the Brood… and Quill… and *everything else*. Flark *everything* and *everybody* and…"

"Rocket, cool your jets, man!" Quill tried to ignore the fact that now they had adjusted to the darkness, the sounds of the encroaching Brood were becoming more urgent, more hungry, and infinitely more enthusiastic. "What do we do now? Come on, we're the Guardians of the Galaxy, man! We've *got* to have a Plan B. Let's think it through. How about if I press this button…" He reached out and Rocket slapped his hand away.

"OK, *you* press that button."

"Oh, there's a Plan B, Quill." Rocket's expression was grim, his eyes narrowed, and his paws trembled slightly. Quill wisely decided to not mention it. He looked expectantly at Rocket for the revelation of the plan.

Rocket revealed the plan with two clipped words. He unslung the rifle he wore across his back. "Blasters out," he said and flicked the switch. The power-up cycle began its low drone, and he altered his posture to prepare to fire. "As soon as that door gets breached – and believe me, it's gonna happen any time now – don't take your finger off your trigger. They'll crash over us like a wave." He raised his voice as the Brood renewed their efforts to break into the bridge. Their howling and screeching had risen to fever pitch.

"Maybe we can find another way out," said Quill, loudly. "The vents?"

"I was gonna open the airlocks vessel-wide," shouted Rocket. "Flush the Brood out that way. If *that* failed, I was gonna uplink the navigation system to the *Milano* and remote-pilot it over to this hunk of junk's emergency hatch. But no game, Quill. No *flarking* game! No juice, no solution. We're screwed on both fronts."

"Why don't you just use the remote-pilot option that you built into your gauntlet?" Quill's voice was a bellow by now.

"Because my gauntlet's still on the *Milano!*" It came out as a scream and Quill was temporarily rendered speechless.

"Excuse me," said the recorder into the gap, but she was neither heard nor listened to.

"How could you forget something that important, Rocket?"

"I didn't forget it! I left it there! I've been having an arthritic flare-up in my wrist, OK? It *hurts* to wear the thing!"

"And you have the nerve to mock *me* for getting old? Rocket!"

"Excuse me?" the recorder tried again, to much the same result.

There was a repeated heavy thudding outside; rhythmic, steady, and keenly indicating that the Brood had found something to slam against the door to finally break it down. Possibly each other, given their hunger-driven frenzy. Quill was losing his cool now.

"We can't just blast our way through the Brood, Rocket! There's hundreds of them! This ship is a *hive*!"

"Finally, we agree on something," said Rocket, shifting position again. The rifle had completed its power-up cycle and as Quill reluctantly took his own weapons out of their thigh-holsters, it winked a steady green light into the darkness. "Our mutual screwedness."

"Excuse me!" The recorder adjusted her own volume to be heard and, as one, Quill and Rocket wheeled on her.

"What?" both said in a disjointed unison.

"I wanted to say that if you feel it could be useful, I could act as the relay for a remote-pilot link."

"What did you say?" Rocket stared.

"I wanted to say that if you feel…"

"Why the *hell* didn't you say that before?"

"Until you explained your strategy, I did not know what

you were planning. And unless I am directly in peril, I am programmed to be an inactive participant in history. I am a recorder. I do not create history or participate in it. I simply record it as an impartial observer."

She said all this over the background sound of shredding hull as the door finally began to yield. Quill gripped his pistols tighter. His heart hammered in his chest, and he nodded vigorously. "Oh, God. All right. They're nearly through. I can see teeth. I see 'em, Rocket. They're coming!" He squeezed the triggers and the double-blast of the discharge was intense in the enclosed space. They were rewarded with a squeal as the shots removed the lower jaw of the unfortunate Brood forcing its way through the new hole in the door.

"OK, skinbot," said Rocket, trying his hardest to ignore the sounds of Brood-hunger. "How do we do this?"

"I am picking up the *Milano*'s signal," said the recorder, and for a moment, her eyes glowed bright white, surrounding her in an aura of light that filled the bridge. A holographic keyboard appeared before her, and her fingers flew over it. "I am projecting a command station. Please enter the encryption key for the *Milano*."

"That is… OK, I got it." Rocket tapped in the code on the keyboard, pushing back his curiosity as to the inner workings of the recorder for later. If there *was* a later.

"They're breaking through!" Quill's occasional declarations of their encroaching doom were distracting, but at least it kept Rocket apprised of the scale of screwed-uppedness. "Come and get a piece of me if you're brave enough!"

"Encryption key entered. Decoding."

*"They're breaking through, Rocket!"*

"I hear that, thanks, Quill. How long will this take?"

There was a terrible sound of rending metal and then the bridge erupted in chaos as a flood of starving, rapacious Brood broke through the barrier that had been protecting Quill and Rocket. They forgot about the *Milano*, they forgot the recorder, they forgot Plans B through Z.

They engaged.

# CHAPTER TWO
## FALLEN WORLD

Entry D1491R7P

Location: *The Earth solar system. Near Saturn. On board the Milano. Hyper-speed.*

Context: *The Mighty Star-Lord, Rocket Raccoon, and I escaped the Brood after a surprisingly brief firefight and are none the worse for the experience.*

A thumping bass beat played, accompanied by a simple guitar riff. There were vocals, but they were probably less important than the nosebleed-inducing reverb of the bass. The mix of the music was heavy enough on the lower registers that a small table in the middle of the living area was shaking papers all over the floor.

Rocket reached for Quill's so-called boombox and flicked the power switch.

"Hey, man, why did you do that?"

"You've played that same song about seventy-seven thousand times already."

"Yeah, that's because it's *awesome*."

"Sure. But I figured you'd want to know that we're only fifteen minutes or so from Earth."

"I am surprised that your ship has made such good time." The recorder had been silent for much of the trip, reviewing the material she had recorded whilst aboard the *Prosperity*.

Rocket narrowed his eyes at her. "Why 'surprised'?"

"Because it is poorly maintained and outdated." Both Rocket and Quill bristled at the insult, but the recorder's observation was punctuated by a sudden scream from the engines. "It has made that same noise approximately six times every cycle. It is a noise presaging the death of an engine. I have heard it before."

"You know what, skinbot? You wouldn't look so great yourself if you'd navigated your way through a quantum asteroid field, or survived a firefight with a fleet of Kree omniships, or…"

"Wait, are you talking about the *Milano*? Or yourself?" Quill smirked.

Rocket scowled. "I'm just saying that the *Milano* might be old and outdated, *much like Quill*, but it's also your only ticket outta here. Show her some respect."

The recorder looked at Rocket for a few moments. Rocket felt uncomfortable; a sense that she was somehow stealing his soul. Then she turned away again.

"I wish to hear more about the Collector and your quest to obtain the thing you called the Black Vortex."

"Quests?" Rocket snorted. "Quests are *heroic*. This ain't heroic. This is a dumb-assed treasure hunt."

"No, she's right. It's a quest. The Guardians' Epic Quest for Cosmic Glory." Quill emphasized each word.

Rocket's eyes rolled so far back into his head they practically fell out. "Would you please *stop*? It's like you're constantly giving yourself a group hug."

"But it's *great*."

"Now tell the rest of it, Quill. Tell the skinbot about what happened with the Collector. About how it's more humiliating than it is exciting."

"Of course! The Collector had just shown me the map…"

The images flashed by again. The planet. The continent. The state. The words. The shattering. Quill watched it several times, then looked up. "A map?"

"Part of a map. Hush, Mr Delicious." The little dog had resumed its incessant yipping. "The whereabouts of the rest of this map are unknown."

"What's at the other end of it?"

"What do you find if you look into any mirror, Peter Quill?"

*Was this a trick question?* No, he didn't think it was. "A… reflection?"

"Exactly. The map, when whole, will lead you to the location of the next piece of the puzzle."

"Another mirror?"

"Yes, but larger. *Much* larger. The size of – shall we say – a coffin. This would be the Black Vortex."

Quill's senses tingled and he scratched at the back of his neck. "The Black Vortex? Huh. I feel like I've heard of that."

"If you recognize the name," said the Collector, "that would be because it is the stuff of myth and legend. A battery of cosmic power to all who submit to it. A relic that could, so it is rumored, turn those who submit to it into a *god*…"

"Yeah, yeah. What's it worth?"

The Collector looked from Quill to Rocket and back again. "Has your associate, Mr Raccoon, not explained the details of my offer?"

"Not a raccoon. Yeah, I told him."

"Yeah, he told me. But that's not what I'm asking here. I know how much you're paying us. I want to know what this Vortex thing is actually *worth*." Quill crossed his arms across his chest, assuming a casual stance. Age had a lot of drawbacks, certainly. But for all that time had stolen from him, the reward had been an extraordinarily shrewd sense of business, of value and, perhaps more pertinently, when he was being taken advantage of. As the confidence oozed, he changed the inflection of his words, and the small dog ceased yapping and growled, instead. It was too small for a sound that *big* to be coming from it and the Collector did nothing to quell its obvious anger. Rocket took a step back, holding out his paw in a conciliatory gesture.

"C'mon, Quill. This is a great gig. How about you don't open your mouth anymore and *flark it up*?"

Quill shrugged, his eyes still on the petite, purple woman. "Just curious, is all."

"Curious. Yes." The Collector's eyes narrowed. "You're thinking about keeping it, aren't you?" When Quill responded in the emphatic negative, she continued. "Perhaps try to shift it on the black market?"

"Absolutely n…"

His denial was interrupted by the dog's growl shifting to a bark. Not the high-pitched little yap that it had thus far offered, but a deep throated, frankly terrifying *woof*. The Collector set the dog down, her eyes never leaving Quill's.

"You know," she said, conversationally, "Mr Delicious might *look* like a fluffy little ball of delight…"

The barks continued to grow deeper and far more menacing.

"Oh, hell, no," said Quill.

"But as you can see," she continued, her tone cheerful, "he's *so* much more than that."

Not only were the sounds getting increasingly demonic, the physical form of the small creature swelled and expanded, whilst it categorically did not *actually* get any larger. Again, Quill had the fleeting idea that he was seeing what the Collector wanted him to see, but he had little time to ruminate on the subject.

"Good doggie. Nice doggie! What… big teeth you have!"

"I don't know what the hell that thing is, Quill, but that ain't no dog!" Even Rocket was backing up now. As they retreated, Mr Delicious crouched, then lunged, eliciting cries of alarm from both Guardians.

"Mr Delicious?" The Collector's voice rang out like a bell. The dog – if indeed that was what it was – turned its head and let out a curious whine of interest. "Come here. Come back to Mama, sweetie pie. Aren't you just the *sweetest*, most *darling*…" The dog trotted back to the Collector, flopping down onto its side and daring to waggle its legs. "What a *good* boy. That's my *best* boy!"

It was nauseating, but at least it wasn't trying to eat their faces. The animal took up the Collector's attention for a few moments and gave Rocket a chance to say what he was thinking.

"Quill," he said, keeping his voice low, "I'm thinking we ought to split."

"You might not be wrong, old buddy," Quill replied. He wrinkled his nose as the creature slobbered all over the Collector's face. *No* amount of credits was worth this. They took a single step backwards and instantly the Collector returned her attention to them. "See those necklaces on the pedestal to your right?"

They looked. They saw. They nodded.

"Good. Put them on."

"Uh... I'm not really your typical jewelry guy..."

"Quill... what did I say...? Just ignore him." Rocket laughed nervously, but Quill was already at full speed.

"I mean, I thought about getting an ear stud for a while, but then I looked at myself in the mirror and I had to question that logic. 'Quill', I said, 'Quill, is an ear stud *really* who you are...'"

When the Collector spoke, it was with that same resonant boom that had greeted them on their arrival; the reverberating echo that shook their very bodies. It was accompanied on this occasion by the devilish barking of Mr Delicious.

"Put them on."

"What if we don't put them on?" Even in the face of the Collector's obvious strength and power, and the thought of what Mr Delicious might *actually* be, Quill was defiant. He'd *always* been defiant. Nothing the Collector could say or do would...

She leaned into him and drew a single fingernail down his cheek. It was sharp enough that he felt the prick of blood dribble in the wake of the motion. He swallowed. In that one motion, she made her intent quite clear.

"Are you threatening us, lady?" Rocket attempted his own defiance.

She spared him a glance. "Would you like it to be a threat? Because if you don't put those on, that's what it will be."

*Doomed if we don't, doomed if we do.*

Reluctantly, now acutely aware that any choice had been taken from them, Quill and Rocket snatched up the necklaces, dropping them over their heads. The Collector's smile was sweet as honey-coated rat poison.

"*Thank* you."

Quill inspected the one on Rocket's neck with interest. "Hey, are they made of *silver*?"

"Adamantium, actually."

"Adamantium?" He paused. "And what would you say *these* are worth?"

"These got trackers in them or something?" Rocket was interested in spite of himself.

The Collector laughed. It was not a pleasant sound. "Oh yes. *Something*. Gentlemen, these are the guillotines of Zanbarzan Supreme."

Rocket stared at her as the implications of the word "guillotine" sank in.

She continued with that same self-satisfied smirk on her face. "He used them to ensure *loyalty* in his subjects." She reached into a hidden pocket of her robes and immediately the two strange necklaces began to shrink, reducing in size until both Quill and Rocket threw up their hands in an effort to stop themselves being choked to death. "Because Zanbarzan Supreme knew that every *good* dog wears a collar. Isn't that right, Mr Delicious?"

Mr Delicious barked his acknowledgment.

"Look, lady," said Rocket, his voice made hoarse by the

jeweled garotte presently trying to divest him of his mortal shell. "Being your loyal dogs ain't what we signed up for. Now quit kidding around and take these things…"

The necklaces tightened further, cutting Rocket off in mid-flow and both he and Quill dropped to their knees, choking and gasping for what little breath they could pull in.

"I can tighten them more if that's what you want." There was true malice, real spite in the words and Quill reached out a hand to her, wordlessly mouthing *please stop*. She studied him, mentally noting the shade of puce he had gone. Her smile became amiable again and she released the guillotines. As Quill and Rocket coughed and gasped to get their breathing back, she studied them. "Or I can choose to let you off the leash."

There was no reply. She'd not expected any, neither did she care to hear one. "You have one week to get me what I want. After that, the necklaces will tighten in a single, rapid movement, severing your heads from your shoulders. Very quick, very tidy, very, *very* convenient."

Quill shuddered inwardly. In the space of a few moments, this whole thing had gone from being a promising money-earner to a life-or-death situation. Quill was a fan of life-or-death situations, but usually he dictated the terms. This was something else. All the fun had gone from the job. Now it was *serious*. He didn't have to voice his opinion because Rocket did it for him.

"Oh, come *on,* this is *bull*!" Rocket's protest was weak, but there was fire beneath it. "We don't go back on our word! You don't have to…"

The Collector held up a hand to silence him. "I'm afraid I do have to. Because I have trust issues. You see, my darlings, you aren't the first people I've hired to do this job for me."

"Really? Who had the gig before?" Quill had his breath back, but still knelt on the floor.

She turned and looked at him. "Your father, actually."

"I'm sorry, what?"

"Hang on," interrupted Rocket. "You hired J'Son to find this Black Vortex?"

"Yes. J'Son and his crew of Slaughter Lords. They had a certain reputation…"

"Yeah," said Quill, bitterly. "As losers and scumbags."

"Perhaps. But also as men who would ruthlessly see a job to its very end."

"What we regular people call 'murderers.'"

The Collector idly stroked Mr Delicious's silky, furry little head as she continued. "One does not simply *acquire* what is, after all, a weapon of mass destruction. Death surrounds objects of great power. The Black Vortex leaves a trail of blood in its wake. A trail that even – what was that phrase… *losers and scumbags* should be able to follow with ease."

"What happened to him, then?" Quill was interested despite that part of him that didn't care one bit. "What happened to my father?"

"This is the thing, Mr Quill," she said. "I was rather hoping you might be able to tell me once all this is finished. J'Son and his crew apparently stole the Black Vortex from the Shi'ar before smuggling it to Earth for their own benefit. So here I am, many years later, without my prize." She curled a hand into a fist and Quill felt rage boil from her in a wave. She relaxed and mastered her emotions. "It's quite possible your father is dead at this point. But if he isn't, well…"

Her smile was predatory.

"For an additional fee, you can most certainly kill him for me."

"I did wonder why you and Rocket were wearing matching accessories, but I was too polite to enquire." The recorder had been silent throughout the remainder of Quill's tale, but now spoke. "I believed at first that perhaps it was a totem of some kind, perhaps a mark of your affection for one another."

Rocket snorted. "As if," he said. "We prefer to limit our marks of affection to dirty curses and kidney punches."

"I still can't believe she hired that piece of garbage," said Quill.

The recorder turned her gaze on him and tipped her head to the side. "You do not have fond feelings for your father?"

"Best not to go there," said Rocket.

"Yeah," supplied Quill. "Let's not go there, Cora."

"Wait, what? Cora?" Rocket stared.

"Yeah! Like... re-Cora-der. Cora." Quill was pleased with the play on words. Rocket was not. "She needs a name, man! She's gotta have a name!"

"Oh, here we go again. It's the Naming Things Stupidly Game. Look, skinbot. Do you know where he got the name of this ship from? The *Milano*? This chick on some TV show called 'Who's the Boss'."

"Shut up, Rocket. Cora. That's your name now. Do you like it?"

"Cora." The recorder considered for a few moments. "Yes. I like it. My ass likes it very much."

"That's not *quite* how you use the expression, Cora, but good try."

"Give it up, Quill. Why bother with a name? It's not like it's coming with us."

"Why not?"

Rocket glowered and looked between Quill and Cora. "When we get to Earth, we dump it. We don't need a third wheel."

"If it suits you both," said Cora, her tone sweet and measured, "I would prefer to follow you for a while. Record your heroic victory..." Quill punched the air. "Or your tragic failure."

"She's coming with us," asserted Quill.

"It's not a she. It's an *it*. It's... a trashcan with googly eyes."

"She. Cora. And she's coming with us. And that's the end of it. Welcome aboard the *Milano,* Cora. You're one of us now. I'm *right* about this, Rocket. And you *hate* it when I'm right."

"How would you know? We've never had the chance to find out."

"Are you kidding? I *said* we should respond to that emergency beacon, and *you* said we should ignore it. And if I hadn't gotten my way, Cora would never have saved us from the Brood..."

"She only saved us from the Brood because we answered the flarking beacon in the first place, Quill!" Rocket had switched Cora's pronouns without even noticing.

"Exactly my point!"

"Am I in hell? Is this actually *hell*?"

But Quill was just getting started. "And I bet I'm right about stealing the Black Vortex, too. Yeah? You with me on that one, little buddy? We should totally steal it from J'Son."

"Quill. Whatever this thing is, we are *not* stealing it."

"Oh, come *on*. Since when do we do what we're told?"

"Since right now. Since our money and our lives are now the stakes."

"We're the Guardians of the Galaxy, man! We aren't gonna let some cosmic baseball card collector boss us around."

They bickered a little while and then Rocket ran his claws through the fur on his head, ignoring the fact that a clump came away with it. "We're not the Guardians of the Galaxy. We ain't... guardian-ing *anything*. We're just trying to survive."

Any further reflection was interrupted by a series of chimes, indicating that the *Milano* was now well on its way to journey's end. Grateful for the distraction, Rocket turned away and studied the readings. "We're starting our Earth approach. May as well take a seat. No doubt we'll have the defense agencies on the line any time now."

Quill slid into the pilot's seat and leaned back comfortably. "Hey, do you think Nick Fury is still alive?" He didn't even wait for a response before he continued, his mind working at a rapid pace. "You know what? I don't even care. I just want to get a bacon double cheeseburger, maybe pick up some new vinyl... catch up with some pals..."

"Oh, yeah. We'll have *loads* of free time." Rocket tapped over-dramatically at the collar around his neck. "So much free time, Quill. Yeah, that sounds *totally* wonderful."

"How long has it been since you last visited Earth, Star-Lord?" Cora joined them in the cockpit, standing in the doorway. Quill looked over and waved a hand in the air.

"Oh. Ages. Longer than you were on that space freighter."

"Long enough that there's likely to be some people down there who are amazed we're still alive."

"I see. And will there be a hero's welcome for the Guardians of the Galaxy?"

"A hero's… ha!" Rocket snorted. "Not a chance, skinbot."

"I mean, it's not *impossible*," said Quill, hopefully.

"It's *quite* impossible. Nobody can know why we're here, remember? The Collector made it quite clear that our focus is getting what she wants. We deviate from that, she'll know about it."

"How will she know about it?"

"Quill, you really want to question what that psycho is capable of?"

Quill didn't. It was a good, well-made point.

"So we keep a low profile. We do our job. We go in, we come out, we get the cheesewire removed, the Collector gets her heart's desire, we get to keep our heads, hooray!"

"I guess," said Quill and mused for a moment. "Hey, how about Alyssa Milano? Do you think *she's* still alive?"

"If I may ask," said Cora, "who *was* the boss?"

"What?"

"Earlier, Rocket told me that was the name of her television program. Was she the boss?"

"Oh my *God!*" Quill was excited by the subject and turned away to look at Cora. "That was the fundamental question of the show! You never *know* who's the boss. It's a constantly shifting power dynamic among this broken family, and…"

His enthusiasm was crushed beneath Rocket's next observation. "Wait a second. There's something *weird* here."

Quill trailed off and turned back to the console. "Weird? What's weird?"

"Nothing."

"Nothing's weird?"

"No, I mean, I got *nothing*. No hail requests. No transmissions. No worried broad from S.H.I.E.L.D. demanding to know my business. Nothing. Zip." He reached up and flicked at several switches on the console, cycling through several frequencies. Quill frowned.

"Maybe the monitor's damaged?"

"The monitor is not damaged," said Cora. "There are no signals being broadcast."

"See? She can be helpful. I think that…"

Whatever it was that Quill thought was interrupted by the alarm blaring out of the console. All thoughts of frivolity disappeared, and Quill finally paid attention. "What's that?"

"A warning," replied Rocket, his eyes darting back and forth along the readouts. "No salutation, no greeting, no vectoring of inbound aircraft, just… a warning."

"Well, where's it coming from?"

"The signal originates in the upper atmosphere," supplied Cora. "An orbital ring of satellites."

"Helpful again!" Quill slapped his knee.

"It makes no sense, Quill! There's been no attempted communication at all! Something's very, very wrong."

"Transmit our flight data."

"I'm *trying*." Rocket's claws flew across the console, and he shook his head. "Something's off. I'm getting *very* itchy." Quill leaned over and put his hand on Rocket's arm. "This is *not* fine, before you try to reassure me. This is…"

A second alarm sounded, more urgent than the first, lacing through the underlying siren with all the care and elegance of a stampeding elephant.

"If I am not mistaken," said Cora, "we are being fired upon."

"What? Why? Why would anyone fire on us? We are the Guardians of the…"

"They are flarkin' well *firing on us, Quill*."

The sirens continued blaring, then a light winked on the console. All eyes were drawn to it as it blinked on and off faster and faster, until all the hairs on the back of Quill's neck stood on end.

There was silence. The light winked off one last time and then came on, steady and glaring.

"Oh, *crap*."

The projectile struck, the impact throwing all three occupants of the *Milano* to the deck. Bodies that had once withstood far worse but which were now getting too old to weather rough treatment protested at this new abuse. The front windows of the ship blew out and the roaring wind drowned out everything but the final shout of Rocket Raccoon.

"Brace! Brace!"

Then there was nothing.

Light and sound suddenly blossomed. Then pain. A lot of pain. Every part of him hurt abominably. *Am I dead? No. If I was dead, I wouldn't be in pain. I'm not religious, but I'm pretty sure that's a thing.* Quill's moment of existentialism was curtailed by the sound of coughing and the hissing of steam venting from torn conduits. The coughing continued unabated for some time.

Quill was lying on hard earth, not the metal of the *Milano*. He remembered crawling free of the wreckage before unconsciousness had taken him. He didn't know how long he'd been out, neither did it seem important right now. He turned his head to look at the smaller figure a few feet from him who was coughing up his little lungs.

"You OK, Rock?"

"Yeah, yeah, never better." Rocket's cough slowly faded. "I'll live. What about the skinbot? She OK?"

"I don't see her," said Quill and he cautiously got into a sitting position. "Wait, I think that's her over there. I can see a leg. Oh, man. She's buried. Must've got flung when we hit the ground." He dragged his aching body upright and staggered to where the recorder's body lay. He hefted the debris clear. "Her eyes are open, but heck, man, I don't know if she even closes them. Cora. Hey, Cora? Can you hear me?"

Nothing.

Rocket joined him and stared at the recorder, then up at Quill. "Well, here we are back on Earth. Just like we planned. Just not *like* we planned."

"Where are we, exactly?"

"South Dakota. Just outside the Black Hills. Just as you plotted."

"No way, man." Quill squinted into the surrounding area. It was a vast, empty wasteland of blasted landscapes and sun-dried grasses. "This isn't Dakota. It looks like *Arizona*. The coordinates must've been off. This can't be right. This is desert, not plains. You can't be right."

"I'm right. Look. Over there." Rocket pointed and Quill's gaze followed. "That's... what do you call it? Mount Rushmore, right?" He moved around to look at what had once been the *Milano*. "Look at this, man. What a flarkin' mess." He picked up a piece of metal and immediately dropped it as it was red hot. The air was filled with the stink of burning fuel. Here and there pieces of rough glass protruded where the sandy ground had fused in the heat of their engines. Quill was standing, staring at the hills.

"Rocket…"

"What now?"

"I know my eyes aren't exactly as good as they used to be, but that's not Washington. Or Jefferson. Or Lincoln. Or… or…"

"Roosevelt." Rocket sighed. "I know your own stupid planet's history better than you do."

"Roosevelt. That's not him, either." Quill squinted and focused and his blood ran cold as he finally began to make out the particular features of the carvings. Four faces, right enough, but none of them renditions of former presidents. Not even close.

"Doom," said Quill and it was little more than a whisper.

"What are you on about now, Quill?"

"Doom, Rocket. Look!" Indeed, Mount Rushmore had been given over to new carvings, each a perfectly detailed and beautifully worked relief of the face of Victor von Doom. "Doctor Doom."

Rocket's earlier assertation was, it transpired, one hundred percent correct. Something was very, very wrong.

# CHAPTER THREE
## THE WASTELANDS

Entry C1451Z2F
Location: *Earth. South Dakota, or at least the state formerly known as South Dakota. Travelling in the vehicle of a local who saved us by the name of Red Crotter. Situation: tenuous.*
Addendum: *My recording is a little muddled as, on arrival, my systems were compromised. I have pieced together what occurred based on what I heard from Rocket and Star-Lord during the journey to this point. The fact that neither of them ever stops talking has assisted this process.*

*I will try to do better in future.*

The truck might once have had suspension, but the years of tracking over the rocky, broken landscape had rendered such luxury entirely useless. Rocket, sitting in the front of the vehicle, scanned the inky darkness beyond the chipped and dirt-smeared windscreen. Beside him, driving the truck with intense determination, sat a dark-skinned, wiry older man who reeked strongly of stale alcohol.

On the back seat behind them, Cora sat with an unconscious Peter Quill. The recorder's body jolted with every bump and lump in the road, but she demonstrated no discomfort at all. Instead, she kept a hand on Quill's shoulder, keeping him as still as she could manage.

"Can't this heap go any faster?" Rocket barked out the words and the driver shrugged lightly.

"How about you make yourself useful instead of being ungrateful? Do you see anything? Are we being followed?" His voice was a deep, bass rumble and, despite the tension in the truck, Red Crotter – unlikely savior and unexpected ally – seemed calm.

"Nothing. Not seeing nobody out there." Rocket squinted into the darkening night.

"What's the last you seen of 'em?"

"Few miles back. Torches in the dark. Nothing since."

Red nodded and released his foot on the gas a little. "Could be they're waiting till morning comes round. There's things out here in the Wastelands."

"Excuse me?" Cora finished her self-diagnostics and resumed conversation. Red continued talking over her as though she had said nothing.

"Things that you definitely don't want to risk runnin' into at night."

"Excuse me? Hello? Mr Red Crotter?"

"How's Old Man Quill doing back there?" Crotter continued to ignore her.

"Him?" Rocket snorted. "Still sleeping off his hangover."

"Be fair. It's more than just a hangover. He got beat up real good back there. Took his punches, got a bottle broken over his head..." Red whistled through missing teeth and looked at the road ahead.

"Can't blame him for choosing sleep over engaging with this world. Some homecoming, huh. Quill? Quill! C'mon. Wake up!"

The curled-up figure in the back of the truck mumbled something. "Don't wanna get up. Just let me sleep a bit longer, Mom."

"Excuse me?" Cora continued trying to be heard and continued to be ignored.

"He's an idiot when he's awake," said Rocket, poking at the sleeping Quill with a foot. "But he's a *moron* when he's asleep."

"Excuse me!" Cora tried affirmative action and silence descended. "I have information that could assist."

"Then spit it out," said Rocket, seemingly reluctant to engage with the recorder.

"If you stop the truck..."

"We ain't stopping this truck," said Red. "Not with a deputized posse hot on our heels."

"But if you stop the truck, Mr Red Crotter, I can use my seismographic sensor to determine whether or not we are presently being pursued."

There was a brief pause, then Red tipped his head to the side. "She can use her what? What did she say?" Rocket glanced at the recorder, then at Quill, before deciding.

"Stop the truck, old man."

"Hey. Hey! Call me Red, or believe me, my generosity will end with you being dumped out on the side of the road!"

"Fine. *Red*. Stop the truck. Hit the brakes."

With a screech suggesting the truck had more disc than pad, it came to a shuddering stop. Red switched off the engine and the silence of the desert night enveloped the vehicle and its occupants like a smothering blanket. Rocket shook off his unease, considering Cora with more interest than he had before.

"Seismographic sensor, huh? What *else* are you capable of, skinbot?"

"I have over one thousand recording functions. I can list them for you if you wish."

"No, that's fine. Just… do your thing." Rocket's words were punctuated by another snore from the sleeping Quill. He kicked his friend again for good measure, but still no response. "Go on, Cora. See what's out there."

It was the first time he'd voluntarily used the name Quill had given the recorder, but he sternly reminded himself that this didn't make them friends.

"Of course, Rocket." The lights behind Cora's eyes switched from their usual green to a deep violet. A pulsating hum emanated from her, radiating outwards in a rippling wave. Whenever one of the pulses throbbed, the hackles on Rocket's neck stood up. She kept this up for a few moments before Rocket interrupted.

"What are your sensors telling you, then?"

There were another three pulses and then her eyes returned to green. "Something *is* out there. Something is coming."

"See?" Red's voice with triumphant. "I told…"

"It is not the men you fear."

"Oh," said Rocket. "That's something, I guess." He tapped Red on the shoulder with one claw. "Let's go."

Red started up the truck and they proceeded, a little slower. The only sounds for a while were those of Quill's snoring and an occasional cough from Rocket. Cora sat peacefully, just watching, and Red's eyes were on the road. After a while, he said to Rocket, "So... what ya got for equipment back there?"

"Quill's got his helmet and his rocket boots. I've got my blaster."

"How 'bout you, Cora? You got some way to defend yourself?" Red's eyes met those of the recorder in the rearview mirror and she nodded.

"My gripping force is four thousand PSI. I can easily lift one thousand pounds in weight above my head. I will happily provide further strength data for you if you are curious."

"Not necessary. That sounds fine. Just so long as you ain't afraid to use it."

"I do not experience fear in the way organic life forms do. Nonetheless, if my safety and continuation is threatened, my programming allows me to terminate my assailant. However, if those around me are threatened, that same programming dictates that I must stand as witness."

"No disrespect, ma'am, but I sure hope that means it's you in the crosshairs." Red shuddered briefly, the dispassionate statement having unnerved him. Rocket watched the exchange, thinking, plotting, calculating. It was not in his nature to trust anybody new, and that held true for the introduction of Red Crotter into his environment. Sure, Red was helping them – but for how long was anybody's guess.

"So, Red. Much as I'm enjoying the first-class comfort of your truck here, I'm gonna admit to feeling impatient. How much farther to this farm of yours?"

"See that quarter moon now shining up there?" Rocket looked and replied in the affirmative. "When it drops behind that horned peak off to the northwest, we'll be home."

"Well, that didn't answer my question at all, but thanks."

"Approximately thirty minutes, Rocket," supplied Cora. "I vectored the coordinates of the moon's path, factored in the median speed of our progress and extrapolated that thirty minutes – approximately – will be the time of arrival." The pause was miniscule, but Rocket caught it. "Assuming we are not delayed by an attack."

"Thirty minutes is time enough for you to catch me up," said Red. "Tell me everything that happened before you busted me and Quill out of that jail cell."

"Let me summarize," said Rocket. "We crashed our ship. We hiked across this forsaken boneyard you probably like to call home. We encountered a few problems at Outpost 13. Blah blah, something, blah. Here we are. End of story."

"Cora?"

"Yes, Mr Red Crotter?"

"Got a hunch you can do better than that."

"Of course. Allow me a moment to cycle back to my recordings following our arrival on Earth."

### EARLIER...

There was no time to ponder the meaning of the changes to Mount Rushmore. Well, that wasn't entirely correct: there *was* time. Given the current state of the *Milano* (what Rocket referred to in technical terms as "flarked up beyond all repair"), there would be plenty of time. Armed with that knowledge, Quill turned his attention back to the key issues at hand.

Kneeling before the Rigellian Recorder, he checked her inert form for signs of activity. He heard her internal systems ticking over, so she wasn't dead or whatever passed as death in her kind, so that was something. As he continued examining her, he mentally reviewed their situation.

*Milano* down. New companion: also down. Guillotine necklaces – *in situ*. Chances of success on this mission, rapidly decreasing. Sun, unrelenting. Signs of life in the immediate vicinity, zero. Likelihood of death, almost entirely certain. Optimism levels, low. He tried shaking Cora, but she had nothing to say. Rocket came up behind him.

"It's bust, Quill. We may as well leave it."

"I'm not leaving her, man!"

"For the love of… just *leave* her. It. Leave it."

"She saved us! If not for her, we'd be Brood food!" His stubbornness was born of his own anxiety around their situation, and it was more than Rocket could bear to let slide. He balled his paws into little furry fists, preventing a full explosion of his not-inconsiderable temper.

"Come *on*, Quill! In the state she's in, she's just gonna slow us down! Think about it. We have *less than a week* to find this Black Vortex and get it back to the Collector. Less than a week, Quill. If we don't sort this problem out, these guillotine necklaces are gonna pop our heads right off our shoulders – or did you forget that detail?"

"No, I hadn't forgotten. But… we don't leave people behind." Quill's tone was achingly reasonable, and Rocket hated him for it. His temper cooled a fraction.

"That's what this is about, huh?" He sighed. When he continued, the rage had ebbed, to be replaced by a hint of sympathy. "Look, the past is the past. That was a long time ago. You can't change what happened."

"No one gets left behind, Rocket." Quill hunkered down, sliding his arms under the inert Cora, picking her up. She was surprisingly light for a being made mostly of metal, but that was probably for the best given the state of Quill's aching back. After several seconds of standing there holding her, he revised his opinion on her heft.

She was *heavy*. But he was making a point, so stood his ground.

"Don't you *dare*. Put her down, Quill, or so help me…"

"There's emergency evac sleds in the hold. They probably survived the crash. I'll strap her down and drag her. I'll do all the heavy lifting here, Rocket, because she's coming with us. Because unlike you, I am a *really good person*."

Something in Quill's tone stayed any further comment from Rocket and he went to check over the hold. Everything was miraculously intact and after retrieving one of the evac-sleds, Rocket used the opportunity to look for anything of use in this gods-forsaken wasteland.

Because that was exactly what had become of the area. What had once been a lush, green sea of waving grasses and fresh breezes had become a barren desert. The air was so hot that whenever either of them breathed in, it was like inhaling a furnace. By the time Quill had strapped Cora down to the sled, his shirt was soaked with his own sweat. That highlighted another problem to add to the Jenga-stack they were already dealing with. They needed water and they would need shelter.

There was little point in staying here at the *Milano*'s wreck: help would not be forthcoming any time soon. They had to travel. But which way?

Rocket sorted through what could be salvaged. They managed to get a little water, some food cubes, changes of clothing for Quill and a slightly elderly medical kit that someone had long ago taken anything useful out of without making sure to replace it. Once they'd stacked their now-meagre possessions, along with Rocket's rifle and his precious box of tools, alongside the recorder on the sled, Quill applied his knowledge of navigating by the sun to pick a direction.

Which is to say, he took a breath and pointed.

"That way," he said with such confidence in his tone that Rocket didn't even stop to consider that maybe, just *maybe*, Quill might be making it up.

The wind picked up dust particulate, swirling it around them as they walked, and it was, frankly, Quill's vision of what hell would be like. He dragged the sled behind him, making good on his promise that he would be responsible for Cora. She still showed no signs of movement, but there had been a series of clicks and whirrs that suggested *something* was going on.

Around them, skeletal branches of long-dead trees stirred vaguely in the wind. Long since stripped of leaves, they stood as ghostly reminders of what had once been, things that now just created ominous silhouettes against the sky. They afforded no shelter from the relentless heat, which according to Rocket's gauntlet climbed to a sweltering one hundred and ten degrees.

They walked for about two hours in the heat before Quill halted, his breath ragged in his chest. "I think I figured it out, Rock," he said. "What's wrong with Earth. Something about the gravity, for sure. It's got stronger. My thighs feel trembly. My throat feels like it's full of fire ants and there's every possibility that my liver has dissolved and is dribbling down my leg. Gravity problems."

Rocket squinted at Quill. "You don't think any of that is because you're getting old and out of shape, then?"

"Nope. I'm in *great* shape."

"Round is a shape, I grant you."

"It's a gravity problem."

Rocket snorted and they resumed their trek. After another hour passed and the sun showed little sign of giving up, they came to another halt. This time, though, there was something more positive.

"OK, I've got noise," said Rocket, studying his gauntlet. "Electronic emissions, that direction." He indicated. "According to the data I programmed in before we crashed, it's the site of a town your Earth maps call Rockerville."

"Never heard of it," said Quill. "Let's keep going."

The asphalt had long since fractured into small, gray, dusty islands. Abandoned vehicles – cars, trucks, motorbikes – littered the highway. Most were empty, but every now and then there would be a shape at the wheel and that shape was almost always a skeleton. Added to that were the fleeting glimpses they caught of snakes and other local wildlife – none of which fit Quill's memory of how big a Terran animal should be. They were incomprehensibly *huge*. It was the stuff of nightmares and had his muscles not been screaming out in agony, Quill might have stopped to wonder further what had happened here to cause this horror. Instead, he asked the most important question on his mind.

"Why is it so *hot*, Rocket? It's like... it's like I'm sucking on the tail pipe of the Mars explorer."

"Oh, for the love of... will you suffer in silence, please?"

Quill managed another ten minutes of silence before he suffered vocally again. This time, when he spoke, his voice was small and tight: angry and upset in equal measure. "Rocket?"

"Yeah? What?"

"Earth officially sucks."

Rocket didn't reply, simply shook his head, and sighed again as they trudged on for another half hour or so. Finally, they found the old town sign. "Rockerville" was clumsily crossed out and daubed above it, in slightly wonky writing, was "Outpost 13".

Someone had also thoroughly scrubbed out the word "Welcome".

It was approaching noon and the heat was at its worst. Quill was beginning to think that the day couldn't possibly get any more miserable. Then it got more miserable.

"So that gets you to Outpost 13," said Red as Cora finished her story.

Rocket stared at her. "You heard *everything* we said?"

"Everything, Rocket."

"Well, that's just *great*."

"Carry on, Cora. What happened when you got to Outpost 13?" Red prompted for a continuation before things devolved to squabbling again.

"Things got complicated."

As they approached formerly-Rockerville, the two Guardians

became aware of the loud, tinny voice. The quality was poor, putting Quill in mind of his childhood days at the state fair. Maybe a PA system of some kind. Moving into the boundaries of the settlement, the voice settled into something that they could understand. Or at least something that they could *hear*. Understanding it was far more complex.

"Outpost 13 is taxed on a bi-monthly basis," the voice announced. "Today is taxation day! All payments must be made by sundown or punishment will be rendered. For the greater good of your community, alert all those you know."

The voice belonged to a humanoid figure moving along a long line of people. Some of them had goats or pigs on makeshift leashes. All of them looked dirty, harassed, and tired. But Quill's eyes were on the humanoid figure.

"Outpost 13 is taxed on a bi-monthly basis," it repeated.

Rocket grabbed at Quill. "It's Doom," he said, his voice a low growl.

Quill glanced down. "It's not that bad yet, Rocket. We've been in worse situations."

"No, man! I'm not talking about my state of being! I mean it's *him*! Doctor motherflarking *Doom*! Not *actually* him, but those… things. You know. Those *things!*" Recall was not as sharp as it had once been, and Rocket struggled to finish his sentence.

The figure continued its monologue. "All payments must be made by sundown…" It passed a pig which began squealing, setting off a chain of cacophonous animal noises.

Quill shook his head in disbelief. "Tell you what, Rocket, something does *not* make sense here. Why is a crazy, powerful, objectively mad scientist collecting goats and pigs and…" he looked. "…carrots… Why is he collecting those in a bunghole in the desert called Outpost 13?"

"Let's be fair, some people might have similarly insulting things to say about *our* fall from grace." Rocket was distracted by his own thoughts.

"Hey, Rocket?" Quill squinted. Such an action worked before and it worked now. "Look at the way he's moving. Those stiff arm swings?" Recollection tickled at the back of his mind, a memory floundering and reaching for rescue. With an effort, Quill retrieved it.

"A Doombot. Remember that Doombot we encountered once?"

"Doombot! That was the word!"

"End of recording," said Cora, leaning back. "Unfortunately, I have yet to fully collate everything that has happened so I cannot explain our presence in your vehicle."

"Don't worry about that, Cora. We'll get to that." Rocket shifted his gaze to Red. "OK, that's the bulk of what happened and it's pretty much accurate. So before we say any more, it's your turn. What happened here? To Earth, I mean?"

"Don't know what to say, buddy," said Red, turning onto another dusty road. "Except that sometimes, the bad guys win. Guess what? The bad guys won. Look around. Isn't that obvious? Dirt starved for water. Radiation from the Chamberlin reactor sets the woods north of here glowing green at night. Most folks wear bandanas around their faces to keep the dust outta their lungs." A sudden heavy gust of wind, apparently a frequent thing in these parts, buffeted the truck, rocking it uncomfortably in the silence following Red's words.

When Rocket spoke, there was something achingly sad in his tone. "So that's it? The world's just… doomed?"

"That's it. Sometimes, things have exactly the right name, y'know? Like… oranges. Or sloths. On that basis, Doom is perfect, wouldn't you say? We're all doomed. Or Doomed." He somehow successfully pronounced the capital D. Rocket didn't know how. Neither did he much care.

"Yeah," he said, disconsolately. "I guess."

"Doom is a feeling," said Red, now clearly into his stride. "And Doom is a man and Doom – depending on whose opinion you get – is our president, or our dictator. He's sometimes even a god, or occasionally our devil…" Red was interrupted by Quill's snoring, a sound akin to a walrus being attacked with a buzzsaw. Rocket turned and delivered another swift kick to the man's ribs. The walrus won a brief reprieve.

"How does someone like Doctor Doom end up running the country anyway?"

"Not the country. There *is* no country, least as far as I know. Doom runs the Wastelands. That's what everyone now calls what *used* to be the Midwest and the Great Plains."

"OK, so what's on either side of the Wastelands?"

"Different places," said Red, grimly. "With different troubles."

"Query," said Cora. "Because at the time I was strapped to a sled, I could not get a clear view of the thing you call a Doombot. What does it look like?"

"Good question, Cora," said Red. "He kinda looks like… a medieval weapon that took the shape of a man wearing a mask. Also wears a heavy, hooded cloak. Y'know, just to *really* drive home the point that he's a bad guy."

"But what does he look like beneath the costume? Beneath the mask?"

Red shrugged. "Don't know. Nobody knows. You might as well as ask what the inside of a sword looks like."

"Curious," said Cora. "I look like a bipedal organism, but I am synthetic. Doom looks like a weapon, but he is a man."

"Oh, he's become more than that," said Red. "He's… a *force*."

"He's always been one of the worst dictators this world's ever known," said Rocket. "Like… *really* bad."

"Now there's an army of him," agreed Red. "Doom is everywhere. He's carved up the Wastelands into numbered territories. Hence, Outpost 13. Each territory has at least one permanently installed Doombot."

"And what about the *actual* Doom? Where's he based?"

"Doomwood."

Rocket shook his head. "Do you mean Deadwood?"

"Once. Not now. Doomwood. I guess you could call it his capital city. Or his factory, maybe. Or if you *really* want to embrace the villain trope and I mean by now, you may as well, his stronghold."

"Then that's where we need to go," said Rocket. "Right now."

Red laughed without any sort of humor. "You can't go there. I already told sleeping beauty there as much."

"No choice. Clock ticking, life-depends-on-it sort of situation. We gotta go to Doomwood."

"I would like to meet this Doctor Doom," said Cora. "He sounds like a powerful and fascinating individual worthy of my study. Could you perhaps introduce us, Mr Red Crotter?"

Rocket's patience, already wafer thin, stretched to breaking and he turned on the recorder. "What are you talking about? Are you flarking *nuts*?" The pitch and volume of his shouting was enough to stir Quill from his slumber and he provided valuable input into the discussion.

"Shh. My head."

"Glad you chose to join us, old man."

"My head. My teeth. My kidneys. Even my fingernails, man. It all hurts." Quill very slowly got himself up into a sitting position, pressing at the more painful parts of his anatomy. "Urgh," he said. "My spleen."

Rocket glared at him, daggers in his eyes. "In case you've woken up wondering what happened, we rescued you from certain death."

"Hey, how are you doing back there, buddy?" Red called back over his shoulder. "You gonna live?"

"It's tenuous," replied Quill thickly. "But yeah. For now."

"Well, now you're awake…" Rocket moved in closer between the front seats to the back, whispering conspiratorially into Quill's ear. "You sure we can trust this guy?"

"Of course we can trust him," replied Quill, making no attempt whatsoever to speak quietly. Rocket groaned and put a paw over his eyes. Red looked into the rearview.

"What's that now?"

"Rocket was asking if we can trust you."

Red chuckled. "Smart question. Can you trust me? It's a good thing to consider. I mean, I'm a total stranger leading you through the dark and the dangers that lurk in it. Maybe, once we reach the farm, I'm gonna poison you both and put you in a stew. Meat's a pretty scarce commodity."

Quill laughed, but he was feeling like he had been hit with

a truck full of trucks, so his heart was not in it. "This guy's *hilarious*."

"Query." Cora spoke up again. "If you poison them, would the stew not become inedible?"

"Good point," said Red. "How about I just slit their throats instead?"

Quill slapped a hand on his knee, laughing weakly. "Slit our throats. Oh geez, this *guy*!"

"This is an interesting style of humor in which you choose to engage, Star-Lord," said Cora. "I am unsure I understand your reaction. Is death not supposed to be a horrifying prospect for an intelligent life-form?"

"Key word there is 'intelligent'," said Rocket under his breath, moving back to the front seat. "It's hard to explain. It's like… when things are so bad, you've got no choice but to laugh out of one eye while crying out the other."

"A coping mechanism, then."

"I guess. Or a distraction from the truth."

"Then I will continue my efforts to understand your mannerisms." Cora turned to Quill. "I will murder you all by picking up a pointed stone from the ground which I will then use as a bludgeon!"

Silence descended. Undaunted, Cora continued.

"I will strike you in the temple – because that is where the skull is thinnest – and this will most likely cause a traumatic and fatal brain injury!"

More silence. When Rocket spoke, there was a surprising level of kindness in his tone. "We'll work on your jokes later, Cora. For now, don't even try. OK?"

"Understood. Thank you, Rocket."

Further discussion was curtailed by an unholy shrieking rising from the darkness. It set every hair on end, grated against sanity, and churned horror out the other side. It curdled blood and elicited sharp intakes of breath and fear from Red, Quill, and Rocket. It was a banshee howl, heralding some terrible end.

"What is that noise?" Cora was the only one unfazed by the sound.

"You can hear it?" Quill's voice shook. "I thought it was in my head. It *feels* like it's in my head! It's going right through me…"

"Shut it!" Red rolled the vehicle to a stop and snapped off the truck's engine. The occupants sat in silence for a few moments. Even breathing seemed too loud, but Quill realized after a few seconds that he had very little choice but to breathe. Not for the first time, he felt a flare of envy for Cora's automation. There was no further sound and emboldened, Quill spoke again.

"What was that…"

"Shhh!"

"I believe I already said that there was something else following us." Cora's tone had not changed, but in deference to the tension, she had reduced her volume.

"Yeah," said Red. "The Ghost Riders."

"Ghost Riders?"

"Yep. Bandits. They're the reason I couldn't pay my taxes today. Ripped me off on the way to my delivery at Outpost 13."

"It's way too dark out there. I can't see a flarkin' thing." Rocket clambered over fully into the back seat, between the two of them. He nudged Quill, none-too-gently. "Activate your helmet."

"Good thinking, buddy." Quill reached up, flicking the switch behind his earlobe. With a soft hiss and whirr of hidden mechanisms, the helmet shuttered around his face. Cora watched with interest.

"What are the exact specifications of your helmet, Star-Lord? My preliminary analysis suggests that the technology far supersedes that of this planet. It is quite alien to Earth."

"It's more of an implant, really," Quill replied, his voice muffled and distorted by the helmet's presence. "Fits behind my ear. Adapts to my face. Contains a universal translator, oxygen regulation and..."

"Night vision," interjected Rocket. "What ya got, Quill?"

"I see them," he said. "Ten o'clock. We got multiple bogeys. Looks like..."

"Let me guess," said Red, his tone hollow. "Sloppy white skulls painted across their faces. Nasty black armor on the horses they're riding."

"There's another detail you missed," said Quill. From the darkness, there was a skittish, nervous neighing. "They've all got bows and arrows."

"OK," said Rocket, scooting over Quill so he was near the window. "They're armed." He took up his rifle, sliding it to a live charge. "Should I start blasting?"

"No!" Red put out his hand, then calmed his reaction. "No. Wait. Just... wait." He swallowed nervously, reaching into his inner jacket pocket. He retrieved a hipflask, took a swig of its contents, and then yelled into the darkness. "I got nothing! You took it all earlier. OK? You get it? You took it all!"

No reply was forthcoming from the darkness and then a double blast shot from Rocket's rifle tore through the night, briefly lighting up his face. His expression was one of contorted, barely contained fury.

Red turned on Rocket. "What are you *doing*?"

"Relax. It was just a warning shot."

The moment disappeared into chaos as the horses in the darkness reared in response to the sound of the weapon discharge and once again, the unholy banshee shriek rose out of the darkness. Quill leaned forward, allowing himself the luxury of a closer look at what he could see in the distance.

"Uh, guys? I don't want to spread any unnecessary panic or alarm. But… they're lighting their arrows."

"Good job, Rocket," snapped Red. "You've done it now." For the first time since they had met him, there was real fear on the old man's face.

Three arrows arced through the night – an oddly majestic sight. Majestic, that was, until they thudded into the side of the truck, one of them barely inches from Rocket. He stared down at it.

"Oh, flark me."

There was a sudden *whumph* as the arrows ignited the sacking in the back of the pickup and the flames began to spread swiftly.

"Fire. We're on fire, Red!" Quill's voice was a shriek.

"Of course we're on fire," bellowed Red. "I never should've offered help to a pair of deadbeats like you! My day started out fine, went rapidly downhill, and now *you* have ruined it entirely!" The engine revved alive. He put his foot flat to the floor and the flaming truck shot through the night.

Rocket snarled furiously. "Now I'm *angry*," he said. "Suck on my blaster, Ghost Riders!" He unleashed several more blasts and was rewarded with the sounds of more panicked whinnying and the increasingly distant gallop of hooves as the bandits retreated. "Yeah, that's right! You *run*, you cowards. Run!"

The flames continued to do what flames did best.

"Quick," said Red, snatching up the water bottle on the seat beside him. "Splash this over the flames. Should be enough there." He threw the bottle at Quill, who grabbed it, dousing the fire. It sputtered out with an angry hiss, and he let out a deep breath.

"We're good back here," he reported. They were also out of water, but that was probably less of an issue than being on fire.

Red turned his temper onto Rocket. "Didn't I say to wait? What were you *thinking*?"

Rocket shrugged. "Itchy trigger finger," he said. "It needed a scratch."

"Well, that's just great. Maybe I *will* carve you up for stew!"

"Watch your words, old man, or I'll…"

"Guys, I can still make them out. The Ghost Riders. They're kicking up flames in their wake."

"The horses are shoed with flint," said Red, not taking his eyes off Rocket. "So they spark and flare like that. Nice little special effect they've adopted to help put the fear of God into their victims."

"To be fair," said Quill, "it looks more like Rocket put the fear of God into *them*. They're out of here."

"Yeah," said Red. "But maybe they just went to get their friends."

Quill flicked the helmet's switch again and it retracted. He looked from Red to Rocket and back again. Red eased them back up to their previous speed as they resumed their journey.

The mood had hardly been genial to start with, but it was clear that tensions had shifted further. Without anybody speaking, there was palpable regret coming from Red. It loaned an air of uncomfortable awkwardness that stretched into an extended silence.

"Excuse me, Star-Lord?" The recorder broke the deadlock.

"What's up, Cora?"

"I can't help but noticing that you are tugging at the guillotine collar more frequently."

"Yeah," said Quill. "I'm feeling a little constricted by this thing. A little bloated. Just wish I could loosen it a bit. You know. Like a belt."

"Perhaps it might be helpful for you to be reminded that if you do not complete your mission for the Collector, the collars will contract and decapitate you in five days, sixteen hours, forty-three minutes and..."

"You know what, Cora? That's fine. That's no help at all, but thanks anyway."

"You are most welcome."

The truck drove on through the night and, little by little, Quill's hangover departed, leaving him feeling simply drained and exhausted. Much like the hangover, in fact, but without the thumping in his skull. He began to take more interest in their surroundings; specifically something that caught his eye on the truck's dash.

"Is that a *tape deck*?" He reached into his jacket pocket and pulled out a well-loved, often played cassette tape. "Well, I am just gonna slot this right on in there and..." The tones of Eighties music blared out of the speakers and Red wrenched the volume back down – but not off altogether. Quill practically beamed. "That's more like it. That sounds _great_. And you know what else sounds great? Breakfast. A plate of ham and eggs. Soak up all the acid slosh in my gut."

On cue, he belched loudly.

Rocket, who had finally set aside his rifle, reassured that there was no immediate pursuit, punched Quill in the shin. "Now that you're fully awake and maybe at least semi-coherent, are you actually capable of telling us what happened to you?" He clambered back into the front.

"What's to say, Rocket? I did exactly what you told me to do. _Go gather intelligence. Go get us help._"

"Help. Right." Rocket glanced at the driver's seat. "This old guy and his rusted junk heap of a truck are your idea of help. I get that. But I'm telling you this for your own good. I am not detecting a _hint_ of intelligence."

"All right, smart pants," retorted Quill. "What did _you_ do that was so, so important?"

"What did I do? What did I do, he asks? Well, let's see, shall we?" He started to list off his adventures one by one, ticking them off on his claws as he did so. "I ran a diagnostic on an alien interface, no offense, Cora."

"None taken, Rocket."

"I located a junkyard. I dug up a bunch of old phones and computers and pirated the copper and silicon out of them. I got Cora up and running again…"

"Thank you, Rocket."

"You're _welcome_. And then, when we realized you hadn't arrived at the rendezvous point, because you'd gotten your dumb self _arrested_, we _saved_ you. So I think I did quite a lot, Quill, don't you?"

"Oh." Quill scratched his nose. "Well, that all does sound kind of busy. And helpful."

"Query. I am curious as to your motivations, Rocket." Cora leaned forward, her voice pitched in that way that demanded some sort of response. "You made a most concerted effort to help me after you had previously threatened – several times – to abandon me. Why is that?"

"Don't for a second think I didn't seriously consider scrapping you."

"But you did not."

"No," said Rocket, deflated. "I didn't. And I'm sorry for saying it." He sighed and stared up at the heavens. "I have no idea why I'm telling this glorified transistor radio that I'm sorry. It's not like she's got feelings." He looked back at Cora. "It's bad out there, OK? Every mile we travelled, it got more and more blatantly obvious that something went *seriously* wrong while we were off planet."

Cora didn't respond, waiting for Rocket to finish. "I figured… we'd need all the help we can get and that includes you."

"You saved me."

"Only for my own self-interest, don't get excited."

"You are truly a Guardian of the Galaxy, Rocket. And so is Star-Lord."

"Please stop calling him that."

"Why?"

"Because it's embarrassing, all right? It's like he's a kid pretending he's a king just because he's wearing a paper crown."

Quill stared at Rocket and when he spoke, it was with more

than a little sorrow in his tone. "Why do you have to be such a *hater*, Rock?"

Rocket looked at his friend and something unspoken passed between them. "Just telling it as it is, pal," he said, and there was a great weariness in his voice.

Quill folded his arms across his chest defiantly. "Well, just you wait. Before this is all over, I'm gonna prove that I'm just as good as I was. Maybe even *better* than I was."

Rocket watched him without comment for a few moments and then turned back to Cora. "You know what? Call him what you want. I don't care."

"Seeing as we are going to be on this journey for a while yet, perhaps you could fill in the missing information for me," said Cora. "What happened at Outpost 13, Star-Lord?"

"Well, I am *glad* you asked," said Quill. "But before I tell you my story, I need you to keep in mind that I was *extremely* thirsty. I'd just hauled you and the sled across several miles of desert. So I needed a drink. I was *parched*. So maybe because of that, I drank just a *little* faster than I should have done."

From the front seat, Red chuckled. "Oh, this will be a good story."

"Then hush up and let me tell it, pardner." Quill leaned back and tipped an invisible hat back up from his eyes. Rocket and Red exchanged glances and for the eight billionth time since they'd met, Rocket's eyes rolled.

"Every town's got its waterin' hole," said Quill. "Don't matter how poor the town, that's the one truth. So when I spotted it, I figured it'd be the best place to go gather intelligence… and to wet my whistle. And hoo boy, if my whistle didn't need wettin'."

"Why is Star-Lord talking like that?"

"Because he's an idiot, Cora. Shh. Let him tell it."

They let him tell it.

"I walked into the saloon through swingin' doors. They're real bad at keepin' the elements outside, you know. Anyway, I walk in and the old guy in the corner who'd been playin' mindlessly on a *real* out-of-tune piano looked up and stopped playin'. He was probably impressed."

As Quill continued, the faux accent dropped slowly, much to everyone else's relief, and the story unfolded normally.

"It was just me and the silence. As I entered the saloon, all you heard were the spurs at my heels clinking as I crossed the room. There was a long, polished bar dominating the far wall and there was this tall, thin guy eyeing me up suspiciously.

"'What'll it be, stranger?' he asks me and I don't hesitate. 'Two fingers of your finest sippin' whiskey, barkeep.' He pulls the cork right outta that bottle with his teeth and pours. I knock it back in a single pull and set the glass right back down for more." Quill was well into the swing of his story now.

"'Say,' says the bartender. 'We met before? Ya look kinda familiar.'

"'How 'bout you top me up there, buddy,' I say, 'and think about it some more.' He pours more whiskey, staring me the whole time, then snaps his fingers. 'I got it,' he says. 'Star-Lord! I knowed ya the *second* ya walked through them doors. Well, would ya done look at that? A gen-you-wine hero and celebrity in our mix! How 'bout that?'

"'Hey buddy,' I say, holding up my hands. 'Chill it. Calm down. I'm just here looking for information.' Then he looks over to the corner of the saloon.

"'Hey! Rattlesnake Pete! See this guy here? This is Star-Lord! One of the greatest heroes the galaxy's ever known!' I mean, I'm standing right there, you know? And here's this guy, bigging me up. I was *so embarrassed*, you know? So anyway, this guy comes over. Big, muscles, dark hair, straggly beard... and he looked real impressed.

"'Well, I'll be,' he says. 'Star-Lord! Should I be starry eyed? Should I ask for your autograph?'

"'Why do they call you Rattlesnake Pete?' I ask. I mean, to be fair, I probably should've worked it out from the staggeringly obvious lisp, but he smiles at me to demonstrate his point.

"'Because I got two teeth and nothin' to lose.' And then he laughs."

"I still do not understand why they called him Rattlesnake Pete."

"Because he hissed like a snake, Cora." Quill looked at the recorder, a look of mute appeal on his face. "He only had two teeth. You're ruining the story!"

"Please," said Rocket. "Stop. Enough of this."

"Aw, Rocket, I was just getting to the good part!" Quill pouted, like some petulant teenager who'd *really* let themselves go.

"Yes, Rocket. You should allow Star-Lord to continue."

"The flark I should. It's all baloney."

"Even inaccurate, prejudiced, and wholly fabricated records are important to consider," asserted Cora. Rocket shook his head, faintly amused despite himself, and turned to Red.

"Whaddya think, Red? What do you think?"

"Let's see," replied Red, his eyes focused on the road. He

allowed a couple of moments to pass before smirking. "My feelings are that that story is the biggest load of fetid horse dung I've smelled since I fertilized my fields back in the spring."

Rocket clapped his hands together. "Finally! Some truth."

"All right then, Red. Why don't *you* tell the story?" Quill's pride was dented, and he folded his arms defiantly across his chest.

"Sure," said Red. "But this is what *actually* happened."

"Proceed," said Cora and they all looked at her. "Please," she added.

"Fine."

Red had been in the saloon that day, because *everyone* had been in the saloon that day. On tax day, everybody had the uncontrollable urge to drink. It was the only real way to numb the pain of their existence. In Red's case, he had double the reason to forget. Not only was he in the doldrums over having to pay his taxes, he *couldn't* pay his taxes on account of having been waylaid by the Ghost Riders on his way into town.

"I had a real thirst on," he said. "And they got this special drink on tap. Real popular around these parts. Snakebit."

"Snakebit?"

"Yeah," said Red. "Imagine, if you will. There's an enormous tank behind the bar with a spigot in the bottom. Inside that tank is a huge snake. Fifteen, twenty feet easy. A prairie rattler." Quill thought back to what he'd seen on the trip to Outpost 13 and didn't doubt Red's account. Red continued his story.

"Every now and then, one of the bartenders bangs on the tank..." Red emphasized this by banging on the steering wheel of the truck. "*THUNK! THUNK! THUNK!* That makes the snake mad, see? It spits its poison which drips down through the caging and is extracted via the spigot. Mix that concoction with whiskey and you have got one *wild* ride ahead."

"That does not sound particularly hygienic," observed Cora.

"Maybe not, but it does what it's meant to," replied Red. "So that's what we were all drinking when I overhead Old Man Quill there bigging himself up to the bartender."

"No, the bartender was bigging *me* up."

"Whatever way you want to believe it, buddy. But this is where our stories meet. *Where is everybody*, he was asking, despite the fact that the bar's full."

Quill nodded and picked up the story. "'What do you mean, 'everybody', he replied, and I said, 'You know. Everybody *good*.' Boy, you could hear a pin drop. 'What's the matter,' he says, and I…"

"Can I finish?"

"What's the matter? Don't like the company of scum like us, Starsword?"

"My name isn't Starsword, it's…"

"Moonsword?"

"No!"

"Moonlord."

"No!"

"Shatterstar! That was it, that was what you said your name was!"

"No, man! I definitely, one hundred percent did *not* say my name was…" Quill sighed, leaning on the bar. "Look, man.

Where's Cap?" The question was met with blank looks and head shakes. "You know who I mean, Cap? Captain America? Cap. Tain. A. Meri. Ca?"

"Oh." The bartender's response became defensive and cold, his eyes narrowing in deep suspicion. "Oh. *Him*."

"Yeah. Cap's a buddy. You know who I mean?"

"Oh yeah, I know who you mean." The bartender leaned on the bar and studied Quill with a renewed interest. "He's dead."

Hearing the words sent a shockwave through Peter Quill. It felt as though someone had just stolen the ground from beneath his feet. He felt as though he was falling into a bottomless pit of *what is happening* and he did the only thing he could do. He went straight into denial.

"No way, man. He's not… you can't tell me… no, he's not *dead* dead, right? Captain America doesn't just *die*. Maybe he's just… you know. *Retired*."

"Nope. Dead and buried thirty years since. Along with the rest."

"The… rest?"

"The self-styled police of the old world. The fallen fascists." He spat a gob of phlegm onto the bar right in front of Quill, who jumped back instinctively. "All dead."

"Fascists? No, you gotta be wrong. You're confused. What about…" Quill sought around for an example, then snapped his fingers. "Iron Man."

"Dead."

"No *way*! OK, how about… Thor?"

"Dead."

"But Thor's like, an actual *god*."

"Demi-god." The correction annoyed Quill beyond measure, but he gathered his senses and stared at the bartender.

"When did this happen? *How* did this happen?" Slow, dawning awareness came over him and he shook his head. "Doom. It was Doom. Was it Doom?"

"In part, yeah," said the bartender, and spat another gobbet in front of Quill. "But not just Doom. Whole bunch of them. Kraven, Baron Zemo, Red Skull. I could go on for hours. Everybody who was sick and tired of getting endlessly policed. Folks who wanted a change. A new world order."

"Give me a break. This is *crazy.* It makes precisely *zero* sense. Are you telling me that one day, all those guys woke up and decided to go on a killing spree?"

"Of course not. It didn't happen in one day. It took time and planning. Careful planning. Like every other war."

"This is *bull,*" said Quill. "I'm not buying this. A bunch of two-bit villains ganged together and wiped out the greatest heroes the world has ever known?" The bartender leaned forward still further, close enough that Quill could smell his rancid breath. He recoiled slightly.

"Might wanna watch your terminology there, pal," he hissed. Quill became acutely aware that he was approaching a potential minefield and he proceeded in true Quill style: straight ahead without caution.

"What, villains? I'm not allowed to say *villains*? Doom…"

"Doom provides," said the bartender and the words were echoed around the bar.

"Doom provides?"

"Yes," said the bartender, not taking his eyes off Quill. "Doom provides."

"What is that, a catchphrase? Like… he's some sort of cheap fast-food joint? What *is* this? What *is* Doom to you people?"

"Doom rose up in a time of chaos," parroted the bartender. "He gave us order. He protects us. Doom provides. Doom…"

"Is a *jerk*!"

If you could bottle silence, then what followed in the wake of Quill's pronouncement would stock an entire shelf. The bartender pointed a thick finger at his ear.

"What did you just say?"

"Doom is a *villain*, man. A villain! Capital 'V'! The *works*."

"Say that again and you won't live long enough to pay your tab," said the bartender. "There's folks a-plenty who will see to that. Or maybe Kraven will hunt you down and put an end to your blasphemy."

It was at that point that Red Crotter, drinking himself insensible in the corner, intervened. He'd witnessed the entire exchange and felt driven to step in to prevent things getting any worse. He sidled up beside Quill, nudging him with one shoulder. "Don't mind him," he said to the bartender. "He's just yanking your noodle. Ain't that right, *Starsword*?"

"I…" The reality of this situation was suddenly all too much for Quill to bear. He sagged visibly and pushed the whiskey glass towards the bartender. "I am gonna need you to pour me more whiskey. A *lot* more whiskey."

"Keep an eye on him, Red. There's too many folks taking an interest in his yap and you know what happens to folks with big mouths in these parts. I don't want to clean up the mess. Not in my bar. You got it?"

"I got it. More whiskey. This one's on me, friend," said Red. "Let's move it to the corner, hey?" The drinks were replenished, the moment of tension broken and Red brought Quill over to the corner booth where he sat down heavily, his head in his hands.

"You OK in there?" Red asked.

"Dead? How can they all be *dead*?"

"Come on, pal. Here. Let's drink a toast."

"To what?" Quill's voice was hollow. Everything he'd ever known about Earth had overturned in a heartbeat. His entire *existence* was crumbling around his ears and this stranger wanted to drink a *toast*?

"To the end of the world, of course."

They clinked glasses and they drank.

"May I ask," said Cora, "what you spoke of?"

"If I could remember, I'd tell you," replied Quill. "Red here had me drinking that Snakebit stuff and it did a real number on me."

"We did what any two old men do when they get together and drink. We reminisced about the past. What had happened, what had changed, what we missed – and there's a *lot* to miss about the world we used to live in." Red took off the baseball cap he'd been wearing and ran a hand over his balding pate before putting it back on.

"I remember bits of it. It was fine. I was mellowing out a bit. And then Rattlesnake Pete got up in our grilles." Quill shook his head. "What a slimeball."

"To be fair, you *were* making fun of his teeth."

"I was only doing that because he was telling you about how you should be paying your taxes! I was standing up for you!" Quill held his hands out in mock-protest.

The smallest hint of amusement lifted Red's serious expression into something akin to a smile. "You made yourself all *big*. Stood right up to him, you did. Practically bounced him back with your gut, sending him back five paces and telling him to lay off. Then the fight started."

Quill rubbed at his jaw and winced as that revealed another of the bruises he'd picked up that day. He frowned. "Did I throw the first punch? I don't think I did. Did I?"

"Yeah, you did, but only because there were a bunch of guys trying to stab you."

The two older men looked at one another and there was a brief silence, a moment of shared recollection. Then Quill grinned. "So there was a fight. A good ol'-fashioned bar brawl."

"Excuse me?" Cora attempted to cut through, but Quill was caught up in his story now.

"There was a fight. Punches flew. People were flipped across tables and everything, and then I threw a chair at the tank behind the bar."

"Smashed it in one," supplied Red.

"I have something to say, please."

"Red, did you see the look on Pete's face when that snake came sliding right on out of that tank?"

"I didn't," said Red and the two began laughing. "But man, did I smell the piss dribbling down his leg." The truck veered slightly as the wheel wobbled beneath the laughter. "And then I said I'd meet you at the stables and *you* said, 'Get down', because that was when the pistols came out…"

"Everyone? Hello? Excuse me?"

Quill was by now laughing so hard he could no longer

speak. Eventually, he shook his head and wheezed slightly. "Anyway, I don't remember much after that point because of the Snakebit."

"For *real*? You don't remember getting locked up? I mean, you were demanding a lawyer and you were singing what you insisted was your prison playlist. Cash. Elvis. The Clash."

"Excuse me!"

The laughter was cut short by the intensity of Cora's tone, and they all turned to look at her. "Excuse me," she said again, more calmly this time, "but my antenna is picking up on some communication that may be of interest to you."

The spell broke, the story ended, and the harsh light of reality dawned once again. Rocket looked between the two old men and shook his head. "Go ahead, Cora," he said, softly.

"I will share the transmission," she said. "It is being broadcast on a loop."

The next sounds to come from the recorder were in the hard, synthetic tones of the Doombot, or at least *one* of the Doombots, as it made a pronouncement.

"...two fugitives at large. Last seen in Outpost 13. Identification: Red Crotter and a man going by the alias Moon-Lord. Both described as elderly, males – one white, one a person of color. Both have thinning hair and scruffy beards." Quill looked outraged at this but said nothing. The transmission continued. "Accused of: failure to file taxation, destruction of property and general disturbance of the peace. Local citizens have been deputized. Suspects, when located, should be detained, questioned, and summarily executed. All Doombot units in sectors 10-14 should be on alert."

The transmission ended and this time the silence was

painful. Finally, Quill broke it. "Great," he said. "Just *great*. Now *we're* the bad guys. How are we the bad guys?"

"Let's not linger on the how here, Quill. Let's think about the 'what'. As in, what the *flark* are we gonna do now? Get kitted out and move onto Doom?" Rocket's voice held a hint of despair. The matter was settled by Red's next words.

"Well, that's my farm up ahead. Here's my advice as to what you do next. You get some sleep, some food, and you get ready."

"For what?"

"For what's gonna come next."

# CHAPTER FOUR
## BLOOD FARMER

ENTRY C1451Z2G

LOCATION: *Near the edge of the Black Hills, in the region now known as the Wastelands. This fifty-something acre farm – owned by Red Crotter – has proved to be an oasis in an otherwise blighted environment.*

Red Crotter's farm was nothing more than that. A *farm*. Although the decidedly dilapidated shack that Red led them towards was barely worthy of the name "farmhouse", it still successfully gave off that vibe. It was dark when the truck pulled up and they heard the soft, background hum of a generator. At their approach, security lights flared into life. Quill made out the shapes of other low farm buildings nearby: a cow shed, a barn… the usual.

"I ain't much used to having guests," Red explained, swinging open the door and ushering the group inside. "So, you'll have to make do with what I have." Once they were all in, he lit a fire and a few old-fashioned oil lamps. The firelight lent a strange ambience to the proceedings and Quill felt a curious sense of otherworldliness that his many adventures on other planets had never brought him. Once the fire was established, Red reached for a shotgun mounted on the chimney breast, before settling in an old, battered rocking chair facing the door. He lay the weapon across his lap and then rocked gently, a beatific smile on his face.

"Hey, Red?" Quill was watching him. "You're cutting quite the picture of contentment there. Gun in your lap, smirk on your face…"

"Well, pal. It's been a long while since I felt this good."

Strange, but Quill could definitely get behind that feeling. He switched his attention to Rocket, who was looking for all the world like he had just smelled something particularly disgusting. He'd taken up a position by the window next to the door, staring out into the farmyard. He looked up as he sensed Quill's gaze on him and scowled even more deeply.

"What? I ain't moving from this window until the sun comes up. I'm telling you this for nothing. If I see so much as a prairie dog out there…" He slid his rifle to charge. "…I will knock the glass outta this window and blast it to space."

Quill said nothing and Rocket resumed his vigil. Cora spoke up from where she stood in the center of the room.

"The transmission from the Doombots went quiet an hour ago." She made the announcement quietly, sensing that volume was not required in this rustic setting.

Red nodded. "If they ain't come yet, they won't come until full light," he said.

"How do you know for sure?" Rocket didn't shift his gaze.

"Because nights out in the Wastelands will eat you up. On top of that… well, I'm an old man. Where would I go? They know that. Hey, Quill. Toss another log on the fire, would you? Days might be hot here, but the nights are cold."

"Sure thing, Red." Quill picked up a cut log from beside the grate, throwing it into the crackling flames where it was quickly subsumed. He stared into its glow for a while. "Feels kinda good, sitting by a fire. You know, I can't remember the last time I did this."

"Did what?" Rocket looked round. "Stayed awake all night waiting for local vigilantes to find and kill us before feeding our guts to a Doombot? Me neither."

"No, Rocket. Just took time to sit by a fire. With friends. While there's that, well, there's still good in the world."

"Amen to that," said Red, and Quill sat on the floor between him and the fire. Rocket grunted in disgust, turning away. Cora just watched them. A silent observer, just as she had said. After a while, Red's voice shattered the companionable moment. "I've helped you this far. But you gotta give me something here. What are you after? Why do you need to get to Doomwood?"

"We can't tell you," said Rocket from the window.

"Hold on, Rock," said Quill. "We aren't supposed to. That's not the same as *can't*."

"Well, I could maybe help you out some more. Get those guillotine collars off your necks for one. I got an anvil out back that I use for shoeing horses. Maybe…"

"They're adamantium, Red, and real tight against our throats. Don't think anything you've got here is gonna help us with that one."

"You've helped enough, old man," said Rocket. "Don't worry yourself about what we've got to do next."

"That's rich," said Red, and he stopped rocking, which was somehow more ominous than when he'd been in motion. "I spent the last few years ducking every time a drone passed overhead. I've got vested interests in things changing around here. When the Guardians of the Galaxy turn up in the Wastelands making demands and creating chaos... hoo boy. You bet I want to be part of whatever plan they got."

"Your trust is appreciated, Mr Red Crotter," said Cora.

He flapped a hand at her. "Just Red, OK? Just Red. Maybe *you* can tell me, if they can't. What the heck are they after?"

"I have observed how things work and as such I suggest a trade may be in order. You tell us more about what happened to Earth, and Star-Lord and Rocket will tell you more about..."

"Hey, hold on, skinbot!" Rocket turned. "You don't speak for us!"

"Hang on, Rocket. Cora's got a point. Face it, buddy, we're running blind here. We need all the intel we can get if we stand any hope of pulling this off. Fine. Let me show you what I've been hauling around in my pack." Quill picked up his bag from the floor and rummaged around, producing the mirror-map they'd got from the Collector.

Rocket made a low, threatening growl. "You show him that, then some Doombot is gonna get it out of him. They'll *torture* it out of him. They'll cut off a toe, maybe. Or get him to eat a wasp's nest. Or whatever else they do for fun around here."

In response, Red racked his shotgun. "You see this? When – *if* – I go down, it'll be guns blazing. There won't be any discussion." Quill handed him the mirror and Red set the shotgun down to take it. "What the heck does a broken mirror have to do with any of this?"

"Take a look," said Quill, quietly. "You'll see a lot more than your shriveled-up old face in the glass."

Red snorted, partly insulted, partly amused. "Fine," he said, peering into it. His brow creased. "Stars. I see… stars." As he watched, Quill opened his mouth to explain what was going on, but Red interrupted him before he even started. "It's a map. A route. Through the stars to Earth, to *here*." He looked up at Quill, something between surprise and interest in his eyes. "What does it lead to?"

"The Black Vortex," said Quill, feeling only *slightly* robbed of his moment to explain things. "Doomwood is where we need to be according to the map."

"A map." Red snorted. "You're following a treasure map?"

"Kinda," said Rocket. "But not for us. It's a job, see? And if we don't retrieve the treasure, these guillotine necklaces…" He pulled a face. "I don't imagine I gotta get graphic on you here."

"No, you're good." Red looked up at Quill again. "What *is* this Black Vortex, anyway?"

"Some sort of super-famous, super-powered, cosmic artifact of ultimate power. You submit to it, it turns you into a sort of god. Wait. Wait! I have just had a *genius* idea!" He sprang to his feet – slowly. Things in his body didn't work quite as well or as efficiently as they'd once done.

"I hate it when he gets a genius idea. Look at him. All excited like he's solved the problem. Sit down, Quill, you're embarrassing yourself."

"Hush up and listen. Remember how we were desperate to

get the Black Vortex back to the Collector and then I had that great idea about collecting it ourselves before we sold it on the black market?"

"An idea which I *immediately* shot down."

"Well, I take that idea back."

"Take it back? You can't take it back, I shot it down. Nothing's ever been more shot down than that dumb idea. Look, Quill. We agreed to the job and we're gonna follow it through."

"No. No, we're not. Hear me out, Rocket, hear me out." Quill danced from foot to foot, excited and engaged with whatever madness was playing out in his head. "We'll *submit* to the Black Vortex!"

"No." Rocket had seen it coming. Frankly, he was amazed it'd taken Quill so long to get there.

Quill shrugged. "Fine. Then *I'll* submit to it."

"No, Quill. No, no and *no*."

"C'mon, Rocket, can't you see this is *it*? This is how we become the Guardians again. This is how I bring back the glory days of Star-Lord! This is…" He had to raise his voice to be heard over Rocket's repeated denial of this solution. "This is how we save ourselves *and* the Earth!"

Rocket smacked a paw over his eyes, groaning in disapproval. "This is gonna be a long night."

"Well then, let's get some more specifics down, shall we?" Red dropped down into his rocker. "Mount Moriah, huh? That's where your map tells you the Black Vortex is buried?"

"Far as we can tell."

"Maybe," said Rocket, "but the mirror's bust, so we might be missing something crucial."

Red rubbed at his bearded chin. "Don't know of any

mountains named Moriah. The highest peak around here is Black Elk Peak. Highest point east of the Rocky Mountains."

Rocket shook his head. "That's way too far off," he declared. "Why would the mirror send us to Doomwood, only to then send us somewhere else? This Mount Moriah? That's gotta be a part of the town."

Red shrugged. "I'll keep thinking. See if the memory dredges anything up." The kettle began to whistle and Red creaked up from his rocker to attend to the important business of making coffee.

Quill rubbed at the back of his neck. "How about the Slaughter Lords. You ever hear of them?"

"The Slaughter Lords? Can't say that I have. But with a name like that, they'd sure fit in around here."

"True." Quill laughed humorlessly.

And so the long night passed.

As it happened, the night was no longer than any other. It just *felt* longer. At some point, first Red and Quill and then Rocket dropped off into a doze. None of them were relaxed enough to allow themselves proper rest. Red woke first. He moved straight to the window, looking out at the gray line on the horizon that suggested dawn would not be too far behind.

"Not much of the night left," he said, loudly enough to stir the other two from their slumber. "Anybody want some fresh coffee before our absolutely unwanted guests arrive?" The easy acceptance with which Red acknowledged they would be hunted down was faintly disturbing but not unexpected. Everyone round here knew where everyone else lived, after all. It was a miracle they'd not been found already.

"Mm," said Quill, rubbing at his eyes. He'd fallen asleep on a chair at the table, his head resting on his hand. He felt a terrible ache across his shoulders and stretched them out. "We're drinking if you're brewing."

"I do not require coffee or any other form of refreshment," said Cora. "But thank you."

"Rocket?"

"Meh." Rocket smacked his lips and hacked a couple of times, a dry cough shaking his small body. "I'll pass."

Red shrugged, filling a kettle from the pump by the sink. He took it and hung it from its hook over the fire. "I still only got chicory nut," he said. "Don't pack much of a punch, but it's better than nothing."

"Thanks," said Quill, finding he absolutely meant it.

"Mr Cro... Red, I mean," said Cora. "You promised us that if you learned why we were here, you would share your information with us."

"I did, didn't I? Sure we have the time?"

Rocket, who had taken up his rifle and his place at the window again, turned and looked over his shoulder. "There's a couple hours before full sunrise. We'll head out then. Spill the deal, Red."

The old man nodded, pouring boiling water into a coffee pot. The smell of chicory wafted around the interior of the room and then he sat down to tell his story.


There was a time they called "before" and there was what some people called "after". Still other people just called it "now" because they didn't know any better. They didn't remember life before the broken, burned-out husk the world had become. But Red Crotter remembered. Oh, he remembered. There were recollections that he clung to, keeping him from losing what little sanity he had remaining. Small things, really. Sprinklers that made tiny rainbows in the neighborhood yards. Cornfields stretching as far as the eye could see. Regular sports games, the stadiums filled with cheering fans. Sure, there were bad things too – crime, politics, reality TV… but in hindsight (which everyone knew was twenty-twenty), the good far outweighed the bad.

"I was just a kid in Sioux Falls when a tornado tore through the state," Red remembered. "The sun was shining and the next thing you know, the sky went this violent shade of green – wicked witch green, y'know – and the tornado hit. We had a tree in our front room. A neighbor's car ended up in someone else's front yard. Just like that. In the blink of an eye, things went from fine to not fine. Nothing made sense. Everything just flipped upside down and spun sideways. Literally, in some cases."

Red took a sip of the bitter coffee, grimacing. It wasn't the greatest of morning brews, but it was hot and kept the chill off his bones. "Thirty years ago. So long, now."

The old man scratched the side of his nose and continued. "I was working for an agriculture firm at the time. Crop research and the like. Took me out down a lot of country roads. Loads of big sky days, you know what I'm saying?" He took another sip. "Had my little girl with me that morning. Megan. She was only four and wasn't in school yet. Heh. She loved riding with me. She'd bring a coloring book, fiddle with the stereo. Some days we'd stop for a hamburger." Red closed his eyes for a moment and set his mug down on the table.

"She saw it first," he said, looking up at Quill. "'What's that in the sky, Daddy?' That's what she said. I looked up."

His eyes closed at the memory. "I thought it was a plane. I watched its shadow streak across the crop fields. Then, the shadow and the shape became a single object as it hit the ground. Even from that distance, we felt the shock of that impact. No flame. No fire. Just a huge plume of dirt thrown into the air. From half a mile away, we saw the crater.

"We watched and there was nothing. Then, two figures emerged. What we called Elites here in the Dakotas. Darting this way and that way… swinging and blasting at one another. Defying every normal law of physics. A war among gods." He shook his head. He could still hear the sounds if he tried hard enough. The crashing of metal, the blasts of advanced weaponry, the shouting. The crying of his little girl.

"The sun caught one of the figures," he continued. "Red and gold armor. I realized that it was whats-his-name. Stark. The Iron Man. I'd only ever seen an Elite on the news. Always felt like something that happened somewhere else. I'd never thought to see them here, but here they were. I didn't recognize the other guy. Somebody wearing a red cape and I tell you this for nothing, he had the look of the devil about him. Something that maybe fell out the back end of the Bible. I don't know. Maybe my old mind is remembering it wrong."

He picked up the mug again, taking another sip before staring off into the middle distance with the effort of recall. "There was a blast of energy and then off they went, totally new direction. I switched radio stations, looking to hear something on the news, and I picked up all sorts of stuff. One station reported that the city was a war zone. Folks running and screaming. Another reported the power grid had been hit, that there had been a coordinated strike. It was utter chaos."

Rocket, Quill, and Cora were completely caught up in Red's story, hanging on his every word. He became aware of their intensity and looked up, suddenly seeming both very old and very tired. "It was happening everywhere," he said. "Iron Man and his opponent were just a single, tiny battle in a greater war. News started coming in that the Elites were gone. One after the other. Captain America. Thor. Black Widow. They fell like bowling pins. Dead. Dead. Dead." Red ticked off the names on his fingers. "People were being told to seek shelter."

He took Megan straight back home to his wife, Angie. From years of experience, they followed survival protocols. The bath was filled with water. Red did a grocery run. They double-checked their ammo. There was a load of crop seed in the back of the pickup that made him feel like he was carrying valuable currency. Angie played along with her husband, but…

"She thought I was being paranoid," he said. "But I knew in my gut what was gonna happen. I wasn't wrong. I wish to God I had been. Because it wasn't very long before it happened."

"What happened, Red?" Quill's tone was soft. He was horrified.

"There's a nuclear power plant not so far from here – the Chamberlin reactor. Later that afternoon, the power grid went out and the station switched to emergency generators. But they only lasted so long. Then…"

"Meltdown," said Rocket, grimly.

Red nodded. "Catastrophic meltdown. A good way to

describe what was happening everywhere. Here, in South Dakota, the skies lit up red and green. The dawn of the Wastelands. It all happened in a single day. We all woke that morning with a sense of blue-sky security. The Avengers. S.H.I.E.L.D. The Fantastic Four. Those mutant kids who showed up occasionally. They were all here, protecting us. By the time the sun set that night, most of them were gone."

The fighting went on for weeks in some places, but every day the window of hope grew smaller. One thing was for certain, though. Nothing was ever going to be the same again. Red rubbed at his upper arms as he came to the end of his tale, a chill in his bones despite the residual heat from the fire.

"You know that song, Quill? The one about the day the music died? It was like that. That same feeling. The day the heroes died."

A heavy quiet settled after Red finished his story, interrupted by Rocket's occasional coughing and the soft spitting of the dying embers of the fire that had burned through the night. Quill stared into what little light they offered but found scant comfort there. Nothing about this job was easy and every passing hour brought more doubt to the near-toppling pile of trepidation building in his gut.

When the first hint of red appeared in the eastern skies, Rocket turned from the window. "We've gotta go," he said.

Quill shook his head and looked over at their host. "We need to thank Red properly, Which we're gonna do by building up his perimeter defenses. Keeping him safe."

"But we should leave, now." Rocket was stubborn.

Red tried to placate. "You don't need to do this. You should get going while you've got the chance," he said.

Quill shook his head. "Feels like the least we can do."

"The old man's got the right of it," said Rocket, clinging to the final vestige of hope that Red's words had offered.

"Really, Rocket? What kind of hero walks away from a friend in need?"

"Oh, so now we're *heroes* again. I see."

"You bet your furry butt we are," said Quill, enthusiastically.

Rocket sighed. "For years, you've been slumming it around. And now, when we're on the run from the gods-only know what, with our necks *quite literally* on the line? *Now* you decide to take a stand?"

"The good guys always win, Rocket. It's a *rule.*"

"Based on the story Red told us, it appears that such an assertion has been contradicted, Star-Lord," said Cora. The recorder had been silent for so long that Quill had forgotten she was even there.

"We'll be fine. Trust me." He reached over and patted Cora awkwardly on the shoulder.

"Look, Quill," said Rocket, exasperated. "I'm really glad to see that you actually still have a heartbeat. But this mission of atonement you're presently on? Quill, listen to me. It's gonna get us all killed."

"You in, then?"

A long, heavy pause.

"Fine."

"You wanna shout at me while we build up some fortifications?"

"Sure, why not?"

"Booby traps?"

The two began walking away, squabbling like siblings. Red

watched them go and called after them. "I need to get the animals fed. You know. Before the bullets start flying."

"Yep," said Quill, not even looking back. "You do that. Let's go! Guardians go!"

Rocket paused and shouted back at Cora. "For your benefit, that is *not* our catchphrase."

"But, Rock, it *could* be…"

The two disappeared out of earshot, leaving Red alone with the Rigellian Recorder and a head full of confused and uncomfortable thoughts. Telling his story had been draining and he'd been unprepared for the onslaught of memories and associated emotions that it had brought. He looked at Cora and shook his head.

"While those two jokers are out doing whatever they're trying to do, you want to help me with a few farm chores, Cora?"

"I would be more than happy to assist you, Red Crotter."

"Just Red, I keep telling you. All right. We'll start with the chickens. Come on."

The chicken house was home to a small flock of bantams, who clucked at the arrival of Red and Cora, ceasing their endless scratching to look up with interest. They seemed content to cluster around Red's legs as he busied himself with their feed. One fluttered down from the top of the coop to sit on the man's shoulder.

They avoided Cora, but the recorder didn't mind. She didn't understand chickens. They seemed far too complex. She turned, hearing Red calling her, and he beckoned her over. Carefully, she picked her way through the flock.

"Listen up. Just in case things go real wrong and I get killed…

when you get to Doomwood, the guy you need to ask for is Sebastian Warn. I'd tell Quill but it seems that everything's in one ear and out the other. This is *important*, so I'm telling *you*."

"I will remember."

"Are you sure?"

"It is my purpose, Red Crotter." Cora played back an audio recording of the conversation they'd just had. Red nodded, satisfied.

"That works. All right, now pay attention. Warn is a hunter and trapper. He knows the Black Hills better than anybody else. If this mirror thing is right, and you're looking for this Mount... whatever..."

"Moriah."

"Yeah, that. If anybody knows what, or where it is, it'll be Sebastian Warn. As long as you mention my name, he'll be on your side. Probably."

"How is it that you know this Sebastian Warn?"

"Old friends. From a long time back. He's a good guy. There's still some of us in this world ready and willing to fight for what we believe in. What we think is right." He continued his way through the chickens to the feed bin and their clucking grew in intensity. Cora followed him.

"There are forces of insurrection at work?"

"Yep. Now you're a part of it." A silence lingered and Cora said nothing to fill it. Red moved on with his chores. "These are some hungry chickies, no? Here you go, girls, enjoy!" He scattered the scoop of feed around the coop and the chickens went into a pecking frenzy. "Latch the door behind you. Make sure none of them get out."

"Of course." She did so, then looked back at him. "Query: if you are so certain that things will go badly, that your farm will be razed to the ground and that you will cease to exist, why is it that you are feeding your chickens?"

"Because they're hungry." He continued to scatter feed and realized how preposterous his response must sound. "Listen, Cora. If there is one thing I've learned in this awful, broken world, it's that you can sometimes survive the most terrible things."

"You have hope, then?"

"Hope, the bright side, call it what you will. But every night has a dawn, right? It's good to take the rough with the smooth. But I like to look on the dark side."

"Could you please explain? Looking on the dark side gives you hope?"

"Well, it's just that whenever I hit rock bottom and think things can't get any worse, I try to imagine things *getting* worse. My farm bursting into flames. The moon explodes. I start pissing oil. That sort of thing."

"I would suggest that urinating oil might require the intervention of a medical practitioner."

Red smiled briefly. "Then when I pull myself out of imagining all that, I think to myself, hey gee, Red! This life ain't so bad after all. You understand?" He leaned over to pat one of the chickens on the head. "Isn't that right, Baldy? This life ain't so bad. Looking on the dark side. You should try it sometime."

"How?"

"Well…" Red considered for a moment. "Imagine that ants colonize your body and every time you went to talk, they spill out of your mouth. A tide of ants."

"That would be unfortunate. And inconvenient."

"See this farm? I spent years growing this plot of land. I expanded the land, and I took care of my family and I survived. Even when drought and blight ruined my crops, I kept going. When the Doombots shaved my profits with their taxes, I kept going. Even when…" He broke off and looked away for a moment. "Even when I lost my wife and my daughter to the cancer that the radiation brings with it. I kept going."

"I am sorry for your sadness, Red Crotter." She sounded as genuine as was possible for a synthetic life form and it was curiously touching. He smiled, even if only fleetingly.

"You want to know why I brought you and Quill and the critter here to the farm?"

"Should my answer be influenced by looking on the bright side or the dark side?"

"Try both."

"You brought us here because you are a good person who sought to help us."

"All right, that's one possible answer. How about the dark side?"

"You brought us here with a plan to keep us here. Every day you will make us toil in the fields and milk the chickens and collect cow's eggs. Every night, perhaps your plan is to have us dance and perform lewd comedy skits for your entertainment."

Despite himself, Red grinned. "That's it! Don't you feel better knowing that's not likely to happen?"

"I am." Cora thought for a moment. "I am also grateful that my mouth is not colonized by ants." Red gave a short, gruff laugh and nodded his head. He was going to say something else, but Cora's entire body stiffened and the light behind her eyes glowed a sudden, ominous red. "We should proceed with alacrity," she said in a serious tone.

"What you got, Cora?"

"My seismographic sensors indicate that there are several horses approaching. About a mile away – but heading in this direction."

"Guess it's time, then. Fight or die."

It wasn't hard to locate Quill and Rocket: the pair were engaged in digging a trench which Quill envisioned filling with sharpened spikes. He insisted that it would be a great booby trap and nobody addressed the fact that between their bickering and the need for Quill to stop every five minutes for a breather, they'd only dug about eight inches.

"We've done other stuff too," said Rocket, whether to save face or not. Red relayed Cora's warning and the two Guardians set down their shovels. The group trailed back to the farmhouse.

They were swiftly ensconced in the house, each of them – except for Cora – fully armed and barricaded behind whatever they could find to shove up against the doors and windows. Between a gap in the wood, Rocket made the first spot.

"Five of them," he said in a low growl.

"Five?" Quill nodded, his expression determined. "We can handle five."

"Oh, yeah," said Rocket, his eyes glittering. "Get yourselves to where you can see, because this is gonna be great. Wait for it."

Red peered out through a knot in the wood. "What are we waiting for?"

"Watch closely. Watch that patch of dark dirt and what happens when the horses get to it." Rocket peered out. "C'mon. Closer. Closer!"

A hiatus. Then…

"Now!"

The horses suddenly came to a complete halt, whinnying loudly as their riders flew forward over their necks, crashing into the dirt. There were shouts of pain and confusion and panicked neighing from the now completely stationary horses. Rocket began to laugh, slapping his paws against his thighs.

"What did you do?" Red was impressed despite himself. "Those horses stopped on a dime."

"Did you see the way those goons flew right out of their saddles?" Quill was more alive than Red had seen him so far. "Outstanding work, Rocket."

"What did you do?" Red repeated the question.

Rocket glanced at him and smirked, baring his sharp little teeth. "I magnetized the ground," he replied with a barking laugh. "Stopped their horses mid-stride." His laughter gave way to coughing and he wiped his streaming eyes. "Worked like a dream, huh?"

Outside, they heard the men – five distinct voices – grumbling and groaning from their impact injuries and the unmistakable lisp of Rattlesnake Pete was among them. Rocket peered out again and continued. "We weren't sure what was coming after us. Figured it'd either be a Doombot, or a posse of Wasteland cowboys. Either way… metal shoes. Win-win."

"But how did you manage…"

"Just appreciate my brilliance, Red. Don't question it. Bask in it."

Outside the cabin, the five men picked themselves up off the ground. Rattlesnake Pete, who appeared to be the nominal leader, stepped forward and bellowed Red's name.

Quill peered out and a flicker of recognition passed over his face. Red joined him and a sigh of resignation passed his lips. "Hey, I know that guy. From Outpost 13, right?"

"He ain't one to pass up a fight. Everyone, just stay low at the windows, all right? The logs on this cabin are solid. Thick. Ain't no bullets getting through those."

"Red Crotter!" Another shout from outside.

Quill turned to their host. "You OK for ammo there, Red?"

The old farmer shucked his rifle and nodded. "I'm good. I got enough."

"Music to my ears," said Rocket as the men outside continued to holler Red's name, demanding his exodus from the cabin. "I mean, not *that* bit."

"Bright side," said Red, more to himself than anything. "A crowd of bloodthirsty, drunken idiots is a better prospect than a Doombot." He glanced briefly at Cora. "Dark side: they'll probably cannibalize our remains."

"Red Crotter! We know you're up there, old man. You might as well give up and come out!"

When it came, the shout was so close that Red, Rocket and Quill actively jumped backwards. Then they turned to Cora, from whom the sound was emanating. She looked at the others. "I am picking up their conversation quite clearly," she explained. "I thought it might be helpful to amplify it so you could hear them."

In the ensuing silence, they heard the men muttering to each other. The sound Cora projected was crisp and perfect. Quill's eyebrows rose.

"Solid sound system, Cora," he complimented. "Remind me to get you play some tunes later."

"They ain't comin', Pete," they heard someone say. "Just tell 'em we're here to collect what's owed and then we'll be gone."

"If by 'what's owed' you mean a pile of broken teeth, maybe a still-beating heart and a new money-purse sewn from his unmentionables…" Pete's lisp sounded through Cora's projection perfectly and the accompanying laughter was enough to chill them to the core.

Red stared coldly out through the window. "Oh, I got some buckshot that says otherwise."

"Is that other old guy still with him?" The question came from one of Pete's cronies. "Shatterstar or whatever his name was?"

"Star-Lord," muttered Quill. "Why is it so hard to remember?"

"I hope so," responded Pete. "I'd be more than happy to gut that old sack of trash." He increased his volume, shouting again to the cabin. "Come on Red, enough of this. Come on out here and we'll talk it over. You pay us your taxes and we leave. Simple as that!"

Nothing.

"He ain't gonna take the bait, boys." Pete's tone was one of bored indifference. "How about we smoke 'em out instead?"

"Good plan. That old cabin looks like it'll be perfect tinder. What do you reckon they got up there in terms of firepower, Pete?"

"Nothing much, I'll wager. Neither of 'em did anything but run yesterday, like the cowards that they are. So here's what we're gonna do. We…"

His plan never got further. A shotgun blast sounded around the hollers of Red Crotter's farm, sending a flock of birds panicking into the air and bringing a fresh round of terror from the trapped, magnetized horses. Rattlesnake Pete hit the ground, screaming and pawing at his thigh. "My leg! That son of a… shot my *leg*!"

Up in the cabin, Rocket clapped his paws together. "Outstanding shot! I like your style, old man." He peered out the window and laughed again. "Oh, man, his thigh looks like a platter of raw meat."

"Holy *crap*, Red." Quill was aghast. "You could have at least *warned* him first."

"That was meant to be a warning shot," said Red, without taking his eyes from the sight. "Aim's not so good as it was."

Cora shut off her projection of the sounds of Pete's whimpering and they were all grateful for that.

"They're out there talking openly about skinning us alive, old man," Red added.

Red's incredulity fired Quill's indignation.

"We should have warned them first," he said. "It's standard good guy practice…"

"Good guys. Huh." Rocket snorted. He turned back to watch the scene outside. "They're fussing around him now, looks like they're trying to stop him bleeding out… What's he saying, Cora? Play it for us."

"Of course, Rocket." She opened up her speakers again and the sounds of panicked voices flooded through the room.

"…no, Ned, forget me. Just light that place up. Burn the bastards to the ground."

"Kill them?"

"Oh hell, yes."

"Oh hell, no," said Rocket. "Oh hell, yes. Duck!"

Gunfire immediately filled their air, bullets ricocheting from the protection of the heavy lumber of the cabin. One bullet zinged through the window, shattering the glass. Quill ducked down, letting out a shout of alarm. Rocket let out a short, barking laugh.

"What do you reckon, Red? Think I should open up and roast these goons? Or would that be decidedly unheroic of me?"

"Always been a fan of the anti-hero, myself," replied Red.

"Good answer." Rocket rose up. "*Right* answer." With a bellow of delight, he unleashed a blast of fire from his rifle in the direction of the men shooting at them. "One down, four guys left. This is no problem. Go on, time me!"

"Cora," shouted Quill. "Now's the time to play that music!"

An orchestral swell filled the fighting zone as Cora played the opening bars of a classic Rigellian symphony. Quill stepped forward, looking disheartened, holding up a hand to stall proceedings and exchange a few quick words with the recorder. The beautiful tune faded away and the heady backdrop of a pounding bass beat rolled out to take its place.

"Now *that's* what I'm talking about," said Quill.

It was a brief battle, even more so than the one with the Brood. Then, it had been a case of thinning numbers enough to make good on their escape. Here, it was five men. It transpired that while Pete's posse were reasonably seasoned and well-armed to boot, they were unprepared for the ferocity of Rocket Raccoon's counterattack. After more glass was blasted out, Rocket burst out of a now empty window frame, moving with such speed and ferocity that the posse were startled into confusion. Rocket rained fire down on them and two fell before they could react. Their injuries weren't fatal but didn't leave a lot of options for survival later.

Then there were two. Emboldened by the change of odds in their favor, Quill left the cabin. A bullet zinged right by his ear, close enough to lift his hair. His heart leaped into his mouth, and he offered up silent thanks to whatever deity might have been watching him at that moment. He allowed himself to circumvent all the brain circuits telling him he was too old for this kind of thing and opened fire with the pistols Red had loaned him. He grazed one of the two men across the shoulder, enough for him to drop his gun. Then he and Rocket were standing together laughing uproariously as the men gathered their weapons and their wounded, fleeing into the Wastelands, leaving their horses behind.

"Well, at least we got ourselves a ride," said Quill as he lowered his weapons. Beside him, Rocket still had his rifle raised.

"Yep," he said, finally lowering the weapon once the two enemies were long gone, and Quill could hear the wheezing in his friend's lungs. "We sure have. Let's get them freed and rubbed down. Then we can get to Doomwood."

Several minutes later, the panicked posse horses had been calmed and led to Red's shabby stable area. They were grateful for the feed, and while Quill and Red headed back outside to check the area was clear, Rocket remained behind to water the animals. As he did so, he inspected them for injury. They had miraculously escaped unharmed and as he rubbed them down, they settled.

Rocket paused as a coughing fit assailed him and Cora spoke up. "Are you quite all right, Rocket?"

"Yeah," choked Rocket, waving irritably. "It's the straw in this stable, that's all. I got… allergies. Stop fretting and help me with the saddle on this horse, would you?"

"Of course, Rocket." Cora moved to help him lift the saddle and buckle it back onto the horse. At first, the straps were a puzzle, but she soon worked out how the saddle functioned as a mechanism and her fingers worked deftly. As she did her work, Rocket's cough started again and he turned away from her, spitting into the straw.

"Rocket."

"What?"

"That was blood you spat out onto the straw." Rocket looked up at the recorder, unblinking and without speaking. "There are several other occasions where I have recorded the sound of you coughing so harshly."

"Oh, great. Yeah, good for you, lady."

"So I do not believe that you have allergies." Rocket didn't respond and Cora supplied a secondary comment. "Neither do I believe it is the straw."

"OK. Listen, Cora. Just… don't say anything about this to Quill, all right? Promise me."

"I promise, Rocket."

"I just… I just wanted to square all this away. Get the Black Vortex, take it back, collect the fee and satisfy myself that Quill's gonna be OK, you know? Before I shuffle off this mortal coil." He spat another gobbet of blood into the straw and passed a paw over his eyes, his little body showing far more than he was saying.

"Are you sad about this, Rocket?"

"Sad? Of course not. I'm not sad. I'm pissed off. Yeah, that's a better phrase. Pissed off. I guess it happens though. You live long enough and death catches up with you, even though you've done a great job of avoiding its gaze." He sighed and looked up as he heard approaching voices. "They're back. Shut up." He hoisted himself up – with great difficulty – onto the back of the horse as Quill and Red came into the stable.

"Woah, Rocket on a horse! That's not a thing I ever thought I'd see," said Quill, his face lighting up with sheer delight at the extraordinary vision of Rocket sitting astride a stallion as Cora patiently adjusted the stirrups for his reduced height. Just for a moment, Quill considered making jokes about Rocket's height, but then he forced it down. It wasn't the time.

"Yeah, yeah," grumbled Rocket, but it was good natured.

"Sure you know how to work the controls on that thing?"

"Oh, shut your yap and open up the doors, please." Laughing at his own joke, Quill did as Rocket asked and nudged the horse forward. It trotted obediently and Red cast a critical eye over it.

"Those horses have been poorly treated," he observed and it was impossible not to hear the anger in his tone. "They're slat-ribbed, they've got sores in their mouths and they're skittish. It's gonna take some doing, getting them used to you."

"I can pilot *anything*," said Rocket, repeating a phrase he'd used countless times across the years. "And that includes a dumb horse."

"Whatever you say, Rocket." All thoughts of teasing him fled as Quill became acutely aware that there was now something oddly poignant, perhaps even *dignified* about the small raccoon Rocket holding his aging body up so very straight on the horse's back. "Whatever you say. Let's get out of here."

"Wait," said Red. "Before you leave…" He fumbled at his gun belt, unbuckling it, and the weapons that he wore there. He held up the holsters, studied them for a moment, then laughed lightly. "These were my grandaddy's. Then they were my daddy's. Then mine. Now, I guess…" He chewed his lower lip, taking in a mouth full of beard as he did so. "I guess they're yours."

Quill took the gun holster, his expression one of incredulity. "Seriously?" He swapped for the pistols he'd been using and Red nodded.

"Seriously. You aren't gonna last long out there without some sort of decent peashooter. Go on. Try one on for size."

His face quizzical, Quill drew one of the weapons from its holster. It was a thing of beauty, fitting into his grip as though it belonged there. He looked at its design carefully: sandalwood grips, a blue steel finish and a six-inch barrel. He slid it back into the holster and drew the other, its perfect twin. They were perfectly balanced, and he was rendered speechless at the gift. He opened up the cylinder and rotated the barrel. Fully loaded. As he snapped it back in and slid it into a fully stocked gunbelt, he nodded at Red, awkwardly.

"This is the point in the story where I say 'Man, I couldn't' and you say…"

"I say, 'I insist.'"

The two old men exchanged sudden, warm smiles. Red put a hand on Quill's arm. "Where you're going – Doomwood – it's about as dangerous as it gets. I'd be a poor man if I didn't give you a fighting chance."

"No offense, Red, but we've been in some pretty hairy situations over the years," said Rocket from atop his horse. "Shot our way out of them all."

"Sure, sure. Big talk all right, Rocket. Talk it up all you want – but this is Doom's *home* you're planning on strolling into. His headquarters. Out there, he's got folks digging into the Black Hills, mining for precious metals. He's got refineries there, purifying raw ore and churning out steel. And that steel goes straight to the assembly lines where he's cranking out weapons and materials." He looked up at Rocket, then to Quill. "Believe me, you'll smell Doomwood a while before you see it. Furnaces everywhere. A factory that got out of control."

"You're a walking advertisement for the Wastelands tourism bureau, aren't you?"

Red ignored Rocket's scathing remark and continued. "Second thing. Sebastian Warn. That's the guy you're looking for. Tell him I sent you. Ask after him at the Heaven and Hellfire."

"The Heaven and…"

"Hellfire. It's the drinking hole he favors. He knows the Black Hills better than most. And this is the important bit. He's not just someone who can help you, Quill. He's someone you can trust." He clapped Quill's shoulder and stepped back. His gaze took them all in. "But the key thing you need to look out for? Kraven."

"Kraven?"

"The Wastelands have a million ways to kill you and Kraven is at the top of the list. He is the number one danger out there. He's Doom's right-hand man. An enforcer."

Rocket made a dismissive kind of noise. "We took care of that posse right enough. We can take one guy."

"No. You can't. This is *important*. Killing is more than just a pleasure for this guy. It's a way of life. It's his…" Red sought for the words.

"Raisin deeter?" Quill attempted to provide what he thought was the right phrase and his terrible pronunciation brought a brief quirk to Red's lips.

"Close enough, yeah. It's his whole way of life. The Wastelands are his prime hunting grounds. So you listen up and you listen *good*. You keep a low profile. You get in, you get out. Because once Kraven's got your scent, you'll be two more carcasses hanging up in his butcher's window at Totem Hill."

The harsh truth settled over the group like a particularly uncomfortable blanket as Quill moved to mount a second horse. After a few failed attempts, Cora also managed to mount up and the three of them moved into a small group.

"Well, on that cheery note… Red, are you sure you won't come with us?" The question came from Quill.

Red shook his head. "Tempting as it sounds, I'm going to have to decline." Red walked with them to the boundary of his farm, opening up the gate so that they could all leave. "Got a date with a Doombot," he said. "Gotta protect what's mine."

"Maybe it won't come," said Quill, but his heart wasn't in it.

"Oh, it'll come," said Red, looking up and shielding his eyes against the rising sun. "Doom controls the Wastelands for a reason. He has to keep the fear alive and, in this instance, that'll be by making a lesson out of me." He waved the shotgun he still carried. "Or at least trying to."

"All the more reason for you to come with us, man."

"Don't worry, Quill, I'm not going to go down without a fight." Red smiled. "Gonna get this place ready for a proper showdown. It might even be fun. You boys – and you too, Cora – you lit a fire under me. Gave me hope that maybe the good guys *can* still win. And I'm grateful for that. Maybe…

if you finish this job and your heads don't pop off… maybe you should consider coming back here. World could use more folks like you."

Quill reached down to clasp Red's forearm in his own, a grip of alliance between two men who, while they were of an age, had been complete strangers the day before. Now, they were friends. "Maybe," he said and both knew they'd probably never meet again. Red nodded and stepped back.

"We'll see you down the trail, Red."

"Sure. Just stay clear of the roads and whatever you do, keep away from Kraven."

He watched as they left, walking the horses away from the farm at a steady pace. He couldn't hear them anymore, but he saw Quill turn to Cora and say something. A moment or two later, he heard the distant sound of electric guitars as she played the music he'd clearly asked for.

"See you down the trail, Star-Lord," he said, shaking his head and turning to go back into the cabin to face whatever else this crazy world threw at him.

# CHAPTER FIVE
## DEER ON A SPEAR

Entry C1451Z2H
Location: *The Wastelands. At the southern edge of the Black Hills, en route to Doomwood.*

"How much further do we have to go?" It was the seventeenth time that Quill had asked the question that morning and he knew, even as he said it, that he sounded like he was whining. He also knew what Cora's response would be. He was correct.

"The distance is variable, Star-Lord," she said, mildly. "Dependent on the difficulties of our route."

"Starting to get a bad case of saddle-butt," he complained. "Also, probably my imagination, but it feels like every mile we travel, this guillotine collar gets tighter." He rasped to emphasize his point, perhaps a little more than the situation demanded, but he hated this trip. Rocket rode on ahead, having insisted on scouting forward.

"You still have four days, twenty-two hours, thirty-five minutes, and seven seconds before your mission and your life are set to end."

The matter-of-factness knocked Quill off kilter and he rubbed at his nose. "Right? The clock is ticking. So we need to giddy up and get to Doomwood. If we don't sidetrack, how far is it?"

"Approximately five point seven miles."

"The route Rocket's taking us feels like we're doubling – maybe tripling that."

Cora nodded. "All the time we follow a more circuitous route, that estimate is accurate."

Quill made a noise of exasperation, throwing up his hands before taking the reins back. "Dumb detours. Never known him to be so cautious."

"I suspect, if you do not mind me hypothesizing, that he is concerned for your life."

"My life?" Quill was surprised. "What about *his*?"

"I am making my observation based on what I have witnessed. Let me replay for you what he said to me when you were busy urinating off a ledge for three minutes and seventeen seconds earlier in the day."

"Three minutes and… you *timed* me?"

"I am a recorder, Star-Lord. I record everything."

"Yeah, of course you do. Look, things don't… flow as well as they used to, OK?" Cora didn't respond and Quill heard the now familiar click and buzz of her accessing a recording. Rocket's voice floated out from her speakers.

*"So while Quill's off taking care of business… I've spotted at least three drones since we left. Lot of these hills are cut clean, logged*

*right down to the stumps. I say we avoid riding in the open. Stick to the forest. Stay in the shadows. We can't let them spot Quill."*

The recording ended and Quill chewed his lower lip. "I mean... I guess I am a wanted man. But I'm uncomfortable with him riding out alone like that. Smell that air. It smells like burned cancer. Who *knows* what this radiation's done to the local wildlife?"

"My Geiger counter indicates current levels are 10 mrem 0.1 mSv."

"Ah," said Quill. "Numbers. What's normal?"

"1.5 mrem is the standard background radiation for this planet."

"Oh, great. Just *great*. We're getting slow-cooked. Another threat." He paused, chewed his lip again and spoke again. "On which note..."

He pulled the horse to a stop. The wind blew around them, accompanied by the creaking of the weirdly twisted and misshapen trees. Cora copied his motions. She had learned quickly how to manage the horse, although for the most part they trotted along at a sedate pace. "Look, Cora, there's something I've been meaning to ask you."

"I am listening, Star-Lord. I am always listening."

"Yeah," said Quill. "It's about that. It's just... well, something's been bugging me about when we found you. Up on that mining freighter." When she didn't respond, he continued. "You said you were *en route* from Alpha Centauri, right?"

"Correct."

"What were you doing there?"

"Recording, Star-Lord. That is what I always do."

It was glib. Too glib, perhaps, for an automaton, but even so, it pushed Quill to keep asking questions. "What was the name of the planet you were recording?"

"Siege Centauri."

Quill frowned.

"If you have not heard of it, Star-Lord, perhaps it is because that is the name given to it by the Rigellians."

Quill nodded, still doubtful. "All right," he conceded, "so that's where you were stationed. But what was it that prompted the change of destination? Why were you headed to Earth?"

"Because..." She paused. It was infinitesimal, barely noticeable to the human ear – but to her own highly sophisticated aural circuits, it seemed like an age. "Because my work there was done."

Quill nodded as though a curiosity was satisfied. Leaning forward over the neck of his horse, he lowered his voice, sharing his thoughts in a hushed whisper. "Here's the thing. When I look around this place and see all these clean hillsides, or when I hear about Doom ruling over and ripping up the Wastelands, I get a thought."

"What is that thought, Star-Lord?" She mirrored his movement, leaning closer to hear what he had to say.

"The Rigellians. You specifically referred to them as an empire."

"Correct."

"I hear that word. 'Empire'. I hear the word 'Siege'." He leaned back again and studied Cora. "You called a planet 'Siege'. That just doesn't sound right to me."

"I am perplexed as to where this line of questioning is leading, Star-Lord. How does it sound wrong to you?"

"Are the Rigellians like... planet eaters? Are you a scout? Sorry, Cora, I'm sorry how that sounds. I like you! You've done all right by us. But with everything that's going on, I've got bumper-level paranoia. Everything is upside down, inside out and back to front. What I'm saying, Cora, is…" He swallowed, then got it out. "Can we trust you?"

"That depends how you use the word, Star-Lord."

It wasn't the response he'd anticipated, and it wrong-footed him briefly. He rallied like a champion. "Isn't there just one way to use the word?"

"Allow me to explain for you," she said, and paused briefly. "What if I were to tell you that the Rigellians could make a world better? Make it safer? What if I were to tell you that the empire is good-willed and altruistic in its ongoing efforts to share its resources and designs with the galaxy at large?"

"I don't know what I'd say," said Quill. "Don't empires always start with that line, though? You know. The whole greater good schtick? Next thing you know, they're raising their flag, changing your national anthem, and killing the populace."

"I have a question for you, Star-Lord. Do you believe that the Earth has prospered without the oversight of a benevolent power?"

"I…" Quill shook his head and sighed. "No," he admitted, reluctantly. "I guess not."

"Look around, Star-Lord. This green and pleasant land is green no more. There is no hope. Or very little hope. I was trapped on that mining freighter for three decades. During that time, my connection to the Rigellian collective was severed. They cut me loose, as you would say. I was tossed aside. Just like you and Rocket, I do not know where I belong anymore. So just like you, I will continue to do what I do best. In my case, that is recording the promise of new worlds."

It was a long speech from the recorder and Quill considered it. Finally, he nodded, satisfied with her response. He lifted his eyes to the skies above. A slight heat-haze distorted everything and the acrid heat of the day left his throat parched and his eyes sore. He took a sip of water. He snapped the reins, clicking his tongue against his cheek, urging the horse forward.

"Well, I plan on saving this no-longer-green or pleasant land," he said as the horse moved on once more.

Cora tugged her horse's reins and attempted to copy him. "Then I will be there, alongside you, to record this great act," she asserted. "Come on. Click, click. Giddy up." For a few moments, it appeared that the horse was going nowhere, but eventually it got the idea and they resumed their trek through the forest. After a few more moments, Cora spoke, addressing him. "Star-Lord?"

"Yuh-huh?"

"I have made an observation about you and Rocket."

"Oh?" He shot a sideways glance at her. "Shoot. I'm listening."

"When you are alone, your tone becomes much more serious." He laughed in response to that and waved it off. "No, it seems that you become less…" She sought her databanks for the most appropriate word for the moment. "Less *silly*."

"No way," said Quill. "I'm still silly. Watch this." With that, he pulled an assortment of ridiculous faces, made several strange and unlikely sounds, ending by putting his thumbs to his ears and waggling them at her. She stared, unblinkingly and he put his hands down. "See? Still silly."

"In turn," she continued, completely ignoring these hijinks, "Rocket is far less theatrically outraged by everything whenever you are not around."

Quill laughed at that. "Oh, now I *know* you're wrong," he said. "Rocket's *always* angry." As though to punctuate his words, their companion's voice called out from the forest.

"Hey, morons! Get your dumb selves over here. Pronto!"

Quill shrugged and then grinned. "See?" He turned the horse in the direction of Rocket's voice. "He's always mad, or impatient or disappointed. Sometimes he's all of those things at the same time. It's his thing."

"His... thing?"

"Like a hobby or pastime. His *passion*." Cora was just about managing the increased pace of the trot and, as they approached Rocket, she was being bounced in the saddle. In a human, that might have been uncomfortable. But she didn't have that problem.

"I have also observed," she said, between jolts, "that you have your own private language and customs. Like a couple." There was no time for Quill to respond to that particular piece of wisdom because Rocket emerged from the woods, still seated atop his horse, and beckoned to them.

"Come on, already!"

"Oh *now* you want to hurry? After spending all day slowing us down? Go left. Go right. Go forward. Go backward. I mean, have we even *left* Red's farm?" Quill ceased his grumbling, peering a little myopically at Rocket. "What's the problem?"

"We're gonna have to double back," said Rocket, grim. "Take a different route."

Quill shook his head in exasperation. "C'mon, Rocket! We don't have *time* for that! We're racing *death* here!"

"Listen, Quill." Rocket looked at him and his small face was earnest. "Don't think I don't know that. But death's a lot closer than you might think, particularly if you don't listen to me."

"What do you mean?"

Rocket hesitated, then reached a decision. His shoulders sagged and he moved away. Or at least would have had the horse cooperated.

"Come and see," he said with great weariness. "Come on. Right round this next bend." The horse remained static, and Rocket tugged and clicked to no avail. "Come on, you dumb horse. Move! It's defective, Quill! I swear to god. Come on, horse. Move."

"Nope, it's fine. You're just a terrible cowboy."

"It's probably scared of the blood, you idiot."

"What?" Quill's moment of humor froze, and he felt a prickle of apprehension.

"The horse is scared of the smell of blood... woah, here we go." The horse pressed forward, but the noise it made suggested Rocket's guess was accurate. The wildness in its equine eyes was fearful. The sound of flies, ever-present, became louder as they followed Rocket around the curve of the hill. All color drained from Quill's face as the pervading stench hit his nostrils.

"Oh my god..." he said, for once devoid of witty commentary or sarcasm. Rocket nodded.

"Oh yeah. Hit me about a quarter mile back," he said, quietly. "There's no mistaking what it is."

Moments later, the stink was overpowering. Choking back the urge to vomit, Quill covered his mouth and nose with the sleeve of his jacket, taking in the gruesome sight before him. A figure was staked to a tree, the remains hanging a few feet from the ground. A thick cloud of black flies surrounded it like a shroud. "This is…" He couldn't find a word in his vocabulary to truly express his utter disgust for what he was seeing. "This is *nasty*. He's mounted like a trophy."

Cora leaned forward, her eyes scanning the corpse. "Given the high ambient temperature of the area, the rate of decomposition leads me to deduce that this individual has been dead for three days."

"Do you think they spiked him before or after he died?" The question came from Rocket, and Quill stared at him over his sleeve. "What? I just wondered. But look, Quill. This ain't it. This poor bastard isn't alone. Look at that tree over there. And the one just past it."

Quill looked. He wished he hadn't.

"Oh, man," he said, quietly. Rocket moved down the line as though travelling through some kind of grisly waxwork exhibition.

"*And* this tree here. And all the way back to the canyon entrance. You see? *This* is why we have to double back. We've gotta find another way, Quill." In his heightened anxiety, Rocket began coughing. If Quill noticed, he didn't say anything. He swatted irritably at the flies.

"Flarking flies. Huh. Just realized. Haven't had to swat at a fly in *years*." He grimaced. "You know my own world sucks *majorly* when I'm yearning for the fly-free nothingness of space."

"Who is responsible for this?" Cora verbalized what Quill was wondering and he *really* wished she hadn't. Rocket re-joined them, wrinkling his snout.

"I can make out one set of tracks…"

"Size fifteen feet."

"Yeah, well, size is one thing, Cora, but there's a critical detail I think you're missing." Quill studied the tracks Rocket was indicating and awareness wallowed in the swamp of his intellect.

"No boot prints. Bare feet."

"Got it in one. I'm impressed." Rocket's cough had lessened. "In this terrain, I'm gonna reckon that means we're talking about a special sort of specimen. A true predator." He looked up at Quill. "A hunter."

"Kraven." Cora supplied the name. Again, Quill *really* wished she had just kept quiet.

Rocket nodded. "Seems like a solid guess on the back of what Red told us."

"No, Rocket. It is not a guess."

"What do you mean, Cora?" Quill looked at her sharply. "What you got?"

"I have picked up a local radio transmission. A news program of some kind. Do you wish to hear it?"

"No," said Quill. "Yes. No. What? Yes. What's it saying?"

"You know we're gonna regret asking that question, right?" Rocket lowered his voice as he moved beside Quill. Cora's speakers began playing a tune; tinny and indistinct to begin with. Quill was immediately put in mind of the start of the old Saturday sport programs he'd listened to with his grandfather as a kid in the pickup. The tune died away and a voice broke through. It had all the hallmarks of a sports commentator: older, male, filled with enthusiastic energy that could be wound up or reeled in as the situation demanded.

"There's still sport?" Hope flared. Perhaps this world wasn't a *total* loss…

"Shhh."

*"Welcome, loyal citizens of the Victorlands, to another exciting edition of Deer on a Spear! This is Brandon Best reporting to you live from Doomwood and the hunt, folks, is on. I'm here in my studio tracking the drone monitors but let me tell you this. Even from here, I am feeling the adrenaline in the air. Doomwood never disappoints."*

"That's not promising," said Quill. Rocket shushed him again.

*"Totem Hill is packed with patriots ready for some justice. Just listen to that crowd!"*

A sudden cut away from the commentator introduced the sounds of a loud, boisterous crowd cheering loudly. Quill and Rocket could make out the chant, *"Kraven! Kraven!"* They exchanged worried glances.

Cora spoke up. "Should I keep playing?"

Quill nodded. He both did and didn't want to hear what happened next. As he listened to the commentary, he became so engrossed in what he was hearing that he could picture what it was like to be right there…

The voice of Brandon Best continued. *"That's right, folks. The sharks out there are in a frenzy because there's blood in the water. I've got a report here from Lord Doom which informs me that today's contender is a member of the underground terrorist organization calling itself the Second Dawn."*

"Contender?" Rocket snorted. "Cute."

*"You heard that right. How disappointing, folks. How disgusting that these hostiles and agitators have no appreciation for what we have here in the Victorlands. We have protection. We have purpose. We have Doom!"*

Another cutaway to the crowd, who screamed Doom's name over and over. It was reckless insanity and it made the hair on Quill's neck stand on end.

*"On that note, folks, if you suspect anyone in our community, please, please don't hesitate to report them to your nearest Doombot. Do they keep odd hours? Do they complain about their job? Have you ever heard them use the slur 'the Wastelands' to describe our beautiful home? Then those are some clear indicators that they may not be on your side."*

"I can't believe I'm hearing this," said Quill, his face white.

Rocket shook his head. "Believe it, Quill. It's happening."

*"It's a shame that some people don't appreciate what we've got and correct me if I'm wrong, folks, but we've got a lot! We're blessed beyond measure with what we've got here. We're spared the lawlessness and violence and poverty and hunger others experience and all because one man stood up in a time of chaos and need. He takes care of us. Because Doom provides. Remember that. Doom provides."*

"I'm not sure I can listen anymore." Quill leaned back in the saddle staring up at the sky. At this hour, it was blue and cloudless. Perfect, were it not for the knowledge that the background radiation was slowly killing everything beneath it. He felt sick, not just from the stench of the corpses and all that implied, but from the words of the commentator. His own world. Reduced to this nightmare.

"Shall I stop, Star-Lord?" Cora paused the transmission.

Quill took a breath and shook his head. "Invested, now," he murmured. "Keep playing." He'd probably regret saying that, but he *had* to know the extent of it. Rocket rubbed at his horse's neck, as grim as Quill had ever seen him.

"Very well," said Cora and she resumed, uninterrupted.

Beyond the studio walls, the crowd were chanting and shouting. "Deer on a spear! Deer on a spear!" The four syllables were picked up and overlapped, creating aural chaos until Brandon Best's voice cut through them once more.

*"The people have spoken! Now. Earlier today, I was able to get a few words from the living spear. The most accomplished predator the world has ever known. Kraven the Hunter!"*

The cheers were explosive and the horses started, their nervousness shifting into brief terror. The three riders were able to calm them enough to pick up the narrative once again.

*"I visited him at his home where I was surrounded by skin rugs. There were mounted horns and taxidermized carcasses on every wall and surface. The full interview airs tonight, but for now, a taster of this brief, cozy fireside chat."*

The tone of the broadcast changed. The overlapping roar of the crowd faded out, replaced by a warmer ambience with the crackle and pop of a fire in the background. It was oddly intimate, given the subject matter.

*"Tell us, Kraven."* Best inserted himself into the scene. *"How do you feel about today's installment of* Deer on a Spear? *Is it a fight for justice? To punish the terrorists who live among us? To showcase your undying loyalty to Lord Doom?"*

A few moments passed before a slow, well-measured and heavily accented voice responded. It was deep and without warmth or any hint of empathy or emotion whatsoever and no effort was made to respond to Best's question.

*"This morning, I walked through the forest, and I happened upon a dead man. His face was purple. Blotched and swollen. His*

veins were black. Vomit coated his cheek. He had been poisoned. On closer examination, I saw the fat of his arm had been gnawed right to the bone. I crouched down to observe the killer, hiding nearby."

Another pause.

"It was a spider scorpion the size of a dog. It, like me, was crouched – but in the shadow of a bush, waiting for me to pass by so that it could continue what it had started. But understand this. There is no predator greater than man. This creature had bested its superior opponent only through trickery. By hiding and only darting out at an opportune moment to sting its enemy. The coward's way. Well, I drew my knife…"

There was the distinct scrape of a knife being drawn from a sheath. It may only have been audio, but the sound made Quill's skin crawl without even knowing why. Just the very sound of this apex killer unsheathing his weapon was enough to make him want to go spend another three minutes urinating from a ledge.

"I drew my knife and considered my enemy. I did not want to kill the spider scorpion, you understand. I wished only to maim it. I moved too fast for it to avoid me, and the knife severed its tail. Milky ooze dribbled from the wound. It had no escape. I took the spider scorpion, took its mewling, squirming body and I carried it over a mile away to a location where I'd previously noted a chest-high pile of fire ants."

"Sheesh, this guy," muttered Rocket.

"I kicked the dust to stir their rage. Then, right before I dropped the spider scorpion into the swarm, I plucked off each of its legs. Its demise was a beautiful thing."

Quill held his breath, caught up by the passionless horror. Kraven continued, finishing his tale.

"*In the face of the dead man, I saw the cold indifference of an uncaring universe. In the swarm of fire ants, I saw that there is no natural justice in this world beyond that which we reap.*"

Silence descended. Even the horses stilled, magnifying the tension as Kraven's words faded. Once more, the background of the screaming crowd swam back into the audio landscape and Best spoke, his tone appropriately somber.

"*Let those words sink in, folks. It was like poetry, wasn't it?*" He allowed a suitable length of time for the question to linger, before adjusting his tone back to the cheery and enthused sounds of the sports commentator. "*Now, we all know that Kraven the Hunter is unstoppable, but nobody likes a blow-out, am I right? That's why today's match-up is especially exciting! Now. You might know Sebastian Warn as a local hunter and trapper, but guess what, folks? It recently came to light that he's nothing more than one of those terrorists. A part of that Second Dawn organization. Now that's the bad news. But the good news is that this should be a great match. Warn weighs in at one hundred ninety pounds against Kraven's two-fifty – but Warn has spilled his own share of blood and knows how to navigate these hills.*"

Rocket and Quill shared another alarmed glance as they heard the name, but neither spoke. The commentary continued.

"*From the time Kraven sounds his horn… let me check the stats here. Kill time is an average of ten minutes and fifteen seconds. If I was a gambling man – and I know plenty of you out there like a wager – then I'd bet you could bump that by a good five minutes today. Let's move into the thick of it now, folks. As is our custom on Deer on a Spear, Warn got a thirty minute head start with the option to select a weapon from the usual choices of a knife, a dagger, a sword, an ax, a bow and arrow, or a crossbow. He went with the crossbow, with one bolt locked and loaded, and set off at a full sprint into the southern hills."*

"Isn't that where…"

"Shh."

*"Our drones are with him and have been with him the whole time. He's made it a full mile into some pretty rough territory, but now…"*

A distant sound came, something like an airhorn, but with a lupine undertone. The sound echoed moments later from Cora's speaker. *"I don't know about you, folks, but whenever I hear that horn, I get chills of excitement. He's off, folks! Kraven the Hunter has sounded his hunting horn and the hunt is on! Warn is sprinting – huffing and puffing for breath as he runs into the woods…"*

"Enough," said Quill.

Cora shut off the broadcast and for a moment the only sounds were those of the horses and the buzzing flies. Quill swallowed slowly and the noise seemed to reverberate around the clearing.

"He's coming," said Rocket.

"Rocket," said Quill, his throat dry. "Kraven is going after Sebastian Warn."

"Yeah, ain't nothing wrong with my hearing. Come on, Quill. We've gotta get out of here."

"Sebastian Warn," said Quill with a hint of panic in his tone. "That's our contact. Our chance to find the Black Vortex."

Rocket grabbed his arm. "Listen to me. You're a wanted man and right now you're wandering through a garden of corpses.

You want to run right into the arms of the enemy, Quill? It's not just Kraven out there, man! It's the drones."

"My helmet," said Quill, as though experiencing a sudden revelation. Rocket's eyes narrowed as Quill reached up to deploy the implant helmet behind his ear. His words became immediately muffled. "Should've done this soon as I smelled the blood. Anyway. My helmet, Rocket. With this on, they won't recognize me. Won't know who I am."

"They won't *need* to know who you are, Quill. If you get in the way of this hunt, Kraven's gonna gut you. You know. For sport."

"It'll be fine. I've got my six-shooters." He unholstered the twin weapons that had been gifted to him by Red Crotter and thumbed back the hammers. "I've got my booster boots."

"Oh. Oh, no."

There was a sudden sputtering, like an engine trying to fire when it was long out of gas. It choked and spluttered for a few moments more.

"What do your booster boots do, Star-Lord?" Cora was curious.

"What it says on the tin, baby! They boost!"

"No, Quill. They boost-*ed*. Past tense. They barely work now! They're too old. Like the idiot wearing them!" The sputtering became a wheeze and then finally, there was ignition. His face was hidden beneath the helmet, but Rocket could absolutely sense that Quill had a dumb grin plastered to it as he slowly began rising from the saddle. "Quill," he said, his tone commanding. "Quill, get back here, now."

He sounded like an irritated parent chastising a child.

"Look, man." Rocket tried reason. "The last time you used

those things, you ended up with a concussion and a broken arm. Come on, get 'em off. Here, I'll get them off you. Quill. Come back down here and let me… Quill!"

"I've got this," came the defiant reply. "Guardians, go!"

With a roar, the booster boots shot Quill skywards, leaving Rocket and Cora in his wake. Rocket clenched his fists furiously.

"That is *not* our catchphrase!"

"Folks, welcome back!" Brandon Best was fully into the swing of the show, caught up in the drama of the hunt and delivering lurid descriptions to the eager, listening populace. He'd been doing this job for years now and he was good at it. He had to be good at it, so it was probably for the best that the sadistic streak that ran through him supplied the passion in his commentary. "If you're tuning into our drone footage today, you will no doubt have noted Kraven is barefoot as always. Even with those size fifteen feet, he still moves silently as a whisper. He is, for the benefit of listeners without video feeds – wearing a new loincloth which looks to be sewn from… yes. From elk hide, I'd guess. Very form flattering. Replicas of this design will be available from tomorrow through our storefront. You too can look this good."

Many things were dead in the Wastelands. Capitalism was not one of them.

"Let's return to the action. The hunt's underway, so let's cross to the drones and catch up with our prey. Our *contender*." The slip was brief and he covered it with the practiced ease of decades. "There he is, folks, Sebastian Warn! Running hard but starting to look like the exertion is taking a toll. He's closing in on the Canyon of Shadows. Now he certainly isn't the first –

and I'm sure he won't be the last – to try to use this landmark as part of a defensive strategy."

A clear smile crept into Best's voice as his commentary continued. "He is climbing now, struggling up a craggy precipice. His fingers continually lose their grip sending rocks tumbling down beneath him. His boots scuff against the cliff face. He is slowing down, but he must keep moving.

"His fingers quest for another handhold and he inches his way upwards. He's going up the walls of the canyon! Would you look at that? The crossbow's over his shoulder and he is going for it, ladies and gentlemen! Sebastian Warn is trying to take the higher ground. I imagine it'll give him a protected vantage to fire down on Kraven."

The crowd roared.

"I know! It's a good idea. Maybe even a *smart* one. But we all know that Kraven never misses his mark. Let's see where our spear is… yes, there he is!"

Kraven ran with an easy gait through the same woods that Warn had previously traversed. There was no gasping for breath though. The lashing branches didn't bother him in the slightest. For such a powerfully built man, Kraven was stealthy and near silent. His eyes scanned constantly for signs of Warn's passing. He smelled the man's sweat and fear and it gave him a desperate hunger.

"He's reached the canyon, folks. Where we know Sebastian lies in wait. What's Kraven going to do?"

What Kraven did was to begin running up the hillside parallel to the canyon. Best screamed with excitement. "I do declare Kraven has predicted Warn's move and is planning to turn it to his advantage!" He dropped his voice to a conspiratorial hush.

"He's approaching the rim of the canyon now. Slowly. Slowly."

Slowly.

Sebastian Warn was ready for him, swinging the crossbow up and firing with a whipcrack echoing back from the walls of the canyon. The bolt struck its target with a loud, meaty and infinitely satisfying smack.

"I don't believe it! I don't believe it! Kraven's hit right in the face. He brought up a hand to block it, but it looks like... wait. Wait! What's this? What? Is? This?"

No.

"No! Kraven's torn the bolt away!"

There was blood, of course, plenty of it. It streamed down Kraven's face from the gash on his cheek, but the wound looked superficial.

No.

"Look at that, folks! Kraven's skill is astonishing. His reflexes so sharp that he *caught the bolt*. That was a kill shot for sure and Kraven *caught* it in the nick of time. That, everyone, is why he doesn't bother with armor and only hunts with his knife. Who needs weapons and armor when you *are* weapons and armor? He is the ultimate weapon. He... Wait, what's this? Warn isn't giving up!"

Sebastian Warn, robbed of his one shot at taking out the relentless hunter, stood, then dropped from the ledge. He hit the ground with a *thump*, rolling several feet down to the forest floor. He had probably cracked a couple of ribs in the fall, but the adrenaline was coursing now.

He ran, but without purpose. Soon, he was swallowed by the forest.

"The drones struggle down there, folks, so it's hard for us

to keep track of his progress. Kraven's pacing the rim of the canyon… he's taking out the hunting knife. He's aiming it! He's going to throw it at the contender. Surely such a throw, from such an angle, is impossible? Now he's running. He's broken into a sprint."

The knife flew from Kraven's hand and seconds later there was a loud, strangled cry somewhere in the shadows. Two drones whirred in closer and, on the screens where the hunt was broadcast, it was apparent that the knife had struck Sebastian Warn in the leg, bringing him down. He dragged himself onwards, despite the injury. He reached down and…

"He's pulled the knife out! Oh, this is one of the best hunts we've had in weeks!" Best was overjoyed at the drama.

"Come and get me, Kraven!" Warn's bellow sounded clear, only a little breathless. Kraven appeared in shot, prowling like a wild animal on the clifftop above him.

"Looks like Warn is going to get his wish," said Best as, against all probability, Kraven took a standing jump from at least twenty feet. The cry he emitted was primal and he landed heavily near the fallen Sebastian Warn who looked up at him, then at the drones buzzing in to capture the moment. He directed his comments to them.

"You don't have to do this. None of you watching or listening… you don't need to do this! You're living in a trap! The Second Dawn is coming!"

"It's always sad, isn't it?" Best's voice was low and filled with an entirely fake sorrow. "To see someone meet their end without a hint of repentance."

"The Second Dawn is coming," repeated Warn. "You can be a part of it. Just… wake up!"

Kraven approached Warn slowly and deliberately, relishing the moment. He was ready to claim his victory. Every muscle in his body tensed.

There was a spluttering noise.

"The Second Dawn is…"

*PuttputtputtPOPputtputt…* and punctuating the sound came a long, loud shriek.

"What is this?" Best sat forward in his chair and stared at the drone footage as a speck appeared on the edges. The sound of failing engines and faint screaming became gradually louder. "I… I'm not sure exactly what I'm looking at here, folks, but it looks as though someone is flying towards our combatants…"

One of the boots gave out.

"…very badly. I don't know what to tell you, folks. But this gatecrasher is out of control! He's… yes! He's collided with one of the canyon walls! Ouch, folks, that *had* to have hurt, but whoever that is refuses to quit. He's hit the opposite canyon wall…"

A loud *thump* could be heard across the transmission and then a shot rang out.

"He's armed! This interloper is armed with a gun and… yes! He's firing on Kraven! A fellow insurrectionist, perhaps. One of Warn's supporters. He's powered by what appears to be rocket boots. Or boot, I should say, since only one of them is working."

For a few moments, the only thing that could be heard was the sound of the newcomer crashing into canyon walls and swearing as he entirely failed to make an impressive entrance. He careened into the canyon floor, bounced back up and then off the wall again.

He fired a second time, with a slightly winded shriek of delight. "The Guardians of the Galaxy are back!" He fired a third shot, then reached down. "I got you, Sebastian! Come here now! Come on!"

Incensed, Kraven took off at a loping run towards this "guardian," clearly changing his plans. As he reached out with a snatching hand, the guardian's boots fired again – both of them – accelerating the newcomer up faster than he'd anticipated. He smacked his head on a rocky overhang, then bumped into the wall again. Then the boots sent him shooting out of the canyon as any semblance of control was tossed heedlessly to the four winds.

As he departed, the airwaves were filled with choice expletives.

"Well." Best composed himself. "Well, that was… I don't *know* what that was. But that very strange and completely ineffective interruption appears to now be at an end. Kraven's shrugged it off and so should we, folks. He's moving in for the kill."

"You don't have to do this," said Sebastian Warn, but his voice was resigned, a man accepting his defeat. Kraven sneered, snatching him up from the ground. Warn screamed as the hunter plunged his thumbs into Warn's eyes. The pain must have blossomed to something unbearable, then into something exquisite…

And then the world was no longer Sebastian Warn's concern.

The drones buzzed. Kraven breathed heavily.

It was done.

"He's done it, folks. Kraven has ended the hunt in a matter of minutes. Unbelievable." Best's voice dripped with awe. "It's hard to even put into words what we've witnessed here today.

So you know what? I'll let you do it for me. Let's hear from our friends on the streets and on Totem Hill where Kraven will soon return with a physical ornament severed from his prey to hammer onto a new post as we celebrate another edition of *Deer on a Spear!*"

The crowd was crazed. "Deer on a Spear! Deer on a Spear!" The chant lifted and carried, voices raised in frenzied delight as Brandon Best signed off.

"Sebastian Warn is dead. Our community is safe."

It was twenty minutes before Peter Quill reunited with Rocket and Cora, and ten of those were the time it took him to descend from the embrace of the tree in which he'd landed. Rocket squinted up as he clambered down, coughing.

"You OK there, Rocket?" Quill appeared none the worse for his misadventures and Rocket scowled.

"I'm fine. I'm not the great human pinball."

"Oh, I'm fine. A few scratches." He waved it off indifferently.

"Yeah, well, I'm good, too." The coughing suggested that Rocket was anything but and Quill steered the conversation down a different route, avoiding talking about what had happened with Warn.

"You know, I was telling Cora earlier it felt like these collars are getting tighter. Is that what you've got going on? Because me…"

"No. I'm fine. It's the air. Just the dust. Breathing's like choking." He took a swig from the water canteen on his belt. "See? I'm fine." Indeed, the coughing seemed to settle. He fixed Quill with a cold, dispassionate stare. "You know you almost went and got yourself killed back there."

Quill held up a finger. "The key word there is 'almost'."

"Dumb move, Quill. Seriously. We can't take risks like that when we get into Doomwood."

"Look. If someone needs saving, then I'm going to save them. That's what we *do*, Rocket."

"You didn't do anything except make even more of an idiot out of yourself than usual."

"I just need to get my boots fixed…" But Rocket was in full flow.

"You were *seconds* away from getting your guts ripped out through your throat and watching Kraven floss with them."

"The whole thing," said Quill, his volume increasing, "could have turned out *very* differently if *someone* had fixed my boots."

Their eyes met. Wills clashed. Eventually, the tension dissipated a little. But only a little. "Look, Quill," said Rocket. "Let's concentrate on saving ourselves. Don't flark this up. Don't even *look* at anybody else. Stay focused. Eyes on the prize, remember? We get the Black Vortex, we get out of here."

"In case you missed it, Sebastian Warn is dead. He was our only lead."

"I know. Tell me what I *don't* know." Rocket folded his arms across his chest. Quill dusted off his jacket, noting as he did so that there were several new tears in the fabric. He sighed. That jacket was his *favorite.*

"Here's what we're gonna do," Quill said. "We're gonna have to reach out to some people in Doomwood. Find some friends. We've got no choice."

"Find some *friends*? Did you hear the people on that broadcast? They're all psychopaths. There's no friends to be found here, Quill."

"Brandon Best sounded friendly and well connected," said Cora, brightly. "Perhaps we should try to speak with him?"

Rocket and Quill stared at her. Rocket went to say something but shook his head. Quill gestured as though patting down a fire. "Look, it's fine. We're gonna be fine here. We'll just head into town, and…"

"Hah! We're just gonna saunter into town? Because of course you know this place *so* well! When was it you visited here? How old were you? Five? Because that, Quill, was a flarking long time ago!"

"It was more recent than that. Five. Huh."

"Well? How old?"

"Six."

The moment broke the discomfort between the two and Rocket relaxed, a small twitch on his lips. "Six. Well, by all means, lead the way to the candy stores and the diaper-changing stations."

"Here's the plan," said Quill, clapping his hands. "We hit the go-kart track. Maybe some putt-putt mini-golf. Then, we go get a root beer float."

"This is humorous," said Cora. "Star-Lord is being funny."

"No, Cora, he *thinks* he's being funny. There's a whole galaxy of difference."

But the recorder was caught in the moment and clapped her hands in the same way that Quill had just done.

"When I get to Doomwood, I am going to eat a banana and wear pants and sit in a chair!"

Had there been any tumbleweeds, they would not have gone amiss in that moment. Cora sounded so hopeful. "Was that humorous?"

"See what you've done, Quill? Your *stupid* is infectious."

"All right, I'm sorry. Let's discuss the real plan." He rubbed his hands together, thinking. Then he struck Quill-gold. "Here it is. We split up and enter the town separately and without attracting attention. Then we rendezvous later."

"A repeat of the Outpost 13 plan? Because of how well it worked? No way, Quill. You'll just get sauced and run your mouth off again. Bad plan. No deal."

"I promise, Rocket. Not a *drop* will touch these lips. Not a single dribble."

Rocket sighed theatrically. He pointed. "It would be a whole lot easier to take you seriously if you didn't have pine needles in your beard," he said.

Quill slapped at his beard, dislodging the better part of a branch's worth of needles and sending them showering onto the ground. He straightened up his torn jacket and considered their options further. "Cora, what kind of audio capabilities do you have for a crowded space? Say… about a hundred people? Would you be able to listen in on that?"

"Yes, Star-Lord. I can easily monitor the conversations of one hundred people simultaneously."

"Great. Then your job is to find and head for the most popular bar in town."

"And I ask them all many questions!" There was more enthusiasm in her voice than Quill had been expecting and he shook his head.

"No. You listen. Just… *listen*. Because people go to bars to complain and brag and spill their secrets. You listen for a while during primetime hours. That way, we'll get a good cross-section of people. Potential allies, potential enemies."

Rocket shook his head all the way through this "great plan" and finally spoke. "No. You can't send her into a bar. Not in a town where hunting people is a *sport*."

"Don't worry, Rocket, she'll be fine. Right, Cora?"

"I will be fine, Star-Lord."

"See? Just don't, whatever you do, under *any* circumstances, tell anybody who we are or why we're here."

Rocket turned, murmuring beneath his breath so that Quill had to strain to hear him. "Seriously, Quill. Do you really think we can trust her?" No reply was forthcoming as Quill thought back to the conversation he'd shared with Cora earlier that day. He studied her now as she stood there, patiently waiting further instruction.

"Hello? Quill?"

"What? Yeah. Oh, yeah. We can trust her."

He hoped so, at least.

The Heaven and Hellfire Club was the largest, most ostentatious and, judging from the number of people coming and going from its doors, the most popular drinking establishment in all of Doomwood. It was a large, timber-framed building – as were most of the buildings in the settlement – but it was painted with a fresco depicting flames on one side and fluffy clouds and blue skies on the other. There were two main entrance doors; one labeled "Hell" and the other labeled "Heaven".

After studying her options for a few moments, Cora chose to enter through the door marked Heaven, believing it would be friendlier.

It was not.

Inside, the room was crowded, filled with people drinking and talking with equal enthusiasm. It was loud and hot and uncomfortable – or at least would have been had Cora been organic. The heat washed over her without issue and her aural filters began the task of separating out different conversations. They also filtered out a loud belch as a drunk man stood in front of her.

"Who are *you*?"

"Hello," she said. "I am a Rigellian Recorder. Who are you?" The question confused the inebriated individual. He sized up her gleaming metal appearance and an expression of pure hate filled his eyes. He hacked up a gobbet of phlegm and spat in her face.

"How's that for an answer, skinbot?" A few people close by laughed uproariously, but Cora took it fully in her stride.

"Thank you for sharing your saliva with me," she said, sweetly. "I will be able to use this DNA sample dribbling down my face to study the effects of pollutants and radiation on your biology."

"Go to hell."

"That is the other side of the building. I will speak with someone else now. Hello." She moved past the confused man, coming face to face with a voluptuous woman who appeared to be short in the clothes department. "Hello, large woman who is only in possession of a single eye."

"Don't speak to me," retorted the woman, venom in her tone.

"My name is Cora. I am a Rigellian…"

"You're a trashcan on legs is what you are," said the woman, her voice rising dangerously. "Get away from me before I take you outside and curb-stomp your… your… fake-ass ass!"

"Oh dear, that does not sound like something I would enjoy. No thank you."

Any further discussion was drowned out by a sudden swell of noise and shouting. The word traveled inside from the street, firstly as a whisper and then as a delighted cheer.

"He's coming! Kraven's coming!"

"First round's on me!" This came from the drunk who had previously spat in Cora's face, and he stumbled to the bar. "Top rail vodka, whatever he's drinking!"

The crowd chanted as Kraven entered, covered in dust and blood and still wearing just the elk-skin loincloth that he'd worn while hunting down Sebastian Warn. The people parted before him, fear and admiration rippling through them like a wave. The chanting continued until the drunk held up a hand. Instantly, the crowd fell silent and Kraven sat at the bar.

"Pour the man his drink," the drunk hollered. The bartender took down a bottle from the top shelf and popped the top, pouring a generous measure into a glass which she set down in front of the Hunter. The drunk held up his own glass – filled with a considerably cheaper liquor. "Cheers to Kraven. For spilling blood and keeping us all safe!"

The crowd dutifully cheered as Kraven downed the shot in a single pull, slamming the glass back down expectantly. "Another! Pour him another!" The drunk was in his stride now. "It's on me. Pour him the whole bottle if that's what he wants!" More spirit was poured, another hush fell as the crowd waited, expectantly. "What are we drinking to this time, Kraven?"

The bar fell so silent that you could have heard a pin drop. Kraven shifted position slightly holding the glass up to the light. "I raise my glass to my next hunt." He looked around the room, his voice still entirely devoid of emotion, and finished the toast.

"To the death of Peter Quill."

# CHAPTER SIX
## HEAVEN AND HELLFIRE

Entry C1451Z2I
Location: *The Wastelands. Just outside Doomwood.*

The ridge was high above the settlement of Doomwood. It overlooked the town, positioned above a winding valley, nestled idyllically in the hills. It was quite scenic if one ignored the fact that the town was a hive of industry. There were mine entrances, factories, a sawmill, and a refinery belching black smoke into the air.

The spot was prominent enough that it had been the agreed rendezvous point. The three companions arranged to meet after three hours and then set off to achieve their separate goals. Quill and Rocket arrived back first, with fifteen minutes to go before their imposed deadline. Cora was not far behind, and as she climbed up toward them, the two were already talking. Quill was animated, his hands waving excitedly in front of him, his straggly hair blowing in the wind. Rocket, however, looked entirely disinterested – although that may have been a deliberate affectation.

"You know why I'm excited?"

"Don't know, don't care."

"I care," said Cora as she joined them. "Why are you excited, Star-Lord?"

"Don't encourage him," said Rocket automatically, but his heart wasn't in it. Quill turned to the recorder.

"I'm excited because I heard our names while I was in town. In Doomwood, people were talking about us. The Guardians of the Galaxy!"

"Quill," said Rocket. "I hate to burst your bubble…"

"You *love* to burst my bubble."

"…but that ain't exciting. All *that* means is that we've got a big, fat target painted on our backs." Rocket wasn't impressed by Quill's revelation, and he watched as some of the excitement drained from his friend, replaced by an emotion Rocket couldn't place.

"Look, man. I couldn't save Sebastian Warn. I admit I screwed that up. But I still helped. There's something in the air, I'm telling you. *Hope*."

Rocket made a noise that effectively communicated his supreme indifference to this.

"Star-Lord is correct. There *is* something in the air," Cora said. "A transmission."

Rocket turned to her. "What are you talking about?"

"I am picking up a Doombot transmission. It seems that they have located the *Milano*."

Rocket groaned again and put his paw over his face. "Oh, great. That's just *great*. Perfect." His hand dropped as he moved to the edge of the ridge. "So, tell me. What next? Fling myself off here right now and splatter my brains on the rocks? Because we're already dead, folks."

Quill hesitated, unsure if Rocket's threat to throw himself off the ridge would be exacerbated if he approached. He stayed where he was – just to be safe – and resumed talking.

"No, Rocket, *no!* Think. Imagine how the people in Doomwood feel. Imagine..." He fished for a metaphor. "Imagine if you had been in a dark hole for a long time. Say, thirty years. Suddenly, a candle flares in that darkness. That's us, Rocket! We're the candle!"

"A candle?" Rocket scoffed and waved a dismissive paw. "Listen, buddy. If you were a candle, you'd be one of those joke gift types. Scented with farts and body odor."

"Mock as much as you want," said Quill. "But you know I'm right."

"I know you're completely delusional." Quill sagged a little. "Look, Quill. The Doombots are after you. *Kraven* is after you. The *Milano* is now not only wrecked but is likely to be impounded. In three days..." He put a hand to his collar. He did not need to expand on what would happen in three days. Cora, however, supplied additional data.

"Three days, fourteen hours, twenty-two minutes, and fifty-three seconds."

It was hard to follow that up and a gloomy pall fell over the group. Quill broke the silence, thrusting a finger in the air, *eureka* moment style. "Unless..."

"Unless I shove *you* off the ridge before I take a dive?"

"Unless," said Quill, ploughing on through the quagmire of Rocket's pessimism, "I find the Black Vortex and submit to it."

Rocket was incredulous. "You're still going to... stick your head into a cosmic microwave and hope for the best? Great plan, Quill. Great plan."

"It'll be fine," reassured Quill with the confidence of the completely ignorant.

"Quill! It's called the Black Vortex! I don't know about you, but that is *not* a name that inspires confidence!" Rocket's exasperation increased with Quill's every word, but the man was undeterred.

"Look. We've seen what Doomwood is like. Garbage everywhere. I saw dogs eating a dead body in an alleyway. There were kids with cauliflower-shaped tumors growing out of their necks. Hundreds of people who've been left blinded by the radiation."

"Yeah," said Rocket, softly. "Yeah. I saw that, too." It had been awful, even for a seasoned cynic like him, to witness such terrible conditions. But Quill was in his stride and kept on going.

"Refineries pumping out black smoke. Mills... chewing their way through what remains of the forest..."

"I said I saw it, Quill."

"Rocket..." Quill's tone become imploring. "They *need* us!"

"You know what?" Rocket stared. "I take it back."

"Take what back?"

"I have a way..." The recorder interrupted, but the argument was now in full swing.

"Hold on a moment, Cora." Quill put up a hand. "Take *what* back, Rocket?"

"All those times I've complained about how lazy and worthless you've gotten over the last few years? I take it back.

I prefer that Peter Quill to the Quill who's standing here, pouring sunshine out of his backside."

"Ah, cut it out. You love it."

"I don't even recognize you!"

"I'm like a tree, old buddy." Quill beamed at him. "A good, stalwart tree!"

"A stalwart… what does that even *mean?*"

"Look around," said Quill, making a sweeping gesture. "This forest. Look at those trees with their leaves and needles falling off. The key thing is that they're still alive."

"O… K," said Rocket, dubiously.

"Imagine… the heartwood of one of those trees. The core. You know what that looks like, right? Rings growing round it to mark that tree's age. Rings that tell *stories*. A drought in one ring. A fire in another. Good years, bad years… they all make up the whole. One after the other. But the heartwood, the core? That's always there." He tapped his chest after this unexpectedly profound take. "*Star-Lord* is always there."

Rocket stared, his sloe-black eyes that gave away nothing. "Are these lyrics to some dumb new song you're writing?"

"No!" Then, "Maybe." Then, "Yeah."

"Promise me you'll never make me listen to it," said Rocket, patting Quill on the arm. "Now we need to get you hidden, and we need to do it fast."

"Hide? Hah!" Quill puffed up his chest. "Heroes don't *hide*."

"I know where we can hide," said Cora. She had not spoken during the dramatic soliloquy but had watched with great interest. "I have already made the necessary arrangements."

"Wait, what? You've done what? With who? How…"

Further discourse was interrupted by the unmistakable

sound of a gun hammer being thumbed into place, and a deep voice addressed the group. "Hands where I can see 'em."

The voice belonged to a thin, spindly man with sun-darkened – or possibly irradiated – skin, with a head that was completely devoid of hair. Even stubble was not visible on his pate. Nor did he have eyebrows. It was the most striking feature in an otherwise average-looking, pock-marked face. He was wearing an oversized work shirt and trousers, with standard-issue boots. His weapon was trained on the group and there was calculating intelligence in his eyes.

"I said hands up. Hands up, knees on the ground!" He gesticulated with the pistol and Quill stared at Cora in horror.

"What did you *do*, Cora?"

"You instructed me to find friends. So I did."

"Get down!" The man's voice raised irritably. Rocket reached for his rifle, flicking it to charge. The low thrum vibrated through his small body like an old friend, and he met the newcomer's stare head-on.

"I'm sorry, what did you say? Can't hear you over the itch in my trigger finger."

"I said, get down, vermin."

"*You* get down, you old bald idiot!"

Quill stepped forward, hands out to the side. "Hey, come on. Everyone calm down. Deep breaths. Everyone, chill for just a second."

"You're in my way, Quill."

Quill ignored Rocket, turning to the man. "Cora said you're a friend. We're looking for friends right now and friends don't point weapons at other friends." He wondered briefly if he'd overused the word friend, but what the heck. It emphasized his point. The man glanced at him, then back at Rocket.

"Tell that thing to lower its weapon."

"This *thing* will do no such… thing." Rocket's indignation was spoiled only marginally by the ludicrousness of the situation. Quill maintained his conciliatory tone.

"Come on. Let's talk this through. Let's start over. Why are you here, man? What do you want from us?"

The man slowly lowered his weapon and Rocket followed suit reluctantly. "The White Queen requests your presence," he informed them.

Quill blinked. "Who?"

The stand-off continued and Cora added plenty of new expletives to her expanding dictionary of human words and phrases. Eventually, the whole thing fraught with tension, Quill convinced Rocket that they needed to trust that Cora had done the right thing. They let the man – whose name was Rick – lead them from the ridge. "Leading" in this instance meant that he walked *behind* them, one hand on his gun. As they walked, Rocket and Quill continued their endless bickering.

"I told you from the start that we couldn't trust that flarking skinbot!"

Quill glanced at Cora. "C'mon, Rock. She was just trying to help."

"How is this helping?" Rocket was enraged. "We almost got shot and now we're wasting time we don't have, going somewhere we don't need to go to meet who only knows who?"

"We need friends," said Quill and then fell silent. They

moved onward, not towards Doomwood, but some distance away from the outskirts. Quill recognized the hallmarks of a disused mining facility and Rick pushed them towards to the mouth of a tunnel. In a caricature of every cartoon Quill recalled watching as a kid, there were warnings and boards suggesting that death lurked ahead.

"Someone really doesn't want us to go into that tunnel, do they?"

"Yeah, well, that's where you're going. Move it." Rick nudged Quill with his gun.

It was a slightly embarrassing squeeze for Quill to get through the gap that Rick indicated and for a moment he wondered how it would look in the history books that Star-Lord, intergalactic hero, had died of starvation, wedged in the mouth of a tunnel.

He pushed through eventually, brushing his pants down nonchalantly as though he hadn't just been squirming like a stuck pig. Rocket didn't even snicker at Quill's misfortune. It had been too sad.

"Where are we going, anyway?" The question was directed to Cora who trotted behind Rocket and Quill and who had not spoken for a while. They moved deeper into the tunnel, brightened only by what little sunlight trickled in from the entrance.

"He is taking us to the secret entrance that lies beneath the Heaven and Hellfire Club," Cora explained. The tunnel curved around to the right and they saw the pump car on steel tracks waiting for them.

"I wonder exactly who's gonna be expected to work *that*," muttered Quill as they boarded the cart. Rocket was too small to help, so he and Cora took the handle and worked in tandem to get them moving – albeit slowly – down the tracks.

Rocket attempted to engage Rick in conversation but was met with a snarl in response. "Who is this White Queen, anyway?"

"Quit barking at me, dog. Or I'll kick you."

"I may be able to help, Rocket," said Cora, who had no need to take a breath during her labors, unlike Quill who was huffing like a steam train. "The Heaven and Hellfire Club is the finest drinking establishment in all of Doomwood. It is owned and operated by the White Queen, the most beautiful and powerful woman in the Wastelands."

"Oh?" Quill wiped the sweat from his brow, clearly interested in this development. "Tell me more."

"She is a highly savvy businesswoman, with an ability to read minds. She is blessed with extraordinary intelligence and…"

"Yeah, yeah. Now tell me more about the beautiful part."

"Well, that is what everyone says about her. I was told that to look upon the White Queen is to study the summer sun."

"Stare at the sun and you'll go blind," muttered Rocket to nobody in particular.

"They say her voice is as delicious as fresh cream poured over a ripe peach."

"Rawr," said Quill. He'd tried for a purr, but he was too out of breath to manage it. So he just said "rawr".

Rocket shook his head. "Oh, stop. Do you have any idea how ridiculous you sound? Stop."

Cora continued. "They say her body should be bronzed for all to behold in its absolute perfection. A thing of beauty that should be revered through the ages."

"I don't know about you, Rocket, but I have got a *good* feeling about this White Queen chick."

"Whatever, Quill. Cora – how did you find her?"

"I did not. She found *me*."

# CHAPTER SEVEN
## ALLEGIANCES

### DOOMWOOD
### EARLIER

Kraven's departure took most of the rowdier crowd with it and Cora was largely ignored by most of the Heaven and Hellfire's clientele. She made her way through the still-thronging crowd, occasionally offering polite greetings and ignoring the colorful insults hurled her way. Those who did answer her questions told her far more with the things that they did not say than with the things they did. She learned that the club was owned by a woman known as the White Queen. She adjusted her questioning accordingly.

After an hour or so of these largely futile efforts, a young woman approached. Cora became aware she was now being followed by this newcomer and turned to face her.

"If you are trying to attract my attention, all you need to do is to say hello."

"Hello."

"Hello. My name is Cora. I am a Rigellean Recorder."

"Hello, Cora. My name is unimportant and you should come with me. Someone wants to talk to you."

"Of course." Cora considered her response only momentarily. Nothing about this young woman gave her cause for doubt or alarm and while others may have seen such easy acquiescence as naïve, it was a calculated trust that took mere nanoseconds to achieve.

Cora followed the young woman through the club, ascending a staircase to the higher levels and along a corridor. The muffled sounds of the bar below faded the further they walked and Cora detected an entirely new noise. The song and chirrup of birds came from up ahead. She was curious as to their origin.

"Wait here," said the young woman as they came to a large, oak door at the end of the corridor. She knocked three times then entered, closing the door behind her. The recorder could not fully make out the discussion beyond: the thickness of the wood functioned as an excellent insulator and the voices were low. A few moments later, the door re-opened, disgorging the same young woman. She glanced at Cora, left the door open and hurried off down the corridor.

"Come in, Cora," came a voice from inside. The recorder stepped into the aviary that was the office of the White Queen. Birdcages lined the room, each occupied by a different species, each more colorful and exotic than the last. Their bright plumage was a stark contrast to the dark wood of the office and the woman sitting behind the long, elaborately carved wooden desk at the end. She wore all white and her long hair was pale gold. Her blue eyes were the color of ice and the subtle makeup that she wore enhanced the classical, well-defined lines of her cheekbones.

"I understand you are asking questions about me," said the woman, beckoning Cora inside. "Close the door."

Cora obliged and the woman rose from her seated position. She was tall and slender, moving with sinuous grace as she approached the recorder. Her eyes roamed up and down the synthetic body with apparent disinterest. "I don't like strangers asking questions about me, so how about you start by telling me what you are doing in my club?" Her voice was husky and mellifluous.

"Are you a villain?" Cora's question was something the woman appeared unprepared for, and she laughed in that same dusky tone.

"What an unusual question!"

"Why is it an unusual question, please?"

"Well, *Cora.* Because there was once a time when people might have called me that. But no. I am not a villain. I do what's right." She returned to her desk, pouring a drink from a crystal decanter. She lifted the glass and swirled its contents. "Right for *me*, anyway."

"From what we have so far observed," said Cora, "only people with compromised morals and villainous tendencies seem to prosper in this place, or to be in positions of power."

"How *beautifully* alliterative," purred the woman. "By 'we,' I am going to assume you mean Peter Quill and Rocket Raccoon?"

"Yes," acknowledged Cora and looked around. "I appear to be in a room filled with cages. Query: Does that mean that I am also in a cage?"

The woman – who Cora had deduced must logically be the White Queen – laughed again. "Well, darling," she said, "let me explain something about cages. These birds wouldn't last long if I were to let them outside." She studied the recorder again and shook her head. "Your programming seems willfully naïve. You seem to have no concept whatsoever of the danger you're in."

Cora considered this before she responded. "I encounter obstacles," she said. "I do not experience fear."

"Why don't you take a look out of my office window?" The White Queen moved to the large picture window at the back of the office. "It offers what might be called a *fearful* view of Doomwood."

"The glass is obscured by a black glaze," observed Cora.

"That's coal dust. Open it."

Cora unlatched and opened the window. Noises from the street below mingled with the background birdsong in a sudden wash of sound. Carts rumbled along the muddy roads, there were the all-pervading sounds of inane chatter among the citizenry and in the distance, the rhythmic clanking of machinery at work.

"Doomwood," announced the White Queen. "In *all* its glory. Take a good, long look, Cora. Consider what you see."

Cora looked and she considered. The streets had a layer of filth that looked as though it was similarly ground into the skin of the people who walked along it. Drones, like those which had recorded the fate of Sebastian Warn, flew through the air constantly, causing people to cringe whenever they came too close.

A little way beyond the vista, Cora saw black smoke belching from refineries. She was not programmed to be needlessly imaginative, but the smokestacks and towers could have sprung from a factory where nightmares were manufactured.

She saw it all. She recorded it all.

"Over there," pointed the White Queen. "Trucks coming down from the hills loaded with ore. Do you see, Cora? Do you see how Doom has consumed *everything*?"

"Yes," said Cora. "I see."

"Then understand that he will consume *you* as well." She put a hand on one slim hip. "Welcome to Doomwood."

"Thank you."

"I was being sarcastic, darling."

"Oh. In that case, no thank you."

The White Queen closed the window, mercifully shutting out the sounds and sights of the blighted town. She turned to Cora. "Now allow me to tell you about the things that you *couldn't* see. You can't see the radiation in the air from the Chamberlin reactor. You can't see the corpses fed daily to the pigs. You can't see spies who lean into every conversation. You certainly can't see the stronghold in the hills where Doom resides."

"Is this the danger we face? Is this what you seek to protect me from?"

"For now," said the White Queen. "But I have many questions, so let's get back to my first one. What are you doing in my club?" She sighed theatrically, much as Rocket did when he was at his most melodramatic. "Normally I don't have to do tedious back and forth. I just look inside a mind like I look into these cages."

"You can see inside of people's minds?"

"I can."

"You are implying that you are a telepath."

"Actually, darling, I am *so* much more than that. But yes. Telepath will suffice."

"Nobody else knows about Star-Lord or Rocket, but you do. Query: Are you a friend or an enemy?"

"Let's keep the questions trained on you for now, shall we?" The White Queen's cold expression became positively frozen. "You're going to tell me everything I need to know about what exactly Quill and Rocket are doing here or…" She seemed to founder, if only momentarily.

"Or?"

"Or I'll feed you *all* to the pigs."

"Pro tip, Cora." Rocket shook his head. "As a general rule, friends don't feed people to pigs."

"Stop the cart. We're here." Rick had said nothing during the short journey, but his aggressive presence had certainly been felt.

"Where's here?" Quill stopped pumping the cart with no small amount of relief.

"Get out onto that platform, go up the stairs and through the trapdoor at the top."

"Hey!" Rocket's patience was spread extremely thin. "He asked you a question, Rick! Where's *here*?"

"The cellar of the Heaven and Hellfire." They reached the top of the stairs and, grunting with effort, Quill pushed the trapdoor up. It moved with a long, slow creak that must *surely* have attracted people from miles around. "Touch nothing," Rick warned.

Quill walked the few steps up to emerge into a vast cellar, closely followed by Rick. He took a moment to stare, turning in circles. "Look at all the booze! Barrels. Bottles. Tanks!" He peered at a few. "Cabernet. Chardonnay. Whiskey, rum, vodka, gin, moose piss..."

He did a double take.

"Moose piss? What's that? Some local moonshine?"

"No," said Rick. "It's moose piss."

"Oh," said Quill. "Man, the apocalypse is *weird*."

Rocket emerged from the trapdoor followed by Cora who closed it. Rick looked them over with a scowl. "Keep your hands off the hooch," he said. "I'm heading upstairs to fetch..."

He was interrupted by footsteps heading towards them. The steps became creaks as the person who owned them walked down the cellar stairs. Halfway down, a tall, blonde woman came into view.

"Well, well," said the White Queen. "Isn't *this* a delightful sight?"

Rick dropped his head respectfully. "My queen," he said, a level of awe in his voice that Quill couldn't help but feel had been seriously lacking in his previous interactions. The White Queen continued her descent and waved a hand laconically.

"Thank you, Richard. You can leave us now."

"Are you sure, my queen?"

"Oh, I'm positive they'll do as they're told from now on. Isn't that right, Quill?"

"Look lady, we make *no* promises."

She ignored Rocket's little outburst and focused all her attention on Quill. *"Isn't that right, Quill?"*

His head felt momentarily fuzzy as though someone had

poured sherbet through his ears and then followed it with liquid. His brain *fizzed*. He stared at the woman in confusion. "I... do I *know* you?"

"My queen," protested Rick. "He's armed! What about..."

"I said leave us," she replied, and it was not a suggestion but a command. The man's eyes glazed and he clattered up the cellar steps before disappearing. Quill was still studying her.

"I... know you," he said. "How do I know you?"

"You're here for something..." the White Queen prompted, and Quill snapped his fingers in sudden understanding.

"I don't think we ever officially met, back in the day, but I *do* know you. You're *Emma*."

"Will you share the map with me, Quill?"

"Emma Frost!"

She continued relentlessly. "The map that leads to the Black Vortex. I would *so* love to see it."

"But you haven't aged a day in over thirty years. You look... wow. I mean, like *wow*."

"The map's in your satchel, Quill. Just reach in and hand it to me."

"Don't listen to her, Quill," said Rocket, urgently. "She's trying to mess with your head."

Quill paid him no attention and looked at Emma instead. "You're right. The map. In my satchel. I'll just reach in and..." He moved his hand towards his bag and then he changed its direction, pulling out one of Red Crotter's pistols and cocking it in a single, swift move. "Oh, man, look at that! I reached for my gun instead!" He smacked his free hand against his forehead. "Am I *embarrassed?*"

"The *map*, Quill. The mirror."

"Star-Lord," said Cora. "I do not think you pointing a weapon is a good idea."

"No? Well, it seems to be working pretty well so far," he said. "I'm on the right side of this deal."

Emma sighed. "I really don't like doing this sort of thing, you know."

"Yeah? What *are* you doing? What *is* this, exactly?"

"It makes me *terribly* tired. And I don't get anywhere near enough sleep as it is." She flashed a brief glance down at the revolver in Quill's hand. Quill followed her gaze and then snapped his eyes back up.

"What are you *doing*?"

His hand, against his own will, was turning, bringing the weapon upwards and away from Emma. He was fighting the urge, but he simply could not resist the desire to redirect the gun.

"Hey, hey, Quill, what are you doing?" Rocket was alarmed. "Don't point that thing at me, point it… hey!"

"I can't… stop it," said Quill, his teeth gritted. He fought with everything he had, but he was *losing*. Something inside him was telling him to point the gun at Rocket and he was obeying. "I can't… Stop it, Emma!"

"I'm not the one aiming a revolver at your best friend's skull, Quill." She shrugged one slender shoulder. "Don't blame me."

Rocket began the charge cycle on his own blaster. "See this, Frost? Take a good look. Because even if he shoots me, my last *millisecond* of existence will be spent taking *you* out."

"Don't you get it?" Quill's voice was strained as he continued to resist. "We're the good guys! We're the… the… Guardians of the Galaxy!"

Emma shook her head. "I see only two of you. Where are the rest of the Guardians?"

Quill swallowed. "They're gone."

"Gone?"

Quill hesitated. When he spoke, the words came dredged up from the very core of his being, stained with pain and loss and terrible guilt. "Dead, OK? They're *dead*."

"Leave him alone, Frost." Rocket moved forward to place his small, furry body between them.

She sneered slightly, a mar on her beautiful visage, then smiled, a cruel, unpleasant smile. "Even if you still consider yourselves to be the Guardians, you're thirty years too late to make a difference."

"This blaster is gonna scorch the smirk right off your face, lady," said Rocket in a cool, mild tone that carried far more threat than boast. "Now leave him *alone*."

"Oh fine," she said, releasing her hold on Quill's mind. He felt as though he had suddenly burst free of physical restraints. He gasped, drawing in a sudden breath, and released the hammer on the gun. He stared at it before putting it back into its holster.

"Now that you've put the toy away, we can talk properly," said Emma, folding her arms across her chest. Then she relaxed a little. "Without interference, hmm? How does that sound?"

"Yeah," said Quill as the fizzing in his brain started to lessen. "Yeah, fine."

"Good." She unfolded her arms again and held out a hand to him. "Then I'll repeat my request again. The map, please." He tried to stare at her but couldn't hold her gaze for more than a couple of seconds. He capitulated.

"Fine." He reached into his satchel and pulled out the mirror. She took it from him and turned it over in her hands.

"How curious," she said, looking back at him. He was trying to appear nonchalant, not wanting to give off the vibe of "defeated loser" that he was presently feeling. He waved a hand vaguely.

"Look into the mirror. Closely. Do you see how it pulls you deeper and deeper? All the way until you arrive…"

"Here," she said, nodding. "In Doomwood. Except at that point, the way is broken. Shattered." She was peering into the mirror so closely she was in danger of pressing her nose against it.

"Yep," said Quill with more than a small air of self-satisfaction. She moved the mirror from her face and looked at him.

"You don't know where the rest of the map is, do you?"

"Nope."

"And you don't know where to go."

"Nope."

"I see." She moved away from him, still holding the mirror, and tapped a long, perfectly lacquered nail against her chin. "The Black Hills are a warren of mining tunnels as I'm sure you must have figured out by now. But here's the strange thing: they don't all line up with the geological surveys. Sometimes, Doom just has people out there digging for the sake of digging."

"Looking for something?"

"That much is obvious, yes. That's been clear for a *very* long time. I fully intend to find it first. The Black Vortex is going to be *mine*."

"No way, witch," interjected Rocket. "Not happening. We're

here in this hellhole for a job and we are *toast* if we don't collect the Black Vortex and deliver it."

"Well," said Quill. "The fine print's negotiable on that last part."

"Don't listen to him," said Rocket, "he's an idiot."

"I'm going to find the Black Vortex," said Quill. "But then… I'm going to *submit* to it, see? Then I'm going to have all sorts of sweet cosmic powers and *then* I'll take down Doom and save the world! Easy peasy." He positively beamed. Emma treated him to a slow smile. It put Rocket in mind of a predator offering its prey a final chance of escape. When she spoke, her tone dripped honey and unspoken promise.

"You want to submit?" She stepped closer and ran a finger down his cheek, tangling her hand in his untidy, graying beard. "That's something we could do together, if you like the idea of… *submission*."

"I… well…" Quill let out a sudden explosive giggle, like a schoolchild. The spell was broken by the crashing of the door to the cellar and Rick's re-appearance.

"My queen!"

"I'm busy here," she said, not taking her eyes from Quill. "I'm… negotiating."

"I'm sorry, my queen, but you need to come upstairs. Now."

"Are you deaf? I'm occupied." She twisted her fingers in Quill's beard again and he smiled at her beatifically.

"My queen," said Rick, his tone urgent. "It's *Kraven*."

"What?" She released Quill who made a faint moue of disappointment. She stepped back, turning toward the man on the stairs. "What about him?" There was a hint of panic in her voice that made Rocket instinctively reach for his blaster.

"He's *here*. Upstairs in the bar. He wants to talk to you."

"What about?"

Rick looked uncomfortably at Quill and, in lieu of a response, simply pointed. Emma may have gone pale: her skin was already alabaster white so it was hard to tell, but there was something sickly around the edges. "Oh," she said, finally. "That is... most unfortunate."

"Query." Cora's voice cut through. "Should you not already know all of this given that you are a telepath?"

Emma glared at her. "I was distracted."

"An Omega-level telepath, even."

Emma turned on Cora and let out an explosion of rage. "I said I was distracted!"

"Please, my queen. Hurry."

Emma took a few breaths and settled her clearly ruffled feathers. She patted Quill on the cheek and thrust the mirror back at him before turning to nod at Rick, who looked immensely relieved.

"You think he knows we're here?" Rocket was all business.

"That remains to be seen," said Emma in response. "If I can convince him to leave, then we will continue this conversation later."

Quill caught her arm as she stepped away, releasing it when she turned to glare at him. "What if you *can't* convince him?"

"Then we will all be as good as dead," she said, matter-of-factly.

It came as no surprise when they heard the lock turn in the door. Despite the evidence, something compelled Rocket to attempt opening it anyway. The fact Emma Frost had locked them in the cellar *infuriated* him. He slapped his paw against the door for a while and then sighed heavily. "All right, so we're stuck down here." Rocket tapped a claw against his cheek, his usual gesture when he was thinking. "Work with me here, Quill. How about shooting the lock off the trapdoor? Try our luck down in the mines?" Quill shook his head. Rocket tried a different approach. "Head upstairs? Guns blazing kind of thing?" Quill shook his head again.

"Nope," he said. "I reckon what we do is *nothing*."

"Nothing?"

"Nothing. We stay right here."

Rocket stared at him, incredulous. "Seriously, Quill? Are you just content to sit here on your old-man rear and leave our fate up to a white witch who just tried to make you *shoot* me?"

"Don't you get it, Rocket?" When the question garnered no response other than a cold, icy stare, Quill continued. "She's got spies, and secret entrances. She's a telepath who gets people drunk and listens while they spill their secrets. She's told us that she wants to get the Black Vortex before Doom."

"And?" Rocket *didn't* get it. Cora spoke up and they both turned to look at her. What she had to say was surprising.

"Emma Frost is part of the Second Dawn."

Rocket blinked. "You mean the same group of terrorists they were talking about during that *Deer on a Spear* broadcast? The one Sebastian Warn was allegedly a part of?"

"They're only terrorists from the viewpoint of Doom and his cronies. You know. The *bad guys*. Which we are *not*. We should join them."

"Quill. We're not looking to join a resistance. The Black Vortex. That's all we care about, OK?"

"What if they're one and the same?" Quill was agitated about the situation.

Rocket shook his head repeatedly. "Quill," he said, grimly. "She put a gun to my head. Well, you did. But she did. You get what I'm saying?"

Quill rubbed at the back of his neck. "She's playing rough, buddy. Trying to figure out where we stand. Whose side we're on."

It was a reasonable assumption and Rocket had no immediate counter. He moved away from the trapdoor, pacing the cellar, his short legs making this take far longer than it might have taken Quill. Eventually, he shook his head.

"I don't know, man. I just… don't trust her and what it comes down to is a question of trust. I don't trust Milky White up there and I don't trust the skinbot."

"Would you *please* call her Cora? She's a *person*."

"Quill, for flark's sake, she's *not* a person! She. Is. A. Skinbot!" When Quill went to retort, he charged on relentlessly. "Look, man! We're locked in a basement with no strategy because of that thing that's 'like a person.'"

Quill could feel the anger radiating from Rocket; a palpable, hostile thing and he looked from one to the other in desperation. He needed to get Rocket to understand. "Cora?"

"Yes, Star-Lord?"

"Would you please convince Rocket that you're on our side?"

Rocket ceased pacing and glared. His arms folded across his chest again, a picture of grim defiance. "Not gonna happen," he said, firmly.

Cora stepped forward. "I have a recording that may help,"

she said. "From six hours ago, from the office of Emma Frost."
Her speakers clunked and whirred softly as she accessed the
appropriate files. The sounds of birdsong filled the cellar and
Cora replayed the conversation.

"On the one hand," came Emma's voice, "you appear to be
a *very* clever thing. And on the other, you strike me as a fool."

"How am I a fool?" It was Cora's response and it was just a
little unnerving to watch how the recorder's mouth moved in
synch with the recording.

There was a tinkling, humorless laugh from Emma. "You
moved through the town completely openly. No disguising
who – or what – you are. But tell me this, Rigellian Recorder.
Did you happen to see anyone else in Doomwood even
*remotely* like you?"

"Of course. The Doombots."

"Let me explain something about Doom. Not only did he
systematically burn all the books in town, but he also scrapped
every robot for a thousand miles, replacing them with his
own. He did both of those terrible things for the same reason:
he does *not* want any sort of intelligence, let alone artificial
intelligence, influencing those under his control."

"So that is why you imprisoned me here," concluded Cora.

"If Quill and Rocket are blundering about as stupidly as you
are…"

*"Hey, I'm not stupid!"*

*"Shh. Listen."*

"…we need to get *them* here. Soon. Before they're
imprisoned or killed."

"If you will promise to protect them, I will bring them to
you."

"Curious. Your loyalty, I mean. Why are you so loyal to them? Have they adapted you? Are they piloting your programming?" There were footsteps and it was easy to picture Emma stepping closer to Cora to inspect her.

"No. They have not adapted me at all. Star-Lord is a hero who has the potential to shape history."

*"Very hidden potential. Invisible, even."*

*"Shhh!"*

"You like heroes then, Cora?"

"It is not that I like them, any more than I like – or dislike – villains. One of my core directives is to align with the powerful. That is why I was in your club asking questions about you, Emma Frost. Because from all that I have learned, you would appear to be one of the most powerful people in Doomwood."

The laugh came again, but there was genuine amusement in it. "You *are* a clever thing, aren't you?" Cora's system closed off the recording and silence returned to the cellar. Quill looked faintly triumphant while Rocket looked faintly irked.

"Well, I don't know about you, Rocket, but I *like* what I'm hearing. We can work with this. Right?"

"Still not convinced. I bet she's upstairs right now arranging the specific terms of our death sentence."

Cora spoke up at this. "I can fully assure you that she is not."

"Oh, yeah? And how, exactly, do you know that?"

"Because I am a recorder, Rocket, and very good at what I do. I record. Which means I *hear*. I can hear Emma Frost and Kraven talking right now. I have been aware of them for a while." Her eyes glowed a pale blue for a moment. "When she left us in the cellar and walked into the bar, Kraven was seated at a table. She dragged a chair across the floor and joined him until they were mere inches apart." The blue glow faded. "My recording sensitivity allows me to detect most conversations throughout this building. When I choose to."

Made uncomfortable by the number of times he'd thought he was talking out of Cora's earshot, Rocket rode the moment. "Well, why didn't you say so before? Come on, let's hear it!"

"Of course, Rocket." Again, that blue flare behind her eyes and the cellar was filled with the sound of clinking glasses and general bar hubbub. It was more hushed than Quill might have expected in a well-attended drinking establishment. Chairs were pulled into new positions and creaking under the weight of people taking their seats. Above it all came the now-familiar voice of Emma Frost.

"If you want something from me, darling," she oozed, "then you're going to have to *earn* it." This brought a rousing cheer from some of the people in the bar. Cora tipped her head to the side.

"There are around a dozen people or so gathered around Emma Frost and Kraven," she said. "Watching."

"Watching what?" Rocket's curiosity rose to the surface.

"Watching them play a game. A drinking game. Called…" She paused a moment, clearly tapping into the collective that she was listening to upstairs. "Rattled." The playback resumed. The cheering faded to excited murmuring. Cutting through the entirety of the aural landscape, a distinctive hiss and rattle was heard.

"There is…" Cora concentrated. "A bottle of vodka, two glasses. Shot glasses. In addition to this, there is also a white rattlesnake."

"Hang on, hang on. How can you work all that out just from

*listening*?" Quill was fascinated by Cora's skills, but this seemed too good to be true. The recorder looked at him and he had the distinct feeling that she *pitied* his ignorance.

"I am listening to everybody in the room, not just Emma Frost and Kraven. I am doing this while recording sonar and seismographic influences. This enables me to build up a picture of what is transpiring that is around eighty-five to ninety percent accurate."

Rocket grunted in response to this, reluctantly impressed. "Guessing that must be one of those snakes like they had back in Outpost 13. Eech." He made a noise of bitter disgust. "Poisonous tastes for poisonous times."

"The rules of the game are being explained," said Cora, continuing. "Every round, you have a single opportunity to touch the rattlesnake's tail. If your attempt fails, you drink a shot of the vodka. If you succeed, then your opponent drinks a shot."

"How long have they been playing this game?"

"This is the twentieth round," replied Cora, looking at Quill. "Thus far, neither has missed."

Her transmission continued and the loud, drunken tones of a man bellowed that he wanted to put twenty Doombucks on Kraven, while someone else countered with twice that on the White Queen.

"The Doombuck is the local curr…"

Quill interrupted, waving his hands to shush the recorder. "Yeah, I figured."

There was some more excited noise culminating in the swell of the crowd letting out a roar and hiss of their own, enough to rival the sounds of the rattlesnake.

"Kraven missed," said Cora. Quill and Rocket punched the air. Now, complete silence fell. "The crowd is now afraid of what he will do because of it." There was another shake of the rattlesnake's tail; a warning across the airwaves that made Quill's blood run cold.

"I believe it's your turn to drink," said Emma, coolly. There was further silence while Kraven contemplated his response, and every heartbeat drew out the tension. When he finally spoke, there was cold calculation in his tone. Every word was deliberate; his Slavic accent thick and heavy and every one of the three syllables weighted with menace.

"I will not."

"I believe there are *rules* to this game. You missed, therefore, you drink."

"Rules? Heh. Yes. Rules that *you* have broken."

"How dare you imply…"

"The snake was there…" There was a soft *thump* as he smacked his hand on the table "Then it was not. I never miss."

"Yet you did."

"You are using your mind on me, woman. You *made* me miss."

Kraven unsheathed his deadly knife and even safe in the cellar the whispering sound caused Rocket and Quill to put their hands to their respective weapons. Cora did not need to provide her narration for them to know that things had become serious. There was a sudden thump, an anguished hiss, and a dying rattle, like someone half-heartedly shaking a maraca.

"He stabbed the snake," said Rocket.

"Yes," confirmed Cora. "He has pinned it to the table." There was an outcry of fear from the audience.

"As I said," came Kraven's slow tone. "I never miss."

Emma's response was cool to the point of icy. If she was shaken by Kraven's murder of the reptile, it didn't carry in her voice. "Well, that's several gallons of poison I won't be selling this month. How tiresome."

"Maybe I'll hunt you another one down. *If* I'm feeling generous. Or maybe…" The hunter's chair scraped back from the table. "If I'm *not* feeling generous, maybe I will take this bottle of vodka and drop it to the floor where I stand. Then, perhaps I will take a match to it and burn this whole building to the ground."

Voices grew quieter as the crowd dispersed. It appeared that people no longer wished to be near Kraven. "It depends," continued the hunter, "whether you are going to give me what I came here for."

Rocket and Quill leaned forward unconsciously, as though they were right there at the table. Cora's playback was so ambient that it felt as though they were upstairs rather than ensconced in the cellar. Kraven's next words came out as a husky near-whisper.

"Where is Peter Quill?"

Everything hung on Emma Frost's answer to that question. Quill felt his heart hammer in his chest, more painful than it had been when he had been younger and had enjoyed adrenaline racing moments like this. Now, it just made him feel sick.

She took barely a beat to respond, her tone still icy. "I know nothing about him."

"Hah." Kraven growled slightly. "The woman who claims to know everything is claiming to know nothing."

The sound of a second chair being pushed back. "Get out of my club."

The pause was pregnant with purpose and did nothing to still the pounding of Quill's heart.

"If you insist," said Kraven, finally breaking the spell.

"Oh, I do," said Emma. "I *insist.*"

"Then I am going hunting," said Kraven. "But let me leave you with this, White Queen. If your pretty songbirds tell you anything and I find out that you have neglected to tell *me*…"

Cora's speakers were suddenly awash with the sound of smashing glass, breaking wood and alarmed shouts as Kraven hurled aside the table at which he and Emma had been drinking. The sounds of his heavy footfalls grew softer as he retreated from the destruction.

"Listen to your birds, Emma Frost. And when I come back? You will sing me their songs."

The blue behind Cora's eyes faded. "He has gone," she said.

Funny how those words did not bring Quill the relief he'd hoped for.

"Great," he said, but his heart wasn't in it.

# CHAPTER EIGHT
## TRUST EXERCISE

Entry C1451Z2J
Location: *Doomwood. The Heaven and Hellfire Club. The living quarters of the so-called White Queen, Emma Frost.*

It did not take much for Emma Frost to convince the clientele of the Heaven and Hellfire Club that there was something infinitely more interesting to pay attention to than the three people she moved from the cellar to her personal quarters on the second floor. They were, she informed them, her honored guests. She would, she also informed them, help them.

Honored guests, perhaps, but that didn't stop her from locking them into her quarters when she departed to "attend to business".

Rocket was coughing again. A deep, racking cough that started at his toes and worked up through his small body before its explosive escape. He struggled to draw breath. It was a distressing sight. Over the years of their friendship, Quill had never found Rocket receptive to concern, but seeing him like this was enough to prompt Quill into addressing it.

"Hey, Rock?" Quill put cautious care and empathy into his tone. No response was forthcoming; Rocket was still coughing his lungs up. Anxious and concerned, Quill put out a hand to his friend who swatted it away.

"Back off!"

The fit eased and Quill chewed his lip. "Is it… Emma's perfume? It's a bit much, isn't it? Like a rose garden threw up a bottle of champagne." It was true enough. The spacious living area had a pervading scent of roses. Quill wondered absently if this was what the books called a boudoir. He moved around, picking things up, putting them down, picking them up again and eventually stopped by the window. He stared out while Rocket got his breath back. "Come over here. By the window. The air's clearer."

Rocket wiped his mouth, scowling at the hint of scarlet on his fur. He rubbed at it vigorously, blending it into the rest of the muck he'd picked up since they'd been travelling. "You don't have to talk to me like I'm a child," he grumbled as he joined Quill.

"Geez, sorry. I'm just trying to help." Quill lifted the latch on the window which swung open with a soft creak. The street noise was muted up here and a few carrion birds squawked on a nearby rooftop. The stench of the refineries suffused everything, so it was hardly fresh air, but it did let out a little of the floral perfume. Cora joined them.

"The air quality is probably worse out there than it is in here," she observed.

Rocket gave a brief chuckle and cleared his throat of the phlegm stuck there. "It's these collars, is all. That's all it is. Ain't you felt the same, Quill? Breathing feels like choking."

Quill didn't reply immediately. He'd experienced that same sensation of the collar literally closing in on him, but he didn't want to be needlessly pessimistic. "Not for much longer, buddy. Once we find the Black Vortex, we'll figure out how we can…"

"No." The reply was certain and emphatic.

"But I'll have cosmic powers, man! I'll probably be able to rip these things off with my bare hands – maybe just a blink. While doing a triple backflip and shooting purple lasers out of my bellybutton at the same time."

Rocket stared. "I see," he said, drily. "This is supposed to reassure me *how*? Listening to you talk about this with your seven year-old's understanding of what cosmic power means? Look, Quill. Quit fooling yourself. We're not going to find the Black Vortex in time. Our focus now has to be finding a way to get these collars off. Surviving. *Screw* everything else."

"We do that, the Collector is gonna be *furious*."

"I'm sorry, do I look like I give a flying *flark* about that at this point? I must have got my wrong face on."

"Emma said she'd help us."

Quill's naivety was infuriating. Rocket drooped. "Yeah. Sure she will."

"She's *got* to know someone in Doomwood who can help. All that mining and construction…" He waved a hand in the direction of the window and the industry beyond. "Someone out there must have, I don't know. A laser welder. A diamond saw. *Something*."

"Quill, Frost is not a friend. She's our warden."

"She wants to work with us, Rocket. Besides." He preened, just a little. "She's clearly got the hots for me."

"OK, fine. If that's the case, why are we locked in this room?"

"Excuse me," Cora spoke, only to once again be talked over by the endlessly squabbling duo.

"We're locked in here because she's shielding us." Quill's insistence, while foolish, was nonetheless admirable. "We're being hunted in case you forgot. Also…" He held out his hands and adopted a faux-serious expression as though what he was about to say was deeply profound. "If you think about it for a second, are we *really* the ones who are locked in? Or is everyone else *locked out*?"

"I'm not even gonna *try* to make sense of the nonsense you're spouting."

"Excuse me, Star-Lord."

"Yeah, Cora, what's up?"

"Events are transpiring in the street below that may be of interest to you."

Intrigued, he stopped arguing with Rocket and turned back to the window. "Yeah? Well, scootch your booch and let me see."

"What is a booch?"

"He means move over," said Rocket, also coming to the window and holding onto the ledge. He heaved himself up so that he could see – just about. "Something coming?"

"Yeah," said Quill. "There's a huge group of people down there. Maybe thirty or forty." He watched Rocket struggling with the ledge. "Want me to pick you up so you can see?"

"Do *not* pick me up. Ever."

"I've got you. Here." Ignoring the words, Quill reached

down to pick Rocket up. He squirmed, protesting until Quill dumped him on the ledge. The little creature's dignity was squashed like a bug, but he looked out the window anyway.

"Looks like a parade," he said, doubtfully.

"It is a protest," clarified Cora.

There wasn't much imagination in the chants floating up from the street below, but they were accentuated by pounding drums, whistles, and an enthusiastic volume of shouting. After listening for a few moments, it became starkly apparent that the protestors were against taxation, starvation, predation, and, gloriously, Doom. In that order. By the time they reached their last item of protest agenda, they were whipped into a frenzy. The chant rose like the promise of dawn.

"Down with Doom! Down with Doom!" Quill joined in from upstairs much to Rocket's irritation. "I told you!" He turned to Rocket in delight. "See? We obviously inspired this march."

"Oh please. You couldn't inspire someone to get out of bed in the morning. Maybe you inspire fans of beard mites and elastic waistbands…"

"Rocket! Seriously! They've heard about the trouble we caused at Outpost 13. They heard or saw me dive-bombing Kraven. They've heard the Guardians are back and they're so ready for it!" His excitement was childish and not remotely infectious and Rocket shook his head.

"You know something? That sort of airhead thinking is what's gonna see us get our heads clipped off."

"Which will occur," said Cora, "in forty-seven hours, fifty-five minutes, and eighteen seconds."

Even Quill was irritated this time and he turned to the recorder. "How many times," he said, "do I have to tell you I do *not* want to know? How many times have I got to say…" He was interrupted by a new series of chants coming from the street below. "Do you hear that?"

"Who are the Guardians?"

"We are the Guardians!"

"Go, Guardians, go!"

Rocket winced. "I can't believe my ears," he said.

Quill beamed. "Our catchphrase!"

"Go, Guardians, go!" The crowd helpfully punctuated Quill's statement with a repeat of the chant and the beating drums died out. The shouting became a susurrating murmur allowing a single voice to rise, perhaps amplified by some kind of bullhorn, or just a particularly excellent set of lungs. It was a young, female voice with the sort of undisguised determination and enthusiasm of one who understands the certainty that they will be heard and understood and who doesn't think for a moment that their views might not necessarily align with those of others. Particularly those in authority.

"We march today because we want you to know something, Doomwood. You are not alone!" Cheers. "We are *all* depressed and hungry. We are *all* exhausted. We are *all* dying in the mines, the mills and even in the streets. Because we are *all* being worked to death. We are being poisoned to death by the air we breathe and the water we drink!"

More cheers and shouts of agreement. Quill's eyes were bright with an energy Rocket had not seen in many years. He felt nauseated by what Quill said next, even though he anticipated it.

"We should join them!"

"No!"

The young woman in the street continued, fired up and ready to fix a broken world with words alone. "There are heroes walking among you, Doomwood. I'm not just talking about the return of the Guardians, but I'm talking about *you*! All those of you making a stand here today as part of the Second Dawn!"

"Go, go Guardians! Yeah, baby!" Quill punched the air with his fist and Rocket reached up to grab his arm.

"Will you just shut up?"

Cora was watching the scene below. "This will end poorly," she observed.

Quill lowered his fist, shaking his head. "Why would you say that? This is *amazing*!"

"Something is approaching," Cora replied and she turned to look at Quill. "Allow me to amplify the sound of its progress." Her eyes glowed as she tapped into the world outside and the unmistakable clanking and hydraulic joints of a Doombot could be heard. "It approaches from the east," said Cora as the voice rose back up from below.

"Doom led an uprising thirty years ago. Well, let there be another one now! A new dawn, my friends. The Second Dawn!"

Quill's delight at the protest turned to something new when he heard the approaching Doombot. He felt an urge to lean out of the window, to shout a warning, but a dagger-sharp look from Rocket killed the words before they left his mouth.

"We've all come to accept that it's fine that we're screwed. That we have nothing left to hope for. But no more!"

*Run*, urged Quill silently, hoping that perhaps he had

somehow caught telepathy from Emma Frost. *Run.* He looked at Cora and tried grasping at straws. "It's just one Doombot, right? It can't arrest them all."

"Doom doesn't provide," cried the lead protestor. "He takes! He takes and he takes and he *takes* until our bellies are hollow and empty as the hills we live on!" Jeers and boos met this statement as the crowd of protestors got caught up in the passion of it all.

"Why aren't they doing anything?" Quill's anxiety peaked. "They could throw rocks. Make a break for it. Run, guys. Go, Guardians, go!" But by now, the Doombot was upon the crowd. The young woman pointed a finger at it, letting out a shout of laughter.

"Here he is now – or at least, his proxy. How about it, Doombot? Are you going to tell us to shut up and go home? Well, folks? Should we?"

The crowd roared defiantly and the leader, emboldened by their support, pressed her assumed advantage. "Hear that, Doombot? We aren't going *anywhere!*" Her chin jutted outward.

The Doombot clanked to a stop, projecting its voice loud enough to be heard quite clearly two stories above the ground. "Ordinance 12-F. Public demonstrations are illegal. Ordinance 1-A. Recriminations of Lord Doom are illegal."

"We're just making ourselves heard and seen," said the leader, but there was an edge of doubt in her tone.

The Doombot clanked forward. "Ordinance 17-Z. Failure to show up for work is illegal." It shifted its position, moving until its arms were straight down, slightly away from its body. "You are in direct violation of all listed ordinances."

"Quill," said Rocket, spotting something. "Quill. The Doombot's hands. Look."

Quill looked and wished he hadn't. A blue glow began forming around the Doombot's open palms and the glow was sparking and jumping. An electrical charge bloomed there, and it was clear what its target would be.

"No," said Quill, softly. "Oh, no."

"Go on, Doombot! Arrest us! I *dare* you! Just try it."

"This Doombot is not here to arrest you." It raised its hands and too late the protestor saw what was coming. She stared at the dancing motes of electrical energy visible on its palms and heard the last words she would ever hear. "This Doombot is here to punish you. Doom provides!"

The energy discharged and leaped to the lead protestor, whose flesh blistered and burned. Then the storm arced from her to those nearest, who joined in an unholy chorus of screaming and pleas for mercy. The Doombot's response was to intensify its attack. The stench of cooking flesh added to the miasma already pervading the Doomwood streets. Above them, staring down at this massacre, Peter Quill was helpless to act.

"We've got to do something, Rocket," he said, urgently. He pulled the revolvers from their holsters and thumbed back the hammers. Rocket reached up.

"Put them away, Quill. There's *nothing* we can do!" Quill tugged back from Rocket in much the same way as Rocket had pulled from him when he'd been coughing. "It's too late."

"He's killing them!" Outside, the agonized cries had faded to just a few voices – some even weakly calling out their words of protest to their very last breath. "He's killing them all."

The street fell ominously silent as the Doombot ceased its attack. Quill said nothing, but a choked sob tore itself from his throat.

"I know, pal," said Rocket and there was an infinite sadness and sympathy in his voice. He caught Quill's arm again and gently, very gently, lowered his friend's hand. "I know."

Quill wallowed in his anguish for a moment. Then he raised his head and there was a spark of fury in his eyes.

"I've got an idea," he said.

"Oh, no."

"Run that by me again," said Emma, her tone dangerously moderate in a way that suggested a full-on tantrum was only a handful of syllables away. "What do you mean, they left?"

Upon discovering that the recorder was the only one left downstairs, Cora had been brought back up to Emma's office on the first floor where birds trilled and sang happily. Cora followed the woman's prowling progress around the room.

"They left, Emma Frost. They climbed out through the open window, crawled across the roof to the lower building next door. Then, they hung from the gutter – although I am unsure that was part of their plan – before dropping to the street. They left."

Emma curled her hands into fists and with immense effort of will managed not to scream her frustration aloud. Her voice, however, carried more than a hint of steel in it.

"Do you realize just how reckless that was? They haven't put just themselves at risk. If either of them was seen leaving this building, then absolutely everything I've done here... everything I've worked for will all be for *nothing!*" She calmed herself after the last word came out as a shout. "You need to tell me where they went."

"They did not tell me where they were going. Not precisely."

"Then what, precisely, did they tell you?"

"They have split their efforts. Rocket has gone to find a way to remove the guillotine collars that are programmed to destroy them in two days."

Emma shook her head, frustrated. "Didn't they appreciate that I was going to help them with that? What's *wrong* with them." It was a rhetorical question, but Cora didn't appreciate rhetoric.

"There is nothing wrong with them, Emma Frost. Because you have chosen not to be forthcoming about your own plans, they have no reason to trust you."

"Hah, trust. Well, I don't trust *them* not to blow up this one advantage we have against Doom." Emma sighed, sitting back. She slowly crossed her long legs and looked up at Cora. "So how about Quill? Where is *he*?"

"He continues the search for the Black Vortex."

Emma laughed. "That *fool* won't live long enough to find it." She tapped a finger lightly against her chin. "What does he know? What other leads does he have?"

"I do not know. He did not tell me." Cora studied the woman behind the desk. "But… Emma Frost, may I ask a question?" Emma waved a hand, lost in her own thoughts, and Cora continued. "You are a telepath. How is it that you neither knew of, nor anticipated, their plans?"

Emma flinched as though she had been slapped, then stood once more and turned to gaze out of the window. Eventually, she sighed. "Peter Quill isn't the only one getting older," she said, quietly. Cora did not comment, but let Emma speak her piece. "There was a time, you know, when I could have every person within a ten-mile radius fall into a seizure with just a wink of my eye."

"Your left eye or your right eye? It is important to provide accuracy and context in my records."

Emma ignored the question. "I've lost some of my *pizzazz*. My sparkle. Why else on this *Earth* would I be wasting my precious time interrogating a human-shaped bag of bolts? They must have told you something."

"No," said Cora and her tone was serious. "Neither Star-Lord nor Rocket felt in the mood to talk, and they are *always* in the mood to talk. There were no more jokes, no more insults." She indicated the window. "What happened outside – with the Doombot – upset them. A great deal."

"But *you're* still here, darling."

"Yes, Emma Frost. I am still here."

"Why is that, I wonder?"

"I will answer your question," said Cora, "but I would ask another of my own first. When you were playing the game with Kraven, and he missed the snake. Did you cheat?"

It was such an honest question that Emma nodded. It deserved an honest answer. "Of course I cheated," she confirmed. "Kraven weighs easily a hundred pounds more than I do. I wasn't going to let him drink me under the table in my own club." Her lips quirked in a smile.

"Then why challenge him if you know you cannot win honestly?"

"That's more than one question," countered Emma, but humored the recorder anyway. "He's blood crazed. The adrenaline of the hunt leaves him on a permanent high. He's always looking for trouble. Kraven is absolutely a weapon of Doom, able to do whatever he wants without consequence. It's a rare day when he visits the club and doesn't leave at least one body behind. I'm the only one who's capable of not just challenging him but subduing him should it become necessary."

"Then you deceived him," said Cora. "Just as you have deceived Star-Lord and Rocket."

"By locking them up, you mean? That wasn't *deception*, darling. That was keeping them safe. It was for their own protection. It may have been unkind, but it was necessary for us all."

"A deception. Yes." Cora changed tactics. "You are deceptive about your own appearance."

"Be very careful where you go with this, Cora." The low purr of threat did not go unnoticed.

"When I asked questions about you, everyone agreed that you were the most extraordinary woman they had ever seen. Let me play you some examples." Her eyes glowed and voices rose from her speakers, recordings of some of the many people to whom she had spoken when originally in the club.

*"The White Queen's legs? Them's some quality legs."*

*"Oh, man, I get the dizzies every time I think about her..."*

There were other, similar compliments, and the faint smile on Emma's lips grew briefly larger. Then Cora stopped the playbacks. "But that is not an accurate description of who you really are, is it?" The recorder was interrupted by the slap of Emma's hand as it came down on her desk. The White Queen lost her legendary composure and screeched into Cora's face, her visage made ugly by the moment.

"I said shut *up*! Shut up right *now*!"

Silence descended, during which Emma composed herself once again. She crossed to a drinks cabinet along one wall and popped the cork on a bottle, pouring herself a drink. "I'd offer you a drink, but I don't have any oil."

"The power you have that allows you to read minds, also allows you to *change* minds. Am I correct?"

"Present company excluded, it seems." Emma held up her glass. "Cheers, darling."

"Thus, you control how people see you. A visual deception. A lie."

"It's not a lie," said Emma, taking a sip of her drink. "I used to be a *lot* of things that I'm not anymore."

"That is the way of the world," offered Cora, surprisingly sagely, and Emma laughed.

"It's not exactly like you're any better," she suggested. "Your entire appearance is nothing more than a camouflage for silicon, bolts, and circuits." She looked the recorder over, taking in the female form that would never change, that would never be ravaged by the cruel passage of time that always took and never gave. Emma sighed, feeling oddly defeated.

"You asked me why I am still here, Emma Frost: it is because I am a test. Star-Lord and Rocket need to be sure that they can truly trust you."

Emma snorted. "Look around you. This is the kind of world in which trust is a luxury."

"Then you have failed the test."

"Oh, for God's sake," snapped Emma. "How in the name of… how would anybody in this world *ever* pass a test like that?"

"If you are the ally you claim to be," said Cora, moving a step closer. "Then you must bring Kraven here."

Emma stared and set her drink down. "I had to chase him out once already," she said. "Now you want me to bring him *back*?"

"Yes," said Cora. "Bring him here. That will enable Rocket and Star-Lord to move freely throughout Doomwood without threat of being hunted."

It was simple. Ridiculously simple. Emma stared for a moment, then shook her head. "What am I even supposed to say to him to get him to come back?"

"You are a clever and powerful woman, Emma Frost. That much is not a deception. I am sure that you can figure it out – but I suggest that we play by their rules."

"What do you mean?"

"I have a recording that may explain. Let me play it for you."

Emma moved back to her seat, leaning back as she listened to Cora's audio. The dulcet tones of Brandon Best filled her office, momentarily silencing the songbirds.

*"Hello, loyal citizens of the Victorlands. This month is off to a great start. Mining quotas have been filled and every outpost has met its taxation goals."* His tone became kindly, fatherly, and proud. *"Folks, let me be the first to congratulate you. Your productivity will be repaid in full by the loyalty and protection of our own Lord Doom. As a thank you, he has authorized that everyone receives an extra half-gallon water ration. That's right! You heard it here first!"*

There was a pause, long enough for anybody who found this news truly life-altering to get loudly excited over it.

*"Now. After the upsetting news of insurgents on our streets, I'm sure you're all interested in finding out the answer to the same*

*question that I have: how do we restore good old-fashioned law and order? Well, no need to fret, folks, because Lord Doom – and Kraven – are on the case. That's right, Kraven is out on the hunt for the wanted terrorist known as Peter Quill!"*

Cora snapped off the transmission. Emma shrugged. "I'm not sure what that was meant to accomplish," she said.

"Do as the hunter does, Emma Frost. Bait the trap." The recorder studied the woman behind the desk. "You are smiling. Why is that?"

"Because, darling," purred Emma, "I'm about to receive some *very* good news." She leaned back in her chair again, glass in hand, and took a long drink. "My mind may not be what it used to be, but neither am I a dead antenna."

"I see," said Cora, who *did* see. "You are communicating with someone outside of this room."

"Oh yes," she confirmed. "Since the moment I learned that Quill and Rocket had left, you've only been receiving about half of my attention. Any moment..."

There was a loud knocking.

"...now."

A voice came from the other side of the office door: another female voice, but unlike the honeyed tones of Emma Frost, this one was gruff, deeper in pitch and with a sandy rasp to it. "Found your talking rat."

"Do come in, Joanna." Emma got to her feet, brushing non-existent dust from her outfit. The door opened and the office was once more filled with noise that drowned out the birds. This time, it came from two sources. Firstly, the hiss and clank of the woman who entered. Easily six and a half feet in height, just about every part of her appeared to have been replaced by cybernetics. There was still just enough humanity left to differentiate her from an automaton. Her hydraulics and systems whirred and turned in much the same way as the Doombots.

The rest of the commotion came from the hissing, spitting Rocket who she held in her arms. One of her metal hands clamped his jaws firmly together. His paws were tied in front of him and he squirmed relentlessly in her grip. The woman stepped before Emma and inclined her head. "My queen."

Rocket managed to free his jaw from her grip, shrieking in no uncertain terms about how he was going to kill her. She casually clamped his mouth shut again.

"Dearest Joanna. I can always count on you, can't I?" Emma beamed at the new arrival who brandished Rocket like a trophy.

"Here you go. Don't let him scurry away." She tossed Rocket to the floor unceremoniously. He hit the ground with a thump that knocked the wind clean out of him for several moments before he looked up, growling.

"You flarking piece of… The hell you think you're doing, disrespecting me like that?"

"Shut up, rat," said the woman named Joanna.

"Rat? *Rat*? You really think you can insult me by calling me a *rat*? Have you looked in a mirror lately? What the hell are *you*, anyway? Did your mother get drunk and rub up the wrong way against a Doombot?"

"This, Rocket," said Emma, "is Joanna Forge and I recommend you don't get on her bad side. I once saw her tear a tree out of the ground with that arm."

"Yep," confirmed Joanna. "A quick squeeze with this hand and I could make soup out of your skull."

"Joanna is a maker – and a breaker – of things."

"Rocket," said Cora. "Shall I untie your bindings?"

Rocket shook his head. "Better not," he said, his voice a threatening growl. "Otherwise, you'll be an accomplice to murder, because that is what I am gonna do to this Forge freak. Tear her apart, metal codpiece and all!" He continued ranting for a while.

Joanna Forge stared down at him, then up at Emma. "Is that all, my queen? Can I go?"

"I have some pressing business to attend to, Joanna. I would be *grateful* if you could watch over these two for a short while. They present a serious risk."

"I've got better things to do than babysit a rat and…" She looked over at Cora disdainfully. "A skinbot."

"I know, darling, but this is important. Kraven is on his way here."

The words had an immediate effect on Joanna. Her remaining skin, darkened by the sun and aerial pollutants, paled visibly. "Kraven?"

"Yes. So for all our sakes, let's keep this little arrangement under lock and key, shall we?"

Joanna looked cowed for a few moments, then sighed and nodded. "As you request, my queen."

"That's a good girl," said Emma. She stepped from the room, firmly closing the door behind her. Joanna leaned against it, a clear physical barrier, glowering at Rocket and Cora.

"Joanna Forge, may I ask you a question?" Cora's voice was curious, a tone that Rocket had, truth be told, come to dread. The powerful woman turned a cool gaze on the recorder.

"No," she said. "You may not."

"Oh," said Cora, clearly surprised by this. "Then I will not." She allowed a moment to pass and then continued, innocently. "I will not ask whether or not you consider yourself to be a cybernetic organism."

Joanna's eyes hardened. "Don't talk to me again."

Rocket coughed quietly a few feet away, nodding vigorously. "Yeah, Cora, don't talk to her. It's like talking to an oven. All you're gonna get back from her is hot air." He fell back to coughing, paws covering his snout as the coughs racked his small frame. Cora turned away from Joanna and went to him. She crouched until she was at eye level and lowered her voice, although they were probably far enough away from Joanna for her not to listen. Not that Cora believed the woman was remotely interested in what they had to say, anyway.

"How are you feeling, Rocket?"

"My pride is wounded beyond repair. But I'll be OK."

"You know that is not what I was referring to."

Rocket squeezed his eyes closed as another bout of coughing tore through him. Once it passed, he was able to settle down, at least for now. He wiped his teary eyes and shook his head again. "There's nothing to be done. Forget it."

"You should tell Star-Lord about your ailing health."

"What's the point? What would it accomplish?" Rocket's voice was fierce in its refusal.

Cora chose her response carefully. "I believe that he would want to know that his best friend is dying."

The stark reality of her words brought a flash of guilt into Rocket's eyes. He passed a shaking paw across his face. "It's the last thing he needs, Cora. Given the fact that he's never got over what happened to the others…"

"The other Guardians?"

Rocket slid down the wall until he was sitting. He pulled his knees into his chest. When he spoke, his voice was hollow with weariness and difficult memory. "Yes. Drax. Gamora." A heartbeat, then infinite pain. "Groot. All of them."

"Does Quill believe he is somehow at fault?"

"Oh yeah, the idiot feels at fault all right. He feels it like the weight of the entire galaxy pressing down on his heart. He feels it in the morning when he wakes up. He feels it last thing at night before he sleeps. He dreams about it. You've seen it, Cora. He's always compensating. Trying to make up for the mistakes he's made."

Rocket leaned back, closing his eyes, the recollection of a time when all the Guardians were still alive passing through his mind. It never got any easier, never hurt any less. "Always compensating," he said again. "Whether it's his good-for-nothing dad, or the death of the Guardians, Quill's entire future is based around a stringent and ongoing denial of the past." He opened his eyes. "I hope the idiot's all right."

"Will you tell me what happened with you and Joanna Forge?"

"Sure. Nothing better to do."

# CHAPTER NINE
## BROKEN ANTENNA
### EARLIER...

Rocket traversed the streets of Doomwood utilizing whatever cover he could find. It was not exactly the easiest thing to do to keep a low profile when you were – in the eyes of dumb humans, at least – a walking, talking raccoon, but Rocket managed it. He planned to head for the refinery. He'd find someone or something there to remove the collars, he was sure.

Then his sensitive nose had detected the unmistakable scent of coal dust. He changed direction and followed it. That was what led him to the large, open-air building with a tin roof on the very edge of town. The sign that read "Forge's Forge" easily identified it. He could make out the glow of the coals within the building and a silhouette moving around. There was the sound of a hammer striking an anvil and Rocket's heart swelled with hope. A forge in a town like this would be his best hope of locating something – or someone – who could help him cut through the adamantium collar round his neck. *One tinkerer to another*, he thought, moving towards possible redemption.

It was not until he was close that he realized the large silhouette was that of a woman. Big, powerful, wearing a thick leather apron to protect what remained of her skin from the sparks flying from the anvil. Rocket watched in a mixture of awe and discomfort as she swung a ten-pound hammer around with consummate ease. The engineer in Rocket was impressed with the array of equipment he could see. Laser welders, diamond-tipped hammers, and others were evident among the range of tools. A thousand-pound anvil. A blast furnace so hot it was like staring into the heart of a star.

The woman was distracted, busy with her work, so Rocket took the opportunity to investigate the bench. There must be something here. Something that he could use to…

Then, fortune deserted him. He coughed. Instantly, the ringing of the hammer on the anvil ceased and the woman turned, staring at him.

*Keep it cool, Rocket,* he told himself and met her gaze square on. He thought about smiling, but what with the sharp teeth and everything, that tended to make people more anxious. *What would Quill do?*

Quill, he suspected, would probably flirt his way out of the situation and that was *not* an option for him. She continued to stare, then lurched toward him, her hammer raised threateningly.

"What do you think you're doing? Get off my workbench, you little thief."

"Cool your jets, lady, I'm just looking."

"Oh, it *talks* as well?"

For someone so big, she moved with startling speed. Before Rocket could even think about making a run for it, she reached out and grabbed hold of him. He let out a primal, animalistic growl and squirmed. But he was going nowhere. Her metallic hand of pistons and hydraulics was not going to let go. She held him up and stared. "What are you?"

"Get your stupid claws off me!"

"A radioactive rat, maybe?"

"Put me *down!*" He wriggled and fought against her grip to no avail.

She laughed. "Put you down? That's dangerous in a place like this." To prove her point, she started walking towards the blast furnace. "Where would you like me to put you down, rat? Here? In the coals?" She held him close enough that he could smell his fur start to singe and let out a howl, begging for her to stop.

"Now that you have mentioned it," said Cora, as Rocket concluded his tale, "I can see that your whiskers do appear to be a little charred."

From the door, Joanna snorted. It was clear that she had listened to every word. "He's fine. Stop making me out to be the bad guy in this, rat. You were the one trying to steal from me."

"Shove it down your throat," snarled Rocket.

Joanna laughed. "He skipped the bit where he tried to knock me out with a hammer."

"It was self-defense!" Rocket did manage to look a little sheepish, though.

She snorted again. "You wouldn't have found anything there, anyway. Not to safely cut through that adamantium. Pretty much anything on that table you tried would have just opened up an artery, and then..." She put her hand to her neck, opening and closing the hydraulic fingers to mimic blood spurting.

Rocket winced. "Then where *should* I have looked?"

"Listen, rat. Play by the White Queen's rules and maybe you'll learn something important."

Rocket got to his feet but didn't go any closer to Joanna. He stared at her coldly. "So are you gonna help us?"

"We'll help you if you help us," she said, simply. There was a pause before Cora entered the conversation again.

"How did you come to lose so much of your body, Joanna Forge?"

The blacksmith turned her head to the recorder, a look of disdain in her expression, but the question appeared to have sparked her pride. "I prefer to think of it more as 'how I came to gain an arsenal'. Much better way of putting it."

"Either way," said Cora, "I am curious. How did…"

"The same thing that eats up everything round here, skinbot. Cancer." The word landed in the room with all the implications and harsh realities brought with it. What the people of Doomwood had to live with. "Every time a lesion or a tumor flares, then I perform the excision myself. When necessary, I create a prosthetic to replace what I've lost."

"I see," said Cora. "You are the kind of person who does not accept their fate easily."

"No," said Joanna, proudly. "No, I am not."

"Is that why you are a part of the Second Dawn?"

Joanna folded her arms defensively and her expression tightened. "What do *you* know about it?"

Cora was unfazed by the tone. "Very little. I would like to know more," she said.

Joanna studied Cora carefully, taking her in from head to toe, and then she nodded, opening her mouth to speak. Before she could get a word out, however, there was a brisk knock at the door, which opened immediately. Rocket recognized Rick, the man who had brought them here through the tunnels. He ignored Cora and Rocket, turning his attention instead to Joanna.

"The queen is asking for you," he said. "She's in her room."

Joanna was on alert instantly. "What happened with Kraven?"

"That's what she wants to talk about."

"I'll go straight there." Joanna began clanking towards the door. The man put his hand on her shoulder and pointed at Cora.

"Her, too." Joanna blinked. Cora *couldn't* blink but gave the distinct air that if she could have done, she would have done.

"Me?"

"The skinbot?"

"Yeah," said Rick. "Go on. You go. I'll watch the raccoon."

"My name's Rocket."

"Don't care," said the man. "You'd better hurry, Forge. She's weak."

The bedroom of the White Queen was peaceful. Much like her office, the theme was one of heavy oak with wooden floors made cozier by the addition of scattered rugs that lent warmth and color to an otherwise somber decor. A large, iron-framed bed filled the far end of the room and Emma Frost lay beneath the covers, a frail-looking thing among the linen and pillows. She looked up as Joanna and Cora entered, the creaking of the floorboards beneath Joanna's not-inconsiderable weight alerting her to their presence.

"Joanna?" Her voice was weak, but still retained the regal tone that Cora had noted originally.

The blacksmith's eyes softened. "Yes, my queen."

"Pour me some water, please?"

"Of course, my queen." Joanna moved to the side of the bed where a pitcher and glass waited. She poured a generous measure which Emma accepted gratefully. "Drink this, then rest. You need your rest."

"Thank you, darling." Emma sipped, then groaned softly. Joanna began to bustle around like a mother hen.

"Let's get you comfortable," she said. "Do you need more pillows propping you up?"

"No, I'm fine. Thank you."

Cora took a few steps closer. "Why is it that you are so weak, Emma Frost?"

"Because what I do takes a toll."

"Doing what? What happened?"

Joanna turned on the recorder with a scowl. "Enough with your questions! Can't you see she needs to rest."

Emma raised a hand feebly. "It's all right, Joanna. What happened, Cora, was that I passed your test."

"I see," said Cora. "What happened with Kraven?"

"I have managed to buy you and the others some time."

"How did you accomplish this, Emma Frost?"

Emma laughed, a weak sound that ended in her gasping for breath. Joanna returned to her side, helping her to sip the water. "I broke him," she replied, eventually. Slowly, she got control over herself and continued. "He came here. To the Heaven and Hellfire. To *this* room. Under my guidance, this time."

"You are not a broken antenna," said Cora.

"No," agreed Emma. "I am not. He was caught somewhere between curiosity and confusion when he arrived, and I closed the door behind him. He sniffed at the air and said that he could smell something…"

"I smell something." His tone was deeply suspicious as he turned this way and that. Emma waved a languid hand.

"Oh, that'll be my perfume, darling. I use a lot of it. Helps to cover up the stink of this world."

Kraven shook his head. "No," he said. "I smell *animal*. There has been an animal nearby."

Emma turned to him, releasing the full force of her power on the man who personified fear. He stiffened.

"Kneel on the floor," she commanded, and he shook his head, trying to clear it. He did not do as she said, so she continued. "Did you hear what I said? I told you to kneel on the floor."

"Yes…" Kraven nodded. He sank to the floor, gazing up at her.

She smiled at him, and he just stared. "Good," she said and took a few deep breaths. "Now *remember*, Sergei. Remember the time before *now*."

He continued to stare at her for a moment or two, then his expression became vacant as memories flooded his mind. His eyes widened and he let out a growl. The growl became a grunt and finally, the grunt became a whimper of despair.

"That's a good boy," Emma whispered. Already she could begin to feel the toll controlling the situation would exact. "Remember it all." She closed her eyes and she *reached*…

•••

"You were reaching into his mind?"

"Yes. The very core of who he is."

"A memory?" Cora understood this. Memories were, after all, her stock in trade.

"Not just any memory," said Emma. "His worst memory. Let me share it with you, Cora, for your databanks. He was a boy, only ten years old. He lived out in the frozen wastes of the far north. Both of his parents were professors – biologists working at St Petersburg University. They were conducting a long-term habitat study near the Arctic Circle."

Emma coughed again, and Joanna helped her sip more water. Then the blacksmith fluffed up the pillows and did whatever she could do to help with Emma's obvious discomfort.

"Please take all the time you need, Emma Frost," said Cora.

"I'm fine," Emma asserted and continued. "One day, an ice bear emerged from the freezing fog. It tore apart the family's shelter. Mauled his parents to death in front of him. But he wasn't Kraven back then. He was Sergei. He *ran*. He fled through the fog out into the ice and snow."

"But where did he go?"

"There was nowhere *for* him to go. When the sun made its brief appearance, he used what he knew of navigation to guide him south and for four days, he was alone. He ate snow and lichen, built himself shelters in rocks. On the fifth day, the ice bear came for *him*. Did you know that it's the only animal on Earth that actively tracks and hunts humans? It had followed him all this way, still with the crimson stain of his parents on its muzzle. It lunged for him. He threw his arms up, defiant at the end and then a rifle shot rang out across the ice."

Joanna was caught up in the story every bit as much as Cora

appeared to be. She'd known Kraven for what he was: the cold-hearted, callous hunter who knew no mercy. This was a part of his story that she had never heard. Elements, perhaps. Rumors. But *this* full account of Kraven's shadowed past was extraordinary. Not for the first time, she marveled at the skill of her queen.

"Who saved him?" Cora prompted Emma to continue.

"He had wandered into an oil field. A geologist was out with a crew repairing a vent when they saw the bear. He saved the child's life. Sergei didn't speak for a year. He was traumatized by the incident and deeply ashamed of his own fear. He never saw it as a fight for survival. All he knew was that he failed to stand and fight. He had run away. He made a vow that never again would he be the prey. He would *always* be the predator."

"Where is Kraven now?"

"He isn't Kraven now. He's Sergei once more. I made it so. He'll be Sergei for another day, perhaps two. I imagine he's presently curled up in his bed, whimpering at his own impotence, gripping that knife with the bone handle. The bone of the ice bear." Emma laughed, weakly, and Joanna intervened.

"Enough. You should sleep."

Emma nodded. "Sleep sounds nice," she said, yawning widely. "But first – don't you agree that I've passed this test of loyalty, Cora? I subdued Kraven and bought Quill and Rocket some time."

"I would say that constitutes passing the test of loyalty, yes."

"Good." Emma shifted in the bed. "Then now it's time for you to do the same for me."

"How?"

"You're fitted with a security system. In case anybody attempts to hijack your core."

"That is correct." Emma glanced up at Joanna, who reached into the bag she wore slung across her shoulder. She retrieved a small device and Cora turned her head to look at it quizzically. "What is that?"

"Something I've been working on for a while," replied Joanna. "It's designed to be used on the Doombots."

"Yes," added Emma. "But I think that *you* would be a very good case study in the interim." Joanna stood beside Cora, holding up the device in one hand and reaching out to clamp the recorder's shoulder in her other.

"This," she said, "is an acorn-sized wonder of surveillance and… shall we say… *explosive* technology." She smiled without humor. "I'm going to shove it down your throat, skinbot."

"Understand that we don't want to *hurt* you, darling," said the White Queen. "But we are also not entirely sure where your loyalties truly lie. Are you *really* working with Quill and Rocket?"

"Or are you serving the Rigellian Empire?" Joanna clicked something on the side of the device.

"I'm afraid we can't risk you skipping town with the Black Vortex." Emma smiled weakly as Joanna moved in to plant the device. "Consider it a trust exercise."

"So, we're going to be recording the recorder." Joanna grinned and this time there was humor in it. "If we don't like what we hear?" She paused, for effect. "Boom!"

# CHAPTER TEN
## CATCHING FIRE

Brandon Best not only provided commentary for *Deer on a Spear*, but he was also very much the public voice of Doomwood. The populace listened to him daily as he reported, and they all listened now – Rocket and Joanna Forge along with them. Having left Emma to her much-needed rest, they had traveled to Forge's hidden armory, some miles out of Doomwood. The journey had taken them at least two hours and a change in the weather meant that they had been caught in a torrential downpour. They were wet, they were tired and listening to Best's commentary soured the mood further.

"*There's* always *a good reason to get out of bed in the mornings,*" Best chirped enthusiastically. "*But there's a* particularly *good reason today – it's raining! A rare and wonderful thing in these parched times, folks. Rare and wonderful.*" His voice dipped into seriousness, the tone of the broadcast altering perceptibly.

"*But folks… there's unfortunate news as well. Terrorist activity in Doomwood continues escalating. What I am about to report may shock and alarm many of you, but it is my duty to ensure you know the truth of what's out there."*

"Truth, huh? My furry ass." Rocket snorted and Forge elbowed him in the face.

"Shut up."

*"You've heard about the trenches in the logging roads,"* continued Best. *"About spikes hammered into trees, and horses freed from their wagons. All this pales into insignificance compared with what the insurgents did last night. They soaked a load of timber bound for the sawmill with diesel. The heat of the saw blade ignited it. I'm sure you can imagine how fast that sort of blaze spreads."*

There was a hushed pause, Best building the tension in a credibly impressive manner. *"If it weren't for these blessed rains, well, we might have lost the mill in its entirety."*

Rocket scratched at his armpit as he listened, his expression unreadable. Forge looked both indifferent and troubled, a difficult face to pull. Nonetheless, she achieved it perfectly.

*"That's not all folks. Last night, a driver was delivering steel from the refinery when arrows – flaming arrows – most likely belonging to the traitorous Ghost Riders, struck both driver and horse. We have frontline drone footage from last night. It's my duty to inform you that it is upsetting. If there's children listening, you might want to cover their precious little ears."*

Best's voice crackled off, replaced by fuzzy, drone-recorded voices talking in an urgent exchange. In the background, a horse whinnied in animal fear and pain. There was a woman's voice, frightened, but clearly attempting to be calming and a man whose words were interspersed with sobs and groans of agony.

"It hurts. Oh, God it hurts! I can feel it... grinding against my spine..."

"You'll be all right. Focus on my voice. You'll be all right. You've lost a lot of blood, but we'll get this arrow out of you."

"I ain't got long..."

"Just hold on, Paul. Hold on." The horse lapsed into silence and the man's voice changed, panic now layered on top of the pain.

"My horse! The old girl got hit, too..."

"We'll sort her once we've sorted you. I'm gonna pull out the arrow now, OK? Take a deep breath..."

There was a wet, tearing sound, a heartbeat of silence and then a dreadful scream filled the airwaves. As the vignette ended, quiet descended, possibly across the whole of Doomwood.

"They died," said Best, somberly. "Paul White, a good man and a loyal patriot, and his horse both died. A load of steel was taken. For what purpose? We don't know. Weapons, perhaps. Designed to hurt us, the law-abiding residents of the Victorlands."

Forge chewed the nails on her remaining hand as she listened, intent on what Best was saying. There was a moment or two to allow the horror of the recording to dissipate and the commentator continued. *"Now, I don't know about you, folks, but I can't help but see a connection in the rise of this local violence and the arrival of the terrorist Peter Quill – the self-named 'Star-Lord'."* He played a sound effect of a crowd jeering and booing. Rocket winced.

"For this reason, I must inform you that Lord Doom will be implementing a twenty-four-hour curfew. There are some exceptions – our miners, millers, and steelworkers. All these people will remain on site, provided with food service so as not to interrupt productivity. The rest of you, and I cannot stress this enough, please

*remember to report, report, report if you see anything suspicious.
He's out there, people. Let's find Peter Quill. Let's restore law and
order and, more importantly, end this anxious time of pain and
unrest. In other news..."*

"Turn it off, Forge. I'm done listening."

Brandon's voice snapped off. Rocket looked over at Forge.
She looked right back, the two briefly united in their mutual
sense of unease.

"Let's get on with this," she said, breaking the silence.

Elsewhere in Doomwood, Emma Frost stared out at the
abandoned street. Lightning forked through the sky and in the
distance thunder rumbled loudly enough to rattle the glass in
its panes. The rain coursed down the office window in endless
rivulets, distorting the view – but Emma stood there regardless.
She was still weary from her run-in with Kraven and had one
hand against the wall to prop herself up.

Cora maintained a silent vigil beside the door. After the
transponder had been deployed into her internal organ hub so
that her movements could be tracked, she made a simple – and
accurate – statement.

"Neither of you fully trust me."

There was no reply to that.

Emma sighed, stepping back from the window. "It feels
wrong to lock the doors on a social hub like this. A bar without
customers is like a hive without bees. No buzz, no sting, no
honey." She made her way slowly to her seat and lowered
herself down with a soft groan of discomfort.

"Emma Frost, may I ask a question?"

"You don't need my permission, but yes, darling. Go ahead."

"How long will it take Rocket and Joanna Forge to reach this armory?"

"It's about a two-hour journey, but the rain may cause them delay. The weather is extreme in these parts. Why do you ask?"

"In one day, four hours, and twenty-seven minutes, the guillotine collars will contract, terminating Rocket and Star-Lord."

Emma flashed a brief smile. "Let's hope they hurry, then."

Cora crossed to the desk and Emma looked up at her. "Don't worry. Forge should have the tools to cut through adamantium. He'll be fine. If his endless prattling doesn't mean she kills him first." Emma reached for her drink and took a sip. "Not that it really matters. How sick is he?"

"His heart rate is increasingly abnormal," confirmed Cora. "His respiratory function is beginning a steady and likely terminal decline."

Emma let no emotion show on her face at the news, simply shook her head. "Quill doesn't even know." She let out a brief laugh. "The stupidity and stubbornness of men never fails to amaze me."

"From my observations, men and raccoons have much in common." Cora pondered. "What have you learned from Rocket's mind?"

Emma shrugged. "Oh, he wants to be sure he's alive long enough to save his friend." Her eyes rolled a little at the sheer cliché of it all.

"Query: How does it feel? To have so many thoughts in your head at any one time?"

"Honestly, darling, it feels like madness most of the time. But it is exhausting *all* the time. All this work is so draining."

"You are still weak from your interaction with Kraven." It was a statement, not a question and Emma sighed, setting aside her water. She opened the top drawer and took out a beautifully made, diamond studded hip flask. She studied it wistfully.

"Is it too early to drink?" Somewhere, in the world, she was certain that it was bourbon o'clock.

"You were saying how it feels to have voices in your head," prompted Cora.

Emma set down the flask without opening it. "There's nothing profound about it," she said. "Ultimately, everyone seeks the same basic things. To feed. To procreate. To find shelter. When you really break it down, we're all just animals. Present company excluded, clearly." She waved a hand vaguely at Cora. "But those primary needs being met isn't enough for humans. They need more. They crave more. They are seeking…" She paused, reaching for the right word.

"Happiness?"

"Yes," said Emma, "and no. Happiness is personal, so seeking it is to spend your life trying to track down the unknown. But yes, let's say they want happiness. Wealth. Power. Or fame. Your average human being, darling, seeks to aspire. Without knowing exactly *what*, they constantly want something *better*." She looked towards the window. "But out here? In the Wastelands? Aspirations are worthless. No matter how hard you work, no matter how many hours you put in, you can't get ahead. No, there's only one Victor out here, darling, and his name is Doom." She took up the hipflask and sipped its contents. "Unless…"

"Unless?"

"Unless there is no more Doom."

As though punctuating her words, there was a sudden loud banging at the door of the saloon. Three heavy bangs.

*Doom.*

*Doom.*

*Doom.*

Cora was reminded of the noise of the Brood attempting to breach the bridge deck of the mining ship on which Quill and Rocket had found her. Emma looked up at the recorder as the knocks sounded again. "Perhaps you should answer it," she said. "I'm in no condition."

"Of course, Emma Frost." Cora turned instantly and headed downstairs, through the deserted bar and to the heavily bolted door. She reached up, slid back the top bolt, and then turned the key in the lock. As the door slowly opened, creaking on its hinges, the rumble of thunder and the torrential rain increased in volume.

"I am sorry," said Cora to the figure outside, "but we are cl…"

"I'm tired and thirsty," a voice interrupted. It was cracked and wobbly – an old man's voice – or at least someone making every attempt to sound like an old man. "Make way for an old man in need of his medicine!"

Cora began to close the door against the figure in the battered old coat and wide-brimmed hat. "There is a curfew in place, and you must…" His foot barred the way and he let out a hearty laugh. Cora paused, recognizing the sound, and opened the door again. "Star-Lord?"

"Hah!" He was delighted and he slipped in through the door. Cora pushed it closed but in her haste to record Quill's new adventure, failed to notice that it did not fully latch. "I got you *good*!"

"I admit that I did not recognize you."

Quill took off the hat. His graying hair stuck out in several directions in response to having been smothered for a while. He attempted to smooth the strands back down. "That, Cora, is because I am in *disguise*. As an old man!"

"You *are* an old man, Star-Lord. It is the hat you were wearing. It obscured most of your face."

"You like this, huh?" Quill spun around on the spot. The tails of the raincoat flared out behind him, coming to settle again. "I swiped this from a drunk passed out in an alley. Smells a little like several goats took a piss in it, but it did what I needed it to do – it hid me from the drones. To make it even better, I was walking like this…" He showed her his exaggerated gait, bent over, wobbling a little.

Cora shrugged. "That is not so different from your usual walk when you have been travelling for a number of hours."

"No *way*! I've been *totally* incognito. Kraven can't hunt me if he can't find me, right?" He was exceptionally pleased with himself, and Cora did not reply. Besides, he was already off on a new set of rails. "Hey, you know how this bar has a heaven door and a hell door?"

"Yes."

"Did you catch me knock-knock-knocking on heaven's door?" She didn't react the way he'd hoped, and he was a little disappointed.

"I am sorry, Star-Lord. Is this more of your humor?"

"No," came a voice from the main staircase. "It isn't. Will you stop with all the noise, please?" Emma looked Quill from head to toe and wrinkled her nose in disapproval at the odor he had brought in with him. In return, he stared at her.

"Emma? You look… *different*."

She smoothed down the front of her blouse. "You mean 'old'? Sorry to disappoint you."

He was quick to deny it, although she did look much older than he had remembered. Still beautiful, of course: Emma Frost radiated a poise and grace that age could not diminish. "No! Not at all! Are you *kidding?*" He paused, before curiosity took hold. "Was it an illusion before? How you looked when we first saw you? Guess that's why I couldn't figure out why it was that you'd not aged."

"Psionic armor, I suppose. My own disguise that I just don't have the energy to maintain right now. This is the real me." She flickered a smile. "Warts and all."

Quill shook his head, defiant to the last. "C'mon Emma, knock it off. You shouldn't bother hiding who you are. Really. Truly. I don't mean that in a 'wear sweatpants and drive a minivan' kind of way. But you look *fantastic*, Emma. Like seriously… *wow*."

He was laying it on thick, but there was *just* enough truth in what he was saying for her to arch one eyebrow. "Well, cheers to that, then." She came down the last of the stairs. "I look like this right now because I'm exhausted. But that's because of the good news that Kraven is temporarily indisposed." Quill's eyes widened and she took the thought right out of his head without even really trying. "Yes," she confirmed, answering the unspoken question. "I *did* mess with his head."

"Would you not… I mean, *ouch*, Emma. You doing that brings me all the way back to yesterday."

"Look, I locked you in that room for your own good. Your own protection."

"That's as maybe. But from now on, we work *together*. Are we cool?"

"Much as it demeans me to use the phrase…" Emma looked as though someone had wafted an unpleasant smell under her nose. "We're cool."

Quill clapped his hands together. "Outstanding. I came back here *counting* on your trust."

"Then I suppose you have it."

"Great. Hey, where's Rocket?"

"He's safe, Quill. Safer than you are."

Quill turned to the recorder. "Cora? Where's Rocket?"

"If all goes as planned, his guillotine collar is being removed."

"That's *great* news!"

"It is timely news, especially since you only have one day…"

"I don't need specifics, thanks, Cora." Quill patted her kindly on the shoulder. "I am gonna trust that Rocket will figure it out."

Emma slid sinuously behind the bar. "Do you want a drink, Quill?"

He nodded enthusiastically. "Yes," he said, then immediately changed his mind. "No. Better not. I need to be tuned in if I'm going to see this through properly. You should see it out there. Doombots everywhere. Burned down buildings smoking in the rain. Protest graffiti scrawled everywhere. I even saw an effigy of Doom made from buckets and cans hanging from a tree." He shook his head. "Call me paranoid, but something's happening."

"Is this vandalism the work of the Second Dawn?" Cora asked the question as Emma filled a glass from a bottle behind the bar.

"No," she replied. "No, I think it's you." Both Quill and Cora were puzzled.

"You mean me?" Quill asked.

"You mean Star-Lord?" Cora asked at the same time.

Emma barked a laugh. "When heroes fall from the sky, I'd like to say that's a sign of things to come, yes? Good things to come."

"Absolutely," he said. "I'm here to make up for lost time."

"The Second Dawn has always been an idea more than a movement," said Emma, taking a long drink. "A handful of us working together, gathering an arsenal. Waiting. I don't know what it is that we're waiting for. The right moment, I suppose." She sighed. "Maybe that moment is *now*. Maybe all it took was…" She gestured vaguely in Quill's direction. "…an idiot cheerleader to inspire an uprising."

"I think the word you are looking for is 'amazing hero guy.'"

"That's three words," said Cora.

"You've started a fire, Peter Quill. Congratulations."

"Then let's keep fanning it before it goes out!"

Emma sipped at her drink, studying him thoughtfully. He cut a strange figure, this peculiar man-child with his gray hair and laughter lines and irrepressible, boyish enthusiasm. As much as she did not want to be, she was caught up in his fervor.

"What did you have in mind?"

Another clap of thunder reverberated around the saloon, an ominous prelude or a tiresome coincidence. Quill leaned on the bar, studying Emma's face intently, and lowered his voice conspiratorially. "I figured it out," he said. "I know how to find the Black Vortex. I have got…" He held up a finger. "A Great Plan."

He paused, presumably for dramatic effect, but mostly succeeded in looking as if he had completely forgotten what he was saying. It mattered little because his monologue was interrupted by the sound of an approaching Doombot.

"The reveal of the Great Plan will have to wait, Star-Lord," said Cora, crisply.

Quill let his finger drop. "I am on the cusp of unloading a *massive* game-changer, and you want me to..."

"Star-Lord." There was a surprising amount of firmness in the two syllables. "A second Doombot is approaching."

Emma set down her glass on the bar and scowled a little. "You were followed here," she said.

"No way. That's *impossible*. I was in disguise. They wouldn't have seen me."

Emma stared at him with eyes as hard as diamonds. "You put on a bad hat and a fragrant old raincoat, and you believe yourself to be invisible?"

Quill had no time to argue because the sound of the Doombot at the door was suddenly one of the two crucial issues that needed addressing. The second was the fact that the saloon door was ajar.

He waved his hands frantically. "Down. Behind the bar! Quick! Get down!"

The three figures squeezed behind the bar as swiftly and as quietly as they could manage. There was the scraping of a stool, the scuffing of wood, a couple of briefly whispered curses from Quill and then there was nothing but silence apart from the wind and rain outside. The door creaked open.

It opened with excruciating slowness, admitting a gust of rain and wind. Quill reached for one of the twin revolvers at his side and slowly slid it free. Emma slapped at his hand.

"Put it away," she whispered urgently.

He shook his head, his face dark. "I'm not gonna die on my knees," he whispered back.

"Quill, a bullet isn't going to make a lick of difference. Just stay hidden. It can't see us."

The Doombot paused on the threshold, clearly running some sort of preliminary assessment, before entering and methodically circling the bar with machine deliberation. It put Quill in mind of when, as a child, his great-aunt visited. There'd been that way she'd run her finger slowly across the mantlepiece before giving his mother a piercing stare. It was a strange association of memory, but these were strange times.

"Scanning for foreign individuals," said the Doombot as it traversed the room. A slow *beep* came from its chest as it activated its scanners. Quill felt his heart sinking as the tone increased in both pitch and pace as it circled around and headed towards the bar. The pitch went up.

And up.

And up.

And then…

"It's… right… on top of us…" Quill's whisper was strained and panicked. Emma fiercely shushed him, but released his gun hand, allowing him to prepare for the fight that was surely coming. The Doombot took another step forward and then a second transmission played.

"Unlawful assembly reported near to the north stables. All Doombot patrols report immediately. Repeat, all Doombot patrols report immediately."

There was no pause, no hesitation, no defying the order. The Doombot turned, deactivated its scanner, and pounded at top speed out of the Heaven and Hellfire, leaving the door wide open. Rain sheeted in and puddled on the saloon floor.

Thunder rumbled.

Quill and Emma released the tension they had held. Emma sat back against the wall, pinching the bridge of her nose. "That was close," she said, her voice still a whisper. "I don't like close."

"You've been living on 'close' for thirty years. Look, Emma. I don't want to be a jerk…"

"Do go on, darling. It's what you do best, after all."

"Thanks!" Quill didn't detect the sarcasm and Emma felt as though she'd missed a wonderful opportunity. "Anyway, it's time you did something more practical. Instead of hiding away."

"Then do carry on and share your great strategy, Mister – what was that phrase you used? Oh yes. Amazing Hero Guy." Quill got to his feet – his body firmly protesting at such mistreatment – and offered a hand to help Emma up. As an afterthought, but with no less gallantry, he also helped Cora up.

"The Black Vortex is the key to my plan," he said. "The critical part. I submit to it. I get cosmic powers – which would make me the *ultimate* Guardian – take down Doom and *boom*!" He punctuated this by punching his fist into his hand. "Everything's awesome!"

"As easy as that."

"Yep!" Quill beamed. "As easy as that."

"Then tell me, Quill." Emma fixed him with that same piercing stare. "Will this plan work out as brilliantly as your plan on Mortem Novis?"

"What happened on…" Cora's query was interrupted by Quill 's growled retort.

"Get out of my head."

"I just feel that it's important to remind yourself that rash behavior does not come without consequence."

"Please," said Quill. "Stop."

"I apologize for the interruption," said Cora, "but what is it that we are talking about?" Emma didn't even look at her as she replied. She and Quill were gaze-locked now: both as angry and defiant as the other.

"We are talking about the Guardians of the Galaxy," said Emma and Quill shook his head.

"*Were*," he corrected. "Not anymore."

Emma conceded and sighed.

"All right, not anymore. But please listen to me, Quill. Please. In your rush to power up and engage in what appears to be reliving your glory days, have you ever considered for a moment that you might be playing with fire?"

"Trust me, Emma," he said, taking her hands. He stared into her eyes intently. "I've got this." She returned his gaze and just for a moment, she softened.

"Then convince me," she said, quietly. He beamed at her. It was an expression incongruous with his otherwise aged appearance and for a moment, Emma was treated to a glimpse of the young man he'd been so many years ago. No, she told herself firmly. He's not that man now.

"Right. Convince you." He held onto her hands as he talked, and she did nothing to let go of him. "We know that the Black Vortex was squirrelled away before the world went to hell, right?" Emma nodded and Quill continued. "Deadwood was a town well known for its gold-diggers and outlaws, right?" She nodded again. He released her hands, stepping away.

"Well, that," he said, "is exactly the kind of person who's going to be responsible for finding and stashing a cosmic treasure. You know." That grin again. "A jerk. Jerks tend to make an impression. Jerks tend to show up in newspapers and books and police blotters. And Emma, my father – J'Son – well, he was a *galaxy-class* jerk." Quill clapped his hands together. He was in full flow. "Given the way things are right now, I could hardly find a computer and type 'jerk' into a search engine, so I used my brain." He tapped the side of his head. "I went old-school. I found the library."

"Doomwood doesn't have a library."

"Sure it does!" Quill shrugged one shoulder. "To be fair, you can barely see the brick walls of it. There's a *lot* of vines there. But it's there all the same."

Emma shook her head. "There might be," she said, "but there are no more books. Doom had them all burned."

Quill held up a finger to forestall her. "Maybe," he retorted, grinning. "But he didn't burn the librarian." Emma quirked one eyebrow but didn't say anything. "Her name is Agatha Blackwater. She lives there. In the library."

"I don't know anybody named…"

"Ah, Emma." Condescension didn't suit Quill, but he tried it on for size regardless. It made her want to slap him. "You claim to know everything and everyone about this town, but you paid absolutely no attention to this old biddy. But she's a *meat* computer. Do you want to know what I found out?"

"Do tell me," said Emma, drily. She *really* wanted to slap him. He told her.

There were no books in the dilapidated library, but the musty smell of old ink and paper remained. It was a smell that to Quill, whose life had largely been spent in space and on alien worlds, was uniquely *Earth*. It induced a rush of memories: being at school, going to the town library with his mother when he'd been small. Things otherwise forgotten awakened by a simple scent.

There were rows of empty shelves, thick with dust, and the mournful silence was broken by the arrhythmic tick of a dozen large clocks. None of them were in synch and the *tick tick tock tick tock* was a background constant.

Quill entered through the main doors. They weren't locked and he was able to get inside without incident. He had assumed that the place would be deserted, but he'd rounded a corner and bumped into an elderly lady, arthritic, myopic, and more than a little detached from the present. She showed no fear at his sudden appearance. In fact, she simply reached for the glasses she wore on a chain round her neck and lifted them to her eyes.

"Can I help you, young man?" Her voice was cracked and whispery, like old, brittle pages – or perhaps that was just Quill being fanciful.

So it was that several minutes later, he was seated at a table with the old woman – who introduced herself as Agatha Blackwater: head librarian. She was glad for his company. There were not many visitors these days. She busied herself with a teapot and several cups, carrying a tray over to the table and setting it down.

"Thanks for this, Ms Blackwater," said Quill, remembering his manners as she set down a cup in front of him.

"My pleasure," she said. "You must be *freezing* after being out in that weather. Here. Warm up with some tea. Mullein tea that I harvested from the backyard." She indicated the teapot and Quill picked it up.

"Shall… I pour?" It seemed like the right thing to say. It brought a smile of pleasure to her old face. She nodded.

"Please. Oh, it *is* nice to have some company." She watched as Quill carefully poured the tea. "It's usually just me and the clocks. I wind them to make sure they keep time but some days it feels like that's all I have left."

"So, you were once the librarian," said Quill setting a cup of tea before her. "In Deadwood. Before it became Doomwood?"

"That's right, dear," she confirmed. "Also, president of our local history society."

Quill poured his own tea and made a noise of delight. "Impressive! So you know
everything about this place, then?"

She chuckled, taking a sip. "Well, I know a lot," she admitted. "I can't say that I remember everything. Seems like I remember a little less with each tick of those clocks." She looked up at them, scattered around. "They're good for me. I can't let them wind down, because when time runs out, when I'm gone, well then." She waved a liver-spotted hand in the air. "The last of the library goes as well."

Quill nodded, taking a sip. He grimaced. "I guess it's stupid to ask if you have any sugar, isn't it?"

"Sugar?" She sighed longingly. "Can't tell you the last time I tasted something sweet."

"Yeah," he said and sipped at the bitter brew. "Let's get back to you knowing stuff. Because maybe you can help me."

"If I can, dear," she said. "I enjoy helping people." She gave him a crooked smile and he felt a surge of renewed energy for the task ahead. This was the kind of person he was fighting for. This was what it was all about.

"Here's how it is, Agatha. I'm looking for something incredibly valuable. But Doom is after it as well…"

"A treasure hunt?" Agatha smiled. "There's always been riches beneath the ground here in the Black Hills. It's been the same since the pioneers first came here." She gazed off into the middle distance. Quill leaned into her line of vision to secure her attention.

"So do you think you can help?"

"Oh, where to begin…"

The conversation was long, rambling and went in unexpected directions, often at the same time. Every time Quill attempted to steer the conversation, she digressed. He had the distinct impression that it was what happened when you had too much information inside your brain – it came pouring out like water. She treated Quill to a potted history of the Black Hills, snippets out of time punctuated by the monotonous ticking of the clocks.

Quill retained barely a fraction of it, hearing the words but not absorbing their meaning. She told him about the Treaty of Fort Laramie in 1868 which allowed white settlers to steal the territory from the Native Americans who had been living there. She spoke about how the ground was mineral rich with gas, uranium, copper, coal, iron, silver, and even gold, attracting prospectors across the centuries.

She talked for most of the afternoon, pausing periodically to make another pot of tea and to try to remember where she had gotten up to. Then she finally started talking about something that caused alarm bells to ring in Quill's head.

"...and then Jack McCall murdered Wild Bill while he was playing poker. I remember telling Lord Doom this story when he had me visit him at his house..."

"Hold on!"

"Hmm? What was that, dear?"

"Who had you visit him at his house?"

"Lord Victor von Doom, of course."

"Agatha! Why didn't you mention this right at the start?" Quill leaned forward on the table, his eyes dancing with excitement. She blinked at him and then sipped her tea.

"I suppose I forgot." She paused. "That reminds me of a nursery rhyme my mother used..."

"No, no, Agatha, please. Stay with me here. Eyes on the prize. We're talking about Doom."

"What about him?"

"Tell me about his home. I'm new to these parts. Don't know much about it."

"Oh, that's easy enough," she said and leaned back in her chair. There was a gentle silence for a few moments and the clocks rushed to fill the void. "It's not a home so much as it is a fortress. Carved right into the very hillside. When Doom came here – after the revolution – he chose to build it up there, on a ridge. It's symbolic, I suppose. He's always looking down on everyone else and that means there's no question of authority."

This was vital, critical intelligence and Quill mentally patted himself on the shoulder for having found this veritable treasure-trove of information. Agatha sighed, remembering happy times.

"There used to be wildflowers up on that ridge. I would go up there and pick them when I..."

"OK Agatha, that's wonderful, but tell me more about your visit."

"Mmm, my visit?"

"To Doom's fortress. What can you tell me about it?"

"Oh." She seemed disappointed to have been distracted from her tale about picking wildflowers on the hillside, but it didn't take too long for her mental needle to settle back into the right track and resume the story. "A Doombot brought a wagon to the library with an instruction for me to fill it with every book covering the history and geology of the region." Her eyes clouded with something that might have been sorrow, might have been anger, might have been both. "The rest were burned."

It was an act so heavily connected with the darker periods of human history that even Peter Quill felt the weight of the words settle on him with deep discomfort. He reached for Agatha's hand without quite knowing why. She seemed to appreciate the gesture and patted his hand with her other one a little absently.

"That was all I could think about. Those books on fire. I couldn't stop crying when the wagon took me up that road. The road that none may travel but the Doombots." Her expression misted over with recall. "I don't know if it's the same now, but there were spikes staggered every ten feet or so." She looked at Quill. "Spikes with bodies impaled on them. I can remember their rotting faces." She set down her tea, putting her hands up to cover her own face. "They looked like they were grinning," she said from behind her hands. "They looked as though they were laughing at me."

This time, Quill didn't try to rush her back on track. He sat quietly, allowing the old woman's awful memory to run its course. Eventually, she lowered her hands and took up her tea. He saw how her hands shook and felt a little guilty for pushing her to relive this.

"There was a big, steel door in the hillside which opened to admit us. When I say big, young man, I mean *enormous*. As though it had been made for a giant. By my reckoning, it's made from the same stuff that Doom is. Bolted steel. I went inside and it was a vast, empty space. Like the inside of a cathedral, only with far less of a sense of the devout. I don't remember ever feeling so small. Like a tiny mouse. Far away, I heard the drills and hammers. The compound was still under construction at that time. I stood there for what felt like an age and then this voice came booming into the space. 'Welcome, librarian', was all that he said. But his voice was *huge*. As big as the Black Hills. As big as the sky. I wanted nothing so much as to turn and run, but the Doombot led me into what I suppose you could call a war room."

"What was it like?" He was gentle this time, given how she had reacted to this memory. Peter Quill was many things, but he was not, never had been, nor ever would be cruel.

"Well, he was there, of course. Lord Doom. He was the first thing I noticed. He sat on a metal throne, up on a high platform. I had to crane my neck to look at him."

"What else was there?"

"Let's see. Tables with maps laid out on them. That's why I thought it was like a war room, you see? Piles of books everywhere. I couldn't see too closely, but they looked like maps of the Wastelands. I mean, the Victorlands." Quill rubbed at his nose thoughtfully and waited for a few moments, filing all this information away.

"What was it that he wanted from you, Agatha?"

"The same thing you want from me now," she replied. "Information. He wanted me to tell him all about Deadwood. I was afraid of saying the wrong thing. Afraid he might burn me like my books. I don't know how long I sat there with him. It could have been hours. Days. Weeks, even. It felt like years."

"Was he asking about anything specific?"

Agatha nodded. "Criminals, mostly. People like Jack McCall. But other lawbreakers, too. Prostitutes, opium dealers, murderers. Robbers. Even space pirates."

Bingo.

"What about space pirates?" Quill shuffled forward to the edge of his seat and gazed at her intently. "What about them?"

"Lord Doom wanted to know about them."

"Why?"

"Because they were a part of a long line of criminals who used the Black Hills as a hideout. All the canyons and mineshafts and natural caves – not to mention the lawless history of the place – make it a perfect location for those seeking to escape authority. They were all a part of the uprising, but none of them lived."

Funny how that made him feel. "None of them?"

"No," she replied. "So much death."

"These space pirates," Quill said, softly. "Were they called the Slaughter Lords?"

"That seems right. Yes. The Slaughter Lords. How did you know that?"

Quill shook his head in response. "Not now, Agatha. I need you to go back to what you remember about the meeting with Doom. Can you do that? Can you remember it?"

"Yes," she said simply. "As if I was right there. Doom wanted me to look at something he kept on one of the tables. So I did. It was just a piece of a broken mirror."

A thousand pieces of the puzzle fell into place one after the other. Quill's heart began beating faster. "Where did he get it?"

"I can't remember if he said or not," said Agatha. Her tenuous grip on the present was slipping again and Quill reined in a desperate desire to scream. He'd nearly had it. Nearly closed his hand around this critical, vital piece of information. Now he could sense it slipping away. He could see by that faraway look in Agatha's eyes that she was travelling down another memory highway. It was going to take some hard work to pull her back again. She looked at him. Her voice was low, sad, and scared and he hated that he'd put her through this. "There was something in the mirror."

He leaped on the moment of hope. "What? What did you see?"

"When I looked closely, there was something else in it other than just a reflection."

"What? What was in it?" Quill got up from his seat and leaned across the table. "Agatha, this is really..."

One of the clocks chimed the hour, its melodic tone drawing the attention of both Quill and the librarian, who turned to look at it, her brows knitting together. "The timing is off on that one." She started to rise from her seat, with arthritic difficulty. "I'll need to fix that. We can't have this, dear me, no."

Quill could have howled like a dog, but he kept it moderate. "Agatha, please. You need to tell me what you saw in the mirror."

"Hmm, dear? What mirror?"

*Please, no.*

"The broken mirror. The one that Doom showed you…" But she was shaking her head.

"I don't know what you're talking about," she said and stared at him in confusion.

"You're kidding me! We just spent a full twenty minutes talking about the mirror. You were…"

Then every other clock in the room went off at once, drowning out his words and washing away any hope that he might have had at getting the answer he so desperately needed.

"That was it," said Quill. He was drinking a glass of water now, made thirsty by the telling of his story. "That was all I got out of her. But it's enough."

"So," said Emma. "Doom has the rest of the map in his possession. Interesting."

"Yep," said Quill. "He has it. We're going to steal it."

His grin set Emma's nerves to jangling and she looked at him quizzically. "'We're going to steal it'. Just like that? That's your plan?"

"That is *exactly* my plan," he said, then looked a little sad. "I wish Rocket was here right now. You know there was this one time I dressed up as a female Badoon in order to infiltrate the Sisterhood and take out the Queen, and I was decked out in…" Cora interrupted him mid-flow.

"Are you proposing that you dress up as a female Badoon?"

"No! That was just an anecdote. Look. Here's the deal. We've got to get into Doom's compound and get the rest of that map. Based on what I learned from Agatha, the only way we're going to be able to do that is by hacking a Doombot." He looked from Cora to Emma, to Cora and then finally back to Emma. "So, if there is *anybody* you know who you think might be able to help us, I'm asking you now. Throw me a bone, Emma. Please."

Maybe it was the "please" that did it, maybe not. Whatever it was, she set down her glass of whiskey and drummed her long fingernails on the bar.

"I may know just the person," she said.

# CHAPTER ELEVEN
## BEST LAID PLANS

The person was a young man called Johnny Loomis. He was young: no more than eighteen or nineteen years old, slender to the point of scrawny, with fine, dark hair that wisped across his head as though it knew the effort of growing only to fall out again was hardly worth it. The milky caste to his eyes marked him out as blind – something Quill had noted was more common than not around these parts. He spoke in a gentle voice that had the faintest hint of an accent to it. He was deferential and polite – even sweet.

His youth made Quill feel his years like a sledgehammer to the face and not for the first time, he wondered if perhaps, *just perhaps*, this was all too much for him now. Then he would remind himself what was at stake and he pushed past it.

They'd left Emma behind in the Heaven and Hellfire, still weak, but rallying, and she had put them into the boy's care after explaining to him what it was that Quill needed to do. Crossing Doomwood turned out to be far easier than it might otherwise have been. Whatever emergency the Doombots had been called away to was occupying them fully.

Johnny led them to the back of town, away from the main street. They flitted from doorway to doorway, keeping as low a profile as they could manage. Opening the door to a ramshackle building, Johnny ushered them inside. There were shelves filled with mining gear and appropriate clothing. Quill, encouraged by Johnny, clambered into a set of overalls. If they were spotted moving through town, they would register on first glance as miners and that would be fine. With one small problem.

"I'm real sorry about your mechanical friend," he apologized. "Ain't sure we can disguise her easily."

"I could put on a helmet," said Cora. "Star-Lord said that wearing a hat was enough for him not to be noticed by the Doombots."

"Hoisted," said Quill, gloomily, "by my own petard."

It was a ridiculous notion, but Cora put on a helmet anyway. In the event, they were not spotted and despite his misgivings at the whole "hiding in plain sight" ploy, he had to concede that it had been a smart move. Better safe than obliterated by Doombots.

Now they traversed the upper level of a mine shaft, heading into the Black Hills. The further in they got, the more easily Johnny seemed to move. Quill, by comparison, found the fading light made his progress difficult and he could not help but marvel at how easily a blind boy travelled the workings. Once they'd entered the tunnels, Quill engaged his helmet. It offered decent infra-red, but even that didn't stop him from stumbling on the loose shale underfoot. Johnny moved swiftly, followed by Cora, and Quill did his best to keep up.

He sensed the slope beneath their feet, and it became apparent that they were getting deeper and further away from Doomwood. At least, presumably they were. Quill's sense of direction was muddled down here.

In the end, it was Cora who spoke. "Where are we, Johnny Loomis?"

"A secret tunnel," he said, his voice carrying back. "It connects to the main branch in the mines." The ceiling was getting lower and the space increasingly claustrophobic. "It's not much further – another hundred yards or so – and we'll spill out into the main tunnel. It's tough going if you're not used to it."

Even as he spoke, Quill tripped, putting his hands out to catch himself. He uttered a series of curses muffled by the helmet. Johnny glanced back over his shoulder.

"Are you OK, Mr Star-Lord?"

"I'm fine, kid…" *Kid.* "It's just hard to navigate down here, even with this on." He tapped the side of his helmet. This was immediately punctuated with a loud *clang* as his head connected with an overhang. "For *flark's* sake! Who cut this tunnel? A leprechaun?"

"I cut it," said Loomis, quietly. That explained why he moved so easily down here despite his blindness. This was his domain. Quill felt bad for his derision, mellowing the follow-up. Humor was his go-to defense.

"Isn't there, like, a triple XL tunnel? One that isn't designed for twigs?"

"This is the *safe* way," replied Loomis. "The secret way. There's only one Doombot stationed within this mine system, and it passes by the same spot at the same time every day."

Quill lapsed back into silence, concentrating on his footing. Cora continued her questions and observations.

"I have noticed that there are many who are blind as you are, Johnny Loomis."

"Yeah," he said, not fazed by her observation. "They tell me it's because of the radiation. But it's OK, Miss Cora. I hear. I smell. I can feel… The other senses fill in the blanks for me. That's why they put me down in the mines. It's why the White Queen chose me."

"How did she 'choose' you, Johnny Loomis?"

The boy paused for a moment – something which Quill, still stumbling his way around, was immensely glad for – and turned.

"She came to me," he replied. "In a dream. Except… well, it wasn't actually a dream. I saw her in my mind as though she were standing right in front of me. She looked like an *angel*." The boy sighed a little, the sign of the besotted. "She told me things and, well, I told *her* things."

"What things did you tell her?"

"All sorts of things. But I don't always speak to her. I talk to her with my mind. Does that make sense?" Johnny started walking again, ushering them on. He had slowed now, taking additional care.

"Can you give me an example?" Cora prompted him to continue. She was managing the mine very well. She was lithe and compact with precision instruments that helped her avoid collisions. Behind her, Quill continued to collide with every available surface.

Johnny considered his response before nodding. "Yeah. Before I lost my eyesight, I saw a picture that had been torn out from an old magazine and tacked to a wall. It was a photo of Captain America. There he was, standing on top of a pile of rubble, holding a flag."

"That sounds *right* on brand," muttered Quill.

"I only saw that picture a couple of times," said Johnny, "but it stayed in my head. Every detail about it. It's really hard to explain. But Captain America… I wanted him to be my friend, to be my dad… and I wanted to be him. All at the same time." He laughed, embarrassed at his own words. "Maybe that's dumb."

"It's not dumb, kid," said Quill, with clear sympathy in his voice. "We *all* felt that way about Captain America."

"The White Queen says that you used to be a hero, Mr Star-Lord. She says you actually knew Captain America."

How to respond to that simple line? So much connected to it. Quill sighed inwardly. "Yeah, it was a long time ago. A *really* long time ago but I did know him, yeah."

"He was real? Not just made up?" There was such awe in the boy's tone and Quill wondered how truly awful it must be to live and grow in a world with no heroes.

"Cap was as real as it gets. He was a good man."

"It seems to me that he was too good to be true. Like someone made him up to make the world seem better."

"Don't say that." Quill shook his head. "Look, kid. I do my best, but I'm not exactly an angel. But for Cap – all that boy scout crap about honesty, integrity, bravery…" He punctuated each word with a thump to his chest. "That was all *real* for him. He lived by his principles. He'd starve if he thought someone else would eat. He'd die if he thought it meant someone else might live. I guess he *did* die. For exactly that reason. We owe it to him to keep right on fighting."

Quill didn't know whether to pity the long-deceased Captain America or envy him.

Further discussion on the matter was stalled when Johnny put up his hand. "This is it. The entrance to the main tunnel. We're here." He put his back into moving a stack of stones piled up against the wall. It became clear that its purpose was to hide the entrance to this secret tunnel linking it to the artery of the mine.

Stepping forward, Quill helped without comment. Together, they moved the mass of rocks and eventually the opening was wide enough to allow them all to pass through. They had to crawl to reach the broad tunnel beyond and Quill stood with a grunt as his knees protested, but he was grateful to simply be able to stand up straight.

Somewhere far away, they heard the distant *clink* of mining. Picks and hammers rang out as they struck the rock, digging for seams, or given what Quill had learned, maybe just digging for *something*. There were lights in the tunnel – not many – and they were distantly spaced, but just enough to see what was going on.

"I'm glad I can stand," Quill confided. "I was getting a real case of the scaries back there." He rolled his shoulders with a wince. Even though this passage was high enough to stand, he was acutely aware that they were now deep underground and that brought a level of discomfort with it.

"There could be a lot of traffic passing by. We can't hang around."

"All right. Tell us what to do next, kid."

Johnny nodded. "Have you got the device?"

Quill also nodded, holding up an object. Loomis reached

out and put his hand to it, getting a feel for the shape and size of it. Anxiety clouded his features. "I'm sorry to question you, Mr Star-Lord, but are you sure this isn't a bomb?"

"It's not a bomb, kid. It's an EMP generator."

"What's an EMP?"

Cora supplied the answer. "An electro-magnetic pulse generator built by Joanna Forge. Once Star-Lord detonates it, it will disable all electrical signals within a ten-yard radius."

Quill nodded. "That Doombot is going to go lights out. Cora, you're gonna have to stay outside the zone."

"You're sure that it's safe?" Johnny persisted. "It's just that cave-ins *do* happen. There's about a quarter mile of rock directly over our heads."

That was not a visual that Quill needed, and he paled beneath his helmet. "We get it, Johnny," he said. "There's no Second Dawn if we're lost to the dark." He reached out, squeezing the boy's shoulder reassuringly. It was enough to satisfy him.

"All right. There's an intersection up ahead. About ten steps or so from here. That's where the Doombot is going to be passing by on patrol."

"How long are we going to have to wait."

"Not long," said Johnny. "Any minute, in fact."

Quill nodded. "Cora, keep your distance."

"I will remain here."

This was it. This was where the revolution began. Quill flipped the switch on the EMP and a low hum filled the tunnel as the device began charging. Once it was ready, a steady green light winked on. Quill nodded at Cora and tapped Johnny's arm to get his attention. "This thing is charged and ready to go. The Doombot should drop as soon as the pulse hits."

"Please hurry, Mr Star-Lord," said Johnny, urgently. Quill knelt, setting the device down, then burying it as best he could. "Hurry," said Johnny again. "I think it's coming."

"What?"

"Johnny Loomis says he thinks that the Doombot is coming," said Cora, helpfully. "He is correct." The distant hiss and clank confirmed her assertion.

Quill nodded, his heart hammering in his chest. "All right. Go. Go. Let's go!"

They pressed back into the side tunnel, Quill successfully smacking his head off a beam yet again. Outside, the sound of the approaching Doombot grew louder. Quill took a deep breath. "Almost there…" he whispered.

*Clank. Hiss. Clank. Hiss.* Almost close enough to touch.

"C'mon," urged Quill. They wouldn't know if the device would work until the Doombot's proximity activated it, which would be…

…right now…

Quill had expected some sort of noise. Perhaps the sound of the Doombot crashing to the ground as all its systems stalled. What he had not expected to hear was the hair-raisingly familiar whine of discharging electricity. Neither had he expected to hear the Doombot's voice raise in pitch and volume.

"Emergency. Activating Emergency protocol."

"Something's gone wrong," said Quill, urgently. In the tunnel, the Doombot's voice juddered strangely. Loomis put a hand up to his head in wonder.

"My hair," he said. "It's standing on end."

"Emergency p…p…protocol… 323."

"I think that the Doombot is preparing an attack," said

Cora. A crackle of building electricity could be heard, similar to what Quill had experienced in Doomwood. "The EMP did not work, Star-Lord. At least, not entirely as planned. The Doombot must have a secondary generator."

"What does that mean, Cora?" His tone was harsher than he had intended, but Quill was fairly certain he knew what it meant. He did not like it. Not one bit. Cora turned to him.

"The Doombot has activated an emergency protocol and will defend itself with extreme prejudice. In a matter of seconds, the main tunnel and this offshoot will be flooded with electrical discharge."

"Not the answer I wanted to hear, Cora."

"But it is the answer to the question you asked," she said. There was no time to argue further because what she had described almost immediately happened.

"Emergency. Insurgents must be eliminated!" The sizzle of electricity peaked and lightning arced through the side tunnel. Johnny dropped first, convulsing as the Doombot's assault racked his frail body.

"It hurts, Mr Star-Lord! It burns!"

Quill could offer no words of comfort as the crackling current surged through his own flesh. His bones filled with agony and nerves twitched in paroxysms as his teeth locked in a chattering rictus, and through it all he still heard the Doombot.

"Terminate all... terminat... terminate all surrounding threats."

The snap and crackle of the onslaught was drowned out by the grinding of stone and earth as millions of tons of rock began to crumble above them.

Johnny held out a hand to him. "Please!"

Quill summoned all his strength and powers to resist, and he dove towards the boy. Johnny's fear was his fault and that was the thought that lodged in his mind.

*This is all my fault.*

# CHAPTER TWELVE
## BURIED

The two horses moved as quickly as the broken plains allowed, the bruised skies still recovering from the thunderstorm looming large behind them. Joanna Forge sat atop a huge, thickly muscled animal, riding with the ease of one who had ridden all her life. Beside her, being jolted uncomfortably in the saddle, was Rocket. He was rapidly reaching the conclusion that his horse was the devil spawn and if he ever saw it again, it would be too soon.

"We have to move faster," he said through teeth being clashed together by the horse's gait. He reached up to scratch at his neck where until recently, the guillotine collar had sat rubbing against his fur. Through Forge's expertise, precision instruments and no small amount of sheer bloody luck, she had successfully removed the collar and with it, the imminent threat of decapitation. But now they had a new problem.

There was *always* a new problem.

"Did you hear me, Forge? We've got to move!"

"Do you want your horse to break a leg? Do you want to go sliding off this ridge? Look around, Rocket. This is rough country. We can't go any faster without risking ourselves or the horses."

"We've got less than an hour to get to him. After that…" Rocket drew his paw across his neck to indicate what would happen in less than an hour. Forge shot him a glance that wasn't entirely unsympathetic.

"We've got plenty of time. The mine isn't much further."

Rocket shifted in his saddle and scowled. "If only these flarking horses had nitro boosters. You definitely got the tools?"

"You already asked."

"Maybe. But you didn't check, did you? If you had actually checked when I asked, I wouldn't be bothering you now, would I?"

Forge glowered and with a click and a touch on the reins, brought her horse to a stop. Rocket floundered for a moment with his uncooperative animal before it also came to a halt. Forge stared at Rocket before opening the saddlebag. She lifted the tool free and held it up. "See? The same vibranium laser saw I used on you. Satisfied?"

Rocket shook his head. "What if we're too late? What if we've got the timings wrong?"

Forge put the saw away carefully, twisting her body so that she could study him more closely. "What happened to the tough-guy act?"

"Excuse me for worrying about my friend! Why have we stopped? That's the opposite of what we need to be doing!" He snapped his reply angrily and Forge prepared an equally cutting retort. Before she could speak, a noise sounded from one of the many pouches she wore at her waist. She opened it up, taking out what looked to Rocket's eyes to be a tracker. Her brow furrowed.

"That's unexpected," she said.

Rocket craned forward. "What's that?"

"It's the other half of the transponder I planted on Cora," replied Forge. While they'd been in the armory, she told Rocket all that had transpired with the recorder. Rocket approved – in principle; he'd not trusted the Rigellean since they'd found her. He had then, being consumed with anxiety over the collar situation, forgotten about it. The transponder went off again. "This isn't good."

"What do you mean, *this isn't good*? Give me more than that! What does that even *mean*? Why is it going off? What's happening?" His questions came out in a tumble. Forge pressed a button on the transponder's side, stopping the noise. She turned her attention back to Rocket.

"It's an emergency beacon. It goes off if the host is in a crisis situation." She gathered the reins of the horse and prepared to set off again. "Something's happened in the mines."

"Isn't it a communication device? Call up the surveillance feed."

Forge nodded, pressing another button. There was a crackling sound, suggesting the line was open but that there was nothing to hear. The static-laced silence stretched painfully. Rocket's heart sank.

"Let's go," said Forge, snapping the reins and kicking the horse with her heels. It set off at speed. Rocket grasped for his reins and urged his own horse on as well, but it didn't move quite as quickly.

"Hey! Wait for me!"

They raced towards the mine shaft where they now knew for certain that they would find those they were looking for. Exactly *what* they would find remained uncertain.

What they found was a scene of utter devastation. The cave-in had blocked a vast stretch of the tunnel and as Forge and Rocket moved towards it, having left the horses tied up above ground, the chances of finding anything alive seemed to grow smaller with every step. But the transponder continued receiving the distress message and that allowed them to at least triangulate a position. Without waiting for Forge to direct him, Rocket dove into the dust and rubble and began scrabbling and pulling at rocks.

"You're in the wrong spot," said Forge.

"I know what I'm doing. Help me or shut up." He was furious and terrified and Forge – for once – didn't retort. She continued studying the transponder to locate Cora, which took her to the far side of the cave-in.

"Rocket," she called out. "The geolocater pins her here. Under this part of the collapse."

"You follow your compass, I'll follow my nose," he snarled. He was desperate now to get to his friend and barely paid any attention to her. She considered repeating what she'd said but then decided against it. He was too agitated right now. She moved to the area she'd pinpointed and began hefting rocks.

"Be careful, or you'll bring down the whole tunnel," she observed as Rocket's desperate excavation attempts became frantic.

"You know what I hate more than the possibility of an entire hill flattening my ass?"

"What?"

"Back seat drivers!"

The two exchanged glares.

"I already regret saving your stupid neck."

"We're running out of time, Forge! It'd help if you could do something like use your cybernetics to just… blast through this rock and then get us out of here."

"There was an Elite once who had those kinds of powers. However, we don't have him here. There's just *us*, Rocket – and we are going to do better if we both work together rather than…" She broke off, letting out a sudden gasp. "Hey, hey! I've got an arm! Come help me out here!" Indeed, she had located the slender arm of the Rigellian Recorder. Once she had cleared past the wrist, Rocket believed her and together they worked to uncover most of Cora's body. "Well, would you look at that," she said. "We've struck gold!

"Thank you, Joanna Forge," said Cora, attempting to move from where she was still partially covered.

"Here. Take my hand. I can pull you out the rest of the way." Cora lifted a hand and locked it around Forge's forearm. With a hefty tug, the blacksmith managed to pull the synthbot from her rocky prison. Rocket looked up at her anxiously.

"How do you feel, Cora?"

"I am damaged," she replied, perhaps redundantly given the circumstances, "but functional."

Forge clapped her gleefully on the shoulder. "Good thing I made you swallow that transponder! Otherwise, you'd be lost for another thirty years."

Rocket resumed digging in the area where they had located Cora, hurling rocks to the side.

"I think I've got him!" He was excited to see the hint of fabric beneath the rock. He paused to cough, the dust and exertion momentarily overwhelming, but after a couple of moments resumed digging, calling out desperately to his friend.

"Quill! Quill, talk to me, you flarking idiot!" There was no response. No return jibe, no snide comment. Just... *nothing*. "Quill! So help me, man. If you're dead, I am gonna *kill* you!"

"What happened, Cora?" Forge posed the question as they assisted the frantic Rocket. The recorder paused and replayed the last few moments through her internal systems before she answered.

"After the Doombot short-circuited," she said, "and as the cave-in began, the last thing I remember recording was the sight of Star-Lord throwing his body over that of Johnny Loomis." Rocket let out a strange sound at this. The little creature was rarely bestial, despite his appearance, but it sounded very much like a pitiful whine.

"Quill," he said, and he'd stopped shouting now. The trio continued tugging rocks aside until they finally unearthed Peter Quill, lying still and unmoving on the tunnel floor. He was face-down and from the tangle of limbs it was clear he was lying on top of Johnny Loomis. "Quill! Come on man, wake up. Wake up!" He shook the unresponsive body, turned Quill halfway over. "He's not breathing! Are they..."

"I am detecting a heartbeat," said Cora. "One of them is alive. The other is not."

"Quill!" Rocket roared the single syllable and then there was a sound. A choking, gagging sound as if the man were fighting a losing battle to breathe. Cora shook her head.

"The time has expired," she said.

"What?"

"The guillotine collar will now activate, begin to constrict and terminate Star-Lord. We are too late."

"Forge!" Rocket whipped his head round to the blacksmith. "The laser saw!" But she was already a step ahead of him and had taken the tool from her bag. She moved forward, gesturing to Rocket to get out of her way – which he did without hesitation. "Hurry," he said and there was a plea in his tone. "Hurry."

Forge knelt before the stricken Quill, bringing the tool up to the guillotine collar. There was a sizzling snap as the beam met the adamantium and sparks flew as she began to cut. Beneath her, the man began to make choking sounds again.

"You've got to hurry," said Rocket, wringing his paws together.

"You want me to slip and cut his throat? Shut up and let me work!" She resumed the task, bringing the laser saw back to the collar. Inch by agonizing inch, she sliced the beam through the adamantium band. It was intense, arduous work made more difficult by the struggles of the slowly asphyxiating Peter Quill. Finally, she completed the cut, shut off the tool and set it aside. "There," she said.

She stretched out, tugging the collar loose. It fell to the mine floor with a loud clang, a noise that seemed incongruous with the comparative size of the thing. Quill, freed from its constriction, drew a deep, ragged breath, then let it back out in a gasp. He gulped greedily at the air then began to cough uncontrollably.

"He's OK," said Rocket, then moved to Quill's side. "You're OK! You're alive!" In his relief, Rocket didn't even bother to insult him. Quill flapped a hand at him, then slow recollection came to him. He looked at Cora and croaked out a question.

"What about Johnny?" Nothing but silence answered him. "What about the kid?" All eyes shifted to the broken body of the young man who had been shielded by Quill's bulk. But Quill had not been enough.

Cora started to respond, but Forge silenced her with a steel grip to the shoulder. She reached into her bag and took out a small pack which she unzipped. "This will help with the pain," she said to Quill and stabbed a syringe into a vein in his neck. He yelped at the suddenness of the shot and in a few short moments the powerful sedative took hold of him, and he drifted off into blissful oblivion.

"We need to get back to the armory," said Forge. "Let's get the rest of these rocks off him and head back out there." She paused, just for a heartbeat. "And let's take Johnny home, too. He deserves that, at least."

Annie Creek Falls were located seven miles from the mineshaft and although the ride back was slower, they still covered the ground swiftly. Forge carried the unconscious Quill on her horse while Cora joined Rocket. They moved through desiccated woodlands until the trees thinned. From there, they followed the banks of a sluggish river upstream to the falls.

They followed a narrow trail leading to the waterfall where a small, fenced paddock was set back a little way. Forge led them in and they dismounted. She took the unconscious form of Peter Quill, slinging him unceremoniously over her shoulder. She led the way up the remainder of the path and pressed through the sheet of falling water, emerging into the cave hidden behind it.

By the time Quill began to surface from the drug-induced slumber, Forge had settled him on a makeshift cot at the back of one of the caves. As he bobbed in and out of wakefulness, he was vaguely aware of a fuzzy, monochromatic face filling his vision. Every time his eyes fluttered open, the face spoke his name until he was finally able to fasten onto consciousness and his attendant.

"I feel *terrible*," he said, groaning loudly.

"Easy, buddy, you're safe." Rocket folded his arms across his chest. "I don't *believe* you!"

"What the heck happened?"

"Where to start? All right. Well, an entire *mountain* fell on you. Then the guillotine collar started to constrict and choke you out. We got to you and saved you. Don't thank me, I know I'm good." Quill struggled to rise and Rocket softened. "Let me help you sit up." He put out a paw and hauled his friend up to a sitting position. He offered a drink of water which Quill accepted. Then memory surfaced from the sludge of the post-narcotic quagmire.

"Johnny," he said, softly. "He's dead, right?" Rocket hesitated, then nodded affirmation. Quill shook his head. "He was just a kid, man. Just a kid." He pinched the bridge of his nose and sighed heavily. "I'm an old man. Worthless. Don't you tell me that eight million times a day as it is? I'm still here when I shouldn't be. I shouldn't be the one who walks away alive." He looked at Rocket with anguish in his eyes. "Not again."

"Quill," said Rocket, his tone firm. "Listen to me. You did what you could."

Quill shook his head. "Not again, man. I can't do it again."

"Forget about it, Quill. Just… forget about it."

"But I don't *want* to forget it!"

An uncomfortable silence descended and all that could be heard for a few moments was the distant roar of the falls and the *drip-drip* of the moisture within the caves. Cora broke the stalemate.

"What do you not want to forget, Star-Lord?"

Rocket rounded on her and growled. "Not *now*, Cora."

"Why not now?" Quill rubbed at his eyes. "She's a recorder. She may as well hear it. Rocket's been right this whole time, Cora. I'm not a hero."

"I talk trash sometimes," interrupted Rocket. "But that doesn't mean…"

"I shouldn't have left them," said Quill.

"Left who, Star-Lord?"

"Drax," said Quill, wretchedly. "Groot. Gamora. I shouldn't have left them."

"Will you tell me about it?"

Quill nodded and Rocket no longer protested the revelation. Instead, he sat back on his haunches. "It was a smash-and-grab mission," he began, his eyes locked on Quill. His friend looked grateful for the support in reliving the story. "Some assassin named Rucka had been taking out an imperial family one by one. Then he went dark, and we were hired to hunt him down. There was this star system…"

"Mortem Novis," supplied Quill and Rocket nodded.

"It's called the Mortem Novis, that's right. Makes the

Wastelands look like a walk in the park. There's not a star at its center, but a huge planet. Massive. There's a smaller, molten sun orbiting it." Rocket shook his head. "It's messed up."

"Everything in that place is upside down and sideways. Including time." Quill took up the thread. "There's energy spikes and dips when the suns come in and out of alignment every day... is that how it works, Rocket?"

"Yeah. Exactly that."

"When it happens, it creates... well, the best way to describe the phenomena I guess would be 'time warps.'"

"What do you mean by that, Star-Lord?"

"Things speed up," Quill responded. "Then they slow down."

"*Way* up," said Rocket. "*Way* down. It's one of the things that makes that system one great place to hide out. The planet itself is a maze of underground bays and bunkers. All the time you're underground, you're fine. When you get out in the open air, you risk exposure to the flux."

"So that's where Rucka was holed up," said Quill. He looked at Rocket and the two dropped into silence, reliving the whole thing as though it had just happened.

# CHAPTER THIRTEEN
## MORTEM NOVIS

### THE MILANO, MORTEM NOVIS
### SOMETIME IN THE PAST

The *Milano* decelerated, adjusting course on her final approach. Thrusters flared, adding their own percussive sound to the rhythmic thump of a heavy metal song that Quill had selected for this moment. He checked a few instruments, then spoke into the comms. "How's the crypto coming on that hangar door, Rocket?"

"Already hacked it." Rocket's response brought a huge grin to Quill's face.

"Man, we're *good*. All right. One minute until go-time. Everyone ready? Check in. Groot?"

"I am Groot."

"You absolutely *are*, Groot. Drax?"

"My blood boils and my entire body is turgid with excitement as I contemplate the battle to come, Peter Quill. I will…"

"Great, yep, great. How about you, Gamora? How are you feeling?"

"I'm ready to end this gig. Because once we get paid, *someone* promised a vacation." Gamora's voice fluted across the comms and Quill chuckled.

"Don't worry, Gamora. I promise you that the lavender baths of Echo Moon are just *waiting* for us." The moment of levity was broken before it really had a chance when Rocket spoke up.

"I don't know, Quill. I've got a real bad feeling."

"What, you don't think we deserve a little spa treatment? A little pampering? C'mon, Rock, it's…"

"No, I mean about this job. I've got a bad feeling."

"Buddy, you have bad feelings about *everything*. Let me find a better music track…" The airwaves were suddenly filled with an entirely new blast of music, a pounding, driving rock track that – to Quill's mind, at least – conveyed energy and excitement. It didn't get quite the reaction he expected.

"Turn it *off*, Quill. I'm *serious*." Startled by the depth of anger he heard in the demand, Quill did just that and calm settled. "Thank you! Look, wouldn't it be a safer bet if we just, I don't know, set up a fake job, lure Rucka out, and snatch him then?"

"Rocket, man, we already talked about this. It could be a week. And a week out here is like a million years."

"You have the attention span of a toddler. Anybody ever tell you that?"

"Yeah, you. Look. This is *cooler*. Way more heroic and badass. Way more *Guardians*."

"Fine. All right. My readings suggest we've got ten minutes before a temporal flux."

Quill, the relentless optimist, laughed derisively. "Ah, we'll be out in five," he said. "Easy peasy, lemon squeezy."

There was a pause. Then:

"Don't *ever* say that again."

Quill chuckled, checking the instruments again. "All right, Guardians. The *Milano* is coming into the hangar hot. I'm opening the ramp now. Roll on out and we'll follow. Everybody good?"

Drax responded first, his deadpan tone coming over the airwaves. Quill was fond of Drax in the strangest way and his response now merely fluffed that affection more. "If by 'good' you mean, am I ready to grind the bones of my enemies to dust after I sup on their marrow, then yes, Peter Quill. I am good."

"I am Groot."

"We're *all* good, Peter," said Gamora, bringing the trio of responses to its conclusion.

Quill nodded. "Make sure you stay that way, baby."

"Please. Save it for later," growled Rocket, and Quill turned his focus to the important task of bringing the *Milano* into the hangar. She glided in smoothly enough, and, as she always had done, she responded to Quill's handling like a dream. He banked a little on the landing and the *Milano* came to a skidding halt.

"OK, we're in. Masks on. Stun him with the gas for extraction." Quill flicked a few switches, preparing the *Milano* for their escape. Gamora confirmed.

"Masks on," she said, her voice more muffled than previously. "Exiting the *Milano* and entering the hangar now."

Quill leaned back in his seat, hefting his boots up onto the console. He provided his own commentary as he often did. "So, this is Rucka's safe hidey hole. Chances are, we're gonna catch this guy with his pants down while watching cartoons. Isn't *any* way he knows we're about to hit him…"

Any further discussion on the subject came to an abrupt

halt as a missile smashed into the *Milano* from behind. Quill was thrown forwards, dumped unceremoniously on the deck. Several discordant alarms activated at once, filling the ship's interior with their wailing.

"Quill? What the *flark* was that?"

"That came from behind us, Rocket. Someone's *behind* us!" Another missile struck the *Milano* and the wailing became more insistent.

"The hell, Quill? Weren't you tracking the radar?"

"I was focused on what was in *front* of me, not what was *behind* me! Shut up while I..." Quill was grateful for the fact he'd made enough escape preparations to keep the engines warm, which mercifully responded to his controls. The *Milano* fired up and he wheeled her around to face whatever threat waited for them.

"I told you I had a bad feeling about this," roared Rocket across the comms. Quill saw on the video feed that he was at the door of the cockpit, so Quill got the rage in stereo. "But no! You..."

"It's him, Rocket," said Quill. "Rucka." He pushed forward on the throttle and the *Milano* gathered speed as he headed straight out of the hangar.

"Wait, what are you doing? Stop, Quill! Get back into the hangar right now!"

"He shot us, Rocket. We shoot him back. It's simple *math*." Quill was deeply offended by having been caught on the back foot and he was going to make this son of a camel dealer's daughter *pay*.

"Quill! The team's on the ground out there and our booster is *shot*."

"He's right here, Rocket! Let's finish the job and shoot him out of the sky."

"We have to abort this mission, you hear me?"

"Guardians," said Quill, "close the hangar door and hang tight. We'll be right back."

Rocket slid into the co-pilot seat and put his paw on Quill's arm. "If Groot gets hit by the flux and ends up as bleached driftwood, so help me I'll cut your flarking throat!"

"They'll be fine, Rocket." Quill squeezed the triggers, firing several optimistic shots at the nimble speeder bike that had ambushed them. They streaked across the gulf of space, going wide of their mark. He cursed beneath his breath. "This would be better with music," he muttered. "Hold on, guys. I'll be right back."

"Only I *wasn't* right back," said Quill. The cave had remained quiet while Quill and Rocket had told the sorry tale and Cora had not interrupted. Now, though, she prompted for a continuation.

"What happened?"

"I was outmaneuvered," said Quill, appearing, for the first time since they had found Cora on the *Prosperity*, like the old man he staunchly refused to accept that he was. There was infinite pain in his eyes, a grief he had borne since it happened. "Trying to track a dude on a cosmic bike is like… trying to catch a bee with your bare hands. Ran out of time."

"We had to leave," said Rocket. "Before the next flux. We were gone for an hour. Just… an hour."

"An hour for us," said Quill, then he went quiet. Finishing this story was tough and he struggled to get it out. When he did, his tone was leaden, the pain evident. "It was a century for them."

"'Them'?" Cora sought clarification.

"The Guardians, Cora." Quill looked at her. "The *real* Guardians of the Galaxy."

"The hangar door was damaged during the firefight," said Rocket. "They couldn't close it in time. They got hit by the next temporal flux."

The reality of this revelation was shocking and for once Cora didn't feel the need to fill the silence. She waited until Quill recovered enough to finish. "My friends died because of me."

Rocket laid a paw on his arm. "It's time to move on, man."

Quill shook his head. "This isn't something I can just forget…" he began, but Rocket kept going.

"I didn't say 'forget'. I said move on. Look, Quill, if I've managed to do it, you can as well. They were my friends, too."

"It's not just that day, though. It's all the days before it. It's about who I am, Rocket. My dad…"

"You are not your dad. You are not J'Son. You never were, you never will be."

"I'm *just* like him, Rocket. He's a criminal. A killer." He put up his hands and made air quotes around his next words. "Mister Knife of the Slaughter Lords. I did *everything* in my power to make sure I didn't turn out like him and how did I end up? Just like him."

"Quill, again. You are *nothing* like him. Will you please get that through your thick skull? Sure, you screw up from time to time, but…" Rocket struggled to get the next words out, whether because he didn't believe them or because it was just emotionally difficult was hard to tell. "But you've got a heart the size of a flarking planet. OK?"

"Spare me the…"

But Rocket was in full flow now.

"Shut up, Quill. Shut *up*. Do you think Cora would be here if you'd left it up to me? Hell, no. I'd have sent her straight to the recycling bin. You risked everything to save Sebastian Warn from Kraven even when you were told to stay put. You *always* do crap like that. You know." He waved a paw. "Good deeds." His snout wrinkled in disgust. "It drives me *nuts*. Look. I know I'm not the kind of guy who does this deep stuff, but what you're doing right now is a full reversal of what you did that day on Mortem Novis."

He paused for breath. He knew he had everyone's attention now and while Rocket rarely had trouble speaking his mind, this was *different*. This was *personal*. This was *difficult*.

"That day, you missed that Rucka was behind us. You haven't stopped looking back ever since. Look. Quill, the fact is, well, we aren't the Guardians anymore, just like America's not America. We've got to find some way to – heck, I don't flarking know – honor their legacy, while at the same time chase something better."

"Yeah?" There was such hope in Quill's voice that it almost broke Rocket's sturdy little heart.

"*Hell* yeah. We got folks right here who want to fight. So, let's fight."

"Rocket, what are you saying? You want to stay? I thought you wanted us to get the Black Vortex and bail out of here." Quill was puzzled by this change of heart, but not displeased.

"The urgency to get out of here lessened since Forge got rid of the collars." Rocket folded his arms across his chest. "Someone's got to fix this wreck of a planet, right? You made it out of that cave-in alive. You're still standing, Quill. You've had a sentimental moment, hooray, well done. Now it's time to get off your butt and get back to work. Can you stand?"

Carefully, Quill achieved just that. He looked down at his friend. "What's the plan?"

"Time to meet the crew that's going to help us get our sweet backsides into Doom's compound."

This far behind the waterfall, the distant roar of the water was little more than a muted rumble. Rocket guided Quill into a sandy-bottomed chamber, Cora trailing behind them. There was more space here and it evidently served as some sort of workshop. Forge stood over the recovered Doombot that had brought the tunnels down, systematically deconstructing it. The air was filled with the sound of power tools as she bored out rivet after rivet. Yet it wasn't to this sight that Quill's eyes were drawn, but to the man sitting on a workbench in the corner. A slow grin spread across his face as the unmistakable figure of Red Crotter raised a hand in greeting.

"There he is!" He waved at Quill, a smirk on his face.

"Holy hell, *Red*! How are you even still alive?"

Red laughed and dropped down off the workbench. "Same could be said about you, Old Man Quill. Don't mind me saying this, I'm sure, but you look like *hell*."

"You live through hell, you look like hell, I suppose." Quill scratched at his beard. "It's good to see you again, man. It really is."

"We gonna hug?"

"Sure, Just… gently."

The two old men came together in a brief, fierce embrace

that they held for a couple of moments before covering up their emotion with burly back-thumps that made Quill wince in pain. Red released him and they dropped into silence punctuated with the sounds of Joanna Forge pulling the Doombot apart, slowly spreading the automaton's anatomy out like a surgeon's exploded diagram. Quill turned his attention away from the sight and focused on Red.

"What happened? Back at the farm?"

Red shrugged one shoulder. "They came for me. Just like I predicted. Nighttime raid. A posse of men with their sights set on a bounty. They were looking for blood."

"What then? You kicked out their teeth and stole their lunch money?"

"I mean, that would be great, but no. Not quite. Did do my best though. I unloaded enough buckshot to make my hands go numb. But there were more of them than me. They made short work of stripping me and tying me down. Made me watch as they torched everything. The cabin, the barn, the stable, even the chicken coop."

"How are you smiling after that?"

"Because it was how I'd always imagined going out," replied Red. "I guess I was… ready, you know? To say goodbye to it all and move on."

*Move on.* That phrase, coming again so soon after Rocket's recent words, was hard to hear. "But you're here," he said, pushing through melancholy. "You're *here*."

"I'm here because my cabin wasn't the only thing burning that night out in the Wastelands."

Quill's eyes widened as he instantly jumped to the only available conclusion. "The *Ghost Riders*?"

"You got it. *Thwack*! A flaming arrow took one guy out – hit him right in the eye. Another got it in the chest. Another, in the guts. It was carnage. Then the Ghost Riders came pounding out of the darkness, horses screaming like banshees. I tell you this for nothing – if I'd have been wearing britches, I'd have filled them at that point." Quill was caught up in the story and even Rocket hadn't commented. Red laughed. "Then they just out and asked me if I wanted to ride with them. I said yes. I said *hell, yes*."

Cora spoke. "Now you are dressed all in black. You have a quiver on your back. The ultimate conclusion is that the Ghost Riders have joined the Second Dawn."

The enormity of the recorder's statement was shocking enough that Quill was speechless. Red nodded at Cora. "That's exactly it. Everybody's had enough. Everyone is coming together."

Behind them, the sound of drilling and cutting continued and then there was a sudden loud metallic *clank*.

"I'm in," said Joanna Forge. "Systems are all yours, Rocket."

Rocket bared his fangs in a slow grin. "Well, it's about time."

Hacking the Doombot proved much tougher than Rocket said it would be. After a couple of hours of swearing and muttering, Forge quietly slipped him a pair of magnifying spectacles so that he could better see what he was doing. "It's darker than usual in these caves," Rocket claimed, daring anybody to suggest that the problem was his eyesight rather than the illumination.

Nobody suggested it and Rocket resumed his work. Another two hours passed before he breached the Doombot's internal security, and he began the even more arduous task of reprogramming it so that they could enact their plan.

While Rocket worked, with occasional input from Forge, the others focused on drawing together the disparate strands of what could loosely be referred to as "the plan". There was not going to be much time in which to get everything arranged but Peter Quill had never been the kind of man to give up at the first hurdle. Maybe the third hurdle – or once in a rare moment, when there was no other choice, the second – but never the first. No way.

He was still subdued following the experience in the mines, not to mention the emotional turmoil of voicing his guilt, so when Rocket finally confirmed that he had succeeded in reprogramming the Doombot, he felt a much-needed surge of elation.

"All right," he said, punching the air enthusiastically. "Let's *do* this."

"Is it working?"

"Oh yeah, it's working." The cave was filled with the noises of an active Doombot echoing from several salvaged speakers. Rocket was busy at a set of rudimentary controls that he and Forge had cobbled together and was concentrating on piloting the Doombot remotely. "Just a couple more moments until we get the visual feed online as well and this little baby will be perfect. A pretty good job if I say so myself."

"Yeah. You did good, Rocket." Quill shuffled impatiently, eager to see through the Doombot's eyes. He reached for something to fill the conversational void. "I gotta say... Doom has the *best* bad-guy look in world history, right?" Rocket shrugged silently, so Quill continued. "Something like that doesn't just occur naturally. It takes a whole *lot* of calculated effort."

"You got a point, Quill?" Rocket glanced up from his work.

"Of course I do. My point is… that I bet Doom is compensating for something."

"Excuse me, Star-Lord, but by that, are you implying that Doom is perhaps not as powerful as he seems?" Cora asked the question and Rocket snorted.

"He seems pretty powerful to me."

Quill flapped his hand vaguely. "I mean, yeah, he *seems* powerful. The costume's one thing. But look at the evidence. He's got Doombots roaming the Wastelands. He's got his *whole face* carved into mountains. There's a hidden stronghold that he never leaves… blah, blah, et cetera, et cetera. That is a *lot* of armor, don't you think? Wearing armor's a thing you don't do unless you're afraid of something."

"Joanna Forge?"

"Yeah, Cora?"

"When was the last time that Doom was actually seen?" The question came out of left field and Forge frowned as she pondered the answer. Then she shook her head.

"You know, I don't even reckon I could tell you. Fifteen years, maybe? Twenty perhaps? Maybe more. To be honest, if *I* was a warlord dictator, I'd choose to stay holed up myself – especially with telepaths like Emma Frost out there. He's only one psychic probe away from being a puppet like this Doombot. Speaking of which… visual link online." Forge indicated the cave wall where the dusty path of the Dakota hills flickered into sight.

"This is what the Doombot is seeing?" Quill turned his attention to the grainy visual. The quality wasn't perfect, but they'd been working to a tight schedule. It was certainly more than enough for their purposes. Quill had come, over the years, to expect nothing less from Rocket's handiwork.

"Yes," said Forge. "What you're seeing here is exactly what the Doombot sees. This array..." She indicated the controls and holographic display in front of Rocket, "is the remote pilot's control. It's pretty good. We work well together, Rocket. If you get bored of this loser..."

It was good-natured, but Quill felt a sudden chill. What if Rocket *did* like the idea of staying here and working with her? He put the thought aside and concentrated on the view as the Doombot stamped up the hill towards the stronghold. The path was studded at frequent intervals by torches and at more irregular intervals by corpses fully impaled on spikes. It was a gruesome sight, even secondhand, and Quill shuddered involuntarily. He looked over at Rocket. "We hike him up this gruesome hill, weave him through this avenue of corpses to the stronghold – then what happens?"

"We get him inside and we find the rest of the map. In and out as quick as we can because *someone* is going to notice," replied Rocket, deftly piloting the Doombot.

"A smash-and-grab operation," said Quill and Rocket nodded, glancing briefly over his shoulder. "How do we get inside? Some sort of secret knock? A password at the door?" He was being facetious and so was surprised by the initial reply.

"A password is more or less right. There's a transmitter in the thing's breastplate. Low power, limited range, rolling code. We get this tin can within twenty yards and the doors should recognize one of their own and open. So yeah. A password at the door. You see, Quill? You can be smart when you try."

"Uh, yeah. Thanks."

"OK, the compound is in sight. Here we go. Cora, are you picking up any reports?"

"Yes, Rocket. It appears that Red and the Ghost Riders are right on time and right on target," reported the recorder. "There is a transmission coming in now." She opened her speakers and played it so that they could all hear it.

*"All Doombots in the Doomwood vicinity are to report immediately to the oil refinery. A terrorist attack is underway. Message repeats: all Doombots in the Doomwood vicinity are to report immediately to the oil refinery..."*

"Good job, Red," said Rocket, turning his attention back to the Doombot's view. "All eyes are now looking in another direction." He watched as the vast fortress doors drew closer. There was a brief pause. "OK, this is it. Here we go. Yes. *Yes!*" There was a loud scrape as the doors received the Doombot's electronic ident and swung open. "Let's see if anybody's home!"

The Doombot headed inside, guided by Rocket with expert care, its heavy mechanical footsteps echoing around the huge hall as it proceeded into the compound. Rocket looked up at Quill. "So... this is where you come in, Quill."

"Yeah, right. Agatha – the librarian – she said that there was a high-ceilinged corridor, but I can't remember if she told me whether the war room was to the left or the right. Maybe being hit on the head by a mountain knocked it out of me. Left me a bit fuzzy."

"Huh," said Rocket. "That's not the mountain's fault."

"It was the first door on the left," supplied Cora, helpfully. Rocket nodded and steered the Doombot in the direction indicated.

"Knock, knock," he said and chuckled. The Doombot's

hand swung into view on the visual feed as it pushed the huge double doors open. The view tilted as the bot stepped into the room beyond, the echo of its footsteps fading. Torches lined the walls, their flames filling the chamber with an orange glow and weirdly dancing shadows.

"There," Quill said, pointing. "There. There's the throne Agatha described. The tables."

Rocket moved the Doombot closer. "Maps," he confirmed. "Maps, blueprints and survey reports."

"The War Room. But no Doom," said Quill.

"The torches are lit," pointed out Forge. "So, while he might not be here, I'd be prepared to wager that there's *someone* in earshot."

Quill nodded, agreeing with and appreciating her comment. "Can we make that thing go any faster, Rocket?"

"Enough with the backseat driving," Rocket snarled, clearly ruffled by the sudden urgency that had come with Forge's words.

She put a hand on his shoulder. "You might have seconds, not minutes," she said. Before she could continue, an entirely unexpected voice cut in from behind the Doombot.

*"Hey!"*

"Flark!" Rocket cursed. "Someone's here. Behind the Doombot!"

*"Hey!"* the voice exclaimed again. It sounded male and, as it continued, Quill felt a creeping sense of recognition. There was something familiar about the timbre, but not the tone, a voice outside its usual context. He tried to place it as he listened. *"What are you doing in here?"*

"Who is that?" Forge asked the question first, but Quill moved up to Rocket.

"Don't look back, Rocket. Don't stop now!"

"I'm not stopping," said Rocket in response. "Nor am I looking back."

*"Did you hear me?"* The speaker seemed more commanding now. *"You're not supposed to be in here."*

"I have analyzed the voice pattern," said Cora. "It indicates a match with the voice of Brandon Best."

Rocket stared at her. "That guy off the radio? What the *flark* is *he* doing here?"

Quill gestured at the projection on the wall. "The pedestal, Rocket. Get to the pedestal! The mirror is supposed to be on the pedestal!"

"Will you shut up already? You're *distracting* me!" Rocket was trying – and failing – to keep the panic from his voice. The man who may or may not have been Brandon Best spoke again.

*"All Doombots are supposed to report to the refinery."* The Doombot ignored him, moving towards the pedestal. Quill was practically hopping up and down with poorly concealed excitement.

"There it is! There's the mirror!" What they saw was identical to the mirror that was presently in Quill's possession. Excitement rippled through the room, but their time was growing very short.

*"Hey, Doombot! Didn't you hear what I said? The refinery is under attack!"*

"Lean in, Rocket. Or… zoom in. Or whichever does the job. Just do it quickly." The Doombot's visual feed suggested he had taken a couple of steps forward and was leaning slightly.

*"What are you doing? You're to report to the refinery immediately."* Stern. Commanding.

"I'm toggling the focus," said Rocket. "What can you see?"

"Nothing. I can't see anything."

*"Don't touch that mirror."*

"How about now? I'm focusing further. Can you see anything now? I'm focusing on the mir..." The feed went dark and Rocket slumped back into his chair. "Flark me!" He slapped his paw against the desk. "The signal's gone offline. Can we reconnect it?"

"The signal has gone dark, Rocket," said Cora.

"Well, fix it." Quill was desperate now. They'd come so close. So very, very close. "Fix it!"

"Fixing it is not possible, Star-Lord."

"Well, that's just great," said Rocket, furious now. "We went to all that trouble for absolutely *nothing*."

Quill's response was stained with the same despair that had marked him not so long ago. Rocket's words were right. They'd gone to all that trouble for nothing, but there was something even more personal than that. "Johnny," he said, his voice wrought with anxiety. "That poor kid. What a waste. He died for nothing as well."

"That is incorrect, Star-Lord. I was able to pick up an image in the mirror before the transmission ended." All eyes turned to the recorder and Quill's voice hitched with just a shred of hope.

"Cora? What did you see? What did the map say?"

"It said, in broken, shattered letters, The Slaughter Lords."

"The Slaughter Lords?" He shouldn't have been surprised, but he was. "That was his crew."

Forge held up a finger. "Wait. *Whose* crew?"

"J'Son's. J'Son was my father."

"Correction," said Cora. "It reads 'The Slaughtered Lords'. And then there is another thing. Two-point six. Eight. Six."

"Are those coordinates?" Quill was eager.

Rocket pondered. "Maybe a geo pin. What do you think, Cora?"

"I think that I know where we will find the Black Vortex," she replied.

Forge remained behind while the distraction at the oil refinery allowed the rest of the group to leave the caves and make their way through the woods unhindered, further concealed by the cover of night. Cora led them east, to an overgrown and untended cemetery. A sign hanging loosely from the entrance gate proclaimed it the Mount Moriah Cemetery. Quill stood for several moments studying it. The breeze lifted his scraggly hair, blowing it into his eyes and spoiling what he'd been sure had been a dramatic moment of realization. He was also pausing because he was *hugely* out of breath after the climb up the hill.

Rocket was also grateful for the pause, and he stood beside Quill, coughing as he tried to speak. "All this time… we thought Moriah was an actual mountain. It turns out to be a flarking cemetery." He coughed again and Quill glanced down at him, his brow furrowing briefly with concern for his friend. He knew Rocket well enough not to ask if he was all right.

"Doom did all that digging," he said, between deep breaths as his heart rate started to return to normal. "All that mining. Hundreds of miles of tunnels. But he only had to go six feet under."

"The map said two-point-six, eight, six," said Cora. "According to my search algorithms, two and a half by eight by six feet is the worldwide specification for grave digging."

Rocket squinted up at the sign again, then peered through the rusted railings. "Looks like nobody's been here in years."

"Maybe the local folks realized that all the way up here is *way* too far to lug a coffin?"

"I would hypothesize that it is more likely because Doomwood feeds its corpses to pigs rather than has them buried," offered Cora.

"Wait," said Quill and his stomach lurched. "We ate ham before we came out here."

"Then you probably ate recycled human." Rocket continued to cough and wheeze.

Quill could no longer contain his concern. "Rocket, are you OK, buddy?"

"Yeah. It's just…"

"The dust again?"

Rocket went to reply, but a deeper cough bent him over double. He hacked and wheezed for a few moments and then spat up a mouthful of something.

Quill stared. "Rocket? Was that… blood?"

"Don't be dumb. It was some recycled human, that's all." Rocket wiped at his mouth with the back of his arm and then pointed out over Doomwood. "Look down there. You see that?"

It was enough to distract Quill, who followed the direction of Rocket's point. "Yeah," he said. "The whole refinery is lit up."

"Looks like a volcano being born," said Rocket. "All those

drones, too. Zipping through the air down there. No doubt tracking the faces of everyone who's out tonight."

"Guess there's no more flirting with revolution," said Quill, engaged by the spectacle. "We've arrived. You know what that means?"

"It means Doom will be doing his hardest to quell it."

"Exactly. So, we need to hurry. Cora?" Quill turned to the recorder who was stood looking over the cemetery. She glanced at him. "Are you scanning names?"

"Yes, Star-Lord. Calamity Jane. Wild Bill. Seth Bullock. Belle Star. David Crockett. Tom Horn. Harvey Logan."

"Lots of famous names in that list," said Quill. "But we're looking for the odd man out."

"Jesse James. Annie Oakley. Mister Knife. Tom Ketchum."

Quill held up his hands. "Woah, woah, woah. Go back a bit."

"Tom Ketchum."

"A bit more."

"Mister Knife." Quill slapped his hands together and nodded. "Lead the way."

They followed the recorder as she led them through the overgrown graveyard, stepping carefully over the fallen tombstones. "Three rows down," she said, "and two graves over. There. The stone is shaped like a blade."

They stood, the small group, in the breezy Dakota night, staring down at the grave. "Well, look at that, Rocket. That's him." Quill indicated the grave, then looked down at it himself. "J'Son."

Cora's voice suggested empathy. "He was your father."

"My father? I mean, yeah. In blood, that's who he was. Can't say as there was anything else we had in common." He felt *sad*.

Somehow, standing here above the final resting place of J'Son left him feeling melancholy. *Death comes for us all in the end*, the grave intimated wordlessly. Quill shivered uncomfortably at the brush with mortality. Rocket hunkered down by the grave, studying it carefully.

"Are you sad, Star-Lord?"

"I don't know. In some ways, he's been dead to me for a long time. I suppose there was always a part of me, deep down, that hoped he could change. That he would become something better." Quill heaved a deep sigh. "I suppose…"

"Hold your horses, Quill. Don't get too choked up over daddy because he ain't buried here."

"What?"

"Look. We know your pop died during the uprising, thirty years ago. But look at this date. It predates the revolution."

Quill leaned down and checked the date. He nodded and straightened. "Guess this is it, then."

"I am sorry, Rocket. Are you implying that the grave is not a grave?" Cora asked.

"It's a vault. The burial site for the Black Vortex," said Rocket. Then he stood bolt upright and swore loudly. "Oh, flark me!"

"What now?"

"We came all the way out here and didn't bring shovels!"

Quill could have laughed at the ridiculousness of that statement, but he didn't. "Maybe you could use your sharp little claws to dig with." Rocket opened his mouth to protest but Quill forestalled him. "OK, *hands*. Use your *hands*. They're good for digging and so are mine. Let's go."

"I do not believe digging is necessary, Star-Lord. Just as with

Doom's stronghold, I am picking up on a low-powered, limited range code."

Rocket brightened. "Another coded door? I can hack that! Here, let me…"

There was a sudden groan of old hinges as the hidden door creaked open beneath them. It was unnerving seeing a grave open right under their feet, but nothing emerged.

"I have hacked it," said Cora, much to Rocket's annoyance.

Quill stepped forward and peered into the hole. "Would you believe that there's a staircase? Well, I guess that's where we're going."

"Hold up. I'm… getting that itchy feeling again. Who knows what we're going to find down there?"

"Rocket, we need to hurry. Come on, let's go. We can deal with what we find when – and if – we find it. But let's move."

Rocket shook his head again. "Look, Quill. Between the tunnel collapse and that mining ship that was overrun with the Brood, your track record of wandering into dark places isn't exactly *great*, is it?" He turned to the recorder. "Cora?"

"Yes, Rocket?"

"Stay up here. Anything happens to us, you're responsible for saving us. You got it? Wish us luck because we are going to need it."

"I understand, Rocket." She watched as the pair descended the staircase and were swallowed by the darkness. "Good luck. I hope that you do not die." For a while, she could still hear them, squabbling softly as Quill trod on Rocket's tail, then she added, "I will wait here for your successful return."

"It stinks down here." Quill's distant voice lilted up from the darkness.

"Of course it stinks, you idiot," came Rocket's retort. "It's a graveyard. It's oozing with corpse breath."

Then, the door began to close. Cora stepped forward. "The entryway is closing. Rocket? Star-Lord? Can you hear me? I am unable to open the door again using the transmitter. Hello? Hello?"

The grave crunched closed, and behind her came the unmistakable noise of a knife being slowly drawn from its sheath. Cora did not turn, but simply responded to this new arrival in her usual calm manner.

"Hello. I was preoccupied and did not notice your arrival."

"You know who I am?"

"Yes. You are Kraven. The Hunter."

"And you are my prey."

She turned and studied the broad, powerful man standing only inches from her. "How did you know to come to this place, Kraven the Hunter?"

He snorted derisively. "I've been tracking your scent ever since that fool boy led you into the mines."

"That is most interesting, Kraven the Hunter. Why have you not killed us yet?"

He let out another bullish snort and studied Cora coldly and without real interest. "You don't shoot the calf when you know the bull elk is close by. My hunt is not for you, Rigellian. It is for the real prize." He leaned into her, but his bulk could not intimidate a being unable to experience fear.

"I'm here for the Black Vortex."

# CHAPTER FOURTEEN
## KRAVEN'S HUNT

In the beginning, there was static. Then the static faded into a jingle heralding the arrival of everyone's favorite radio presenter – Brandon Best. The tune reached a peppy, cheerful crescendo, hit a long, final note and Best's dulcet tones filled the airwaves with their unique ability to transform the gruesome into entertainment.

"*This is Brandon Best telling you to rest easy, fellow citizens of the Victorlands. Take a deep breath. Because the worst is over.*" The tone was smooth and cultivated to relax the listener. Brandon Best was a master craftsman, artfully sculpting his words. "*We have faced an unprecedented period of unrest, vandalism, arson and looting here in Doomwood – the handiwork of an outside agitator.*"

The tone dipped into something just a little darker. "*Someone who neither knows nor cares how hard we've worked just to survive – and thrive – in a challenging world. Someone who*

287

*is nothing more than a washed-up old terrorist. Peter Quill."* Best's voice rose heartily. *"But law and order has been restored, my friends, because Peter Quill has been apprehended! That's right! To celebrate this momentous occasion, citizens, for the remainder of this month there will be no taxation. Did you hear me right? Yes, you did! No taxation! Why? I'll tell you."*

Best slipped into hushed, conspiratorial tones. *"Because Doom provides. Always. In times of prosperity and in times of crisis. Now, he will provide entertainment unlike anything you've seen before. The ultimate showdown. A very special edition of* Deer on a Spear *will pit our very own Kraven the Hunter against that washed-up, would-be hero – Peter Quill – and his flea-infested pet raccoon!"*

Canned cheering drummed across the airwaves, filling every home, every space in Doomwood. People stood in the streets where the speakers played Best's announcement to all in earshot. Victorious, pumping music blared and then faded.

*"Now to business! A major battle requires nothing less than a major stage. For that reason – at Kraven's insistence – today's hunt will take place in the Radiation Woods."* A massed hush fell over Doomwood at this announcement. Everyone knew the Radiation Woods hid a legion of dangers, not least of which would be a revenge-seeking Kraven. It did not bode well for Quill.

*"Our drones will be there to record every last second of mayhem, every last drop of blood in full detail. Everyone in the Victorlands will be tuning in later this afternoon, folks. Believe you me, you are not going to want to miss this one."*

The music built to a final crescendo and Brandon Best's speech concluded.

*"Justice is coming."*

Then there was static once more.

Entry C1451Z2M

Location: *Doomwood. The Heaven and Hellfire Club. Emma Frost's office.*

The birds around Emma's office sang their avian hearts out, unaware and not caring of the drama unfolding in the world beyond their bars. Cora stood before the desk of Emma Frost, the White Queen. Rest and time had restored Emma's control of her ability to project the image of the eternally youthful, beautiful woman they had originally encountered. She was also once more fully in control of her temperament. Right now, she stared coldly at the recorder.

"I had that bug installed inside of you for a reason, darling," she said. "Simply put, it was to avoid the *tedious* necessity of asking questions."

"I am sorry, Emma Frost," said Cora. "One of the first things Kraven did after capturing me was to carve the surveillance tracker out of my body. There was nothing that I could…"

"Bull," snapped Emma, not in a terribly ladylike way. "How much does he actually know?"

"At this juncture, I would say that there is very little that Kraven does *not* know."

Emma's eyes narrowed. "Then how is that I am still alive?"

"Most likely for the same reason that I am also still functioning and have been delivered back to you, Emma Frost. We are irrelevant to him."

Emma's eyes flashed dangerously and she half-rose in her

seat to lean towards Cora. "Irrelevant? I'm irrelevant to *nobody*. There should be a swarm of Doombots closing in on me! The Heaven and Hellfire should be burned to the ground!" She slapped her hand down on the desk.

"You sound disappointed."

"Do you have any idea, *any* idea how long I've been waiting for this moment? Just when we reach the critical point, that utter *imbecile* gets himself caught. We had momentum. We were moving from resistance to revolution and then Quill... it's so *infuriating!* Once he gets himself butchered in the woods, it's over. All over." She sat back down, shaking her head. "He was our hope. Stupid, stupid, hope."

"Unless Star-Lord wins the fight," said Cora.

"Oh, please." Emma gave a short, derisive laugh and then turned her attention back to the most important matter on her mind, her own relevance. "I just don't understand. Why am I not staked up on Totem Hill? Or hanging upside down from a tree with my guts in a pile beneath me?" She shook her head. "I don't understand."

"If I may," said Cora. "You are equating what Kraven wants with what *Doom* wants. They are not the same. Kraven is working to his own agenda."

"Which is...?"

"You are the one who has traveled his mind, Emma Frost. You are the one who told me about the boy he was. Sergei. The boy lost in the snow with an ice bear on his heels. What do you believe his agenda would be?"

"He wants to prove he is the strongest."

"He wants to prove he is stronger than the last hero. Star-Lord."

Emma nodded, understanding. Yes, it made sense. Kraven's drive was the need to prove that he was the strongest in all ways and Star-Lord's appearance had threatened to de-throne the apex predator. "Yes," Emma said. "Of course. Well, I might just have a few more tricks up my sleeve."

"Please share your plan, Emma Frost."

She shook her head. "First, tell me exactly what happened with Kraven in the cemetery."

"Kraven had been waiting for us to arrive. He waited until Quill and Rocket had gone underground before drawing his knife on me."

"Yes, so you said. What happened next? Was the whole thing an elaborate trap set by Kraven?"

"No. Not by Kraven."

"Then by whom?"

"J'Son."

J'Son and the Slaughter Lords were the ones who had originally been commissioned by the Collector to retrieve and return the Black Vortex. They had been successful in retrieving it. But the decision had been made to retain it, not return it. To keep it for themselves until they could find a use for it. Then the uprisings had started. One by one, the Slaughter Lords were tortured, murdered, and lost to history, leaving their precious buried treasure behind them. All that remained was their hideout, hidden deep beneath the cemetery. Born of the habits of a lifetime, J'Son had booby-trapped it top to bottom and it was into those traps that an unsuspecting Rocket and Quill blundered, unaware of what transpired above.

On their way down the stairs Quill tripped, stumbled,

stepped on Rocket's tail and then the matter was forgotten. But his misstep triggered the release of an invisible, but potent, gas into the room that waited below.

The tunnel was one of many burrowing beneath the cemetery, an earthen mockery of the stone mine tunnels that threaded the Black Hills. Human bones were embedded in the packed dirt, exposed skulls leering into the low tunnels below. Within the macabre hideaway was a series of chambers: barracks, living areas, an arsenal and, most critically, a safe.

"It was a waiting game at the point Rocket and Star-Lord went through the door," said Cora, pausing briefly in the narrative. "Kraven is good at what he does. He recognized the sound of the trap, waited for the gas to clear, then opened the grave again. With the trap sprung, the door released, and he ordered me down – to go first. To function as a shield against other traps, I suppose."

"What did you find?"

"Firstly, we found an unconscious Star-Lord and Rocket," said Cora. "Then Kraven made a most excellent job of binding the three of us with metal wire. It was not something that I am designed to overcome, so I was also rendered helpless, although clearly not unconscious."

"Clearly," said Emma, drily.

"Then we found a large, square object – some metal composite that I had no time to analyze. It was about seven feet in height. Kraven called it a safe and it was where his attention went.

"He tried to force it open, but it resisted his efforts. He was not remotely perturbed by this, however, and he continued to apply his strength. My audio receptors detected the crackle of corrosion from within the safe, of mechanisms giving way. In the end, he succeeded. The bolt slid free and the safe opened."

Emma leaned forward on the desk, caught up in Cora's tale. More than anything, she was extremely keen to learn what the Hunter had found therein.

"Within the safe were many objects. Stacks of coins, gold ingots, ancient skulls. There was a ring the color of a nebula. I saw a leatherbound book and a blade with a pentagram etched into it. I saw all these things as Kraven furiously searched the safe, tossing many of them aside. He hoped – just as Rocket and Star-Lord had hoped – to find the Black Vortex. But he could not locate something that was not there."

"It wasn't there?" Emma let out a long breath.

"No. The Slaughter Lords had not taken any chances."

Cora paused and Emma leaned back. It was all for nothing. All the work that the Second Dawn had undertaken to reach this point. All the deaths that lay in the wake of their endeavors had been for nothing. Emma's disappointment was palpable. "How immensely disappointing," she said, understating the depth of her personal feeling.

"Kraven did not find the Black Vortex. But he *did* find the next best thing. Another mirror." Emma's hope flared again. "He was thrilled with this outcome. He said that a prize easily won was not a prize worth winning and that the thrill was and always would be in the chase." She delivered the quote in a lightly amusing impression of Kraven's voice.

Emma pondered. "Kraven wants it for himself, then," she said. "The Black Vortex, as I'm sure you've gathered by now, is said to cosmically enhance whoever submits to it. It amplifies their strengths."

"Such a thing would make Kraven the ultimate weapon," said Cora.

"So… where *is* it?"

Cora turned from Emma's desk to look out of the window. "When we first met," she said, "you told me to look out of this window at all the industry here. The machines, the refineries, the mills. You told me how the air was choked with radioactive poison." She turned and looked at Emma. "You told me where that poison originates."

"The Chamberlin reactor." Emma sprang to her feet and joined Cora. "The last place *anybody* would think to look!"

"Precisely, Emma Frost. The mirror revealed that the Black Vortex is located in the nuclear core of the reactor."

"All right, then here's what I don't understand *now*," said Emma. "If he knows where it is, then why doesn't he just *take* it? Why the ceremony? Why bother with the unnecessary theatre of *Deer on a Spear*?"

"Pride, Emma Frost. Right now, Star-Lord is being viewed as the last hero. When Kraven defeats the last hero, he will become the true, uncontested champion of the Wastelands. He wants everyone to be watching." They looked out at the chimneys belching smoke and impurity into the already putrid air.

"Does Quill even know what he's going up against?" Emma was careful not to sound too concerned.

Cora nodded. "He knows. Kraven told him that this will not just be a hunt. This will be a race."

"A grand show so that everyone knows where Kraven sits in the hierarchy. What a ridiculous phallus of a man he is."

"Emma Frost, I have told you all that I know – just as you asked. Will you now please tell me *your* plan?"

Emma pulled the curtains across the window and went to her decanter. She poured a drink, downed it, and poured another. Then she nodded sharply.

"Fair enough," she said. "If there's one thing I've learned from surviving all these years, it's that a little manipulation can go a long way. I propose that Star-Lord, the last hero…" There was sarcasm in the way she said it, but it was more muted than it might have been before all this had begun. "I propose that he won't have to fight alone. I will engage the help of the Second Dawn – and summon the Ghost Riders." She held her glass up to the light and studied the liquid. "Then, of course, there is *your* role in all this, Cora."

"What is my role?"

"Darling," said Emma. "The revolution is not over. It's being broadcast even as we speak."

*"Ladies and gentlemen, this is Brandon Best and this is Deer on a Spear. On this very, very special occasion, our drones are reporting to us live from the front lines in Radiation Woods."*

The woods were eerie, there was no better way to describe it. The trees pulsed with a soft, green glow, concealing things with far too many legs and eyes. Bats roosted in the twisted branches, venomous chiropteran nightmares of fangs and red flesh that hunted even when the sun was high. Spiders, easily the size of dogs, wove oozing, man-sized webs that glistened in the sickly light, and albino rattlesnakes with barbed tails tasted the poisoned air with long, prehensile tongues. They all paled beside the menace of Kraven's keen-edged blade.

*"Normally, we offer our contenders a primitive weapon to defend themselves, but today is different. With Kraven's blessing –*

*or rather, I should say, at his insistence – Quill will be permitted to defend himself with his own pair of six-shot revolvers. Let's check in with our contenders now, maybe hear their final words before they're released into the wild!"*

Quill was shackled, his wrists and ankles bound by strong, short chains preventing his escape. By his side, Rocket was similarly restrained, and he was coughing hard. The wind whistled around them; a strange noise out here where there were so few leaves to rustle. It lifted black dust from the ground, twisting it into short-lived, spiteful dust devils that stung the eyes. Circling above, flocks of tattered black birds could be heard laughing at the whole thing.

A drone buzzed low, hovering a few feet away. Quill looked up and stared. "Rocket," he said, "do you see that drone? I reckon it's talking to us."

"Then say… something back," Rocket gasped out, between coughs.

Quill inched closer to the drone. "Do you think it can hear me? Hey, am I live? Hello?"

He was rewarded with a tinny echo of Brandon Best's voice coming from the drone. *"Hey there, Peter Quill, you washed-up loser! Welcome to Deer on a Spear!"*

"Oh hey, gee. Thanks!"

*"You're minutes away from certain death. Tell everyone, Peter Quill: how does it feel, knowing that after causing so much disruption and damage to our beloved community, you're going to get your lungs ripped out through your throat?"*

"It feels like… let me see. How can I best get this over to you? Eat. My…"

A blaring honk came out of the drone; a noise that was

almost entirely censorship in reaction to Quill's words. He shrank back momentarily, wincing at the sound. When it died off, he leaned forward again.

"Whoever out there is listening to this, you don't have to put up with this anymore. You…"

*"Apologies – we seem to be suffering some interference here in the studio."*

"…and there are moments when I thought about giving up. You're probably having one of those moments right now. But you don't have to put up with this kind of bull…"

*"We are so sorry for the audio glitching. Normal service will shortly be restored."*

"What if you're the one about to make history? What if you're the next…" Quill's monologue was interrupted by a sudden clanking as the chains binding him detached, tumbling to the ground with a rattle. "Hey! My chains are off!"

Rocket, no longer coughing, wiped a paw across his mouth. "Run," he said, his voice little more than a croak.

"Wait, are we *free*?"

"Quill, less conversation and more action. *Run!* This is our head start so we've got to go. Go. Go!"

"Guardians, go!"

"That is *not* our catchphrase!"

They ran.

*"And they're off! Deer on a Spear has finally begun! Please accept our apologies for the glitching, ladies and gentlemen. If you didn't catch what he said, Quill admitted his guilt and regret for all he's done. He wishes he could take it all back and that he feels he deserves whatever he's got coming to him. He hopes Kraven cuts off his fingers and toes, tears out his teeth and tongue… you know.*

*Make him suffer a whole heck of a lot so that death is a gift. Too little too late, am I right? Let's go outside to Totem Hill and check in with our fans, shall we?"*

The broadcast shifted, as it always did at this moment, to the crowd at Totem Hill. This was where the voices of the masses would rise as one, jeering, baying for the blood of the criminals who met their demise at the end of Kraven's blade. Today, the crowd of people was a crowd of person. A solitary, scrawny man, standing alone on the hillside, waving his hands above his head. His repeated chants of "Deer on a Spear" were barely audible above the rising wind.

*"Gosh darn it, folks, that interference is back! But boy, the crowd was wild out there. Biggest gathering ever! Absolutely everything is huge about today's hunt. There isn't anybody who exemplifies outsized danger better than the executioner himself – Kraven… the… HUNTER! Let's check in with him now."*

A drone buzzed up to Kraven where he sat. He was running a whetstone down the length of his knife with a metallic *sching*, the oiled blade gleaming. He glanced up at the drone as it approached, proceeded by Best's voice.

*"Kraven, your prey has been released. Soon, you'll sound your hunting horn and set off on your quest for carnage. How do you feel about that?"* There was no reply; just the *sching, sching, sching* of the whetstone. Best pressed on. *"I have to say that I'm really excited about the bear pelt loincloth you're wearing today – listeners, don't forget, we will be selling that design in our shop starting tomorrow."*

There was what could perhaps be described as an awkward pause which Kraven absolutely did not fill.

*"What does today mean to you, Kraven?"* Best was nothing

if not relentless in his efforts to get a response. "*Knowing that Lord Doom is greatly pleased by your continued defense of his leadership?*"

Kraven finished his work and briefly inspected the weapon's razor edge. Then – *only* then – he turned to the drone. "Today," he rumbled, "is a trial of pain and endurance." He got to his feet. The drone buzzed back a short distance to better frame his big, powerful body. "Today is a day of reckoning."

Outside the armory of the Second Dawn at Annie Creek Falls, a true crowd had gathered. After her discussion with Cora and the revelations that had taken place, Emma sent out a simple telepathic message. It was minimal effort for maximum reward and now the collected groups of the Second Dawn along with Joanna Forge and the Ghost Riders – Red Crotter included – were here and they were ready. Horses snuffled and stamped. Above it, Emma's voice carried loud and clear.

"We've been hiding our intentions, our weapons, and our supplies here for far too long. The time for hiding is over." There was a muttering in response – all in agreement with what she was saying. She looked around at the gathering of revolutionists. "I don't leave the sanctuary of the Heaven and Hellfire often. You all know that. I suppose you could say that for the past few years, I've used it as my own little cage. I hope you all appreciate what it's taken for me to leave and be here with you all today."

Red Crotter spoke up first. "You're with us, Emma. All of us? We're with *you*."

"Thank you, Red. And *all* of us are with Peter Quill." It was a promising start that raised resounding cheers and whoops.

She indicated the recorder. "Cora has a comm link established directly with Rocket's gauntlet. It's allowing her to track the Guardians as they move through the Radiation Woods."

"That is correct, Emma Frost. Presently, Star-Lord and Rocket are traveling in a south-westerly trajectory toward the Chamberlin reactor."

Emma nodded, turning back to the group. "Your task will be to make every conceivable effort to interrupt the hunt and to stop Kraven. Quill and Rocket *must* reach the reactor first."

Red, who had become the group's unofficial spokesperson, replied. "Let me get this straight," he said. "We're heading into a radioactive furnace which in turn will be *surrounded* by Doombots, through woods that are full of creepy-crawlies? All while a half-naked psychopath with a Bowie knife lies in wait?"

Cora inclined her head. "An accurate summation, Red Crotter."

"Right. And if Quill collects this treasure, this Black Vortex, he's likely to become an unstoppable cosmic force? Let's call it a god among grandpas."

"That *is* the best-case scenario," confirmed Emma, her lips quirking slightly at Red's turn of phrase. "You're right. We stop Kraven today and we end Doom tomorrow."

"So... the bright side here is that cosmic Quill overcomes Doom. He ushers in a time of prosperity for all of us here in the long-suffering Wastelands. That's great. That's *grand*."

"The dark side, Red Crotter?" Cora had remembered and it brought a grin to his face.

"Yes. the dark side. I stumble into a den of angry rattlers before Kraven cuts off my feet."

"Do not forget, Red Crotter," said Cora, helpful as always.

"Even if you *were* to survive, the radiation will likely bring about a cancer that takes you slowly and painfully to your ultimate death."

Silence settled like an eiderdown. Even the horses stopped their snorting for a moment. It felt for all the world like time had frozen for this one, crucial moment, holding its collective breath for Red's response.

"Huh," said Red, eventually. "Yeah, well. I've lived too long anyway." He turned to the gathering. "What do you say, everybody?" He cracked the reins of his horse and it let out a terrible shriek. "Ghost Riders! Let's *ride!*" With a thunder of hooves and mingling shouts of defiance, Red Crotter and the Ghost Riders tore into the woods, fully ready and fully enthused for what they might find out there.

They'd only been running for fifteen minutes, but Quill and Rocket were already exhausted. Their initial sprint had become a light jog, then the brisk walk that propelled them. They headed towards a small clearing among the trees and as they approached, Quill spoke up. He was, as Cora had observed, *always* talking.

"Have you noticed how the air tastes here? Sort of... metallic. Reminds me of that time I accidentally left my fork in the microwave along with my burrito..." He paused, aware that Rocket was not engaging in the conversation but was, instead, coughing his lungs up. The absence of a biting response was unsettling. Quill looked at him for a few moments, then tried again.

"Rocket?" More coughing filled the silence, but Quill carefully pressed forward. "Rocket, what does your... what does your gauntlet say? What's it telling you?" He came to a stop. Rocket flashed him a mutinous look that nonetheless had a slight air of gratitude to it.

"Let me... fire it up," he wheezed, taking a moment to catch his breath. He tapped in the sequence on the control pad, scanned the feed and nodded. "This reckons we're about two miles... from the reactor." His words came out in a strangled croak.

"We don't need to run, then." Quill nodded confidently and Rocket grabbed at his arm.

"I already... know what you're thinking... and it's a bad idea."

Quill patted Rocket's hand gently. "I can fire up my rocket boots. I can get there *really* fast."

Rocket let out a bark that was most definitely not one of amusement. "Quill, you'll... you'll break your dumb neck before Kraven has a chance to slit it!"

"I can fire the boots, then pick you up. Carry you!"

Rocket's expression hardened and his snout drew back in a snarl. "Nobody carries me. *Nobody.*"

"Aw, c'mon, man! It'll be *fun!*"

Rocket's retort was curtailed by a sudden, sinister rattle from the barbed thicket at the edge of the clearing. Quill heard it too and for once, said nothing. The two stood stock-still as the pale serpent emerged. It kept coming and coming, easily a full seven feet in length, bigger even than the one that had been in the tank at Outpost 13, what felt like a lifetime ago.

Quill slid one of the revolvers from its holster. "What do you think? Shall I shoot it?"

Rocket shook his head. "Don't waste the bullets. Keep our

distance. Let's go around." Quill nodded at the wisdom implicit in Rocket's advice and they backed away, heading toward the cover of the woods where they could resume their flight from Kraven. They had hardly gone a few feet before a second rattle joined the first.

Then a third.

A fourth.

"Flark me," said Rocket, neatly summarizing exactly what they were both thinking in two words. "We must've walked straight into a nest. I think…" He couldn't elaborate on what he thought because a fresh spasm of coughing racked his body. Quill called his name over and over, warily glancing at the approaching snakes but getting nothing but more coughing in response. Finally, with one great hack, Rocket coughed up a huge gobbet of blood. Quill watched the scarlet trail as it flew from his friend's mouth, a traitor to Rocket's true condition.

"Rocket," said Quill, once again demonstrating his remarkable penchant for stating the obvious. "Rocket, you're coughing up blood."

Rocket flapped his paws in irritation. "Go on, Quill. Just go on."

"Just let me carry you."

Rocket's flap became a full blow, his claws biting into Quill's arm. His words came out as ragged whisper of barely contained rage. "I said. Nobody. Carries. Me."

One of the rattlers surged closer, snapping at Rocket. Quill thrust the smaller Guardian behind him and fired his revolver, the report shockingly loud. "Get back! Get back!"

"I said go on, Quill! Stop wasting bullets and just *go*!"

"No way. We are gonna *fly* together, Rocket. Me and you."

"Please, Quill. Not the booster boots."

"Forge gave them a tweak. We're good to go once I put on some flying tunes. Let me see, let me see…" He checked his music files and found just the thing. "We're going to cruise right on out of here. With me *carrying* you, whether you like it or not."

"You need to learn to carry yourself."

"What?" Quill had flicked the external speaker on his modified Walkman and music blared out, overlaying the furious sounds of the rattlers. "Speak up."

"Let *go* of me!" But Quill had Rocket underneath the arms and had already fired his boots. With a gleeful cry – from Quill, at least – the pair burst free of the rattlesnake lair, rising into the bleak skies above the Wastelands.

"This is *not* hiding from Kraven," shrieked Rocket as his voice disappeared into the distance.

A long, low tone rolled across the woods as Kraven sounded his hunting horn. Any lead that Quill and Rocket had achieved from their head start was now the only lead they would maintain. Brandon Best resumed his broadcast, which, until the horn had sounded, had been replays of old episodes (*"while we deal with the audio problems, folks!"*).

Now he was back. Bold, brassy, confident and clearly quite determined to make the best of this situation.

*"Welcome back, folks. If you're just tuning in, the drones witnessed washed-up loser Peter Quill and his flea-infested pet raccoon narrowly avoid a den of white rattlers. They might have managed to get away from those bites, but they won't get away from Kraven so easily."*

Kraven loped through the wilderness at a full run, crashing through the undergrowth without care for anything trampled beneath him. It was the kind of pace that few but Kraven could sustain.

*"You and I both know, folks, that Kraven can keep that up for as long as he needs to. I bet he could gut an elk on the side of a mountain in the middle of a snowstorm and his heart rate would never so much as dare to go over forty. Looks bad for Peter Quill. Looks perfect for Kraven. Stay tuned. The hunt is well and truly on."*

Five miles from Doomwood, the remaining members of the Second Dawn were on their own hunt. Their intention was objectively simple. They needed to disrupt the drone transmissions. If they succeeded, the next step was to hack the network and take control. Replace propaganda with truth.

*Objectively* simple.

It had taken Cora considerable time to run her scans to isolate the frequency that would connect her to the network. She stood motionless, eyes flickering behind their sockets as she tried to find what they so desperately needed. When she finally spoke, it was with a suddenness that made Emma almost jump out of her skin.

"Emma Frost."

"Yes, darling?" Emma covered her surprise well. She had years of practice on her side.

"I believe I have located the operational frequency for the drones."

Emma clapped her hands together in girlish delight, calling out for Forge, who responded from nearby. The mechanic joined them, cybernetic limbs clanking and hissing at her arrival.

"Yes, my queen?"

"Cora is calling in the drones. Be ready."

"I couldn't be *more* ready. I've put together this net cannon." She hefted the object, a small, broad-barreled launcher, brandishing it proudly. "When I fire, the charge splays out and makes a web, tangling the drone's propellers. It'll come down fast."

"Good work, Forge. Cora, proceed with the plan."

"Of course, Emma Frost." The recorder lapsed into silence and her internal systems clicked softly as she broadcast a recall signal to the drones within range. It took only a couple of moments before the air filled with the buzzing of the nearest drone. It responded to Cora's summons without hesitation and swooped low on its approach. Emma stared at it. For years, they had been the ugliest things in the sky. Now, she had never seen anything so *beautiful*.

"This is it," breathed Emma. "The beginning of the end."

"Be ready, Joanna Forge," said Cora – which the woman already was. She had the weapon trained, finger on the trigger, and was prepared to fire, her aim leading the approaching drone as the distance shrank.

"Steady…" she said, softly, more to herself than her companions. "Steady… deploying net now!" She fired, the net expanding to snare the drone in its embrace. There was an angry whine as the propellers rapidly tangled, then it crashed to the ground with a solid *thump*, ploughing a shallow trench behind it. Forge moved towards it, noting that the device was much larger than she had believed.

"It's ours," she confirmed with a small laugh.

Emma forced herself to calmness. "Good work," she said to the pair. "Now we crack open our gift and make it *truly* our own. Then the Second Dawn will control the voices in the air and the Wastelands will hear the truth."

She looked over at Cora.

"How's it going for the last hero, darling?"

# CHAPTER FIFTEEN
## THE LAST HERO

*"But wait, what's this? Kraven is slowing down!"* Brandon Best's voice was filled with the art of the tension builder. *"He's stopped. He's scented something on the air, or maybe he's heard something... wait. Wait! Now we can hear it as well!"*

As the commentator spoke, an eerie, ululating wail filled the air. The battle cry of the Ghost Riders was not something that had ever intruded upon *Deer on a Spear*, its audience more used to the sorts of cry that abruptly ended.

"Let me remind you, folks," breathed Best. "The Radiation Woods are full of unknown threats. That's what makes it such an exciting venue."

The wail sounded again, and Kraven turned to confront whatever dared approach. He loped over to one of the towering trees, its twisted bulk bowed by its own weight and its scabrous bark glowing with inner light. He glanced up, surveying it critically before heaving himself into the lowest branches and scrambling up the sagging bole. He located the ideal perch from which to watch and dropped into a low crouch, unsheathing his Bowie knife.

Like all great hunters, he waited. Only this time, the hunter was now also the hunted.

The thunder of approaching hooves was deafening, heralding the arrival of a Ghost Rider. Flint-shod shoes sparked as the horseman appeared, stopping directly beneath Kraven's tree, the horse snorting and stamping. A handful of Doom's drones arrived at the same time, buzzing around the scene. The rider, clad in black armor, swatted at them irritably but one managed to snatch a visual, to the commentator's excitement.

*"Our drones have identified the leader, folks. It's another wanted criminal – Red Crotter. Last seen in Outpost 13. Ladies and gentlemen – this hunt just got wildly more interesting and a lot more fun!"*

With a primal cry of bloodlust, Kraven exploded out of the tree, descending on the Ghost Rider below. Best continued his commentary, but his practiced tone became choppy and fuzzed with static as somewhere far away the Rigellian Recorder began to subvert the broadcast.

*"Oh my… stabbing… never seen Kraven so…"*

The scene was utter carnage. Kraven's greater bulk carried the rider out of the saddle and down to the ground with an audible snap of breaking bones accompanied by a cry of agony. The horse whinnied in terror at the arrival of the perceived predator and took off at a gallop, swiftly disappearing into the woods.

"No! No! No, you son of a…!" Red's protests were cut off as Kraven raised the Bowie knife. The blade flashed in the light and as it came down towards his chest, the hunter spoke just one word.

"Yes."

*"Folks, you do not want to miss… total domination… bonus death…"*

The blade flashed repeatedly and try as he might, there was no escape for the unfortunate Red Crotter. Blood drained from him like air from a deflated balloon. His right arm was fractured, probably his leg as well. There was more blood welling up in a deep cut on his temple from the fall. Kraven sat astride him, staring down into the face of his unexpected victim with abject hatred in his expression.

"Who commands you, Ghost Rider?" Red maintained his defiance and spat in Kraven's face. The hunter did nothing to wipe the spittle away. "Who told you to try and stop me?"

Red, growing weak from the loss of blood, could barely speak. When his voice did come, it was smaller than he would have liked for this last stand. Still, he put his all behind it. "Ain't nobody ordering anybody, you piece of trash. That's not how a revolution works."

Kraven dug the tip of his knife into Red's breastbone, piercing the skin. It was a cruel, casual thing and it hurt more than any of the critical wounds that afflicted his body. "How many Ghost Riders are presently in the Radiation Woods?"

Between huge gulps of air, Red replied. "You've seen what's happening… in Doomwood. People are done. Enough." He took a shuddering, rasping breath. "It's time to burn and it's time to *fight.*" He put such pent-up rage into a single word that Kraven sat back. Just a little – but Red took satisfaction in seeing that he had succeeded in a hit. He had startled the hunter. Kraven regained his composure swiftly.

"You talk of fighting? Hah. Your body is broken. You are

bleeding from at least three critical wounds. Your fight is *over*."

"Hardly," said Red, his voice weak now. "The Second Dawn's about to break."

Kraven was silent for a moment, idly twisting the blade of the knife into the wound he'd dug in Red's chest. Then he jerked his head in the direction that the horse had fled. "You shoe your horse with flint so that its hooves spark fire. You costume it in black armor, you muzzle it with an amplifier. All designed to make the creature look and sound more terrifying."

"You got a point?" Red wheezed desperately.

"This is what you are doing now, yes? Putting on a costume. A show. To hide your vulnerability. A *mask*." A slow, cruel smile spread over Kraven's face, and he withdrew the knife. "But I know all the nerve centers in the human body. I know how to tear down your defenses, one careful stab at a time."

To prove his point, he casually and easily inserted the tip of the Bowie knife behind Red's eye. The man screamed in agony as the knife severed the optic nerves. He felt the horror of having his eye cut from his skull, felt the blood and jelly run down his cheeks.

"There is no sense in this masquerade," said Kraven between gaps in the screaming. "Tell me, Ghost Rider. Is Emma Frost your commander? What is her plan?" Red was not forthcoming with an answer and Kraven leaned in closer. "Tell me and I will end this suffering. *Don't* tell me and I will leave you to die slowly over many days."

For a heartbeat, Red was ready to beg for release. Then he remembered all that he had lost. He remembered all that the world stood to gain if they won here today. He found his courage and he found his own inner hero.

He found Red Crotter.

"You don't stand a chance," he said, sealing his own fate. "Not you. Not Doom. This is just the beginning. You won't break me."

"The bitterness of peasants," said Kraven as he leaned back and studied the prone form before him. "It is matched only by their extreme fragility."

For long, agonizing moments, the air was filled with Red Crotter's screams. Then there was nothing.

The Chamberlin reactor was nothing special: in fact, in an ugly world, it was the ugliest building around. At one time in its illustrious past, it had been a vast complex of offices and outbuildings. All these now stood in ruins. The reactor's containment unit was similarly crumbling and slowly being reclaimed by whatever passed for flora these days. There was an audible low-level sound that could be both heard and felt as a bass throb beneath the feet. It was through this mess of jagged concrete and broken glass that Quill and Rocket picked their way. Occasionally, pieces of long-dormant broken rock would fall at their passage, disturbed by the movement.

Their flight had been startlingly without incident: the work Joanna Forge had put in on the booster boots greatly improving their stability. Rocket had, of course, complained the entire way and Quill had in turn completely ignored his friend's protests. He'd been more concerned by Rocket's incessant coughing, something that was going on right now.

Everything about this place screamed "come no closer". That meant that Quill approached with caution, but still approached.

"Rocket," he said, over his shoulder. "Are you seeing this?" Rocket simply continued to cough and Quill took another few steps. "The belly of the reactor is split wide open. It's *really* bright. Can't even really look at it." He lifted his arm to shield his eyes and his jaw set in determination. "But the Black Vortex is in there. Just waiting for us." He turned around and rejoined Rocket.

"No, Quill," said Rocket, finally managing to speak. "It's waiting for *you.*" Then he began coughing again, dropping to his knees, desperately trying to draw air into lungs that could barely manage what he had there already. Quill dropped down beside him.

"What's wrong, man?"

"Oh, come on. You're an idiot, sure, but you aren't stupid. You *know* what's wrong."

Quill did know, but he didn't want to say it. Giving voice to it made it real and he just wasn't quite ready for that. He reached over and absently rubbed Rocket's furry back, hoping it might help the other get some breath. It did seem to help a little and Rocket's breathing steadied again.

The fact there was no complaint at this sudden manhandling set alarm bells ringing.

Scratching at his chin thoughtfully, Quill put a foot forward into this terrifying world he wanted to avoid. "Earlier, when you said I was going to have to learn to carry myself... what did you mean?"

"For the love of... Quill!" Rocket hesitated and then moderated his response, speaking just a little more gently. "You know what I mean."

"No," said Quill, whether as a staunch denial of his

knowledge of what Rocket meant, or a denial of what his friend was *not* saying was hard to tell. "No."

"This is it, Quill. This is the last time we raise hell together."

There it was in all its hideous truth and Quill felt something deep within him burst into flame and blow away on the winds of inevitability. He sat with Rocket for a while, the two of them silent, only the endless hum of the reactor in the background. Finally, he spoke.

"How long have you known?"

"What does it matter?"

"Why didn't you tell me?"

"Oh, come on. What would have been the point? Why would I tell you just so we could sit around and mope, feeling sorry for ourselves?"

Quill was shaking his head vigorously, still denying the obvious. "If you'd told me, I could have…"

"You could have done *nothing*, Quill. You can't do anything when there's nothing to be done." He reached out his paw and laid it on Quill's forearm. "Look. Things come to an end."

"Flark, Rocket. Stop." Quill snatched his arm back and wrapped both around himself. "Stop."

"Things come to an end," insisted Rocket. "But there's one thing you were right about. The Guardians *are* still alive. In you."

"In *us*, man."

But Rocket was relentless now. He was prepared for what was going to happen to him and he needed to communicate with Quill on a level he'd never *truly* managed previously. A personal level.

"I had to get you to the end of the trail, and I did. Here we are. The end. So, I need you to go on now, Quill. Please. For me."

"I don't want to go without you." There was a childish petulance that was at odds with his grizzled appearance. Had he been even ten years younger, the words would have been accompanied with a pout, Rocket was sure.

"Look, Quill." Rocket hauled himself up so he was sitting on a broken slab. "If you don't go, you're gonna end up melting from the inside out like some kind of lava cake. So go." He waved a paw as though dismissing Quill from his presence which, in a way, he was. "Go, already."

"No." Quill released his self-embrace and adopted what could best be described as a defiant stance. Rocket rolled his eyes and wondered which deity might be listening and if there were any out there with an ear on his current plight, would they please give him strength?

"Quill." Rocket's expression hardened. "Kraven is coming. He is going to kill you. The radiation is going to kill you. Or, if you don't get going, right now, I'm going to kill you. So go."

They stared at one another for the longest time, and it was impossible to imagine all the shared moments, the memories that connected in that gaze. Finally, Quill's body visibly drooped and he nodded. "OK," he said, miserably. "All right. I'll go. But I'm coming back for you." He turned to make his way toward the reactor and Rocket held out an arm.

"Woah. Hold on there, princess. Before you go, give me the guns." Quill unbuckled the holster that Red Crotter had given him and offered it to Rocket who took them with a quick flash of his grin. "There. That wasn't so hard, was it? You get going and I'll put a bullet right between Kraven's eyes for you. You're not gonna need these where you're going."

"Rocket…"

"You won't need them at all if this ridiculous plan works out. You'll have the Black Vortex."

"Rocket!" It was plaintive and pleading and Quill hated the sound in his own voice, but still made it anyway. "I can't just leave you."

"You don't need the guns and you don't need me anymore."

"Don't say that. I…"

"Go, Quill." Rocket looked up at him and sighed softly. "Go be the hero you've always wanted to be."

# CHAPTER SIXTEEN
## DOOM AND DAWN

For most of his life, Kraven the Hunter had been running. First, he ran away from threats and perceived danger. But trauma and time tempered that into an uncanny ability to run *towards* them. Not only that, he ran towards them with a nigh-insatiable hunger that would not be denied. Right now, he ran through the cover of the Radiation Woods, heavy footfalls pounding out his progress. All around him were the banshee wails of the Ghost Riders as they closed in on him.

The clash, when it inevitably arrived, was gruesome. Kraven, his Bowie knife gripped tightly, cut low at the first horse to come within reach, instantly crippling its legs. It screamed in pain and toppled, hurling its rider to the ground several feet away. The horse thrashed, trying futilely to escape, and rolled over the stunned Ghost Rider in its desperation. Kraven ignored the suffering animal – it could wait its turn – plunging his knife into the heart of the fallen man. Death was mercifully instant.

He freed the weapon, showering himself in a spray of gore. Kraven wheeled, assessing his prey and their surroundings. He sprang into the lower branches of a nearby tree, seizing a crooked limb. Hauling it back with his prodigious strength, he released it with a whipcrack. His timing was impeccable, the branch knocking another Ghost Rider from his horse. The man left his mount with a *woosh* of air being knocked from his lungs. He barely had time to register Kraven's approach before the hunter was on top of him, knife flashing in the air, cutting short any pleas for mercy with a throat-opening slash.

"*Kraven the Hunter is enraged,*" reported Brandon Best. "*Every part of his body is painted scarlet with the spilled blood of his enemies…*"

An equine shriek.

"*…and the blood of his enemies' horses. He's lost the trail of washed-up Peter Quill because the terrorist cheated. He used those booster boots of his to unfair advantage, leaving no trail to follow.*" The broadcast was interrupted by a sudden burst of static, but then Best's voice floated back. "*Apologies, seems that interference has returned. Perhaps the radiation close to the Chamberlin reactor is too much for our comm systems to handle.*"

There was another squall of static. This time, when Best's voice returned, it was punctuated by a series of clicks and pops that sounded not unlike the tumblers of a huge lock falling into place. "*But here's the good news, folks! Quill has doomed himself! Exposure to the reactor has probably already killed him. Here's what I think…*"

But nobody ever found out what it was that Brandon Best thought because that was the moment that the transmission came to a dead stop. Silence, for the first time in years, ruled the airwaves. The Wastelands held their collective breath in this sudden hiatus before an inevitable storm.

"I am in." Cora's words were manna from heaven and Emma leaned forward, excitedly.

"What do you know?"

"I am still collating information, Emma Frost, but the network signals have been silenced." Emma clenched her hand into a fist in silent triumph. She turned to her companion.

"Forge, you should head into town. When people realize what's going on, they will take to the streets again." Forge moved, her hydraulics a wheezing echo in the confines of the cave.

"What do you propose, my queen?"

Emma smiled. "There's a lot of pent-up rage and aggression out there. I say we should encourage people to put it to the best possible use." Her smile grew broader. "Lead them up the hill to Doom's compound."

Forge's smile matched Emma's own. "Any requests once we kick the door down?" Emma tapped a long-nailed finger to her chin.

"I always find," she said, "that there's nothing more comforting than a well-stoked, roaring fire." Her eyes hardened. "Burn it to the ground."

It was peaceful out here. Quiet enough that Rocket, growing weaker by the minute, could close his eyes and drift into a fitful slumber. He woke with a start a few times as coughing tore at his lungs, but he was able to get a *little* rest. At least he was being allowed to die on his own terms, with a little silence to…

"Rocket!"

Scratch that.

He opened one eye slowly and saw Quill, silhouetted against the backdrop of the light coming from the Chamberlin reactor. "I'm already dead," he muttered, "leave me alone."

"Rocket! I've found it!"

Rocket allowed his other eye to open, struggling into a more upright position. Everything hurt. His chest, his limbs, even his *fur* hurt. "What?" He sounded weak and strained. Quill reached his friend and hunkered down.

"I found the Black Vortex," he said. "It's in the reactor. Come on. Let me help you up."

"No!" Rocket snarled. "Why? What are you doing?"

Quill patted his arm. "There's a change of plan. You're coming with me."

"What? You can't take me into the reactor!" But Quill was adamant, helping Rocket stand. The disparity in height made putting a supportive arm around his small friend difficult – but Quill did it anyway. Rocket's legs were like jelly and their progress was excruciatingly slow. "Quill, wait. I've got to… I've got to…"

"What, Rocket? What do you have to do?"

"The radiation's made my head fuzzy," he said. It was like someone had siphoned his brain out through his ears and replaced it with cotton candy. *This must be what it's like to be Quill*, he thought, then immediately felt guilty. "I've got to stand guard. In case Kraven…"

On cue, Kraven's horn sounded somewhere close by. Despite his struggling, Rocket rallied. "Did you hear that? He's here!"

"That's why we've got to hurry! Let's *go*!"

"No, that's why I've got to *stay*! To fight."

"It's *you*, Rocket. You're going to submit to the Black Vortex."

The statement was dumb enough that Rocket's strength poured back into him in a sudden rush of disbelief and rage. "Me? What the *flark* are you talking about now, you *idiot*?" But Quill would not be deterred, swayed, or otherwise moved from his clearly quite insane course of action.

"Like I said. You submit to it. You flood your veins with its power… it'll reboot your system." Quill tugged at him, urging him forward. "Come on, man."

"Stop!" Rocket, despite his heavily weakened state and his much smaller frame, still managed to slow Quill down. "It's not gonna happen, Quill!"

"Why not, man?" Quill's dismay was clear. His distress at his friend's suffering was writ large across his face and it was obvious that he was struggling with coming to terms with what the near future held for them both. "Why won't you do this?"

"It's *cheating*, Quill! It's a cosmic crutch. Neither of us need it."

"Just come on, Rocket. Kraven's coming. He's gonna…" Rocket snatched his arm free from Quill and backed up a couple of steps.

"Seriously. Powers don't make you a hero. Or a villain, for that matter. Powers, capes, dumb code names… none of that makes you any better. You've got to make your *own* greatness."

Quill sagged, the combined weight of his years and his yet-to-be-spent grief weighing heavily on his shoulders. "Rocket, you're dying. Please. This will *save* you."

"Maybe. But at what cost, Quill? Not one I'm willing to pay. Not ever." Rocket shook his furry head. "I'm not submitting to anything. I've lived my life on my own terms. I'm going to die on my own terms as well."

"That can be arranged," came a heavy voice from behind them. They recognized the sound of the Bowie knife being unsheathed. Turning, Quill went into something of a panic.

"The guns," he squeaked. "The flarking guns! Give them to me now! Give... me the..."

Kraven took a prowling step closer, pointing the knife tip directly at Quill. "You had a head start. There was an army of your allies between us and yet, I have caught you. You had *every* advantage. I have beaten you, Peter Quill."

"Rocket! The *guns*!" Quill felt the press of cold metal in his palm and looked down. Rocket was already pulling back the hammer on one of the weapons.

"You get one," he said. "I get the other." Both weapons were now cocked and pointed at Kraven, whose face split in a slow, hungry smirk.

"Are you ready to meet your end?"

"Not yet!" Quill held up his finger, a "wait" signal if ever there was one. Kraven frowned, momentarily taken aback by the unexpected response. Rocket pulled a face as Quill began fumbling at his belt.

"The Walkman? Now? Seriously, Quill... that thing doesn't fire bullets!"

"Maybe not," came the reply. "But it will take me to my happy place. Hang on, hang on... I've got it."

"Can we get the killing over, please?" Kraven was irrationally irritated by this pair of foolish amateurs, and their antics right now were both tiresome and baffling.

Quill beamed. "Ready!" The sounds of the Beach Boys

"Kokomo" flooded the ruins, making Kraven wince and Rocket stare.

"Out of your annoyingly extensive music library, you choose *this* as your fight song?"

"Enough nonsense," said Kraven, barely audible over the killer combination of the music and the bickering of the Guardians. "Time to die!" He let out a battle cry and sprang towards them.

"The Beach Boys, Quill? *Seriously*?" Rocket shook his head before facing the approaching hunter. "No taste. At *all*."

Mayhem erupted.

"Hello?"

Cora's voice punctured the silence that had settled over the airwaves. She had concluded her work and was now fully in control of the transmission. "Hello," she said again and the musical intro that usually introduced Brandon Best played. "My name is Cora. I am a Rigellean Recorder. Today, this will be the final edition of *Deer on a Spear*."

As though to prove her mastery of the system, canned applause played. "Yay," she said, completely without emotion. "Fun. People of Doomwood, Brandon Best is officially unemployed. Please welcome his replacement – Doomwood's very own Emma Frost. Yay."

The delivery was deadpan, as Cora's interactions generally were. After a moment to allow for a swell in the intro, a new voice took over.

"Hello there, my darlings. I'm sure you're all just *dying* to know what's going on with Kraven and Quill. Don't you worry, I'm here to fill you in. But before we cut back to coverage of *Deer on a Spear*, you should know something about the Chamberlin reactor. There's an object hidden there that many, *many* people seek. One such seeker is Lord Doom."

Cora cued a gasp of surprise. Emma arched one eyebrow at her just ever so slightly.

"That object is the true objective of today's hunt. It's a treasure hunt. It's called the Black Vortex and it is a cosmic relic, which bestows immense power upon anybody who submits to it. Because ultimately, Kraven wants the same thing that Quill wants… that we *all* want." She paused for dramatic effect. "To end Doom's reign."

More scattered gasps and carefully curated applause from Cora's databanks. It was a little gratifying to discover that the recorder had a flair, however annoying, for the dramatic. It was something that Emma could respect.

"I know it's hard to imagine being worse off than we already are," she continued. "But if Kraven acquires the Black Vortex, we will all be denizens of his hunting domain. No, we won't be denizens, my darlings. We will be *prey*. For now, we must put our hopes in Quill and Rocket as they stand their ground. They're doing their best to stop him – and to survive him. Let's re-join the hunt, people of Doomwood."

Mayhem.

Quill and Rocket fired almost simultaneously, but both shots went wide of their mark despite Kraven's proximity – however, it was enough to force the big man in the loincloth to adopt a less direct approach, stalking the ruins like a predator. Two more gunshots rang out and the hunter grunted in pain. Someone's shot had hit – although it was impossible to tell exactly whose – and Kraven was wounded. Not enough to stop him snarling as he closed in on Peter Quill.

"You die now," he growled, and Quill set off at a run. He had no destination in mind – he just *ran*. Dodging, darting, jumping, sliding – he sprinted through the blasted ruins of the Chamberlin reactor in a looping circuit. Kraven set off in pursuit, but Quill scrambled to keep as much of the wreckage as he could between them. Tumbled walls, corroded girders, the burned-out shell of a truck, anything that would keep Kraven from reaching him. He fired three more shots before the hammer clicked on an empty chamber – then there was nothing left but to keep moving.

"Bite me, Kraven," Quill shouted, made gleeful by the adrenaline surging through him. By contrast, Kraven was growing increasingly *furious*. It was *his* task to play with his prey, not the other way around.

"Stop running and fight me!"

"No way! Run, Rocket!"

"I *can't*, Quill. I'm done running."

Hearing this, Kraven skidded to a halt and focused on Rocket instead. He bared his teeth in an unpleasant smile. "Now I have you."

"No," said Rocket. "I'm the one who's got *you*." He squeezed the trigger and was rewarded with a spray of red mist that painted the ruins. The hunter staggered back with an animal howl of pain, blood leaking from his wounded shoulder. Quill, eager to draw Kraven away from his friend, emerged from the rubble.

"Get down, Rocket!"

"No, *you* get down! You'll just get in my way!"

"I've got this, buddy!"

Rocket fired again and Kraven cried out as his leg went out from under him, his thigh shot through with another splatter of gore. Quill reached Rocket.

"He's still coming."

The pair watched in disbelief as Kraven dragged himself upright with grim determination. It was like watching an old horror movie where the zombies refused to stay dead.

"How can he still be coming?"

The hunter stumbled forward. One step. Two steps, a trail of crimson in his wake.

"Quill." Rocket's tone was urgent as Kraven lifted the knife, drawing back his arm. "Quill, he's gonna…"

"Stay behind me," Quill said.

Rocket tugged at Quill's sleeve. "Did you hear me? He's going to throw…"

"Stop pulling at me, Rocket! Stay down!"

Rocket *could* have stayed down, just as Quill had said. He *could* have remained behind his bigger friend as the knife left Kraven's hand. There had been many times in Rocket's life when defining moments had taken on a strange, dreamlike quality as though everything was happening at half speed, and it happened again as his tired old eyes tracked the flight of the blade. Even wounded, the hunter's aim was true, and the knife sliced through the polluted air toward Quill with horrifying inevitability.

"Kokomo" came to its conclusion.

The knife struck flesh, buried itself to the hilt with a meaty *thump*, and an awful silence rushed in after it.

Quill's eyes were wide, huge with fresh, raw pain. "Rocket?"

His voice was no more than a whisper and he reached for his friend at the same moment Rocket slid to the ground, Kraven's knife buried in his chest. It had only taken a small step to put himself in harm's way, but it would carry him further than Quill could reach.

He lay on the ground, blood pooling around him, unmoving and unresponsive. Quill stared for a few moments longer and then snatched up the weapon that had tumbled from Rocket's grasp. He turned to face Kraven. "You... mother..."

Grief and rage sent the first shot wide, but the second struck Kraven square in the chest. The big hunter grunted in pain and finally toppled to the ground. But Quill was not done with him. "No," he said, firing Rocket's gun again and receiving nothing but the futile click of empty chambers. "No. No. No!" Every word of denial was met with another click of hopelessness until Quill finally flung both weapons down and dropped to his knees beside the fallen Rocket.

"Why? Why did you have to go and do that, Rocket? *Why*?"

It took every ounce of Rocket's fading strength to turn his head to Quill. His voice, already hoarse from coughing, was little more than a low rasp. "He... thinks he's such a big man. Size ain't everything. Isn't that what you always..." He coughed weakly.

Quill looked at him in despair. "Can I take out the knife? Can I get it out?"

"Too late," came the whispered response. "Too deep."

"Rocket, no." The denial was pointless, and Quill knew it. "I... can't go on. I can't do this without you, man."

"Shut up. You can." Rocket closed his eyes. His world was growing smaller by the heartbeat, his life now measured in shrinking seconds. He fought past the crushing pain in his chest to say what needed to be said. "You live and breathe dumb optimism. It's brought us this far. It'll take you the rest of the way."

"No." Quill felt Rocket's paw reach out and he took it automatically, gripping tightly to his friend as though he could somehow physically anchor Rocket to the world of the living. He felt the prickling of grief behind his eyes.

"Listen to me. Do me a favor after I'm gone. Save the flarking world." Rocket's eyes fluttered open, and he looked up. "Would you do that for me please, Star-Lord?" His eyes closed once more, never to open again.

"You know I will. You'll be there to cheer and clap for me when I get back." Quill waited for a reply, but there was only the hum of the reactor, no words, no ragged wheezing from abused lungs, no breath. There was no *Rocket*. "Rocket, no. Please. Don't be gone." He knew that it was futile. Rocket's death had been an inevitability, but the reality of the situation was too much to bear.

A scraping sound behind pulled him from his moment of grief as Kraven, relentlessly clinging to life, tried to reach him. "He's dead," exalted the hunter. "Just like all the others. But I am still here."

"He was my best friend," said Quill without turning. "No. He was my *brother*."

"Before you join him, Peter Quill, let me ask you something." Kraven wiped at the blood dribbling from his mouth. "Who is your god?"

That was enough to force Quill to turn and stare at his enemy. "What is wrong with you?"

"Everyone has a god. Everyone in the Wastelands had a god until today. His name was Victor von Doom."

Quill's hands curled into fists. "It's your turn to run, hunter." He launched himself at Kraven, unleashing all his grief and rage. He channeled every shred of hatred he felt for the man through his fists as he laid into the hunter, blow after blow.

"You hit like a little boy, Star-Child." Kraven's laughter was weak, and Quill punched him full in the face. More blood sprayed, but Kraven kept laughing. "God is the one you fear the most, Peter Quill. God is the apex predator!"

Quill stepped back from the prone form of Kraven, wiping at his eyes to clear them of the blood and grief. He grabbed the hunter by the shoulders and, with a whine of engines, activated his booster boots. He tightened his grip.

"You wanted to get to the Black Vortex? Then let's go get it," said Quill, blasting off, Kraven hanging from his grip. He headed for the reactor vault, Kraven held before him like a shield or rather, as it transpired, like a battering ram. The hunter's body smashed through the ruined walls and debris, revealing the core. But Kraven was not going quietly and, even wounded, remained formidable. He fought and struggled, pulling Quill off balance, and the pair spiraled into the wreckage. The boots sputtered and failed as Quill fell and the two men went sprawling, Kraven landing atop the smaller man.

His fist connected with Quill's jaw with a meaty thump. Peter Quill had traveled the galaxy for years, but this was the first time he could genuinely remember seeing stars that closely. But Kraven was not done with him. He hit him again, and then again, tossed him aside like a doll, followed up with a kick that drove all the wind from him and then hit him hard enough to bounce his head against the barren earth. Satisfied, Kraven turned away from the beaten Quill to the exposed reactor.

Dazzling light throbbed within the cracked vault, simultaneously blinding and hypnotic. "Look at it, Quill. It is beautiful, is it not?" Through the unnatural radiance and through the swelling of his black eyes, Quill could make out an archway. A drone came in over his shoulder, feeding back what he was seeing to the listeners of *Deer on a Spear*.

It was like staring into the sun. An archway that was dwarfed by the reactor's core, large enough to allow a single person to pass through into its heavenly embrace. It was mesmerizing.

"Huh," said Quill. "So that's the Black Vortex? It's... so small. Smaller than I imagined for something so powerful."

"When I walk through that archway," said Kraven, "and emerge from the other side, you will know God. His name will be Kraven." He held his arms out and raised his head.

Quill, still on the ground, reached to haul off one of his boots. "If you're a god," he said, punching a control and firing the boosters, "then I'm a God Killer." He released the boot, which rocketed into Kraven's back like a kick between the shoulders. It was a calculated chance, but Peter Quill did those very well – and his luck held. Kraven stumbled past the arch of the Black Vortex, narrowly missing it, heading instead into the heart of the reactor.

There was a blistering flare of white light.

Then, nothing.

"How's it feel, you worthless evil *man*," screamed Quill. "How does it feel to *lose*?" He staggered to his feet and wiped at his face. "How does it feel to lose?" He repeated the question quietly, preparing to collect the body of his friend.

The utterly unholy screech stopped him dead in his tracks.

"No flarking *way*," he said in disbelief, staring at the figure that lurched out of the reactor core, burning as it did so. "No *way*! You're dead! You should be *dead*, man!"

The blazing body of Kraven the Hunter ignored the available evidence, burning fingers reaching for the archway, the choking wail a sound never meant to emerge from a human throat. He managed to shuffle a few agonized steps, then fell, and his body tumbled into the Black Vortex.

Kraven had done it.

Laughter filled the fractured vault. Loud, wild, insane. "I have done it! I am a god! I..." He fell suddenly and abruptly silent.

"Kraven?" Daring to hope, Quill took a step forward. "Kraven? What's going on there, buddy?"

The silence was shattered by a sudden, clear, and terrible scream of the most *exquisite* pain. Quill shook his head and watched as the figure of Kraven the Hunter began to crack, light spilling from within. "Well, I've gotta say – and I'm just helping here, you understand – that look does *nothing* for you, man. I know submission isn't exactly part of your nature, but I'm guessing you just submitted to the Black Vortex?"

The screams continued. The head turned towards Quill and there was nothing but fire where eyes had once been. Quill pushed on, relentless in his hard-earned moment of triumph. "You see, pal, all cosmic contracts come with fine print and the Black Vortex is no exception. You can't control it. You must *submit*."

He paused, savoring the moment.

"Oops."

The screaming finally gave way to weeping, soft and childlike. A voice fluted from the heart of the corona. The flaming mass that had once been Kraven the Hunter was pleading, desperate. It was heart-wrenchingly tragic. "Mama?" A pause. "Papa?" There was more weeping and Quill, his revenge fully exacted, nodded in satisfaction.

All that remained was the voice of Emma Frost across the airwaves.

*"The mask of Kraven the Hunter is gone,"* she said. *"All that remains is a little lost child."*

There was a sudden, blinding flare of light from the reactor as the core pulsed one last time before collapsing on itself in a gale of sound and power. No longer being fed, the core fell dormant. But the Black Vortex remained, an innocuous, oddly sited gateway to destiny.

*"Goodbye, Sergei,"* said Emma, softly.

Quill stood before the Black Vortex for a long time, making no approach but simply staring. Somewhere, deep down, a part of him anticipated Kraven returning from annihilation and coming back to finish what he had started. But he did not.

His old body was battered raw from the final fight with the hunter. His head pounded from his injuries, grief and as a side-effect of standing too close to an exposed nuclear core.

*Ultimate cosmic power. Right there. In my reach.*

Quill let out a humorless laugh, flipped his middle finger, then turned his back on the Black Vortex to return to his fallen friend. Some things were important. Once he was out of the reactor core and back to Rocket, he dropped to his knees and let the grief come as he remembered shared moments. Shared victories and triumphs. Shared frustrations. Shared sorrows. They'd been together for so long that Quill had no idea how he was meant to go on. He was all that remained of the Guardians of the Galaxy.

"*Guardian* of the Galaxy just sounds a bit… *pretentious*, y'know?" Quill said to the cold body of Rocket, knowing there would be no reply. He lifted the unresponsive head and lay it in his lap, bending over his fallen companion and shedding tears for everything that had happened. It felt as though the grief might never stop, but eventually there was nothing left but emptiness and aching, yawning loss. Perhaps, he thought, feeling a great weariness creep over him, staying here and letting the radiation just finish him off was the best ending to this entire debacle. At least he would be with Rocket.

At least he wouldn't be alone.

Since the core was dead, the disappearance of the constant *thrum* left a stark silence. Now a new noise intruded, and not just a sound, the entire ruins shook beneath his feet. Quill dug deep, locating an as-yet untapped well of determination. The tremor had a mechanical quality to it, as though perhaps the Doombots were arrayed in an army and were marching on the Chamberlin reactor. Maybe Doom himself was at their head.

*Let him come.*

Quill rested Rocket's head gently on the ground and with some effort forced himself to stand. Every fiber of his being complained at the motion. His bones, his body, his very soul had been beaten bloody and the act of remaining upright was the most heinous crime he could have committed. But he stood anyway. He retrieved one of the two revolvers and held it with fierce determination.

"You coming for me, Doom? Then you'd best be prepared for a fight because if you want this, you are gonna have to come through me. And I'm warning you, I've got a pocket full of bullets and there's got to be at least *one* in there with your name on!" A bluff, perhaps, but what else was there now for Peter Quill, Star-Lord, Guardian of the Galaxy, the Last Hero, to do but bluff?

A vast shadow engulfed him and for a moment it was as though the darkness itself rose up to claim him. Then, his addled brain realized that the shadow was being cast by a ship coming in to land. He did a double take. He'd seen this ship before. The weird vibe it exuded: that of a haunted castle. A strange choice in aesthetic, but actually, Quill was forced to acknowledge to himself in the privacy of his own skull, kind of *cool*.

"Like I'm in an episode of *Scooby-Doo*," he muttered and then he realized. This was where it had all started. This was the ship that belonged to the Collector.

Thrusters fired, slowing the huge ship's descent, its bulk settling on the ground. Several moments passed as it powered down. Quill lowered the revolver and watched with increasing trepidation as the ramp slowly lowered. Once it touched the ground, the small, yappy dog bounded down and began running around Quill's feet. Then the *click click click* of heels was heard and the Collector descended the ramp, her gaze locked firmly on Quill.

The dog barked in delight.

Quill blinked. "*You*? But how…"

"Oh, it was simple, really," she said, forestalling his question.

"I tagged the pair of you with surveillance trackers." A slow smile spread across her face. "Do you think I learned *nothing* from the Slaughter Lords? I was *not* about to send a pair of simpletons off without some kind of insurance policy." Her eyes flickered to the body of Rocket. "Seems it paid off, given that you've proven *entirely* untrustworthy after all."

"You want the Black Vortex?" Quill jabbed a thumb over his shoulder. "It's all yours, lady."

The dog yipped excitedly and ran to the Collector who stooped to pick it up. "Yes, Mr Delicious. At long, long last indeed."

"You might notice that there's a bit of a charred flesh and bone motif going on around it," said Quill. "I'd recommend keeping your distance."

She looked at him with amusement. "Do you think I'm going to try to submit to it? What sort of insane, narcissistic powermonger do you take me for?"

The words startled Quill and he blinked slowly. "What... Then why do you want it?"

"For the same reason I want anything in my collection," she replied, her eyes taking in the carnage. "To keep weapons of mass destruction out of the wrong hands." Her eyes slid to Rocket again. "Or paws." The dog's yips turned into something darker and more menacing, a deep-throated and threatening growl. Quill's resolve was fading along with the light of day.

"I guess that's it," he said, weary beyond anything he'd ever known. "You're going to kill me now."

"Oh, I've considered it," she said, dismissively, "but as long as you don't stand in my way now..." She seemed to soften. "It looks as though you've suffered enough already."

Quill ran his fingers through his graying hair. "Guess the radiation's probably cooked me clean through anyway. You wouldn't have to wait long for me to drop dead."

"That's true," said the Collector, then shrugged. "Or would be. If you were human. If it weren't for that Spartoi blood churning in your cholesterol-laden veins, you'd be dead already."

"Oh." Quill's nose wrinkled involuntarily. "Yeah. That."

"I know that you have become – how shall I put this delicately – rather *disenchanted* by your father's legacy. But there is a lot more to your history than his mistakes."

Quill shook his head. He was hurting, he was tired, and he simply didn't have the capacity for complex thought right now. "What do you mean?"

"Whatever powers the Black Vortex may have afforded you, had you chosen to submit, you don't need them. You have powers already. They're just waiting for you to unlock them." Her tone changed swiftly into something far more businesslike, and she folded her arms across her chest. "Now. You are late with the delivery, but I imagine that you would like some sort of payment. Yes?"

Quill rubbed at his gritty eyes and startled himself with the next words to leave his mouth. "I don't want the money," he said.

"Well, that's probably for the best, then," she replied. "Because what I have for you is not money." She reached into a satchel across her shoulder, withdrawing a small, black box. There was nothing special about it: it was merely a means to carry whatever lay beneath its lid. Curious despite his own misgivings, Quill accepted the box from her and opened it.

"A *seed*?"

"I'll thank you to remember who you're talking to, Peter Quill. That's not just 'a seed'. It's an extremely *rare* seed. It's yours, if you want it."

He took the seed from its box for a moment and then very slow realization dawned. He stared at it. "Is this... a *Flora colossus*?"

"You're not as stupid as you pretend, are you?"

Quill put the seed back in the box and looked at her. "Like Groot," he said and received a single, sharp nod in response.

"You will have to come up with a title for your new companion, of course, but that's *your* problem. Not mine."

The truth was, Quill was overjoyed by the reward. Whether the Collector had presented him with this gift out of kindness, or whether it was simply for her own amusement didn't matter. He closed his hand around the small box and put it very, very carefully into his jacket. "Alyssa Milano Junior? Rocket's Revenge?" Already his mood was lifting. His grief for his fallen friend was not lessened, but this new arrival tempered the pain. "Groot Two, Electric Boogaloo?"

The Collector stared and he calmed down. A little, at least.

"Your planet, Peter Quill, has become a weapon of mass destruction. To that end, I suggest you save it. Because if you don't, I'll shrink the entire thing down to the size of a marble and add it into my collection. Do you understand me?"

"I do," he said. "I will." A pause. "Thank you."

The dog in the Collector's arms yipped excitedly and Quill nodded earnestly. "That's right, Mr Delicious. Step one is pretty obvious. It's time to take Doom down."

# EPILOGUE
## IN DOOM WE TRUST

### THE WASTELANDS
### SOME WAY OUT OF DOOMWOOD

"Tell me." The figure drew the cloak more tightly around itself, staring into the flames of the crackling fire. It popped and sparked, a single point of warmth in the cold, lonely desert night. "Tell me what happened next. How many people rose up in the wake of all this?" The voice was deep, accented and with a faint edge of cultured intelligence.

"The people rose up in their thousands, led by a defiant and determined Joanna Forge. The throng marched from the town up the hill to Doom's stronghold. They met no resistance along the way."

"The Doombots did not try to stop them?"

"No. The successful hack of the drones had also tapped into the frequency of the Doombots. They passed many on the way up the hill: stationary and useless. Unable to connect to the network and without orders, without the metaphorical lifeline that bound them to their leader, they were nothing more than overly ostentatious mannequins."

"Ha!" The man turned the skewer over in the fire and the smell of roasting flesh filled the air. Fat dripped from its carcass, hissing in the flames beneath it. "Your turn of phrase amuses me. What then?"

His companion shifted position a little and paused for just a moment to collect their thoughts. "The mob stormed the stronghold with a unified goal in mind."

"To find Doom."

"That is correct, yes. They located him, sitting on top of his throne. Just waiting for their arrival. That was all he had left at that point."

"Pathetic." The man spat into the fire. "Clinging to his last moments of power. He did nothing to stop them."

"No. He did not fight."

"Of course he didn't. He was never a fighter. He had people to do his fighting for him." The man took the meat out of the fire and blew on it to help cool it before tearing a chunk off with his teeth. "He was a talker," he said, his mouth full. "A manipulator."

"Yes. That was how I first came to understand that all was not as it seemed. All transmissions – including those of Brandon Best's propaganda network – were channeled out of the same place. The stronghold."

"You are a remarkable creation, Cora the Rigellian Recorder."

"I am exactly what I was programmed to be."

"All this time and not one person thought to look for me."

"They had no need to look for you. Your face was everywhere. *Doom* was everywhere. Staring coldly out from

Mount Rushmore. Collecting taxes in the streets by way of the Doombots. Why would anybody consider that Doom was never who he said he was?"

"It was not my face," he replied, curtly, "but my mask. The one he stole from me. Tell me, Cora. What became of him? What did the peasants of Doomwood do to Brandon Best when the truth revealed itself?"

"There is a place known as Totem Hill," she replied. "It was where Kraven the Hunter used to hang trophies from his hunts. They took Brandon Best there. Would you perhaps like to hear the audio recording?"

Her speakers crackled into life and the sound of a baying, frenzied mob could be heard. In the middle of it all, sobbing and crying like a child, the voice of Brandon Best. He begged, he cajoled, he commanded, he pleaded, but all to no avail. Cora shut off the recording.

"The people of Doomwood took what was left of his body there. When they were done with it."

"I hope, most sincerely, that the vultures choke on it." He tore another strip of meat from his kill and tossed the skewer to the ground. "Your other companions? What became of them?"

"The last I saw of them, they were at the Heaven and Hellfire. They were too pre-occupied with their celebrations to notice my departure. That was for the best."

The sounds of celebration filled the streets of Doomwood, nowhere more so than the floor of the Heaven and Hellfire Club. It was rammed with bodies, shoulder to shoulder, and people even leaned in through the windows. For the first time in three decades, hope had settled on the populace like a winter blanket, and it was intoxicating. So was the liquor, but the thought was there.

Everything had unraveled swiftly in the wake of Quill's triumph over Kraven the Hunter. It had taken a while for him to return to town, particularly with the heavy burden of his dead friend and the injuries he'd sustained, but he had always been resilient. *Intolerably so*, Gamora had told him once. He missed her. He missed them all.

His right arm was in a sling and his face was still swollen black and blue from the beating he'd taken, but Quill forced his way through the crowd and managed to climb atop the bar. "Hey," he called, but nobody could hear him over the din. He took a breath and forced it out again. From the very bottom of his lungs, sending the word out across the crowd and it *worked*. They all stopped talking. A man playing the fiddle was fractionally slower to silence than the others and – aware that all eyes were on him – tried to hide the instrument behind him.

"Everybody? Everybody. Great. Thanks. Nice fiddling there, buddy." The musician gave a sheepish grin. "Listen. I know that all of you, like me, are ready to crank up the metal and party until dawn, but before we go crazy, do me a favor, yeah?" He held up the glass of whiskey he was drinking and let his eyes roam the crowd. "Let's just take a moment to raise a glass and remember my friend. My... *best* friend. Without him, I wouldn't be alive. So here's to you, Rocket."

"To Rocket!" The crowd roared its appreciation and Quill waved his hands for silence.

"And to Red Crotter."

All eyes turned to the man standing just in front of Quill at the bar.

Nobody knew how it was that Red had survived the injuries that Kraven had inflicted on him. Perhaps it had been because the hunter was so concerned with finding Quill that he'd somehow, mercifully, never bothered to finish the job. That wasn't to say that Red was in a good state of health, far from it. But he was alive.

"You lost your family, Red, but that never stopped you from fighting. People keep saying it was me who inspired them, but it was *you* who lit the fire under *me*. Not the other way around."

"Yeah, well." Red shrugged. "You'd better stay out of space and plant yourself right here."

Cheers filled the bar again as the crowd in the Heaven and Hellfire toasted Red Crotter. Quill called for silence again. "Then there's Emma Frost who kept watch over you all and who brought you the truth. And Joanna Forge. And Cora the recorder. We owe *all* of them a toast and a cheer. They're the reason that Doom is done! These are your new Guardians!"

More cheers, more clinking of glasses, more happiness and then finally, Quill pointed around the room.

"And to you. To all of you who fought today. This is *your* win. This is *your* world. That's it, folks. I got just one last thing."

The silence had a personality of its own. He could feel the people in this room hanging on his every word and he loved it. He set down his now-empty whiskey glass and put a hand in his pocket, closing it around the box and its precious contents. Everyone looked up at him, waiting with bated breath for his final pronouncement.

"Let's *party*!"

•••

"I left not long after," Cora finished, and her companion nodded. "After the chaos settled and the celebration was well underway, I returned to the ruins of the compound. When I had been there previously, I had picked up something that I could not initially identify. A tapped, rhythmic code. What the people of Earth call 'Morse code'. Running it through my translators, I realized it was a coded call for help."

"I knew someone would hear. Eventually."

"I located the cell beneath the throne. I found you. I know you are weak…"

He rose up from where he sat on a pile of rubble and faced Cora. He seemed to swell with fury and there was a sudden, strange bite of ozone in the air as though a thunderstorm might break any moment.

"I am *not* weak," he said, his voice large enough to fill the night. He took a step toward Cora, who did not shift.

"I apologize if I have offended you. That was not my intention."

It was enough to calm him, and he took a deep breath before sitting once again. "I am not weak," he replied. "I am in recovery. I have spent *years* in a hole, collared with a power inhibitor. I still have strength, but it has been dormant for so long. Soon, it will awaken fully. You have my gratitude for getting me out of that cell. I had come to think of it as my tomb."

"I sensed you were wea… you were in recovery. But it was important that I get you as far away as I could so that Emma Frost did not detect you."

"Then I thank you, Cora." She inclined her head.

"This ends my recording history. New entry, C1451Z20 is now unfolding even as I speak. Perhaps you could tell me how it is that you ended up as the prisoner of Brandon Best, Lord Doom?"

It was not often that Cora sat while others told her what had transpired, but that was what happened now. Victor von Doom stared into the fire as he regaled her with the events that had led to the ever-changing now.

"We had been planning the uprising for such a long time," he began, his voice low. "Our enemies were incompetence and oppression. Not so dissimilar to what you have seen in Doomwood, but on a larger scale. A much larger scale." His eyes closed as he recalled events three decades old as clearly as though he were living through them again.

"The world order was controlled by a select group of authoritarians. Secret police. People like the Avengers. S.H.I.E.L.D. Reed Richards and the Fantastic Four..." Doom spat on the ground as he said this. "Xavier and his mutants. All of them had brainwashed society into the falsehood that they were all *heroes*." He opened his eyes again and looked up at Cora. "That's the thing with the human race. They need heroes. They need something to fixate upon when the world is in chaos. As a collective, they are incapable of saving themselves. They believed in these heroes, but we knew better. The bridge between scientific and occult expression is the bridge between the new and the old. I am both technology and elemental. I am that bridge."

He stoked the fire, and it flared up briefly, throwing his features into sharp relief. "Of all the *heroes*, in particular the Avengers, there was one we knew who was the greatest threat. The most dangerous. Both to us and to them. There was only one way to end Bruce Banner and that was to make the Hulk immortal."

He was quiet for a few moments and then, without looking at her, continued. "The Chamberlin reactor did not go into accidental meltdown," he said. "The core split and vented its radiation for a very simple reason. It was not a failure of containment or structural integrity. No. It was because…" He looked up and there was a faint smile on his face. "I dropped the Hulk on it."

"Please elaborate, Lord Doom," said Cora.

He nodded. "Of course. The radiation from the reactor flooded his body. It super-charged him." He gave another of those short, barking laughs. "I had created a beast without a leash. A raging, green chaos monster that could never be turned off."

The only sound was that of the crackling fire. Doom thought for a while, then looked up at Cora. "Tell me," he said. "Do you know what I mean by deimatic behavior?"

"Yes," she replied. "Deimatic behavior is a display given by certain creatures in the natural world of many planets. On Earth, for example, there is a species of moth that has the eyes of a snake on its wings. It is a falsehood. A bluff. A lie. A way to scare off predators."

"Excellent," approved Doom. "And that is the case of Brandon Best. But there is another behavior, Cora. Aposematic. Such as when the snake *actually* strikes after shaking his rattle. Sometimes, behind the bluff, there is real violence waiting. This, then, is the Hulk. I should not have lingered at the Chamberlin reactor. But I did."

His eyes flickered shut once again and he swore blind he

could still see the shape of the Hulk, bursting from the reactor, a green star born from the white heat of the nuclear core. "I was hovering at least a hundred feet from the ground but that was not nearly enough. The Hulk ran and he leaped from the ruins, snatching me from the air." Doom shook his head. "I made the same mistake as Kraven in my arrogance. I assumed I was the apex predator in this scenario. That it was *I* who could not be stopped. I was wrong. I share this with you in the full knowledge you will never truly understand – there is wisdom in pain, Cora."

The Hulk had smashed him with enough force to shatter almost every bone in his body. Once he had stopped moving, the green monster had moved on to wreak his own brand of havoc out in the world, leaving Doom for dead.

"What of Brandon Best?" Cora prompted.

Doom's eyes flared open, both angered at the interruption of his thoughts and grateful for the relief from them.

"Indeed," he said. "He was employed to serve as my press secretary when I claimed control of the Midwest. It was he who found me at the reactor, my body broken. He saw his opportunity and he took it. He took my mask, and he took my cloak. He took my *existence*. He took the reputation he had neither earned nor deserved."

"That is why he sought the Black Vortex," said Cora, comprehending. "Because he believed that it would provide him with the power that he lacked."

"Not just the appearance of power," agreed Doom, "but power itself."

"I understand," she said and moved to sit on the pile of rubble opposite him. "Rocket said that you – play recording."

The unmistakable voice of Rocket played from her speaker. *You gotta make your own greatness.*

The two sat in silence for a while longer. It was not exactly companionable, but neither was it hostile. When Doom spoke, it was careful and measured. "So, Cora the recorder. No more secrets. No more masks. How is it that I find you as my ally?"

She had anticipated the question, and it had enabled her to construct the most appropriate reply. She adjusted her posture to face him. "I survey worlds for possible domination and the ultimate extraction of resources. I was sent to Earth as a scout by the Rigellian Empire and was ordered to ally myself with one of the three most powerful people on the planet."

"Who might those be?"

"Baron Zemo, the Red Skull, and you. Lord Victor von Doom."

He shook his head, amused by a small fact. "You must appreciate, Cora, that you have been allied with the other side since your arrival?"

"Quill was a vehicle whose purpose was to bring me to you."

"I see. And now that you are here, what is your role?"

"I will be your assistant and chronicler. To ready Earth for the coming invasion. You will, of course, be rewarded by the Rigellian Empire for your assistance."

He stared at her coolly, then let out a short grunt of acknowledgment, understanding her words but not necessarily committing himself to agreement. "We will see what happens when that time comes," he said. "In the meantime, you will be a most useful resource. Very useful indeed. You may start by handing me my mask."

She took up the object that she had brought with her and stood, moving to him. She offered it out.

"Of course, Lord Doom." He took it from her and turned it this way and that, studying its familiar contours, taking simple pleasure in its weight. Then he raised it above his head.

"It has been," he said, "a long time." He lowered the helmet and it locked into place on the head to which it rightfully belonged. His voice, when he spoke, was no longer simply human, but that of a powerful, commanding conqueror. "Such a *very* long time."

"How does it feel?"

"Like a new beginning, my dear." He rose from his seat and a nimbus of lightning formed between his palms. The increase in pressure whipped up a breeze that lifted the cloak, billowing it out behind him. The sight was inspiring and, had Cora been capable of experiencing the feeling, terrifying.

"What do we do now, Lord Doom?"

"That, my dear Cora, is obvious." The electricity arced around him in a corona, and he rose from the ground haloed by lightning, looking down at the distant lights of Doomwood.

"We take over the world."